ROW WELL *and* LIVE

ROW WELL *and* LIVE

A novel of young love, innocence and espionage during the Cold War

JAMES E. HALEY

iUniverse, Inc.
Bloomington

Row Well and Live
A novel of young love, innocence and espionage during the Cold War

iUniverse books may be ordered through booksellers or by contacting:

iUniverse
1663 Liberty Drive
Bloomington, IN 47403
www.iuniverse.com
1-800-Authors (1-800-288-4677)

ISBN: 978-1-4620-8349-7 (sc)
ISBN: 978-1-4620-8989-5 (ebk)

Printed in the United States of America

iUniverse rev. date: 12/23/2011

Sidney Reilly downshifts and pulls hard at the wheel of the Buick as the big car heels over majestically, tires howling, and drifts wide through the bend of the little country lane. Coming out of the curve, Reilly jams the accelerator and the straight eight engine roars in response. His grey eyes dart quickly to the rear view mirror just in time to see the flickering beams of the pursuing Packard fade and disappear altogether in the enveloping darkness. The road straightens a little and Reilly lets the Buick run all out, hitting seventy five before once again being caught in the headlights of the relentless Packard. At first glance, they are but tiny yellow cat's eyes in the distance, then steadily grow larger as the space between the two cars rapidly closes. Without warning, a half inch hole appears in the windscreen next to Reilly's head and is instantly followed by a distant popping sound. Reilly glances once more into the rear view mirror. Amazingly, the Packard has closed the distance between them and a large man is leaning out of the passenger window, flashes from his revolver punctuated by a series of thumps throughout the Buick's cabin. Reilly reaches down to the seat beside him feeling for the cold steel of the familiar object. His thin lips form a tight smile as his fingers close around the trigger mechanism then shift to pull back the bolt on the Thompson gun. Grasping the heavy weapon firmly beneath his right arm, Reilly hits the brake pedal and wrenches the wheel as the Buick makes a terrifying spin and slams to a halt sideways in the middle of the lonely road. On the highway, Reilly quickly drops to one knee and, aiming directly at the onrushing Packard, pulls back on the trigger of the Thompson gun. The summer night is shattered with blinding light and a long, staccato burst of deafening noise.

I jerked the wheel of the VW Beetle hard over to the right, from where it was straddling the center line, as two motorcycles roared past my open window with shouted curses, flashing lights and the cacophonous roar of souped up Harley engines. The VW wobbled and teetered on the edge of disaster for an instant, bobbing like a cork in a heavy sea; and I sawed back and forth on the wheel to bring her under control, finally settling down to about 35mph while still in an upright position as the red tail lights of the motorcycles swiftly drew away and disappeared in the inky blackness.

HOLY SHIT! Where on earth had they come from? The world was still spinning madly and I tried to clear my head and bravely pushed on in the VW despite pounding heart and trembling extremities.

I had left my home town in southeastern Kentucky at a little after nine p.m. that evening bound for the nation's capital. I had chosen to drive at night when it was cooler and there was less traffic on the 500 mile trip north through the Virginia countryside. Only segmented portions of Interstate had been completed by the summer of 1961 and the prolonged stretches of two-lane road had been my continual habitat for the last six hours. It was now obviously time to pull over for a little rest and a lot of coffee. I needed a break even if Sidney Reilly and his frightening Thompson gun did not.

The decision to spend the summer after graduation from college in Washington, D.C. had been prompted because I had spent a lot of time there over my four years at Hampden-Sydney College, only a couple of hours drive down in Tidewater Virginia, and knew people and had friends in the Washington area. Also, I was vaguely planning on furthering my education at some university in the north east and living in Washington for the summer would provide a good logistical jumping off spot for exploring graduate schools. All I needed to complete the plan was some sort of temporary job. It didn't have to be much, just enough to pay the rent and put gas in the VW. The much anticipated weekly check from my mother would answer for walking around pocket money.

An hour later, I was back on the road feeling somewhat refreshed after coffee and a brief snooze. It was just past noon when the outskirts of Arlington, Virginia hove into view and I found a phone booth at a roadside gas station and spent the next hour or so calling friends, pondering plans and possible jobs and, most importantly, securing lodgings for the night. It immediately became apparent, from discussions with a friend who was doing the same thing, that the job situation could be most easily rectified by driving a taxi cab. Nothing could be simpler:

one merely presented a valid Virginia chauffeur's license to the cab company owner, filled out a few forms and that was it. Uniform and vehicle were provided by the company, shift times and regulations were explained and work started the next day. Well, not quite.

The cab driving job was offered by the Arlington Yellow Cab Company, across the Potomac River from the nation's capital. To be hired, as I have said, all I need do was obtain a Virginia chauffeur's license and show up at the Yellow Cab office just off Glebe Road. Acquiring a chauffeur's license turned out to be somewhat more difficult than obtaining the usual driver's license. I had to prove to the testing authorities that I actually knew my way around the geographical area in which I was being licensed professionally to drive the general public. I was not a native of Arlington, nor had I spent much time there beyond the odd weekend during my college years.

Long a bedroom community for federal office workers in the District of Columbia, Arlington had grown rapidly since the Second World War and was still doing so. Finding one's way among the labyrinth of parkways, boulevards and tiny winding residential streets was almost impossible for native and non-native alike. Unlike Washington's predictable grid of numbered and lettered streets, Arlington required the constant aid of a map to get to a destination. After a while, I was able to absorb enough from such a map to answer questions involving the shortest route from, say, the Pentagon to National Airport.

Upon successful completion of this hurdle, I was fingerprinted and photographed. These bits of identification were affixed to the newly minted chauffeur's license and sealed in a plastic envelope. The envelope was to be worn clipped to my shirt pocket at all times when operating the cab. Because he was forbidden to work without it, each cabbie referred to this innocuous bit of celluloid as his "face." All the drivers were assigned call numbers. My name, Jack Norton, was never mentioned. I was simply #41. Upon receiving it, I recalled that this was the number given to Ben Hur when he was a galley slave: "We keep you alive to serve this ship, XLI. Row well and live."

The dispatcher was a disembodied voice over our cab radios or sometimes over the phones at the cabstands. No one ever saw him. No one wanted to, either. It was rumored that he was an ex-army drill sergeant, and I could believe it. He was a tyrant with the power of life and death over the cab drivers, dispensing favors and punishments by his assignments. From the start of each day I lived in dread of the radio dispatcher's sarcastic voice telling me to pick up a "fare" at such-and-such an address. An enormous bolus of frantic anxiety inevitably underlay the ensuing melee as I tentatively located the customer's address on the city map and plotted a route to his destination, while having no clear, geographic idea how to actually find either.

As a newcomer and a "college boy" I was given the worst possible fares, the ones that required half an hour to get to with their destination just across the street. The two-way radio system in the cabs permitted me to hear the dispatcher talking to all the cabs on the street. I could not, of course, hear the responses of the other drivers.

When I had delivered a fare, I was required to call in and announce my location. The dispatcher would acknowledge with a growl, and I was then supposed to proceed to the nearest cabstand and wait for an assignment. I loved going to cabstands. It meant I could sit in the line of cabs already there and read *The Rise and Fall of the Third Reich* and not worry for a little while about getting called by my enemy the dispatcher to go someplace I didn't know how to get to.

Of course, unlike the small-town cabstands of my Kentucky boyhood, no bootleg whisky or gambling deals transpired when I sat idle. More to the point, no fares or tips were collected; but I didn't care. For a few minutes in the line of cabs I was immune to the scornful invective of the dispatcher. I was safe for a little while from being exposed as the only cab driver in metropolitan Washington who didn't know where he was, let alone where he was going.

Then as now, one lived where one could. I prowled about a good bit during the first weeks of summer, staying with one friend and another, far beyond tact and good manners. It finally became clear, even to me, that I should seek quarters of my own.

I considered my meager income ($20.00 cash at the end of an 8 hour shift) a bonanza; but it was still only $20.00 and did not permit a search of very wide latitude. An apartment, never mind the address, was out of the question; I must seek lodgings in a room.

The notion of confining my living quarters to a single room wherein I should sleep and eat and have my being was not particularly daunting. I suppose when one is 21 years old and has spent the last 4 years of his life in a college dormitory, there is nothing particularly strange about living out of a room. It might even be viewed as romantic and exciting.

4

I conjured up visions of Captain Horatio Hornblower, beached and on half-pay, waiting for 'Boney to come out' making possible a new command; meanwhile having to live in a shabby waterfront rooming house while supplementing his paltry income playing whist with richer but far less clever officers and gentlemen than himself.

My waterfront rooming house turned out to be in Georgetown, just a few feet off Wisconsin Avenue and about a block from Brentano's book store. The Georgetown of 1961 had not quite finished its overall metamorphosis to elegance which had begun in the fifties when it was still a down-at-the-heels backwater.

The oldest part of Washington, Georgetown, founded in 1687, had served as commercial and residential center of the growing federal city nearby until well into the nineteenth century. At that time, metropolitan Washington began to become established. Thereafter, the old colonial village had gradually declined into a sort of genteel slum until rediscovered in the 1950s.

The once grand old townhouses were reclaimed and restored to well beyond their former glory. The senior and not so senior members of the Kennedy administration found the newly gentrified Foggy Bottom irresistible; and soon a Georgetown address was as much to be desired as touch football and 50 mile hikes down the C & O Canal path with Bobby.

I found my own little *pied a terre* while scanning the ads in the Washington Post. It wasn't high style, urban *chic* or a love of the new administration that led me to seize upon this location. It simply happened to be a place in the city that I knew how to find and was in quite close proximity to The Arlington Yellow Cab Company.

I phoned the number given in the newspaper ad and was told by a servant that I had reached the residence of Miss Elizabeth Withersby. After a moment's confusion, Miss Withersby herself was on the line; and an elderly, genteel voice of the sort with which I was long familiar, explained that the room was not yet ready for occupancy. Besides, she was not at all sure she wanted to rent it out to someone she didn't know.

I introduced myself and pressed on, not bothering to wonder, let alone ask, why someone would place an advertisement in the newspaper which was bound to attract people she didn't know. I didn't mind that it hadn't yet been cleaned and re-painted. It wouldn't bother me if the shower dripped and the toilet ran all the time. All that stuff was down the hall in the communal bathroom, and I had just come from having lived successfully in a two hundred year-old college dormitory.

"What college might that be?" inquired she.

"Hampden-Sydney College," I offered, with some trepidation.

"You don't mean it!" she gasped. "My great granduncle, William Henry Harrison, was a graduate of Hampden-Sydney, class of 1790."

"Not *the* William Henry Harrison?"

"Oh, yes," she replied sweetly. "President Harrison."

"President *Benjamin* Harrison," I offered cautiously.

"Oh, no. Cousin Benjamin was much later. Ah knew him as a child."

Was it possible that I was actually speaking to the great grandniece of the 9th President of the United States? Old Tippecanoe?

"You don't mean it!" I gasped in turn.

There followed an outpouring of do-you-know-this-illustrious-family-or-that which covered most of the Virginia aristocracy back through the Byrds and Dabneys to the Lee, Custis, Shirley, Randolph, Jefferson, and Harrison clans. We chatted on, each historical revelation and mutually recognized name eliciting happy little squeals of delight. I was in. I knew it.

"Ah suppose Ah could meet you in front of the house at foah o'clock this aftuhnoon and we could look at the room togethuh," she finally said, right in the middle of an explanation of how a descendent of George Wythe had been a childhood playmate and a life-long friend. I thanked her profusely, bowed gravely to the telephone and gently replaced it in its cradle.

In the Arlington apartment of friends, where I had increasingly come to be regarded as The Man Who Came To Dinner, the news of my phone call brought great rejoicing. I jubilantly showered and dressed appropriately in tan poplin slacks and the light blue jacket from my Brooks Brothers travel suit. I carefully chose a paisley tie, buttoned-down oxford cloth shirt and put a fresh shine on my Bass Weejuns.

CHAPTER TWO

A t the appointed hour, I was standing on the street in Georgetown next to the rooming house when an ancient Packard touring car ghosted up to the curb.

I really had no idea, of course, what to expect or how to identify Miss Withersby. It was clear from our telephone conversation that she was elderly, but, beyond that, I had been given no special signals for recognition. As it turned out, none were needed. When the enormous old Packard rolled sedately down Wisconsin Avenue looking like an apparition from the Coolidge era among the glitzy machines of the go-go Sixties, I knew. This ancient motorcar did not contain agents of the Cheka in hot pursuit of Sidney Reilly. This was something far closer to home and the early childhood of yours truly, Jack Norton. This was a peek into the nearly forgotten, bygone world of grandmothers and maiden aunts, garden parties and lawn tennis. I just hoped I remembered how to behave.

The elderly Negro chauffeur opened the rear door and assisted Miss Withersby as she made the transition from hushed cocoon of polished burled Carpathian elm, buttery leather and rich broadcloth to grimy concrete, swelter and noise. I came forward to introduce myself, but was ignored until she was sufficiently upright and acclimated, had adjusted her clothing and gloves, and had a steady grip on her ebony cane.

"Miss Withersby, I'm Jack Norton," I said smiling, uncertain whether to bow or shake hands.

She merely nodded in my direction. "All right, Alonzo," she said quietly, dismissing the chauffeur.

She turned to me without formality and said, "Ah'm not sure Ah brought the right key," the soft dulcet tones of tidewater Virginia caressing each syllable.

Miss Withersby stood there on the sidewalk and fumbled with a very large bunch of keys held together by a very small ring. She was no more than five feet high, a wizened little creature in black whose body with its hunched back suggested avian comparisons: arms and legs like jackstraws over which was stretched yellowed parchment skin, the claw-like hands picking and plucking at the ring of keys, the cane and black handbag dangling from the crook of her elbow.

Her head was large and wild with a beaked nose and deep set, ancient eyes. It was couched under remarkably thick white hair which surged out on either side of her face from beneath the tiny hat and veil. The mouth was not unkind, but was set in a firm, even line of determination as she battled with the keys, all of which appeared to be identical.

That face seemed so familiar; and, suddenly, I knew where I'd seen it before: earlier that day, when I'd reluctantly handed over three one-dollar bills to the ESSO attendant filling the tank of my VW beetle. She may have been Miss Withersby to the world at large, but, for me she would always conjure up visions of George Washington's twin sister—the one that history forgot.

After a few uncomfortable moments standing on the crowded sidewalk while Miss Withersby fumbled with the key ring, both of us began to move toward the entrance to the old building. Alonzo silently returned to the car and guided the long black machine off of Wisconsin and onto the less traveled cross street in front of the entrance. Miss Withersby and I moved slowly up to the little concrete stoop in front of the door, a step at a time, concentrating with increasing enchantment and incomprehension at the obstinate ring of keys that refused to yield up its secret.

We stood for what seemed a great while at the entrance to the building, both watching with fascination the endless metallic cycling. Finally, weary from the heat and frustrated with the endless parade of keys, I glanced at the door in front of which we stood and found it wide open.

"It's open." I said.

"What's that?" She asked, irritably. Miss Withersby was clearly not the sort of person who suffered fools gladly or liked having her search for truth interrupted by unsolicited comments, especially from someone she hardly knew.

"The door," I added cautiously.

She looked up from her task, a frown of annoyance becoming more pronounced as attention was shifted from recalcitrant key ring to new interruption.

"Ah've told them ovah and ovah to keep that doah locked. No one evah listens."

Miss Withersby continued to ritualistically scrutinize her key ring while making no move to enter the building. After a few moments, in an attempt to sort of stroll about while not actually walking off and leaving her standing there, I casually slipped across the threshold of the old building and into the dimly lighted hallway.

To my left, a second, half-opened door beckoned, and I was drawn to it as iron filings to a magnet. I glanced back to see if Miss Withersby might give up the fruitless key search and perhaps join me; but she was still standing there, peering more carefully than ever at each key and mumbling about people who didn't listen.

I pushed open the interior door and glanced inside at what was clearly a bedroom that had been hastily vacated. The simple furnishings included a rug of some kind, a single bed, a comfortable armchair, a lamp and a bureau, on top of which lay a set of keys. The small frosted window was raised halfway and looked out into a narrow alley. Across the dimly lighted hallway, under a staircase, was a sort of improvised bathroom from which emanated warm, moist odors of steam and mildew, and something more. Something which suddenly made my shirt collar and boxer shorts seem two sizes too small. Involuntarily, I pulled at my necktie and realized that I could actually hear the blood pounding in my ears. Naked wet footprints led across the threshold and along the hallway floor: small, dainty, naked footprints.

Miss Withersby had by now entered the building waving a single key triumphantly. I quickly moved back into the hallway with a series of graceful steps, turns and gestures bringing the news that the bedroom was open and cleaned out. The turns and gestures served as fairly effective cover for what I hoped was an unobtrusive effort to adjust my shorts through my pants pockets. As Miss Withersby thankfully ignored me and peered inquiringly into the abandoned room, I gushed on and said it seemed fine, and that I'd love to take it. Well, I don't really think I said that I'd love to take it, but I let her know that I found it satisfactory.

"He was supposed to mail the keys." Miss Withersby studied the two keys from the bureau which were held together with a short piece of string as if examining them for possible damage. The departed tenant, after all, had taken leave quickly and hadn't mailed them as he'd been instructed to do.

"Might have known he'd simply *leave* them lying about heah in the room. You just don't know about people nowadays," she said, looking straight up at me with what I imagined she thought of as her penetrating stare; the one which sought the truth in men's souls and found it.

"Uh, that's true," I said, nodding agreement. "You just don't know."

Her penetrating stare boring in more deeply, Miss Withersby began to speak slowly and deliberately as if imparting a great secret.

"You *know* Ah only rent these rooms to *gentlemen* guests."

"Uh huh, yes, of course," I said, nodding vigorously and thinking of the dainty, naked footprints upon which Miss Withersby and I were now treading with abandon. *"And he* knew it, too," she added, bitterly.

"Ummm," I nodded, frowning sympathetically, "Of course he did."

"After I had explained everything to him, explicitly," she hissed, disgust escaping from between her tightly compressed lips like wisps of steam.

"You just never know," I added, shaking my head. "Some people . . . ." We both stood there for a moment in silence shaking our heads at the awfulness of it all and what the world had come to.

"And right heah under ma own roof!" She went on, gesturing around the dingy corridor. "Hanky Panky! Ah just won't have it."

From down the hallway, I heard the faint but distinct sound of a door being opened and then quickly shut again.

Miss Withersby sighed and shook her head to rid herself of the unseemliness of the situation which had been visited upon her by this miscreant whom she had trusted. It went without saying that he was not a southerner. He had further proven himself to have been no gentleman, and she had cast him from her house. She moved toward the open bedroom door, then wheeled on me and vigorously launched into what I would come to know as The Hanky Panky Discourse.

It was a lengthy homily on morals, the general unreliability of people one didn't know; and, in particular, the *deceit* practiced by young men lacking in good breeding.

Good breeding or the lack thereof, turned out to be the heart of Miss Withersby's discourse. As a character trait, it was never actually defined (after all, *we* didn't have to be told what it was) and, in our world, an assumed prerequisite to social intercourse. It was only certain *young men* who sometimes appeared to be completely lacking in it and whose actions were a reflection upon *their parents*.

The gist of the Hanky Panky Discourse was that young men who lacked good breeding always practiced deceit. This, of course, led directly to Hanky Panky and was not tolerated by Miss Withersby, who threw them out into the street (in this case, Wisconsin Avenue) without a backward glance. After a moment of personal reflection, I found myself nodding in complete agreement. Miss Withersby certainly had young men and the lack of good breeding firmly pegged.

Throughout the discourse, my thoughts kept turning to the occupant of the room down the hall. Though I seriously doubted that he lacked good breeding, I should have been willing to wager a rubber of whist that he had practiced deceit since that fateful day when he first stood in this darkened hallway, listened respectfully to the Hanky Panky Discourse, and taken up lodgings in these rooms.

Eventually, Miss Withersby wound down and I had a crick in my neck and permanent frown lines from nodding and agreeing earnestly with everything that she said. We moved out of the hallway and into the tiny bedroom while she explained each article of furnishing, the general prohibition about cooking in the room, the idiosyncrasies of the bathroom plumbing and where and when to send the rent check.

Then, without further ceremony, she handed me the keys of the departed tenant and we left. I carefully demonstrated my competent and responsible nature, and the fact that I was *not* one of those who didn't listen, by carefully locking *both* bedroom and street doors behind me. Miss Withersby looked on with satisfaction and approval.

As we descended the three worn steps of the old building, she waved off the proffered assistance of Alonzo and took my arm in a lavender-gloved grasp. I steadied her across the brick-lined sidewalk to the dark gaping maw of the Packard. As I handed her in, a tiny electric fan mounted in the rear compartment blew warm, scented air into my face. She seated and adjusted herself for the ordeal of travel, then leaned forward and peered out at me.

"It occurs to me, Mr. Norton, that you might possibly assist me in solving a little problem." She smiled sweetly in rapt anticipation of my assent.

The unexpected request, coming as it did on the heels of the Hanky Panky Discourse, set off warning bells inside my head that were loud enough to have been heard by the occupant (occupants?) of the room down the hall, fifty feet away.

Sidney Reilly parks amid murky shadows in a black Lagonda, his dark eyes never leaving the silent door of the rooming house as he casually lifts a silver tumbler of cognac. He deftly removes a monogrammed case from the breast pocket of his dinner jacket and extracts a cigarette. Across the street the rooming house door opens just a crack. In the darkened Lagonda, a sardonic smile plays slowly across Reilly's thin lips.

"Of course. Anything I can do," I blurted. "Anything at all."

Miss Withersby fixed me with her truth-finding, penetrating stare and asked if I knew anything about automobiles. "Well, not regular automobiles," she said, gesturing around her to indicate the enormous Packard, "Ah mean those little foreign ones that are all ovah the place nowadays and make so much noise."

Sidney Reilly sitting in his black Lagonda vanished instantly, and I had one of those awful moments when one has heard the words but hasn't the slightest idea of what has been said. I stared back for an eyeblink and then said, beg your pardon, or, I'm sorry, or some such, because there she was repeating with some irritation the question about the little foreign automobiles and my knowledge of them.

I stammered and apologized and made an artful social recovery while modestly admitting that I enjoyed a nodding acquaintance with those little foreign automobiles, which was something of an understatement. She said she had just known, somehow, that I did and that she was delighted.

"Ah have a little project in mind that Ah'd like very much to discuss with you," she continued quietly, as if beginning a bedtime story for an eager child.

Sidney Reilly motors along a tree-lined street at the wheel of an open Morgan, easily keeping in sight the red Alfa Romeo coupe being driven clumsily by a young man of good breeding. The Alfa brazenly whips to a stop in front of an old rooming house to the trill of wanton laughter. Down the block, Reilly expertly pulls over the Morgan and waits cunningly. The Alfa's passenger door pops open and a pair of dainty, naked feet slip down to the worn brick pavement. The trace of a smile begins to form on Reilly's lips.

Miss Withersby was saying something about dinner.

"Dinner?" Once more, I was totally at sea.

"Would Friday be convenient?" she asked, apparently for the second time.

It seemed I had just received an invitation to dine with Miss Withersby at her home on Friday, but I was sure I must have missed something, since the last words I remembered hearing concerned a project involving foreign cars, *small* foreign cars.

Somehow, I bowed, smiled and conveyed my thanks and acceptance. Miss Withersby reached into her purse and withdrew a small, engraved card, which she handed to me through the open door of the limousine. Redolent with the cloying scent of lavender, it read:

Elizabeth Withersby

4000 Connecticut Avenue N.W.

"Come about seven and we can have a nice chat befoah we eat."

She nodded to Alonzo, who quietly closed the car door. I mumbled inanely about seven being just fine and thanked her again and was nodding and smiling as the Packard pulled majestically away from the curb and out into the afternoon rush hour din of Wisconsin Avenue.

For the next several days I was too preoccupied with the little details of living to give much thought to Miss Withersby or her utterly weird invitation. At the rooming house I rose early for a day of cab driving and returned briefly at about 5:00 p.m. to shower and change out of my Arlington Yellow Cab uniform. I was seldom in bed before midnight.

Apparently, the other gentlemen guests kept different hours, for not only did I not see anyone, neither did I hear a peep from behind the mysterious door down the hall. Then, in the waking hours of the morning of the third day, as I was lying half asleep, the sound of a door closing with the simultaneous snap of a lock brought me wide awake. The clip-clip-clip of footsteps right past my own door propelled me out of bed and across the room. In Miss Withersby's rooming house, footsteps along a corridor were supposed to go clump-clump-clump, never clip-clip-clip.

Visions of dainty, naked feet seductively sheathed in nylon and soft leather flamed through my sleep-fogged brain. I quickly reached for the door only to realize that my pajamas, along with the tangled bedclothes, had been discarded in a heap on the floor during the sweltering summer night. In the dim half-light, I frantically sought my robe and had just thrown it on when I heard the street door open and close and the distinct and fading sounds of clip-clip-clip on the worn brick of the old sidewalk.

Peering cautiously out into the shadowy corridor, I realized with bitter disappointment that it had all been there, and that I had missed everything. The warm moist odors of steam and mildew were still fresh from the bathroom, the dainty naked footprints lay in puddles on the hallway floor; and this time something more, the glorious lingering scent of roses.

Like a shot I sprinted to the street door and heaved it open. The pale light of early morning revealed only the neat double row of townhouses and an empty sidewalk. On the corner, the din of the morning rush hour was building on Wisconsin Avenue. Sonuvabitch!!

Feeling dejected at having slept through what might have been the most interesting half-hour of the day at Miss Withersby's rooming house, I showered, dressed and left the building. As I started down the sidewalk, I noticed coming toward me from the corner bus stop on Wisconsin what appeared to be a very tired, red-eyed young man of good breeding. He carried a briefcase and a folded copy of The Washington Post.

He nodded as we passed. I noticed that his tie was askew, his linen suit rumpled and that he needed a shave. In fact, he looked exactly as if he were just coming home from a hard night's work.

Somehow I knew, without turning, that when I did, I would see him mounting the three little steps to Miss Withersby's rooming house, opening the street door with his key and then the other to his room down the hall. I waited a moment and turned just in time to see him enter and shut the street door behind him. Well, well, well.

The twilight shadows lengthen and the last rays of the fading sun glint against the brass hardware of the rooming house door. Apart from the muffled hum of traffic on Wisconsin, it is quiet along the tree-lined street. The door suddenly opens. A young man of good breeding comes down the steps and sets off for the corner bus stop at a brisk pace. His three piece suit is neatly pressed. He is freshly shaven and his hair is still damp from the shower. Down the block, sitting in the black Lagonda, Sidney Reilly notes the departure with a casual glance at the Patek-Philippe on his left wrist.

An hour passes, two. Reilly extracts a Galoise from the monogrammed case and flicks a gold Dunhill. When the lighter flares, he sees a figure approaching from the distant bus stop. It is quite dark now except for the dim street lamps and the figure is indistinct; but, as it draws nearer, Reilly hears the sound of clip-clip-clip. A thin smile spreads across his face revealing an even row of white teeth. Pausing a moment, the figure suddenly darts quickly up the steps of the old rooming house and is through the door in a whisper. Reilly extinguishes the cigarette and leaves the car. Moving in the shadows, he approaches the old building and quickly mounts the steps. With a single glance over his shoulder, he inserts the passkey in the lock and pushes through to the scent of roses drifting softly in the darkened corridor.

I found my VW Beetle where I'd parked it on a quiet street the other side of Wisconsin, executed a swift mid-block U turn and ran down onto M street and the approach to Key Bridge.

The Arlington Yellow Cab Company was about 10 minutes away, and I used the time wisely to formulate a plan. It was just possible that Miss Withersby's trust in the young man of good breeding who lived down the hall, albeit during the daylight hours, had not been misplaced. He had not practiced deceit. He had not engaged in Hanky Panky. Good Breeding had triumphed. He had simply made a practical business arrangement to defray living costs and to assist a fellow creature in finding shelter in this beehive of a city. The word *platonic* struggled up slowly from among the recently buried detritus of my classical education. He by day, she by night, separated always by eight hours of vocational incompatibility.

Why, they probably didn't even know each other's Christian names. Sleeping arrangements? Well, she would obviously use the bed while he probably had a pallet or sleeping bag on the floor. Weekends? This was a tough one. The idea of them having two days to spend languishing in each other's company was simply too painful to contemplate. I dropped the exercise in speculation and took up the business of getting to the cab company on Glebe Road before my shift started.

Later that morning, I was sitting at a cabstand reading *Rise and Fall* when it finally became my turn to answer calls from the dispatcher on the cabstand phone. Reluctantly, I left the cab to answer the next ring and was told to pick up a fare at The Arlington Towers, a nearby apartment building. This was somewhat of a relief, because I knew how to get to Arlington Towers. There were actually two or maybe three towers and they stood next to each other around a semicircular driveway.

At that point, I didn't know the destination of the fare. The dispatcher knew, of course, but he wouldn't tell. I was left to find out from the fare after I picked him up. I would then write it down on my "manifest." I suppose the theory was that if the cabby knew the fare's destination in advance, he might not want to go or might trade off the assignment with somebody else, choices strictly forbidden by law.

As I drove up the winding drive to the Arlington Towers, a young man of about 24 wearing the uniform of a U.S. Navy Ensign, ran out of the entrance and into the path of the cab, shouting and waving his arms. When I stopped the cab to avoid hitting him, he opened the passenger door and jumped into the front seat.

"Take me to the Pentagon!" he snarled, adjusting his white hat as he frowned and looked straight ahead through the windshield.

"Listen, I've already got a fare," I told him. "I can't take you anywhere."

He reached into the breast pocket of his uniform coat, shaking his head as if pitying my ignorance. He thrust an open wallet under my nose. It contained a Pentagon pass with his picture.

"I'm commandeering this cab," he snapped. "Take me to the Pentagon!"

"What about my fare?" I demanded.

"He'll keep. This is an emergency! I'm commandeering this cab!"

I swung the cab out of the driveway of the Arlington Towers and headed out Washington Boulevard for the Pentagon. The trip took only about ten minutes. I had just let the ensign out at the Mall entrance when the radio crackled.

"Forty-One, where you at?" The dispatcher bawled.

"The Pentagon."

"Say again, Forty-One?!" Incredulity.

"I'm at the Pentagon."

"Forty-One, you in big trouble," he declared happily.

"My cab was commandeered by a Naval officer!"

"Forty-One, you shittin' me?"

"No! I swear to God, he commandeered the cab and he showed me his Pentagon card."

"He showed you his Pentagon card? What about his baseball card, Forty-One? Forty-One, are you a *complete* moron?"

MOE-RON. The word oozed out in two long slow syllables, as though Lyndon Johnson were saying it. He continued softly, his voice almost tremulous.

"Don't you know, Forty-One, that this is Amurica, not Rushey, and NOBODY," his voice suddenly exploded in a deafening roar, "NOBODY IN AMURICA CAN'T COMMANDEER NO FUCKIN' CAB!"

My summer career almost ended with the commandeered cab incident. After being told by the dispatcher what apparently every other adult and child in AMURICA knew by instinct, I was required to speak to Neil. This was the worst thing that could happen to a cab driver working for the Arlington Yellow Cab Co. Neil was the son of the man who owned the company. Neil was also a fat, smug jerk. He never spoke to any of the cab drivers except on their first day when he hired them, and on their last day when he fired them. No cabby wanted Neil to speak to him, ever. In the morning at the cab company before going out for their shifts, the cabbies stood around and drank coffee and ate doughnuts and rolls. If Neil's car appeared on the lot, everyone vanished instantly. No one tried to suck up to him the way they did to the dispatcher. Neil was bad news, the kiss of death for any cabby.

I had to speak to him over the cabstand phone where I was directed to go after my Pentagon caper. He heard my story without making a comment. Then he told me, in rather more formal terms, pretty much what the dispatcher had said. He went on to say that my fare had repeatedly called for half an hour until another cab had been dispatched to pick her up. She was thinking about suing the company. Neil told me that if I ever did anything like this again to consider myself instantly fired. For the time being, he was giving me one more chance. Lucky Me.

I went back to the cab seriously considering early retirement. As soon as I'd closed the door the radio squawked and the voice of the dispatcher growled,

"41, you out there somewhere? You got your Boy Scout compass in your pocket today? Where you *at*, 41?"

Where I was *at,* was simply trying to discover where I actually was on a day-to-day basis. I now found myself increasingly looking forward to the dinner with Miss Withersby.

One look at the apartment building where Miss Withersby lived was all that was necessary to let one know that it had been constructed during a Republican administration, probably that of Coolidge. One might even have gone further to infer that it was extravagantly, and with not the slightest thought of the cost of labor, put together sometime shortly before The Great Unpleasantness of 1929.

Four thousand Connecticut Avenue was sited about half-way between the Shoreham Hotel and Chevy Chase Circle. The rolling forested expanse of Rock Creek Park lay just behind the edifice which faced the stately boulevard across a series of cool green lawns beautifully landscaped with flowering shrubbery, huge old oaks and maples. Perhaps four or five stories high and massive in appearance, the building was deeply segmented by dividing wings so that each apartment enjoyed a number of different parklike views from its various windows. The main entrance was discreet and substantial, suggesting a bank rather than a grand hotel. There were great doors of glass and polished brass set into the red brick and flanked by white painted concrete columns, a port-cochere for those embarking in inclement weather, as well as a liveried doorman to assist them.

The long winding driveway veered off beside the building down through gently rolling lawns and swept majestically into a great parking garage located in the basement fastness. Though security was almost non-existent in those halcyon days, a successful entry into the garage demanded the twisting of keys and the raising of steel gratings to reveal a vast subterranean expanse filled with scores of Cadillacs, Lincolns, Jaguars, Bentleys, the odd Rolls, and above them all, an elegant old Packard V12 Touring Car.

There was a small outdoor parking facility located beyond the main entrance and tucked in behind one of the building's many wings. Convenient for the occasional caller who suffered the indignity of having to drive himself, it was, like everything else about the building, discreet and tasteful, and managed nicely to conceal the vulgar from the sublime with cunningly situated foliage, much like a maze in the garden of a great English country house.

It was in the maze that I parked my VW Beetle at about five minutes before seven. I made my way around the corner of the building to the front entrance and presented myself to the doorman.

"Miss Withersby's," I said, the fingers of my left hand toying with her calling card, just in case.

The doorman was already swinging aside the heavy door. He smiled warmly and said, with apparently genuine feeling, "Yes sir, and have a very pleasant evening. Just take the elevator on your left."

I repeated Miss Withersby's name to the attendant and rode up to the second floor in a carriage of mahogany and polished brass. As the door opened silently, he whispered politely, "Number three on your right, sir." The elevator doors shut soundlessly and he was gone.

I walked down the corridor toward number three, sinking into the deep pile carpet and admiring the decor. The place was not at all institutional, not even suggesting a fine hotel. Rather, it had the light and airy feel of a beautifully decorated hallway in someone's home with wallpaper, light shades of painted woodwork and trim, good paintings, and intricate mahogany drop-leaf tables holding exquisite lamps and Chinese vases. A burglar could have made a haul right here in the corridor without entering a single room.

I pushed the buzzer at number three and waited. I had worn my one and only suit, a light blue poplin thing woven with just a dash of some miracle fiber which made it absolutely, positively wrinkle-free. Brooks Brothers called it a travel suit and it certainly was. Not only could it be slept in all night on a train and retain its pristine appearance, but amazingly, it could be cleaned by simply wearing it in the shower and setting it on a hanger to dry overnight.

19

I was greeted by Alonzo who had exchanged his antique chauffeur's uniform for something more comfortable. The knee-length leather puttees and full gauntlets were gone, as was the leather visor cap and splendid double-breasted coat. In their place, he wore a simple black suit jacket that appeared to be made of silk or rayon and reserved exclusively for indoor use.

At the rooming house when I'd first met Miss Withersby, Alonzo had not even acknowledged my presence; which, after a moment, seemed quite natural, as if he were just a part of the old limousine, like the vast broadcloth seats or the great whitewall tires. Now, at the door to Miss Withersby's home, his demeanor changed markedly. He behaved toward me with correct reserve but permitted a hint of warmth and humanness to grace each gesture.

When we entered, Miss Withersby was seated on a sofa near a bank of windows in what I supposed was the living room. The place was enormous by any apartment standards that I knew. Furnished in solid American good taste, money and comfort that the very rich continued to enjoy without a ripple during the nineteen thirties, the rooms did not seem at all old-fashioned or quaint, but enormously substantial and much more than satisfactory in every respect. Each of the seven or eight that I could see was quite large with ten foot ceilings, and the public ones, at least, flowed into each other with no more formidable barrier than an occasional set of beautifully carved French doors.

I presented Miss Withersby with a small bouquet of cut flowers and was suitably thanked and ushered into one of the silk upholstered armchairs. We made the usual chit-chat for the next few minutes, she asking how I was getting on in my new quarters and I trying to say something pleasant and sensible about the place while being quite unable to get my mind off my next door neighbor (neighbors?) down the hall.

Presently, Alonzo appeared with the flowers in a cut glass vase. Miss Withersby admired them and had them set on a big Steinway grand, the top of which was apparently serving a dual purpose as picture gallery with dozens of ancient photographs mounted in ornate frames arranged haphazardly on the polished surface.

One of these included a snapshot of seven or eight young people from the Roaring Twenties attired in old-fashioned bathing costumes. Looking vaguely like comic figures from a Chaplin film, the group was posing, all languorous smiles, draped willowy bodies and tangled limbs, in the spacious cockpit of an old-fashioned speedboat on some long ago summer outing. I suspected that one of the girls might have been Miss Withersby herself, but decided that they were more likely nieces and nephews, as she was probably too old to have kicked up her heels very much during the flapper era.

Miss Withersby droned on about the rooming house and the young men who had occupied it over the years. Alonzo reappeared and fussed around serving sherry and a small tray containing three or four tiny baked *hors d'oeuvres*. I had just begun tentatively to sample one of the cheese and crust things when I distinctly heard the words: ". . . . nice young man down the hall?"

Miss Withersby's idea of conversation was her own monologue in response to which the other person, at appropriate intervals, was required merely to nod, frown seriously, or say, "Uummmm", while doing both. I had gotten the hang of it pretty quickly but found it difficult to remain intellectually engaged, as it were, having only to be attentive to the changing voice inflection and momentary pauses in order to give the appropriate responses. As this could pretty well be done at the thalamic level, the higher neural centers were free to frolic about as they pleased. At the moment when she spoke those words, they were frolicking along following a set of dainty, naked footprints down the hall toward an open bedroom door, the scent of roses filling the air.

I scrambled frantically to reassemble the fragmentary sentence, came up with "young man" and remembered, just in time, that it had been a question.

"Ahh, no. Not yet. Not so far," I said, hoping that I'd answered correctly.

"Well, no wondah," said Miss Withersby. "He works at night, you know, a government job."

"Ah," I said, "A government job. I thought the entire government shut down at 4:30 pm." This was intended to be mildly amusing, but Miss Withersby did not even smile.

"Oh no. Not *these days*," she said, shaking her head. *These days* was but one of Miss Withersby's euphemisms for the new Kennedy administration.

"It all has something to do with this idea of being Vigorous that they're always talking about. Football and hiking and long hours at the office and all," She paused and raised her eyes heavenward, "Ah think it's just dreadful, "she snapped, bringing her lips together in that tight, horizontal line so faithfully captured by Gilbert Stuart.

I said, "Uummm," and frowned in sympathy, trying to duplicate the same straight line with my own lips. "Do you really think he just stays at the office till all hours every night?"

"Oh, no," she quickly explained. "His hours *are* at night. Ah believe he said he had duty then."

"Oh, then he must be in the military," I offered.

Miss Withersby took a sip of sherry and shook her head peevishly as if this sort of talking back and forth was both irritating and unsuitable.

"He is *not* in the military. He works for the highway department, Ah believe."

"The highway department?" I ventured curiously.

"Yes. Bureau of Roads, located out in Virginia somewheah." Miss Withersby had grown tired of the subject and wanted to get on to other topics. She began talking non-stop about her family and her grand niece, Priscilla, in particular.

I made the expected nods and smiles but daydreams of dainty, naked footprints and open bedroom doors no longer frolicked through my higher neural centers. I knew about the Bureau of Roads located 'out in Virginia somewhere'. It was one of the few places I knew exactly how to find. I delivered and picked up fares at the Bureau of Roads almost every day. It was located in a very large building at a place called Langley.

Sidney Reilly silently closes the door of the big Lagonda and glances quickly in both directions as he moves off down the darkened, tree-lined street. He avoids the soft glow of the streetlamps staying easily in the shadows until he is almost at the rooming house door with the large brass fittings. His right hand moves deeply into the pocket of his long cashmere overcoat grasping the comforting weight of the small Browning automatic.

Two hundred feet away, Felix Dzerzhinsky shifts on his chair. The window is slightly raised in the darkened room. He focuses the scope of the heavy Mauser on the lighted center of the rooming house door. Just below, on the brick sidewalk, a slim shadow quietly ascends the three steps and enters the circle of light. Dzerzhinsky's cat-like eyes narrow as his finger gradually tightens on the polished trigger.

"So, you see, it would be tremendously helpful if you could assist me in selecting something suitable for the girl." Miss Withersby folded her hands in her lap.

"Ah, yes. Something suitable," I stammered, trying to instantly replay the last two minutes of monologue.

"Ah don't really know anything at all about young people these days," Miss Withersby was saying, "but they all seem to adoah these little foreign ones that dash about and make all that noise."

"Yes. The noise," I ventured, trying to piece together her words about a grand niece who was apparently a sophomore down at Sweetbrier and who, poor thing, was unable to get away from Charlottesville on weekends, to say nothing of Thanksgiving or Christmas.

Miss Withersby felt strongly obliged to rectify this dreadful state of affairs by giving the young lady an automobile, but not just *any* automobile. This purchase would have to be selected with care.

With some effort, I put Reilly, Dzerzhinsky and the young man of good breeding who did night duty at Langley on a mental back burner and turned my attention to the now waiting Miss Withersby. Despite the fact that I carefully omitted such arcane and boring esoterica as engine displacement, wheelbase, performance figures, prices and the like from my discourse on little foreign cars suitable for rich coeds, Miss Withersby cut right to the chase. Raising a frail hand to halt my discourse on the relative merits of Porsche Speedsters over Alfa Romeo Spyders, she announced that, above all other considerations, the machine must be gay and pretty. She continued to explain for some moments until I began to understand that what she had in mind involved cuteness and color.

I ostensibly agreed and after a few more thoughts on the subject, it was decided that I should take Miss Withersby shopping the following morning for something that would catch her eye, while I pronounced it sound and reliable as men were equipped to do.

The dinner was excellent, if unremarkable, apparently prepared entirely by Alonzo who served unobtrusively through three courses and took his own meal in the kitchen.

I said my farewells and thank you's just before ten o'clock and drove back through largely deserted streets to the rooming house off Wisconsin. There were no sounds from the room down the hall nor was there any hint of a light spilling out from the crack beneath the bedroom door. Disappointed and harboring mixed feelings about Saturday's shopping trip and the Man from Langley, I wearily performed my evening ablutions and retired for the night.

CHAPTER THREE

On the following Saturday morning, the showroom at Manhattan Motors was a veritable cornucopia celebrating mostly the then robust and thriving British motorcar industry. All sizes, shapes and flavors were represented, such marquees as Austin, Hillman, Morris, Riley, Jaguar, Triumph, Rolls, Aston Martin and Morgan, among the better known.

I gently escorted Miss Withersby from car to car pointing out features and advantages of this one and that one. She proved to be largely immune to their mechanical charms. For Miss Withersby, it was very much like buying a hat. She simply approached one of the gleaming little chariots and appraised it from several visual angles. The names meant nothing to her. She looked critically and then moved on, commenting from time to time on color or shape.

I did not try to swing her in the direction of any particular brand, but merely explained about the various cars as we walked past them in the big showroom. Triumph, Austin-Healey, and MG were familiar and popular names then and likely to appeal to the heart of any young person, mine for instance. I was also certain that Miss Withersby's niece would have been captivated by any of them. Miss Withersby, however, did not appear to have been impressed.

"They're interesting but they all look so insubstantial, rather like toys."

I decided that this was not a good time to advance the point of view that they were, *indeed*, toys, toys for wealthy adolescents for the most part. Miss Withersby had now started off by herself across the floor toward a rather odd looking machine that seemed to have been created several generations before the rest of the offerings.

"Now, what is this one called?" She asked, a trace of interest beginning to emerge for the first time since entering the showroom.

I explained that the car in question was called a Morgan, that it was hand built, had a wooden frame and was considered the very epitome of *pur sang* British motoring. I did not include the fact that, although the engine was quite powerful having been developed from a tractor motor, the car itself had remained substantially unchanged from the mid-nineteen twenties when it had been conceived and designed by members of the Morgan family who still owned the firm.

It was raw and primitive and considered by a small number of fanatical purists, myself included, to be the only *real* British sports car currently in production. It was unencumbered with such sissy affectations as roll-up windows or fold-down top.

The body was a beautiful maroon with sweeping blue fenders running on either side the entire length of a very long hood, which was peculiarly rounded at the end and held in place by what appeared to have been a thick leather belt. It had gleaming wire wheels, seating for two in the small leather cockpit with tiny windscreen and two enormous rubber doughnuts hanging out over the rear end. It was forthright and archaic, a genuine anachronism that was, nevertheless, currently the most successful sports/racing car in its class; a sort of automotive equivalent of the Steerman biplane.

"It has charactuh," pronounced Miss Withersby, "and it's rather cute."

A salesman had been lurking nearby and, like an alligator sliding off a mud bank at the first sign of commotion in the water, approached us quietly from behind a large potted palm. Ignoring the man who was now hovering a foot or so away, I tried very gently to explain to Miss Withersby that this car was really for a small group of rather odd young males who somehow derived a sort of sexual gratification from the overtly primitive and mechanical nature of this little beast. The raw power, the exposure, the roaring noise and wind in your face; the thing was, in reality, a four wheeled motorcycle with the same sort of appeal, and more.

From the thick leather belt holding the long rounded phallic-like hood in place, to the roaring, thrusting, brute-like engine, back through the cramped cockpit to the two, big rubber tires hanging off the back end, the subconscious intention of the builders was clear. This was the Oscar Meyer Weinermobile without adornment. This was more than just a mechanical stallion as a motorcycle might be seen to be. You entered into and became a functioning part of the Morgan. This was the real you, enhanced and magnified to your true physical and spiritual dimensions!

Of course, I could not say any of those things to Miss Withersby, much less even hint at them. I could only point out that the Morgan did not have the modern amenities that had, by now, found their way into most of the other cars on the floor. These less primitive offerings might, after all, be more suitable for a young girl of gentle upbringing.

Miss Withersby was not listening. She gazed with apparent fondness at the glistening bulbous hood and nodded in assent when the salesman, with uncharacteristic cunning, made his final approach while obsequiously rubbing his hands together like Uriah Heep and quietly suggested that we might like to take a test drive.

We came down Connecticut and rounded DuPont Circle at least three times before shooting up Massachusetts along Embassy Row, with the mellow drone from the tractor engine reverberating loudly off the stately marble and granite edifices. Suddenly pulling a dramatic U-turn in the middle of the avenue, we sailed down a winding entrance ramp onto Rock Creek Parkway.

Up to this point, I had driven the little roadster sedately, as if Miss Withersby sitting beside me with her hat and purse and umbrella might be a crate of eggs. But when we rolled down onto the wooded parkway from a winding curve and the road ahead was clear and free, I put the spurs to the Morgan and was instantly rewarded with a tremendous burst of acceleration and a sonorous blast from the exhaust pipes.

In one gear after the other, it roared and swelled and spurted ahead with each ramming push of the clutch and shifter. Centrifugal forces built up in each curve causing giddy excitement and a certain queasiness, but the Morgan remained rock-hard as it was meant to be, rooted firmly to the pavement, and squirted out of each bend with a fresh burst of power and noise.

We traveled several miles in this fashion before I felt a prod from the handle of Miss Withersby's umbrella. I immediately slowed the car to the point where conversation was possible.

"It's quite exhilarating, of course," Miss Withersby began by saying, "but Ah'm not altogether certain that it would be suitable for Priscilla. Somehow, it just seems to be so harsh. Ah think, perhaps, something a little softuh . . . ."

I was nodding agreement when, without taking much notice, we splashed into one of Rock Creek's fords which ran right across the parkway and which could be several inches deep, depending on the weather and the runoff from rainstorms.

There had been a great deal of rain that summer and the ford was at full race as we hit the swirling water at about 30mph. Geysers festooned on either side and waves roiled like the Red Sea parted by Charlton Heston. The Morgan and its two occupants also rolled for a few more feet before coming to a complete halt just beyond the center of the ford.

The Red Sea-like waves instantly subsided and though we were not inundated after the manner of Pharaoh's chariots, we were just as effectively immobilized. I pressed the quaint little starter button above the ignition key in the big leather-covered dashboard and was greeted with a cough, a sputter and then the repetitive and hopeless yammering of the motor. Miss Withersby peered over the top of the low-cut passenger door at the sparkling little stream in which we sat.

"Oh, deah," she said.

I pushed the starter button and held it down but was greeted with only the labored whirring sound as it performed its own little English tractor motor version of "I thought I could. I thought I could. I thought I could." repeated ever more slowly and in lower register. After several such "whirring sessions" the register of the cadence was lower still as the six-volt battery came up against its rather modest limits. I shut off the ignition and sat, watching whisps of vapor slowly emerge from the louvers in the long hood.

"Oh, deah," repeated, Miss Withersby, somewhat more urgently.

"It's all right," I said, reassuringly, "the water's just drowned out the ignition. We'll be able to restart as soon as it's dried."

Miss Withersby seemed to take this news philosophically and we sat there for a few moments during which I periodically made unsuccessful attempts to restart the engine. As I was trying to pass the time cheerfully by explaining about coils and ignition points and their aversion to water, the first drops of rain appeared on the tiny windscreen.

Miss Withersby held one of her glove frocked hands palm up to verify what was, in fact, the beginning of a summer shower, and without a word began fumbling with her umbrella. I quickly opened the driver's door, looked down at the swirling water and began removing my shoes and socks. After rolling up my pants legs, I clambered gingerly out onto the pebbled concrete of the roadbed and slogged through the ankle deep stream to the rear of the car.

The trunk, or boot as the English insisted on calling it, was rather like a large metal hamper which had been bolted on behind the cockpit and which I knew contained whatever minimal concession to the elements the Morgan company had reluctantly made. Lying in the bottom of the cavernous boot were several large packages of rubberized canvas. I had just succeeded in pulling out the larger of these and was setting it on the rear shelf of the cockpit for closer examination when the sky darkened ominously. All around us, the light went frighteningly to pale yellow and then brown.

As the wind set in and the rain started down in earnest, I frantically undid the metal snaps and began to paw at the contents. Inside the bag were odd pieces of Eisenglass and canvas and an indecipherable collection of metal struts and rods. This, neatly packaged and stowed away for use in emergencies, was what the English incorrectly called the hood. On a sunny afternoon among pleasant surroundings and with the guidance of an indulgent and mechanically gifted friend, putting this contraption together would have been a daunting task, requiring perhaps half an hour. Now, with the first tenuous drops already discharged and the main torrent very rapidly coming on line, here I was standing alone in the middle of a rushing stream. The thing was impossible!

As the downpour rose in volume, Miss Withersby hunched down in the big pneumatic seat and gamely took refuge beneath her umbrella. Roundly cursing the English for their little private joke on the affluent American consumer, I glanced around in desperation and suddenly noticed a concrete overpass only a little way beyond the ford which might offer at least partial shelter from the storm.

I threw the rubberized package back into the boot and put my weight against the two spare tires that were hanging on the rear of the Morgan. The car rolled forward and up the slight incline without much resistance until it was mostly clear of the water in the stream bed.

By now completely soaked, I ran around to the passenger side and assisted Miss Withersby out onto the pavement and along the parkway to the overpass. Just as we reached the shelter, a heavy sedan mushed through the ford and rolled up beside us. The passenger window rolled down and a man wearing rimless glasses, a Palm Beach suit, a Panama hat and a clerical collar, sweetly asked if he could be of assistance. In what felt like only seconds, introductions were made, Miss Withersby was ushered into the back seat and the Buick disappeared through the underpass and around the next corner leaving me standing barefoot, like a ship wreck victim, squinting through the torrential din at the feckless Morgan which was quickly filling up with water.

Thoroughly soaked and having no hope of ever erecting the primitive top, I located the tonneau cover and quickly buttoned it in place. The rain had set in for the morning and, with resigned effort, I managed to push the roadster the few remaining yards to the shelter of the overpass. Unbuckling the thick leather belt on the hood and using my socks as towels, I managed to wipe dry all parts of the ignition system that I could recognize and, eventually, to bring the tractor motor sputtering back to life just before the little battery gave its last amp.

Back at the showroom I thundered, with great umbrage, to the people at Manhattan Motors that their little English thoroughbred had let us down completely without warning just as it was beginning to pour; that Miss Withersby was fit to be tied; that all our clothes had been ruined and that our lawyers were being consulted.

I neglected to mention, of course, that the breakdown had occurred in one of the fords in Rock Creek Park, as I felt that driving through a few inches of water would not have mattered in the slightest had the car been properly equipped with the same waterproof ignition system that every other car on the road had possessed for at least a decade. Then, mustering as much indignation as I could, I stalked out of the place, wringing wet, climbed into my warm dry VW Beetle, and headed for Georgetown.

A call to Miss Withersby verified that she had been delivered safely home by the clergyman and was, apparently, none the worse for wear.

I decided almost immediately to cut my losses and to spend the remainder of Saturday afternoon in the privacy of my room, snugly ensconced with *The Rise and Fall of The Third Reich* and a six-pack of Heineken's. Along about the fifth bottle, a nap seemed like the perfect idea. I switched off the bedlamp and was just nodding away when I heard a faint commotion down the hall followed by the clump-clump-clump of the young man of good breeding as he apparently started off to stand his nightly tour of duty at the Bureau of Roads.

An hour or so later, the sound of clip-clip-clip lifted me partially from a gentle reverie; and I lay there, half in and half out of a peaceful doze, and began to contemplate the possibilities of the evening.

At the first sound of running water, Sidney Reilly rises swiftly from the narrow bed and stands near the doorway in the dimly lighted room. His naked body is damp with perspiration. A silk dressing gown from Sulka's is draped across the leather ottoman and Reilly slips easily into it as he reaches for the handle of the door.

The hallway is dark except for the fringe of light around the bottom of the bathroom door. Reilly moves silently across the corridor and listens carefully. Above the muffled spray of the shower, his attention is instantly drawn to moist squeaking sounds as dainty, naked feet turn to and fro in the old porcelain bathtub.

Quickly and without hesitation, Reilly moves down the hall and stands opposite the exotic bedroom. He slowly dials the knob and, as the door pushes inward, a smile spreads across his thin lips.

Lit only by a small lamp beside the bed, the room is wreathed in shadow. In three steps Reilly is beyond the light and standing in front of the heavy mahogany bureau. He removes a penknife and a small electric torch from the pocket of his robe, and, gripping the light between his teeth, gently maneuvers the blade into the lock of the top drawer. A muffled click and the drawer is open.

Beneath a tousled pile of lingerie, the thin beam of light reveals a tiny, metallic cylinder. Reilly picks up the diminutive object and slides back the stainless steel tube to reveal the lens of a Minox camera. Beside the camera lie a small leather-bound book and a pearl-handled dagger. As Reilly reaches for the slim volume, the sound of running water suddenly slackens, then stops. Quickly replacing the items, he silently closes and locks the bureau drawer.

Moments later, the bathroom door opens and the padding of dainty, naked feet leaves moist footprints in the darkened hallway. From the safety of his own bedroom, Reilly smiles in the darkness as the telltale sounds fade from the hallway. He slowly removes his dressing gown, lies down quietly and waits for sleep on the narrow bed.

The evening passes silently in the old rooming house. As he tosses restlessly in the early morning hours, the bedroom door opens, and a shadowy figure on dainty, naked feet steals silently across the room and kneels beside the narrow bed. A pinprick of pain flashes at his throat and Reilly is instantly awake.

"Make no sound," she hisses, tightening her grip on the dagger.

Reilly twists slightly on the bed and gazes steadily into her eyes. For a long moment she returns the look, then asks in a hoarse whisper:

"Who sent you to me? For whom do you work?"

Reilly smiles and gently pushes the dagger from his throat. Slowly, she lowers the weapon to the bed, releasing it altogether as his arms encircle her and their lips meet.

As the evening shadows lengthened, I slowly regained consciousness, drugged with summer heat and the Heineken's that had been taken aboard. Confronted by urgent necessity, I rose and fumbled groggily across the hall into the bathroom to shift the cargo and revive for the evening with a quick shower.

Ten minutes under the blazing spray was about the limit, as the temperature then began to fall precipitously and the experience became absolutely bracing. I turned off the water and reached for my towel where I'd laid it on the toilet seat upon first entering the bathroom.

In the steamy half light, I crouched over the side of the tub and thoroughly patted down the wooden lid, then ran my hand up on the porcelain tank top, but encountered only the strangely cold, unyielding surface of the old toilet. Cursing the prospects of toweling my naked body with a warm and fluffy object that had just fallen to the floor of a communal latrine, I gingerly felt around the base of the toilet with the tips of my fingers while peering intently down into the billowing clouds of mist. As the vapor rose and began to dissipate, I realized with a shock that my towel was not there.

Waving through the steam, I clambered out of the tub and stepped across the little room to the peg where I had hung my old flannel robe. The peg was exactly in the right spot, about six feet above the floor just to the left of the bathroom door; but in this instance, instead of having been properly covered by the old flannel robe, it was as starkly exposed as I.

I glanced hurriedly around the tiny converted space and took stock of my few drab surroundings. The three-by-five-foot grotto beneath the stairway contained a tub with shower head, an old toilet with a cracked wooden seat, a diminutive pedestal sink beneath a fogged-over mirror, a large bar of Dial soap and me!

Cautiously opening the bathroom door, I peered out into the hallway. Nothing but darkened silence. The corridor was as still as a painting. Muddled and confused but having no other option, I sprang boldly across the corridor and seized the doorknob of my bedroom. LOCKED! The bloody thing was locked.

Like a basketball hurled against a brick wall, I rebounded to the relative protection of the bathroom. My mind raced. What was going on in this goddam place? Someone's idea of a practical joke? Immediately, I recalled the clip-clip-clip noise that had trotted past my room just as I had been falling asleep. Holding tightly to the doorframe, I leaned my dripping body out into the corridor, held my breath and listened for the slightest sound. Nearby, a board creaked. Was the old house settling after a day in the August sun or . . . ? Suddenly, another creak and I knew it must be coming from the floorboards of my own room.

Was she there now, her robe and towel discarded on the floor where she had cunningly thrown my own, her luscious body lying insouciantly across the narrow bed? Her lips parted in waiting, her dainty, naked feet caressing the damp sheets?

With the sudden thrill of certainty, I threw wide the bathroom door and strode lustily across the corridor, a naked gladiator entering the Coliseum. A chorus of trumpets blared. The crowd roared and Ladies of noble birth ripped scented togas from their bodies and hurled them down into my path. I raised my eyes in acknowledgment and was greeted by a tossing sea of rouged breasts and impassioned cries of ecstasy. I arched powerfully against the unyielding door, bringing my wet body into full contact with the smooth dry wood. My breathing became audible and with my chest pressed tightly against the barrier, the pounding beat of my own heart crossed the threshold and entered the little locked room. For me, she had no name; but it did not matter, we were already known to each other. I smiled and slyly made a clawing noise on the door with my fingernails.

One hour later, I was finally able to enter the bedroom after first unlocking it with a spare key provided by Miss Withersby. An extremely embarrassing phone call had eventually produced Alonzo, who only slightly restrained his amusement at seeing me swathed in a flowered plastic shower curtain and hiding in the telephone nook behind the bathroom.

Miss Withersby had not questioned the story about the wind blowing the door shut, and I did not feel it necessary to explain my unusual attire to Alonzo. Once inside my bedroom, I discovered that my towel and robe were hanging mutely in their usual place on the peg beside the door.

Eventually, I dressed and walked down Wisconsin and along M street to just before it curves onto Key Bridge. At The Pipe and Drum, I enjoyed a large roast beef sandwich and several pints of ale for well into the wee hours of the morning. It was past two A.M. before I got back to the room and collapsed onto the damp sheets of my empty bed.

Just after sunrise, I drowsily heard the street door open and the sound of clump-clump-clump rolling down the corridor. Three hours later, when the merely stifling heat of the night had been superseded by a monster of pure oppression, I rolled off the sweat-soaked bed, fumbled for my robe and staggered across the hall to the communal bathroom to find myself face to face with the young man of good breeding.

He was correctly dressed in a tartan robe and slippers and was carrying a shaving kit and a neatly folded copy of the Washington Post under his arm. It flashed through my mind that, either through haste or oversight, he was not wearing an ascot.

We nodded and grunted at each other quickly without much eye contact, as was proper for males in the vicinity of a lavatory, and pushed on in our respective paths, as if meeting in the hallway of Miss Withersby's rooming house were a daily occurrence.

Once in the shower, I turned on the cold water tap, which was about at body temperature, and stood there a long, long time, thinking, considering the possibilities.

The previous evening, while crouching for what seemed an eternity in the telephone nook anxiously awaiting Alonzo's arrival with the key to my room, I had sadly worked out the feckless sequence of events which had led to my naked and aroused antics in a public hallway and had been forced to discard any notions of involvement by persons other than myself.

The idea of anyone else having been in the building seemed increasingly remote. I had been here for a week and, until a moment ago, had actually met no one. Muffled footsteps and dainty naked footprints in a corridor were the only tangible evidence I really had of the other occupants. I had almost certainly got it all wrong. With the humiliating self-inflicted events of last evening, the notions of intrigue, hanky-panky and new romance had been dashed and seen clearly for what they really were: self-delusional wishdreams brought on by severe hormonal imbalance. Nonsensical fantasies which overlooked a perfectly rational and legitimate, though hidden, explanation. Now, as the tepid water coursed over me, the chance meeting outside the bathroom with a real live flesh-and-blood human brought the intriguing questions and possibilities flooding back as well.

It was time to make an active move. First contact had just been established. He was about my age, perhaps a year or two older. Now that we had been forced to acknowledge each other's presence in the building, I would pop down the hall, knock on his door and introduce myself. A legitimate basis existed for meeting socially and from this might emerge, who could say, the foundation for lasting friendship, or, much more to the point, intelligence pertaining to his elusive roommate: she of the smell of roses. She of the dainty, naked feet!

Not wanting to miss an opportunity, toweled off and determined to plunge ahead, I dressed quickly in tan Bermudas, buttoned down Madras shirt and Weejuns without socks.

The bedroom door was ajar and the sensuous sound of saxophone music was rolling out into the hall when I rapped sharply a couple of times and stood back waiting. After a moment, the door opened quickly and the young man of good breeding was standing there, right in front of me, holding a cup of coffee and the Sunday Post.

I introduced myself and learned that the young man of good breeding was Art Baldwin, a recent graduate of Cornell.

I later learned that he was actually Arthur Thayer Baldwin IV and that his family owned paper. Lots and lots of paper, practically all the paper there was, in fact. But on that August morning, he was just Art Baldwin from Cornell and he rented a room in Georgetown and worked in a government office about which he provided little information.

At least, he didn't mention the Bureau of Roads thing that he had told Miss Withersby. That euphemism was a standing joke in the Washington metropolitan area so that when I said, "You're one of those bureaucrats, I understand?" he simply laughed, nodded and quickly mentioned some department or other that I had never heard of and which I had completely forgotten by the time he had finished speaking.

We chatted about the usual things: Washington, summer jobs, career interests (his was law) and mutual acquaintances which, naturally, brought us to the subject of Miss Withersby. He had declined a dinner invitation from her on the grounds that he worked nights, after which the relationship had remained correct and formal.

I related the aborted attempt to buy a car for her grandniece and this revealed a mutual love of sports cars, each of us reeling off long lists of statistics about this or that favorite model; and, of course, they were *all* favorite models.

After twenty minutes or so of this sort of thing, we were practically best friends, and when Art said, suddenly, "Do you sail?" each knew he had found a kindred spirit and that all the mutual interests which make up the stuff of friendship between males would naturally fall right into line. Preferences in dress, music, booze and women could be explored at our leisure, but it was almost certain that they were likely to be quite similar. Both of us were well educated but, beyond a general interest in politics and history were not of a particularly intellectual bent. When we wanted to be serious, we spoke of the Negro and civil rights issues.

Eventually, as things were going so well, it was suggested that we drive up Wisconsin to the Hot Shoppe at Westmoreland Circle and get a Mighty Mo. It was during the ride that the subject of women arose in conjunction with dating and, in particular, going sailing on the 24-foot sloop Art kept on the Severn River at Annapolis.

"We have to double date next weekend," he said with great enthusiasm. "Do you know any women?"

Do I know any *women?* Not, "Are you going steady with anyone?" So I very carefully said, "Oh, nobody in particular," as if he had asked me if there were anybody in particular, which he hadn't.

"Damn, I don't either. We'll just have to remedy that," he said, lacing his fingers together and staring hard out the car window as if suddenly deep in thought.

Warning bells clang loud enough to wake the dead, and Sidney Reilly immediately springs up from his tousled bed to find himself utterly alone. In the darkness, he calls out her name, but there is only silence. Reilly switches on the light. The small dagger lies mutely on the nightstand beside the heavy ashtray, which contains the crushed stubs of two English Ovals. Quickly, he crosses the room, pausing only long enough to throw on the Sulka's dressing gown, listens for an instant at the door and makes his way down the hall. Her room is empty. The bureau drawers are unlocked and contain nothing but old newspaper lining their bottoms. She has vanished.

As we sat in the Hot Shoppe, Art began drawing up lists of possible names on the paper place mat using what I recognized as a gold Parker pen. As he set down each name with an elegant flourish, I realized that for someone who didn't know any women, he knew an awful lot of women.

After completing a list of some twelve or fifteen names, he began to flesh them out, if you'll pardon the expression, in the usual way: an abbreviated biographical sketch which more or less included how he knew them, where they went to school or worked, what their fathers did, i.e., whether they *had* money or merely *earned* money, their physical and, if any, intellectual, attributes and immediate availability.

This final criterion was usually disappointing and tended to cast a pall over the foregoing description; and it began to appear as if these series of vital statistics were, for the most part, a series of erotic reminiscences, until he arrived at Linda. Linda turned out to have not only great stats (money, body, personality) but was also of the present world. Well, sort of. It seemed that she was the fiancee of Art's best friend and former roommate at Cornell. But, hey, not to worry. He had recently heard through the grapevine that they had broken up less than a month ago. She would undoubtedly be responsive to the tender ministrations of an old and trusted mutual friend.

Apparently ever the man of action, Art pulled a small black book from the breast pocket of his blazer, said he'd be right back, and headed for the bank of telephones in the restaurant lobby. In ten minutes he returned, grinning triumphantly.

We were set: Linda was thrilled to hear his voice, was dying to go out on the boat next Sunday and had just the girl in mind for me. I was, of course, delighted; but not far beneath the surface, a trail of dainty naked footprints which apparently belonged to no one lingered in my mind.

CHAPTER FOUR

The following work week was made lighter by the ever-present thoughts of the Sunday sail. I found myself daydreaming about it even while ploughing through *Rise and Fall*.

As I sat idly at cabstands anxiously awaiting the barking growl of the dispatcher, it was abundantly clear that boats and romance occupied fairly high, almost equal levels of importance in my life and, when considered as a single entity, worked synergistically to produce a whole which was very much greater than the sum of the two parts.

Of course, intellectually, I knew that the real stuff of true happiness lay in devotion to God, family and children, meaningful creative work and a large income. But in the summer of 1961, at the tender age of twenty-one, the abstractions that constituted true happiness did not occupy a great deal of my attention on a minute-to-minute basis.

Rather, boats and sex were the stuff that roused my body and made my spirit soar. The more profound and puzzling of life's conundrums could wait for a while longer; and, since I already had a pretty good idea of what they were, I tended not to spend a great deal of time worrying about them.

Sunday dawned hot as hell like all the other days of the Washington summer. I had heard not a peep from Art Baldwin all week long and even the clip-clip-clip of his non-existent room mate had been absent from the corridors of Withersby Hall. Things had gotten so quiet and the heat so oppressive that I had taken to leaving the door to my room open during the evening hours while I was reading; but the sounds of footsteps, dainty, naked or otherwise were not heard in the land.

I arose particularly early on that Sabbath morn, forced from my bed by the hideous temperature and accompanying humidity as well as the delicious anticipation of the day's events. Fifteen minutes later when I popped out of the steamy bathroom wrapped in only a towel, I almost ran into Art Baldwin. Apparently unmindful of the stifling heat, he was carefully dressed in tartan robe and slippers, his free hand reaching for the door knob while cradling the shaving kit and newspaper in the other.

We exchanged enthusiastic greetings, told each other how hot it was and reconfirmed our plans for the afternoon. I dressed in pullover, shorts and Topsiders then walked down the street for a bite of breakfast and was back within the hour. I quickly packed ice chest, towel and swim trunks and collected Art. Two minutes later, we were in the car and traveling north on Wisconsin Avenue.

We picked up the girls at Linda's home on Foxhall Road. The Townsend residence was a large red brick Georgian with white columns and a winding drive, set well back on about two landscaped and lawn-swept acres of the most exclusive residential real estate in the District.

Picking up the girls involved fifteen minutes of conversation with the Admiral and Mrs. Townsend while we sat around a wrought iron and glass table on the terrace by the pool and were served coffee by a constantly smiling Negro waiter in a white jacket. The talk was of school and mutual friends and families, with Art carrying the conversational ball most of the time. Mrs. Townsend had been educated in Virginia which allowed me to easily pass muster. The Admiral was quite charming as Admirals are supposed to be and bored us with only one little story about sailing on the Severn during Academy days.

The girls were a lot better than all right. Linda was long and slim with dark hair, very fair skin and dazzling blue eyes almost as striking as Elizabeth Taylor's. Darcy was a little smaller, about 5'7". She was very tan and honey-blond with wonderful long legs and ideal proportions.

Physically, they were both extremely attractive, quite far above the average; but what set them off, what made you instantly take them seriously, was the overwhelming force of their personalities. It was as if, having discovered early on that neither was an intellectual giant nor particularly interested in great questions nor would ever have to consider the problems confronting those who must work for a living, Linda and Darcy had consciously selected a plane of existence best described as Beautiful-Sportsy and had decided to be tremendously enthusiastic about it.

They were the most effervescent girls that I had ever met. They positively bubbled over all the time. It wasn't just a silly or childish enthusiasm. They quite simply managed to bring a feeling of delight and enormous importance to whatever they were doing, talking about or listening to. I found this last to be tremendously appealing, since both were apparently enthralled with everything I had to say and laughed genuinely at all my funny stories.

The one hour drive to Annapolis was highly successful. The four of us were matched perfectly for an afternoon of sailing. The big cloth sunroof, which was almost a convertible top, was pulled all the way back on the VW's roof. Darcy bounced to and fro in front beside me, and Art and the beautiful and willowy Linda were snugly ensconced in the tiny rear seat. So snugly ensconced that it pricked a twinge of jealousy and the image of dainty, naked footprints in a darkened hallway rose up out of nowhere and began to demand attention.

As the sun dips into the warm waters of the Black Sea, the big schooner rides majestically at anchor in the shadow of a secluded cove. Seated at a small table on the fantail, Sidney Reilly releases the woman from his gaze and nods with a glance at the uniformed steward. The servant steps forward and lifts a dripping bottle of Dom Perignon from its icy bath. Wrapping it in snowy linen, he pours the bubbling liquid deftly into the long stemmed crystal that has been slowly twirling between the woman's fingers. Reilly continues to gaze at the woman across the table but does not speak. He nods again and the steward turns silently and presents a large black humidor, its lid opened, for Reilly's inspection. Reilly selects a Monte Christo and carefully puts it to his lips for the steward to light. As the smoke swirls above his head, Reilly flicks a bit of ash from his stiff white shirt front, pushes back his chair and crosses his legs. He smiles at the woman.

"What do you know of me?" She asks defiantly.

Reilly's smile does not fade. He rolls the cigar gently between his fingers. "I know you were sent here by Zhakarov to obtain the Ploesti oil field reports."

WW "That's as may be," says Reilly quietly, "but a rich and dangerous one."

The woman slams the crystal goblet down on the snowy tablecloth rattling the place setting. The steward moves silently to take away the plate but Reilly waves him away.

*"And what of the fifty thousand pounds?" Her voice takes on a
hard edge. She glares at Reilly as the flickering light of the candles
dances off the diamond studs of his shirtfront.*

*Reilly slowly extinguishes the Monte Christo, rises to his feet and
adjusts his tailcoat. The steward moves to draw away the woman's
chair. Reilly glances toward the stairs leading forward.*

"It's time we went below. For dessert."

The woman looks angrily at him. "I want no dessert."

*"Bring the champagne," he calls and descends the stairs toward
the main deck and the interior of the yacht.*

*The steward draws back the woman's chair and she stands
smoothing out the lace ruffles of the white evening gown. The steward
lifts the Dom Perignon from its icy bucket and wraps it in fresh linen.
The woman reaches forward to take the bottle from him. She moves
alone across the freshly scrubbed deck and down the stairway toward
the main salon. As she steps into the owner's cabin, moonlight through
the brass ports reflects the moist twinkle of dainty, naked footprints on
the teak and holly sole.*

Upon arriving at the marina, we cast off and pushed out of our
slip just at high noon. Darcy immediately disappeared below to stow
the provisions; and Art and Linda busied themselves like old hands,
unpacking the jib, shaking out the mainsail and rigging the boat. I sat
in the stern and applied my mechanical abilities (Row Well and Live,
XLI) to whipping the crudely eccentric British Seagull outboard motor
into some semblance of motive force.

I had not sailed from Annapolis before, but I spotted the buoys
along the channel, repeated the mantra: Red, Right, Returning, and set
a course for the mouth of the river and the Chesapeake Bay.

We had barely cleared the harbor before Art and Linda had the
mainsail run up and the jib set. As the little sloop heeled hard over on
the port tack, Art signaled to cut the Seagull and the soothing silent
magic of a boat under sail seized us all with the poignancy of a profound
mystery experienced for the first time.

We quickly broke out beer rations and donned swim suits as each
of us made his separate foray into the tiny cabin. The girls' suits were
standard fifties' one-piece Jantzen affairs. With a new girl, one always
hoped for a daring two-piece, maybe even—hope springs eternal in the

male gonad—a bikini; but none of the girls I knew ever wore bikinis and these girls were no exception.

We had a fair breeze and enjoyed lively sailing for the first part of the afternoon. The estuary was full of boats of all descriptions and we set the ship on a reach, close hauled and let her go out away from the sweltering land and into the cool vastness of the Bay. From time to time, Art would point to a buoy or distant landmark along the shore and I'd set the compass course accordingly; but we weren't going to any particular place, feeling entirely self-contained on our little vessel and happy to be where there was wind.

Occasionally, we crossed the course of a vessel of similar size and speed and a roaringly enthusiastic race ensued. Darcy sat beside me at the tiller and Art and Linda lifted the mainsail to its very limits and furiously worked the jib sheets as we tacked this way and that to gain the slightest advantage.

One of Art's less attractive personality traits quickly emerged during these little contests. He liked very much to tell other people what to do. None of us were novices at sailing and each about equally skilled. The races were impromptu and entirely meaningless. We didn't even know the people on board the other boats, but a streak of tyranny emerged in Art as soon as we came within hailing distance of a rival, and he vigorously shouted orders at everyone. No one seemed to take much note of it. The girls apparently thought it went with being male and owning the boat and did not resent it. I didn't resent it either, but I thought he was a little hyper. I wondered about that, along with other things about Arthur Thayer Baldwin IV.

On our way out of Washington, we had stopped long enough at Carl's Caterers on Connecticut Avenue to get the makings for rare roast beef sandwiches, pickles, cole slaw, potato salad, deviled eggs and, of course, a case of Heineken's. In due time, and as the wind began to slacken, Linda and Darcy fetched up plates from the galley loaded with this provender and we sprawled about in the cockpit eating and talking, trying to balance plates against the heave of the boat and the chop of the Bay.

For most of the afternoon we talked as four young people do who have just become two couples. We weren't stuffy enough or really interested in discussing serious political issues or the Civil Rights Question and not yet drunk enough to discuss the Meaning of Life. We found the latest album of Nichols & May hysterically funny and took turns imitating the various skits. We liked what Bob Dylan and Joan Biaz were currently singing about but we were far too self-conscious about appearing to be sincere and affirming, i.e., square, to continue for long in that vein. We were far more comfortable when we sought out acquaintances or people in the public eye and simply made sport of them.

The best of these figures of fun involved a socially pretentious couple known to Darcy and Linda who had been gulled into accepting a phony invitation to a dinner at the White House. This was issued directly over the telephone apparently by Pamela Tenure, social secretary to Jackie Kennedy. It was an extremely cruel hoax engineered entirely by a friend of Linda's who simply happened to have been bored one afternoon. We laughed hard, especially about the part where the couple arrived at the South Entrance in evening dress. We laughed hard because it really was funny and harder still because it was instantly apparent that the story had scored a major hit, binding the four of us together as friends and assuring a successful day.

As the sun became more fierce, Linda of the Fair Skin quickly produced a broad brimmed straw hat and applied liberal doses of *Bain de Soleil* to *most* of the right places. By mid-afternoon, about half of the beer had mysteriously vanished and its effects were being felt equally with those of the sun. When Art took the suntan lotion from Linda's hand midway through her fourth or fifth application, turned her on the seat and began lavishly reapplying the goo to *all* the right places, he did so without even interrupting his gossipy tale of wild sexual escapades around the Capitol Hill office of Jack Kennedy during the President's obligatory stint as the Senator from Massachusetts. The story was made all the more intriguing because the object of Kennedy's peregrinations was a girl known personally to at least three of our little party.

It was about at this point that the wind practically died. The alcohol had dulled our senses; but, for a time, we had known we were moving ever more slowly through the water. At some point during the terribly witty and entertaining anecdotes about Camelot, I noticed that the sails were aback and that we were barely rolling in a calm sea. I stood up and looked around the horizon for signs of meteorological activity. We were several miles off shore and pretty much alone. The only sailing craft that were moving in the far distance were obviously under power. I dutifully offered to start the Seagull.

Art held up a greasy hand and shook his head.

"Hell no! It's time for a swim."

With a great comical flourish, he snatched the towel covering Linda's legs and twirled it over his head like a cape. Amid delighted cries of *OLE* and much exaggerated applause, he jumped, Errol Flynn-like, from cockpit to cabin trunk and along the little foredeck, shouting some ancient Gaelic battle cry and waving the towel like a flag. He was over the side and into the water before the rest of us could react quickly enough to follow.

I went forward and retrieved a little aluminum boarding ladder from the cabin. I had just poked my head out the hatch when Linda, still seated in the cockpit, flinched and raised her hands in defense, looking past me over the side of the boat. I instinctively turned toward the source of the commotion and was swocked full in the face with a drenching pair of wet swim trunks. Everyone thought this hysterically funny. I carefully wiped my face with the trunks, handed them to Linda and said, without cracking a smile,

"So sorry, I believe these were intended for you."

I then hooked the boarding ladder over the side and fell back down beside Darcy as a fresh gale of laughter rocked the boat from stem to stern.

We were all, of course, implored by Art, to join him as he hung off the gunwale and playfully splashed water into the cockpit. The girls protested faintly several more than the requisite number of times and Art turned his attention to me.

"They're never coming in if you're just going to sit there all wrapped up to the neck ogling them."

I was wearing a pair of short boxer trunks and had a beach towel draped over my shoulders. I stood and dramatically cast the towel aside. A cheer went up from all hands. Quickly making my way to the bow, I crouched and dived, hardly making a ripple in the dark water. As I surfaced, I tossed the trunks high in the air in the general direction of the boat where Darcy reached out and caught them.

Art and I swam round and round, all the while issuing little-boy appeals for the girls to join us. Meanwhile, Linda and Darcy had made both pairs of swim trunks fast to a line and had sent them up the mast to gales of merriment. After five minutes of foolishness and teasing, they extracted promises to keep our backs turned while they modestly disrobed and entered the water, deliciously naked.

Now we all swam around and round, and told each other how wonderful the water felt and engaged in a dozen topics of terribly serious chit-chat, including I believe, The Civil Rights Issue, all the while maintaining a careful distance and pretending that we weren't really naked.

In those by-gone days before the Pill, the possibility of actually having sex under such conditions was about zero. The four of us were young and beautiful and sophisticated enough to thumb our noses at most of the sillier middle class mores; but we were not ready to deal with the consequences of pregnancy.

We cavorted in naked splendor for perhaps an hour. At one point the call went out for more beer. Modesty completely abandoned, I boarded the ladder in front of all, fastened the Styrofoam cooler to a pair of life rings, and put the whole thing over the side to serve as a sort of floating bar. I had just opened a fresh, green bottle and was handing it to Darcy, when I heard the motorboat.

It was a mahogany, triple cockpit GarWood, and it was coming straight at us at something on the order of 40 knots. Perhaps a quarter of a mile away when first sighted, it had cut the distance in half by the time the group made the unspoken but unanimous decision to gain the protection of the lee side of the sloop with the greatest possible speed. As we disappeared around the stern of our little craft, the engines of the speedboat were throttled back to a deep rumbling idle, and her wake rocked us violently as she came off plane and settled back down into the water. I swung around the end of the sloop, holding onto the outboard bracket and yelled for them to take it easy. The GarWood was about the same size as the sloop and was drifting toward us in the gentle swell about ten feet away. A man stood behind the wheel while a woman lounged in the leather seat beside him.

"Ahoy," came a voice with a British accent, "Can you tell us where we are?"

You're too damn close, I thought.

We had all been pleasantly drunk and sexually titillated in a harmless sort of way before being invaded by the speedboat. I began to imagine the Admiral's face if these people turned out to be social acquaintances or, God forbid, friends. Darcy's father did something or other on the Hill, and though I hadn't yet had the pleasure of meeting him, I was fairly certain he wouldn't have been particularly enchanted at having his daughter's antics recounted and laughed about all over the Washington cocktail circuit. Now, succumbing to Calvinist guilt at being discovered *flagrante delecto,* we cowed behind the protective hulk of the sloop like small children caught smoking behind the barn. That is, all of us except Art who immediately left our company and boldly swam right out to the speedboat, his luminous white bottom shining through the clear water as bright as a 100-Watt bulb.

They carried on about directions and distances with Art hanging off the GarWood's polished gunwale. The woman left her seat beside the driver, crossed over to the port side and perched on the coaming of the second cockpit just above Art for an unobstructed view.

She was as beautiful as a film star but a film star from another era. Jean Harlow came immediately to mind; or was it Clara Bow, the It girl. What the hell was an It girl? She was blonde. Not honey blonde like Darcy but platinum blonde like Hollywood. There was creamy white skin beneath the short bobbed hair, deep languid eyes of indeterminate color, the seductive bedroom eyes of a vamp. A Vamp? I realized that I hadn't the faintest idea what a vamp was, but this girl definitely had the eyes of one. The angular distinctive features of the face, the short bobbed hair and the willowy figure were the picture of a fashion model in Vogue or, more exactly that of a 1925 Vargas girl, but the breasts were definitely Playboy of the sixties. And with more confusion, I realized that I didn't really quite know what a Vargas girl was, except that this exquisite creature looked just like one. It was the bathing suit, or whatever it was, that was so peculiar and had set off this host of images in my mind: it was a bathing *suit,* not a swim suit like Darcy and Linda had recently worn but a weird antique thing with a sort of tee shirt top which became a frilly skirt and tight-fitting pants which came down almost to the knee. It even had a kind of collar, a dickey such as sailors have on their blouses. I had seen one of these costumes somewhere recently but, at the moment, couldn't remember where or when. I managed to hear Art say that he had a chart in the cabin and he vigorously pushed away from the speedboat. Graphically picturing the view he presented to the occupants, the three of us collectively groaned as we felt the sloop heel over in response to his clambering up the ladder on the opposite side. He disappeared into the tiny cabin and began rummaging in the lockers.

Darcy and Linda took advantage of the lull in the conversation to cleverly retrieve their bathing suits, struggling demurely back into them, a feat not easily accomplished while hanging by one hand off a boat in 40 feet of water. I divided my attention between watching this incredibly interesting exercise and the people in the speedboat.

The people in the speedboat, though only a few feet away, pretended that we did not exist and made no attempt to engage us in conversation. They spoke quietly between themselves in a language that sounded Slavic to me, although most foreign languages, except French, tended to sound Slavic to me.

Neither the driver nor his boat was of our generation. He appeared to be in his forties and wore cream colored, flannel slacks very high on his waist and an expensive looking red sport shirt. He was strikingly handsome and a dead ringer for James Mason in one of his earlier films.

The elegant GarWood speedboat was, I was certain from my voluminous knowledge of such matters, at least thirty years old, maybe even older. On the other hand, judged purely from the way it looked, sounded and ran, it might have been on its maiden voyage.

And then, there was the amazing girl in the weird swim dress or whatever it was. She was about our age, early twenties, and could well have been his daughter; though we later discovered when we compared notes, that that possibility had not even remotely occurred to any of us. I had been frolicking with two very lovely naked girls all afternoon, yet the girl in the antique bathing costume moved me in ways that Linda and Darcy simply had not, for Linda and Darcy were *nice* girls, the sort who became wives and mothers of one's children. It was wonderfully tantalizing and provocative, *risqué* and more than a little sexy to be in close proximity to them in the present circumstances. With a little more time, a little more beer and the inevitable moonlight, physical consummation might well have occurred. But the Vargas Girl as I was beginning to think of her was different, powerfully different. She was clearly, sensually, nakedly, a predatory creature, and a man would stand as much chance with her as a moth with a flame.

Finally Art reappeared, thankfully draped in a towel, carrying a rolled-up copy of a Coast Guard navigation chart, which he handed across the water to the skipper of the powerboat. The Vargas Girl drew them alongside with a boathook. Art boarded the GarWood and poured over the document with the two foreign intruders. Linda, Darcy and I, we lay low.

The three of us lolled in the water behind the sloop and pretended to chat and move about while those on the GarWood apparently found the navigation chart irresistible. After a minute or two, Linda and Darcy completed their miraculous underwater change and made their way back aboard the sailboat.

I continued to pretend that I was enjoying the water and didn't want to get back into the boat. This was a necessary bit of subterfuge for two closely related reasons: I didn't have any clothes on, and I had become so aroused by the Vargas Girl that there was no way I could modestly board the vessel, clothes or no clothes.

Without making a fuss, Darcy went forward and lowered the swim trunks flag from the mast. I took them from her extended hand and began the awkward maneuver now made more difficult by the current arousal.

As I was struggling with the trunks, I couldn't help noticing the general demeanor of Art and the two visitors in the GarWood. Their attention was on the chart, but they spoke, nodded and gestured to each other as if they were, well, friends. At one point the Vargas Girl put her hand on Art's shoulder, and the lack of any response from him made me certain that it had been there, as well as other places on his body, on previous occasions.

The other thing that was beginning to dawn on me was that these people were not Sunday afternoon joy riders or tourists. That vintage GarWood had most certainly not come from a rental marina. It belonged here either as a permanent part of a waterfront estate or as tender to a large yacht. Humbert Humbert and his Lolita were most certainly *not* lost whatever else they might be. Just then, the Vargas Girl curled her legs up under herself on the cockpit coaming and her dainty naked feet came into full view. Adorning one slim ankle was a tiny chain of fine gold. I immediately realized that I was going to have to stay modestly submerged for yet a while longer.

CHAPTER FIVE

A fter the GarWood had started engines and swiftly become a black undulating dot on the shimmering horizon, the four of us sat around in the sloop's little cockpit and finished off the last of the stuff from Carl's Caterers. We were all feeling a little subdued by the beer, the sun and the events of the afternoon. Our earlier daring and the subsequent invasion were now perceived as something of a mild shock which left us feeling down and sobered before we ought to have been.

Of course we discussed the "Foreign Invasion." The girl in the antique bathing costume provoked endless speculation. I simply couldn't recall just where I had recently seen an outfit like that. The skipper of the GarWood was dismissed quickly for what he obviously was: Sugar Daddy. Art dispelled any speculation as to where they had come from:

"Off a yacht, cruising up from Florida to New England," saith Arthur Thayer Baldwin IV. "Dropped anchor in the Chesapeake for a bit of sight seeing."

The talk immediately drifted over into the pleasures of cruising and of long romantic voyages. Each of us had his particular favorite: the Greek Isles, the Caribbean, Micronesia, and so on and on. We spoke eloquently, longingly of blue warm water, white flour beaches, swaying palms and enchanting coral reefs; the Greek Isles gradually losing out to more southern latitudes. And little by little, all talk of "The Foreign Invasion" died away and, apparently, was forgotten.

Of course, I didn't believe a word about the cruise up the east coast. Those two weren't cruising people. They didn't have the salty, weathered look of ocean travelers. And they weren't friendly the way cruising people were. With their pale skins, freshly minted clothes (even the antique bathing costume looked new) and that rich man's speedboat with its immaculately polished mahogany hull and butter soft leather seats, any sea voyage would have had to have been on something approaching the tonnage of the *Queen Mary*, which certainly wouldn't need any additional charts to know where it was. These people were landlubbers. The GarWood was perfect for them. A salty, weathered cruising boat was definitely not. I was also sure that the Vargas Girl had made her one and only contact with a sailboat only a few short hours ago when she'd snagged Art's little sloop with the boathook. And, of course, there was that other thing: Art Baldwin knew both these people. He knew them both a lot better than he knew me, and I was absolutely certain that he and the Vargas Girl had committed serious Hanky Panky on more than one occasion.

Had Art's little sloop possessed a yardarm, the sun would have been well beneath it by the time we dropped sails at the entrance to the marina. I fired up the outboard and we motored up the narrow channel with the Seagull putt-putting along at a stately four knots. Eventually, amid a muddle of slow-motion activity, we managed to stow the motor, bag the sails, hang out the fenders and cleat off the lines in a marginally seamanlike fashion.

Four pleasantly tired sailors pulled back the top of the baking VW. We spread damp towels on the scorching seats, then quickly piled in and left Annapolis without further ceremony.

We sped west in the gathering twilight, Art and Linda once again in the back seat. The two of them immediately pretended to fall asleep on each other's shoulders; while, in the front, Darcy pretended to do the same on mine. Since she smelled like shampoo and salt and cocoa butter and girl and was very soft, this was just fine with me.

The lights of the mansion are visible far out on the Chesapeake Bay. At the rear of the house, Japanese lanterns softly light the broad gently sloping lawn down to the water's edge. On the lawn and along the deck to the boathouse beside the clay tennis courts, couples in formal dinner attire stroll and quietly talk, drinks in hand and plates held gingerly. Near the mansion, on the flagstone patio, liveried servants preside over buffet tables. Beyond the tall stone columns the lively strains of Gershwin and Dixieland Jazz pour out of the great ballroom.

On the long circular driveway in front of the mansion, a yellow Auburn Speedster brakes rapidly to a halt and a Young Man of Good Breeding descends from the car. A footman whisks the roadster away and the Young Man enters the house through the great open doors and gives his hat and cane to a waiting servant. He is drawn immediately by the sound of the orchestra and heads for the ballroom. Along the way, he pauses to deftly lift a glass of Dom Perignon from the proffered tray of a passing waiter. As he enters the ballroom, his eyes drift slowly across the milling throng, searching.

In a secluded corner, Sidney Reilly notes the newest arrival and quickly excuses himself from the little group which has been paying court to the German ambassador. Reilly crosses the crowded dance floor at a relaxed pace, smiling and nodding slightly at acquaintances as he moves among the dancing couples. The Young Man of Good Breeding sees Reilly and his eyes signal recognition.

Reilly smiles and slowly withdraws a cigarette from a silver case. The Young Man of Good Breeding fumbles quickly for a lighter.

Reilly inhales deeply and blows a stream of smoke toward the frescoed ceiling. He glances discreetly around and speaks softly to the Young Man. Behind the tight smile there is a hard edge to his voice.

"It wasn't very smart to bring your friends along this afternoon."

"I know."

"Really, old boy, you might have sent word."

The Young Man of Good Breeding takes a sip of champagne and shakes his head slightly. He closes his eyes for a moment and then speaks:

"It's all right. They suspect nothing."

Reilly smiles again and bows slightly as an elderly woman wearing an emerald green gown and matching tiara passes nearby.

"Countess," he murmurs.

The nod is returned and Reilly swings back to the Young Man.

"I hope that's true, old boy. for your sake."

The Young Man glances nervously around, searching the crowd behind Reilly.

"She's in her room."

The Young Man of Good Breeding glances quickly at the staircase beyond the distant foyer.

"Steady, old boy. I shouldn't be in too much of a hurry if I were you, especially after your antics of this afternoon."

"It was nothing," hisses the Young Man. "You know it was nothing."

Reilly's eyes widen in mock disbelief, the smile never leaving his lips. "Of course, old boy, we could see perfectly well that you were only enjoying a sail and a bathe with friends. No harm in that, surely?"

"It was supposed to look convincing. What else could I have done?"

"You might have stayed undercover like your friends rather than jumping out to greet us so, uh, openly. You might even have affected the transfer without having had to show up here," Reilly gestures around the opulent ballroom, his smile continues to flicker at the edges of his mouth.

"We were drunk. I felt I needed to make direct contact before one of the others did. They thought nothing about it. Just glad you turned out to be someone none of us knew.

Reilly ignores the explanation. "You do have it with you, I trust?"

"Of course I have it with me. Why else would I be here?"

"Why else indeed, old boy? Why else indeed?"

At that moment, with a bold flare the orchestra strikes up one of the newest of the Gershwin tunes and conversation becomes almost impossible. The Young Man of Good Breeding looks anxiously towards the foyer and the broad winding staircase beyond.

"She's waiting," Reilly said. "You know what happens when you keep her waiting."

The Young Man of Good Breeding sets his empty champagne glass on a nearby sideboard and walks away quickly towards the foyer. Glancing back hurriedly at Reilly, he turns and mounts the winding staircase.

The carved mahogany bedroom door is closed and locked against him. Leaning forward, he raps softly: two knocks followed by three more. No sound comes from within, then a familiar voice: "Ein kommst."

The brass knob turns easily now in his trembling fingers and the door swings slowly open to reveal a large room decorated all in white. In the center of the room is an enormous gleaming brass bed made up with black satin sheets and lace bolster pillows. Overhead a large mirrored panel lifts the black sheets to the white plastered ceiling.

The Vargas Girl is sitting at a white dressing table. The bathing costume of the afternoon has been exchanged for a nearly transparent black peignoir tied with a large bow at the throat. She sees the Young

Man through the dressing table mirror but does not stand or turn to greet him.

"Did you bring it?' she asks coldly.

"Yes. I actually had it this afternoon but . . . ."

"I remember zis afternoon," she replied harshly. "Put it on ze dresser."

The Young Man of Good Breeding swiftly crosses to the white dresser near the bed and deposits a small metallic cylinder. He turns and stares at the back of the seated woman.

"I just wanted to explain . . .", he begins, hesitantly.

"I don't like explanations," she cuts him off. "You vill ring for Fraulein Gruber."

The Young Man falters, "But I . . ."

"Silence. You vill ring, At Vonce."

He crosses to the white satin bellpull hanging by the bed and gives it a sharp tug.

"If you'd only let me explain," he begins.

A door set cleverly into the white wainscoting opens silently and a heavy dour woman enters. She wears the severe black uniform of a maid with heavy leather shoes and thick black stockings. Her iron gray hair is pulled back harshly in a bun. Fraulein Gruber does not speak. She walks to the Young Man of Good Breeding and stands silently, her arms at her side. Waiting.

The Vargas Girl applies makeup to her face. Raising her eyebrow pencil, she looks at the image of the Young Man in her mirror.

"You vill remoof your clothink."

The Young Man glances quickly from Fraulein Gruber to the seated blonde woman. He starts to speak.

"You vill remoof your clothink. At Vonce."

Quickly, the Young Man begins to disrobe, handing each article to the silently waiting Fraulein Gruber. When he is finished, Fraulein Gruber carefully folds the clothing over a muscular arm, stoops to retrieve the patent leather dancing shoes and the long formal hose and garters and silently leaves the room. The Young Man of Good Breeding stands completely naked in the middle of the white bedroom.

The Vargas Girl looks up from the mirror. Quick anger is in her voice. "You know vat to do. Vy do you hesitate?"

Obediently, The Young Man of Good Breeding approaches the enormous brass bed. At each corner a golden chain and manacle have been attached and lie brightly dormant against the black satin sheets. The Young Man sits down and slowly lifts his legs onto the bed. He slips a manacle around each bare ankle; the locks snap loudly in the silent room. He lies back on the pillows and stretches his arms over his head. His spread-eagled naked image taunts him from the mirrored ceiling.

The blonde woman rises from the dressing table and moves silently across the room on dainty naked feet. The diaphanous peignoir swishes around her legs revealing a tiny chain of fine gold on one ankle. She is wearing nothing else. She bends slowly over the Young Man of Good Breeding and fastens the golden manacles around his outspread wrists. His eyes widen and his chest heaves involuntarily. From beneath the satin coverlet, the blonde woman produces the single long feather of a peacock. The Young Man gasps. The blonde woman smiles coldly and lightly strokes his naked thigh. She lets the feather slowly drift down between his wide spread legs. There is a sharp intake of breath from the Young Man.

The blonde woman smiles cruelly, "Und now Liebchen, Ve vill talk about zis afternoon, Ja.?"

We came to a stoplight on the outskirts of the District and all passengers stirred and roused themselves. The hour-long naps had apparently had a rejuvenating effect and it was unanimously voted to stop and get something to eat at the Chinese restaurant just on the other side of Chevy Chase Circle. The driver abstained from voting.

Over dinner, I was surprised to note that there was hardly a reference to "the foreign invasion." We ate hungrily, with the girls chattering enthusiastically about almost everything under the sun from Danny Kaye's tour de force at the Arena Stage and Marilyn Monroe's latest movie to the recent death of Ernest Hemingway, which some were beginning to call a suicide, instead, as the family had insisted, of an accident that had occurred while he cleaned his 12-gauge shotgun.

I realized suddenly that I was having some difficulty following this last topic of discussion. Perhaps it was a cumulative effect of the beer and the sun; but, as I recalled with crystalline clarity, Ernest Hemingway was an extremely popular young author living in Paris. He had just recently finished a book called *For Whom the Bell Tolls*, which was already on its way to becoming an international best seller. Why on earth would he want to kill himself? The conversation rambled on and I was left with the confusion of my thoughts.

Then, as I was chopsticking the last of the broccoli beef into my mouth, the whole problem with the foreign invader topic finally struck me: There was no way anyone could discuss "the foreign invasion." Certainly Art wasn't going to voluntarily draw attention to it, and Darcy and Linda weren't going to bring it up with Art sitting there, because they knew as well as I did that he knew the "invaders".

When the bill with fortune cookies arrived, Art and I each pretended to grab for it and ended up splitting it between us. The fortune cookies were broken open and read aloud but none of them contained anything more enlightening than Linda's which said: *"This is the month for ingenuity."* Eventually, along toward midnight, we pulled up in front of Linda's house. Darcy and I said our good-byes and Art walked Linda to the door and went in for about fifteen minutes to say his.

Upon leaving the Chinese restaurant, Darcy had immediately gone from high manic to a state of apparent catalepsy on my shoulder; and her warmth and scent and softness mingled with the memory of the wonderful skinny-dip proved to be a potent mixture. She roused herself somewhat as soon as we arrived in front of the Admiral's digs, but after a few seconds of waiting for Art to return, sighed and went back to pretending to fall asleep on my shoulder. I pretended as well for another two or three minutes while the inevitable forces welled and swelled within me, then leaned down and began nuzzling her hair and cheek. Amazingly, like Sleeping Beauty responding to the Prince, she awoke just enough to do some informal nuzzling of her own.

And so we nuzzled, sleepily and dreamily at first and then we were really into it, groping and French kissing like mad until our ears, which were always keenly attuned during these sessions to the faintest noise from outside the car, picked up the clump-clump-clump of Art finally coming back down the walk. Darcy and I broke apart and I got out of the car so Art could fold himself into the back seat.

We drove without comment the half mile or so to Darcy's house where the two of us made our trip down the walk to the front door and left Arthur Thayer Baldwin IV to cool his heels all by himself for twenty minutes.

Darcy's parents had already gone up so we sat on the sofa in the living room and picked up where we had been a few minutes earlier before being interrupted. Now free of the constraints of the cramped VW and having to keep ears attuned only for signs of activity on the floor above, we worked ourselves into a suitable passion. Darcy called the halt, as was her duty, at just the point where one loses all physiological control; and we broke apart and sat looking at each other feeling the blood pound and the hormones still bouncing off every nerve ending.

It was now time to be earnest and sincere, and I said what a great time I'd had, which was true; and Darcy said the same thing, which was true. We said how much we really liked each other and, in so saying, opened the door to a repeat performance in the immediate future. Then, knowing that the time had come, I popped the question: "What did you think of Art's two foreign friends?"

Darcy looked up without a moment's hesitation. "We were behind the boat with you, frantically trying to get dressed before he introduced us. I was terrified he was going to say: "the girl with her boobs sticking out is my friend Darcy. Pay no attention to her, she's retarded. But he didn't. He didn't introduce us. He just totally lied about the whole scene."

"Did Linda know?'

"Of course, she knew! How could she not know? She was there. She saw them all three together, especially that girl."

"So what is going on, for crying out loud? Why would he try to make us believe he didn't know those people?"

Darcy shrugged and gave me a coy little smile. "Who knows. Art's a spook. He's also an obsessive/compulsive. Spy versus Spy."

"What kind of spook work does he do?" I asked suddenly.

"CIA"

"I know that, but what is it he actually does?"

"How should I know? You're his room mate. Don't you guys talk about it?"

"I am *not* his room mate," I said, emphatically.

"Well, you're in the same building. You're friends."

"Look. I have seen Art Baldwin only three times in my life and two of those were on weekend mornings. I certainly don't know anything personal about the guy."

"His family have money, you know," said Darcy.

"I didn't know. But what difference does it make?"

"No. I mean *lots* of money. You know, big industrial rich, for generations. Paper."

"What paper? The *Post*?

Darcy laughed her wonderful laugh. "No, *paper* paper, silly. They have huge paper mills and own vast tracts of forests and all that."

"Curiouser and curiouser," said I. "So why would he rent a shabby little room in Georgetown when he could buy a house in Chevy Chase?"

"Maybe he has a house in Chevy Chase too. You never know. "The very rich are different from you and me, Ernest." Darcy smiled her bewitching smile.

I told her about my hunches and suspicions which, if you sifted fact from fantasy amounted to little more than that Art secretly had women in his room. Despite Miss Withersby's strict rules to the contrary, there was nothing earthshaking about that. I, myself, for instance, would very much like to have women in *my* room, if only I knew any.

Now, of course, I did and this was far more interesting than any nosy speculation and James Bond fantasy concocted about Art Baldwin. So Art had his weird little secrets. Who gave a shit? He was a nice guy; and, more importantly, he owned a boat which he might be induced to share in much the same way that he shared his room at Miss Withersby's. We got up and moved to the front door where another five minutes of nuzzling and groping ensued, and I managed to secure a promise to see her again the following evening, to do we knew not what. For the truth was that I was rapidly becoming quite fond of Darcy. I began to see a deep beauty far beyond cuteness and sexual desirability. And she was so very much alive with that tremendous enthusiasm which before had been widely cast to cover all things Beautiful/Sportsy, but which now was giving definite signs of being focused exactly where it belonged: On me and me alone.

As Art and I returned to Georgetown and Miss Withersby's, there was little chit chat along the way except for dutiful male bragging; and the loftily restrained references to each of the girls which permitted us to automatically know that each was potentially serious about the person he'd been out with and that this was to be respected.

As we ran down across the city on the Rock Creek Parkway, Art rambled on with genuine enthusiasm for Linda and all of her sterling qualities. He could be quite personable and charming, genuine and attractive when he talked like this. One immediately sensed the presence of character in Art. One sensed it and one liked him for it. I began to feel ashamed of my half-witted James Bond spy fantasies with Art in the starring role, clothed in deceit, perversion and international intrigue. Art was just a regular neat guy and a very nice Rich Person to boot. Nothing in the world wrong with that. Matter of fact, it was great!

And then I realized something that puzzled and confused me. I had not had half-witted James Bond fantasies about Art. I had had half-witted Sidney Reilly fantasies about Art. James Bond was a fictional product of Ian Fleming's fertile imagination. Sidney Reilly had been very real indeed.

So real, in fact, that as an agent working for British Intelligence he had single-handedly almost overthrown the government of the Soviet Union just as it was getting started. A price was put on Reilly's head and he was tried and convicted *in abstentia.* After a fantastic, larger-than-life career as England's most remarkable secret agent and super spy, Sidney Reilly had escaped the Bolsheviks and had lived in England and America for some years, giving his money and his active support to anti-Bolshevik causes. Finally, however, he had gone back into Russia against the advice of friends and was never heard from again. But that had all taken place many years before I was born.

Now, in some sort of utterly fantastic way, I had the weirdest feeling that I had actually seen Sidney Reilly standing only ten feet away this very afternoon, conversing with Arthur Thayer Baldwin IV, an event which was clearly, incontrovertibly, impossible.

CHAPTER SIX

A rt and I said our good nights as we walked into Miss Withersby's
rooming house. I did not waste a minute tossing and turning and
pondering the day's mysteries. Instead, I fell asleep almost immediately
with the sweet scent of Darcy on my cheek and found upon waking
that it had been faithfully transferred to my pillow. After four or five
minutes of inhaling this ambrosia, I decided that I really didn't want to
go to work and set about inventing excuses to give the dispatcher for
not doing so.

Objectively speaking, this was no big deal. The dispatcher didn't
care whether I lived or died, much less whether I showed up for work on
a given day. Subjectively, however, it was a different question. I viewed
the dispatcher as a fierce authoritarian figure who would immediately
know that I was lying and expose me, to my embarrassment and horror.
Nevertheless, I made my way to the phone under the staircase and
dialed the number for Arlington Yellow Cab.

"Not comin' in today." He spoke slowly and deliberately,
pronouncing each word as if writing it down as evidence to be used
against me later. "Awright 41. Whatsamatter, too much bookreadin'
over the weekend?" He cackled wickedly.

"That's it. Done in by Dostoyevsky."

"Whut?"

"Dostoyevsky!"

"Awright 41." And he hung up without another nasty word,
apparently having felt that I'd led him in over his head.

And I was free for the day! Free to call Darcy. Free to go pick
her up. Free to see her, to talk with her and hear her wonderful laugh.
Free to nuzzle and nibble and smell her. Free to inhale her wondrous
softness and beauty. Free!

I took a long, slow shower and consumed as much time as possible shaving, dressing and walking down to Art's room to see if he were in. His door was still shut so I went down to the little coffee shop on Wisconsin for a long slow breakfast and read the *Washington Post*. It was then a long slow walk back to Withersby Hall where my watch, which had been left on my dresser so I wouldn't look at it every two or three minutes, told me it was still not quite eight o'clock and therefore too early to call Darcy. Shit!

Darcy's parents had a house on Chesterfield Street, one of the beautiful little residential lanes just off upper Connecticut Avenue. Washington, at least northwest Washington, was a fairly small town and the house was only about 20 minutes or so from mine. I drove up Wisconsin and had another cup of coffee at the Hot Shoppe at Westmoreland Circle, then took Albemarle across to Connecticut to another Hot Shoppe where I finally made the call.

In the magical way that things always seem to have of working out perfectly the first time, Darcy answered immediately and spoke my name before I had time to say hello.

I was thrilled. "How did you know it was me?"

"My fingers tingled when I picked up the receiver." She laughed that wonderful laugh.

"Are they still tingling?"

"My whole body," she said, feigning breathlessness.

I didn't answer. The seconds dragged.

"What's the matter. Did you hear me?"

"I've been rendered speechless thinking about your body."

Again, that wonderful full laugh. "Are you going to remain mute for the rest of the day?"

"Yep. Struck dumb by your beauty. I'll have to make signs and gestures to indicate what I want."

"Poor baby. I'll just have to read your lips."

"*Your* lips. Uummm."

We went on and on in this inane fashion, until I finally said I'd be there in five minutes and she said, "Good."

I sat and talked with Darcy's mother for half an hour. Her mother took a keen interest in the budding careers of young men who courted her daughter. My career didn't happen to be budding just at that moment;

so, for the sake of peace in the family, I manufactured a small shrub and began to fertilize and water it carefully to see what would sprout.

To my great satisfaction, by the time Darcy made her entrance I was being asked to stay on and teach at Harvard after receiving my Ph.D. in history. This really wasn't too much of a leap, as I had already filled out a number of graduate school applications and, earlier in the summer, had actually driven up to New Haven to talk to the people at Yale. I had accurately explained all this to Darcy's mother. She was the one who sent me to Harvard and offered me the Chair of European History.

So we went off with Mother's blessing, Darcy and I. We went off into that wonderful bright summer morning of 1961. Two twenty-one year olds, wildly happy in that first day of our new being and excitement and discovery, in that first day of falling in love.

One of the nicest things about the Washington of 1961 was that it could be left behind in about ten minutes by fleeing over Memorial Bridge into the pristine wilds of Virginia. South of the newly constructed towers of Rosslyn, the countryside immediately reverted to two-lane roads and lush greenery and winding streams and looked largely as it had forty years earlier.

We were bound for the colonial village of Middleburg in the Virginia hunt country, Middleburg with its very English flavor, its little tearooms, its quaint shops, its winding cobblestone streets and ancient buildings. We did not go as gawking tourists seeking a spectacle or observing an oddity. We went because we both innately identified with the place, with the life of Middleburg. It was the life of country estates, privacy and beauty, hunts and garden parties: the realm of the Land-Rovered gentry. We could both see our future together in focus in this place. When the word Middleburg fell into the conversation seemingly at random, we turned to each other and said, yes.

The drive to Middleburg took something under two hours; and we slowly entered the sleepy little colonial village that had been largely bypassed by time and largely occupied by the rich. We parked the VW carelessly alongside a high cobblestone curb (kerb?) between a mud-spattered Land Rover and an XK140 Jaguar with a tiny cockpit and blue leather seats.

And we wandered. We strolled, ambled, wandered and gamboled. We delighted in each other's company and in the things around us. We paid no particular attention to where we were or what we were doing.

Neither of us had yet reached an age when the acquisition of property might assume some importance. Yet we knew intuitively that adult couples did exhibit such an interest. In this vague social way then, the nesting instinct began to faintly assert itself, and with it the first primal urges of feathering also rose to the surface as we walked around Middleburg and drifted in and out of the little shops.

We delighted in the smells of Middleburg. We delighted in the old fashioned hardware with its sharp aroma of oil and nails and fresh-cut lumber. We smiled at each other upon entering the saddle shop where tack was sold to the horsy set and which smelled like the inside of a Rolls Royce. Lemons and polish and mustiness greeted us in shops filled with fine antique furniture. The warm dust of great age which baked and spread in the July sun was present in the solid Georgian architecture of each eighteenth century building as we passed along the street.

We dropped in at the little real estate office and talked about "places that were for sale." Then, with the sunroof open, we motored up and down the country lanes looking at land.

Finally, there was the private muffled quiet and the cool wet welcoming smell of the little creek beneath the stone bridge where we sat and talked and paddled our bare feet and threw stones. Where I looked for the first time at her elegantly slim and tapered hands and held them in my own and kissed each palm, where she reached over from behind me encircling my waist with her arms and resting her soft chin on my neck for a long, long time. Where I turned and lightly brushed her cheek with my fingers; and she saw me and the light in her blue eyes became the light in my own.

After a time, we climbed back up the bank and returned to the village to the English tea room for a bite to eat and ordered something called the *ploughman's lunch*, which we fell upon like field hands. We managed to linger over dessert and ale and more ale and finally coffee, and still we did not leave. It was as if each sensed in the other the almost palpable need to remain in this time and place, lest the magic of this first experience be somehow lost.

At 4:00 pm, the place began to make signs of wanting to close its doors. We paid the bill and laughed with the waitress, who was also the owner, and bid our farewells. I was holding the door to the tea room open for Darcy, when the unusual sound of hoofbeats on pavement caused me to glance across the street.

Mounted on two hunters and bearing right down upon us were the foreign invaders from the GarWood. Darcy saw the horses first and looked at them and not so much at the riders. As they swiftly passed, the man looked directly down into my eyes, a little too straightly and a little too long but gave no further sign of recognition. The blonde woman stared into the middle distance, oblivious to onlookers or the surroundings. The pair continued down the street to the end of the block where they dismounted, tied the horses to a hitching post and entered a tavern. I was never so surprised in all my life.

"Oh, look! Aren't they beautiful!" Darcy gently touched my arm to call attention to the passing horses, when she suddenly noticed who was riding them. Her fingers clamped onto my elbow and she let out a little squeal of surprise. "Hey, neat! It's Art's friends from the boat." She looked at me, delighted. "Isn't this amazing? Let's go say hello."

Darcy took a step forward with her arm linked in mine. I didn't move and she looked up at me and saw that her own pleasure was not reflected in my face.

"What? What is it, Jack? What's the matter?"

"Nothing." I smiled and shook my head. "I just thought for a moment that we ought to be careful."

Darcy laughed, "Careful of what? You think they're Russian spies? KGB?" She playfully poked me in the ribs. "Or maybe they're involved in recruiting for the White Slave Trade."

I looked down at her magnificent honey-gold hair piled loosely atop her head, then pulled her gently against me and gave a quick peck to the tousled curls.

"Let's go," I said, starting down the sidewalk toward *The Benbow Inn*.

"Do you think they'll recognize us?"

I shrugged, "He looked right at me but I don't think he knew who I was."

Darcy nodded vigorously, "We'll just march right in and get a table; then," she put her hand on my sleeve, explaining her strategy, "We'll wave wildly in complete surprise and rush right over."

I burst out laughing and Darcy joined me. "And then what? What do we talk about?"

She thought a moment. "We ask them if they got back to the yacht without getting lost again."

"Hah," I scoffed.

"What? What's wrong with that? They'd think we were being rude not to ask."

"Darcy love, you're forgetting that they weren't really lost. And since we're all a long way from the Shore today, I doubt they even *have* a yacht."

Darcy shook her lovely head emphatically, bringing her enthusiasm to focus. "*They* don't know that we know. They think we completely swallowed whatever story Art told us. They'll agree pleasantly with anything we say and just go along with it. It would seem weird *and* rude not to inquire."

"You're probably right."

"Of course, I'm right. And Jack?"

I smiled down at her loving to hear her say my name. "Yes, Love?"

"That's the second time today you've called me 'Love'."

I grinned, "Who's counting?"

"Me, obviously. And Jack?"

I grinned some more, "Here we go again."

She tugged my hand. "Be serious. Even if this whole thing is a hoax, who cares? What difference does it make? They're just two silly people, playing some sort of weird game with Art."

"That's what bothers me."

"What?"

"That man doesn't look like a silly person to me."

But Darcy had made up her mind and I let myself be led down the street toward the Benbow Inn with her beautiful hand linked in mine.

The Benbow Inn turned out to be an inn, after all, as well as a tavern with a separate entry door for each. The place was cool and shaded and lit with soft lighting. There was a bar and tables laid out and furnished in a pleasant manner. Several gentlemen were seated at the bar, and no one seemed to take notice of us as we entered. We seated ourselves at the barkeeper's invitation and glanced around at the other tables. None was occupied. Though their steeds were hitched just outside the door, the two riders were not in the tavern.

I nodded my head at the passage way which led directly from the tavern into the hotel. "Maybe they booked a room."

Darcy's eyes widened. "In ten seconds."

"Maybe they already had it booked."

"They went in the tavern door. Not the Inn door. We both watched them."

I shook my head in mild bewilderment. "Maybe they ran to the bathroom. Let's have a beer and see what happens."

Darcy nodded and I got up and went to the bar for two draught beers. For the next half hour we sat and drank our beers and talked in whispers and constantly looked this way and that with quick furtive glances. When I strolled over to the door to have a look outside, the two hunters were no longer tied up at the wrought iron hitching post.

I came back to the table. "They've pulled out. Horses are gone."

Darcy nodded thoughtfully and looked toward the bartender. "It can't hurt to make inquiries."

I was in complete agreement. I slipped over to the bar said that we were expecting friends. Had a couple in riding clothes, a man and a young blonde woman, come through just before us? I was told, quite definitely, that Darcy and I were the only couple that had come in all afternoon. Could they have quietly slipped past him and gone into the lobby of the Inn? They might have gone into the lobby of the Inn, but not through the bar. Nobody went through the bar without him knowing about it. I wondered at that, but thanked him and came back to our table and reported to Darcy.

"Let's ask the hotel clerk," was her immediate response, as I knew it would be.

The desk clerk was female, about fifty and at least sixth-generation Virginian. She was the perfect stereotype of every well brought-up southern boy's mother.

She was terribly sorry to disappoint us, but the answer was no.

While we had been sitting in the tavern having beer and waiting for our quarry to appear, the germ of an idea had begun to form. This brilliant thought loosely involved Darcy and me checking into the Inn and getting a room there for the night in order to keep watch for the 'foreign invaders.' Now, one look at the desk clerk dashed whatever hopes might have lain in that direction. We thanked her and walked out into the fading sunlight.

The trip back to Washington was relaxed and delightful. We speculated for a while about the two 'foreign intruders,' but found we could not sustain the topic. We were much more interested in each other and spent the time shyly opening the many little windows that were mostly kept tightly closed.

The Big Country was playing at the Georgetown Theater and, early in the day, we had planned to see it. Upon our return from Middleburg, we ran straight over to Darcy's house so she could clean up and change and then headed back to Georgetown for the movie.

We parked just beyond and across the street from Miss Withersby's rooming house and crept up the stairs in the gathering twilight hoping that no one would see us violating The One Great Taboo. While I dashed into the bathroom to remove any possible impediment which might take the fun out of being close, Darcy sat in my room and looked at all my things.

When I came out of the bathroom, she was looking at Arthur Thayer Baldwin IV, who was standing in my doorway all dressed to go to work at the Bureau of Highways. To my great surprise, Darcy was telling him about our encounter with the 'foreign invaders.' Art was saying things like, "Really?" and "Isn't that odd?" with an air of genuine puzzlement and mystery. I honestly thought he was as surprised by the revelation as we had been upon seeing the two of them riding down the main street of Middleburg. He began an open musing speculation about the origins of the strange couple. Riding clothes and horses. What about their Chesapeake Bay cruise? Why would they be in Middleburg? Had they actually been staying at *The Benbow Inn*, after all? The horses were possible livery stable rentals? (Hardly. Art hadn't seen those horses.) No. Did they live there? No. Staying with friends? Yes! That must be it. Weekending on the estate of friends. Why did they try to give us the slip? Well, obviously they didn't. We had some preconceived notions and let our imaginations run away with us.

Of course, all this was very much like walking a tightrope, because Art was lying. He was so good at it that if I hadn't known to the contrary, I'd have thought that he was just as puzzled and intrigued as Darcy and I.

We couldn't bring ourselves to say, "Oh, come off it, Art. We know you know these people, and we know you've been getting it on with the little blonde." For some reason, Art did not want us or anyone to know of his relationship with this pair; and he was willing to go to elaborate lengths to lead us to believe that there was no connection.

Yesterday on the boat, he had breezily lied and passed off the whole incident as a chance encounter. Now, he stood in my doorway and compounded the lie a hundredfold. Why? I couldn't imagine, but Art was taking far too great an interest in this whole business for it to be anything trivial.

Finally, he glanced at his watch and said he had to run. We said the same thing and locked all doors upon our departure.

After the movie, Darcy and I walked across Wisconsin and down the half-block to my room where we proceeded to get to know each other better.

It was wild and magical, a trembling, driving, ecstatic milestone in the new miracle of knowing. As we lay momentarily spent with labored breathing after the first frenzied rush, we knew with a deep frustrated yearning that we had just opened the door a little and it must now be immediately closed again. The drifting timeless hours of dreamlike exploration must be deferred.

I glanced over at the Baby Ben and made out a luminous 1:30 am, when Darcy moved her head on my shoulder, warmly nuzzled into my neck and whispered those dreaded words.

"I should go."

"You can't stay?" I whined. "I want to wake up with you in the morning."

She purred in the darkness and gently kissed my cheek. "Me too, but I have to."

By the dim glow of the bedlamp, we managed to find most of our clothes which had been scattered in the oddest places all over the dark little room. After quick trips to the bathroom, we locked up and tip-toed down the shadowy hallway and out the front door.

We had just settled into the VW and rolled down the windows when I noticed movement in the side rearview and shhhed Darcy who, as usual, was chattering away. Across the street on the ancient brick sidewalk a figure was briskly making its way toward the rooming house. In the still summer night, the echoing sounds of clip-clip-clip could be distinctly heard. Neither of us dared to breathe.

The figure ascended the three steps and stood for only a moment at the heavy door before we heard the tell-tale sound of a key being inserted into the very lock that we had just bolted. The door quickly opened and closed and she was gone.

"I knew it," I said. "She and Art."

"Are you sure it's she? I couldn't see. It's hard to tell who it is."

"Darcy, Sweet, who do you think it was?"

"The girl we saw on the boat yesterday and again this afternoon in Middleburg."

"Right. The only question is why is he *lying* about the whole thing? Nobody gives a damn if he has a girlfriend, except Miss Withersby, and I'm sure she doesn't even care so long as he keeps her out of his room.

Darcy put her hand on my arm. "Jack, maybe she's married. Art's afraid the guy will find out about them."

"But why try to kid us?"

"Linda."

"Ah," I sighed. "You're right. Linda." It really was nothing more than clever old Art keeping two girls on the string at the same time. All my exciting fantasies had been an utter waste of time. We sat quietly for a moment in the sultry darkness.

Then Darcy said, "What's the time?"

"Late. We gotta go."

The trip to Darcy's house took less than fifteen minutes, and the house was dark except for an outside porch light. We entered the unlocked front door and went immediately to the kitchen to raid the refrigerator.

After a few minutes a sleepy, feminine voice whispered, "Hi kids," Darcy's mother appeared in robe and nightgown.

She sat for a moment to chat and put us at ease. She was fun and pleasant to be with. After a few moments chit-chat, she wearily smiled, excused herself and went back upstairs having determined that her daughter was safely home and all was well.

There was some talk of my sleeping on the living room sofa since it was only about three hours until dawn, but I could picture the scene when her parents came down to breakfast and I decided to pass. Despite the hour, my heart was light as I drove off. Although I had only about four hours to get some sleep before going off to a job I hated, in the evening I could be with Darcy.

In my room, I shed my clothes on the floor between the door and the bed and collapsed without further ceremony. The sheets were rumpled and damp and smelled of Darcy, and I drifted away almost at once transported by the memory and the wonderful aroma. I did not once dream of the dainty naked footprints still damply visible on the hallway floor.

CHAPTER SEVEN

I roared out of Miss Withersby's rooming house next morning with a giddy lightheadedness which was not entirely the result of hunger and lack of sleep. I was free of the burden of the Great International Conspiracy down the hall. The worrisome uneasiness which gnawed at me for the past several days was mercifully gone.

Also, I wanted Art Baldwin as a friend. I had had disloyal and dishonorable thoughts about him, and these were troubling to me. Now it all slipped away with the single realization that Art liked Linda enough in order to want to deal quietly with his other girlfriend. Perhaps let her down gradually. Who knew? It was his business and certainly not mine. Anyway, I suspected that he would unburden himself to me as we became better friends.

The other reason that I was giddy and lightheaded was, of course, my beautiful Darcy. I plowed through the traffic of the morning rush as one immune to the frustrations of commuting. I was beyond the maelstrom of the Rush and well up Glebe Road when I realized with a start where I was and how far I'd come, and that I'd spent the whole drive thinking of Darcy.

As was almost to be expected, I got off to a bad start with the dispatcher that morning by arriving at the cab company nearly thirty minutes late. This was a serious offense, as it meant a cab was sitting there idle, making no money for Neil and his father.

"I almost give your cab away, 41," was the dispatcher's opening shot. "You still not recovered from that there big weekend? That church recital too much for you?" He chuckled softly at his rapier-like wit.

The impulse to key the mike and shout, **"Fuck You"** was successfully repressed. About five minutes later, I was dispatched to transport an elderly widow living on social security the four or five blocks to the government office to pick up her check.

I then ran empty to the nearest cabstand, which wasn't all that near, sat there for twenty minutes without getting a fare, and finally went back to the social security office to pick up the widow. The fare was the minimum thirty-five cents each way and no one had thought to tell her that tipping was permissible.

Throughout the morning I soldiered on without complaint, knowing that eventually "this too shall pass", and that at the end of the day Darcy would be in my arms.

This sweet reverie was shattered by the squawk of the radio and the guttural base growl of the dispatcher's voice. He yelled out an address with which I was all too familiar.

I had a few regular fares. Several times a week I was called upon to transport The Pink Lady. She lived in an elegant suite in one of the new Riverhouse apartment buildings, a complex of posh high rises down on the Potomac between Alexandria and the Pentagon. The Pink Lady summoned a cab every afternoon, just a little past twelve o'clock.

I always stopped at the building's entrance and gave the doorman her name. She invariably appeared wearing an enormous broad-brimmed hat, a white or pink silk suit and elbow-length silk gloves. A diamond bracelet the size of an ace bandage set off the ensemble. The Pink Lady was a vision of chic elegance. I thought of her as being old. I suppose she was forty-five or fifty.

Several showers had made the morning gloomy, but about eleven-thirty the rain stopped and the sun came out. Steam rose from fresh puddles on the sidewalk as I approached the grand entrance.

She lunched every day at a Washington restaurant called Paul Young's, but started her own personal cocktail hour somewhere around mid-morning. The doorman came absolutely unglued each time she appeared. She proceeded through the lobby approaching the entrance in a series of tacks. Like a sailboat beating against the wind, she veered at about 45 degrees to the entrance. Making a series of short, fast little steps, then abruptly rounding up to adjust the purse on her arm, she cast an imperious gaze, then beat over on the opposite tack for about ten feet before stopping and collecting her dignity once again.

The doorman quietly entered the lobby during this little exercise and followed in her wake with his arms spread, a concerned expression on his furrowed brow. She would not permit him to take her arm or to assist her in any way. As she began another in a series of jumpy little runs, he squinted up his eyes, clenched his teeth, and hissed with a sharp intake of breath each time she swayed or faltered, all the while crouched behind her with arms spread wide. Other people in the lobby turned and stared open-mouthed, thinking the doorman was about to attack this elegant woman who took no notice of him at all.

Everyone was visibly relieved when the doorman at last scurried around her and opened the door. She sailed through like a ballerina, the doorman squinting, crouching and hissing in her wake.

Sunshine broke through the clouds; I jumped a rain puddle and smartly opened the rear door of the cab, as she teetered to a halt. The doorman rolled his eyes heavenward in thanksgiving, sighed wearily, and returned to his assigned post.

"I want to go to Paul Young's."

She spoke with enormous gravity, sounding exactly like Greta Garbo and addressing not me, the driver, but the taxicab itself. Despite not being spoken to, I answered for the cab with a cheery, "Yes, Ma'am" and gave her my winning smile, which she ignored.

Standing on the wet sidewalk, she peered directly into the dark interior of the vehicle, took her purse in both hands, bent her knees, and carefully sat, as if a chair had been drawn up behind her by a perfect servant. Only, a chair had not been drawn up behind her. Nothing at all had been drawn up behind her and she lowered herself into thin air, the look of serene condescension never leaving her face.

Aghast, I think, is the word that best described the doorman who had turned just in time to witness the event. Aghast would do as well for the three or four onlookers who were passing on the sidewalk. I stood there transfixed, clutching the door of the cab. Both of us were also aghast.

The summer shower having just passed, the sidewalk glistened with moisture. The doorman and I sprang to her rescue as though to save a child caught in a swirling torrent.

The Pink Lady, apparently uninjured, seemed nonplused to find herself sitting on the wet concrete still facing the open door of the taxi.

We assisted her to her feet and stood there asking if she were all right, as she adjusted her hat, the once-elegant white silk suit and her gloves. Then, as if in answer to our queries, she raised her head and said gravely to the open door of the taxi: "I must change."

With that, she came about and tacked back toward the big glass doors, the doorman crouching, squinting and hissing behind her like a monster in a horror film. I hastily scrambled back into the cab and radioed the dispatcher that the fare had canceled.

"Which is it, Forty-One? Couldn't find the place, or got kidnapped by another sailor boy?"

"Neither," I responded gravely, "Fare just made a last-minute change."

The afternoon sun was drawing little vapor clouds off the wet driveway of the Riverhouse. I pulled out into the traffic and merrily sculled off toward the nearest cabstand to await the end of the day, and Darcy.

As the summer days passed, we usually met at my place after work. I had a spare key made so she wouldn't have to wait if I were late, as frequently happened. Later in the evenings, after renewing our acquaintanceship, we went out to movies, or sometimes to interesting bars or to hear jazz played at the Charles Hotel, an African American establishment in SW Washington which catered to a mostly White audience. During this phase of initial discovery, I was invited to have dinner with the family in order to meet and be personally inspected by Darcy's father, Charles Harris.

Mr. Harris was a portly man with a warm and outgoing disposition. He was a journalist, the senior representative of the Associated Press covering the doings on the Hill. Like all members of Darcy's family, he was easy to talk to and fun to be around. Apparently, he approved of his daughter's current selection with the usual reservations, and we hit it off reasonably well.

Actually, as it turned out, I was saved from more finely focused inspection by the ominous news about the erection of the Berlin Wall. The East Germans had raised this grotesque symbol of oppression, concrete block by block, over the weekend. Washington and the world was all agog with the news and the response of the Kennedy administration. So far the response had been limited to some rather tough remarks by the President which were echoed in the U.N. by Ambassador Adlai Stevenson.

Charles Harris admitted that there was really nothing we could do about it and the talk centered on Cuba, the Bay of Pigs fiasco just three months ago and the little hints and rumors that had begun to emerge regarding the importation of Soviet advisors to that island in ever greater numbers. We talked of such things, amicably, over drinks until joined by the others. Thereafter, apparently, the force of the initial parental scrutiny was sufficiently blunted to let me off the hook for the rest of the evening.

The closest I could come to reciprocating with the 'meet the family thing' was Miss Withersby. I was not altogether sure that Miss Withersby and I were still on the best of terms, especially since the car shopping fiasco; but I tended to think of her as a sort of great aunt. Besides, I wanted Darcy to meet her.

I phoned a day ahead and asked if my friend Miss Harris and I might call upon her; and, before we knew it, Darcy and I were approaching the grand entrance at 4000 Connecticut Avenue N.W.

Miss Withersby had invited us to tea. I had to leave work early in order to shower, change into my poplin travel suit, pick up Darcy and still get there by four o'clock. Alonzo met us at the apartment door and ushered us in, smiling and even making a little conversation. Considerable softening of the sober and formal demeanor he had always displayed before.

Darcy's presence clearly made a difference. Of course, she was stunning to look at in an elegantly simple white dress with thin rolled straps that revealed her beautiful tanned shoulders. Her shoes and purse matched the creamy looking dress and her golden hair was done up on top of her head in the most devastating manner. The whole thing was set off by a single strand of pearls around her lovely neck. She looked good enough to eat and it was with great difficulty that I restrained the urge to nuzzle and nibble while we stood and waited for the door to open.

Miss Withersby was seated on the sofa in the living room fiddling with a silver tea service on a large tray that Alonzo had apparently just placed on the little table at her knee. When we entered the large room, her deeply creased and folded face lit up and she thrust forth both hands in welcome. "Ah'm *so* glad you children could come and see me," she said with real feeling. I began to feel that I'd somehow been neglectful of her, and that she'd missed me.

The introductions were quickly made and she patted the sofa and insisted that we sit beside her while she began, once more, to fuss with the teapot, china and refreshment. As she fussed, she kept up a gentle patter of questions aimed at Darcy and all designed to ascertain whether or not her initial favorable impression had been correct.

Miss Withersby had just started to comment on some little tea cakes, when Darcy squealed, brought her hands together and looked at the smooth little round objects as if seeing the Holy Grail.

"Ohhhh," she breathed, "Beaten Biscuits!"

It was apparently Miss Withersby's firmly held belief that only ladies of a very special class and background knew anything at all about this Southern delicacy; and, with a single cry, Darcy went instantly from being just another pretty, well brought up American girl to being, well, one of us. The two of them chattered like school girls, laughed and told stories and even whispered together. Darcy scooted over closer to Miss Withersby and they sat together, her beautiful slim young fingers gently cradled by the ancient, liver-spotted hands.

I couldn't get a word in edgewise for the next forty minutes. I might have attended the same school as Miss Withersby's grand uncle, President William Henry Harrison. I might have known the names of the First Families of Virginia. But I hadn't passed the Beaten Biscuit test and, of course, as a man, could never hope to do so.

Thus, while Darcy and Miss Withersby continued to commune on an elevated plane to which I could never aspire, I sat and drank tea and ate the damned Beaten Biscuits smeared with chutney and little slices of Country Ham. Of course, I smiled and nodded and even joined in the gaiety at all the appropriate times, but both of them had already mentally tuned me out after pouring tea and filling my plate with enough food to keep me busy until it was time to leave.

Grateful that I wasn't made to eat in a separate room, I continued to pretend that I was actually there too; and, of course, Miss Withersby's innate good manners would not permit her to entirely ignore me. She glanced my way with a smile or a phrase from time to time, but it was clear to me that she was taking tea with Darcy and her young man and not, as she had said with great enthusiasm during the introductions, "Mr. Norton and his young lady."

The other irritating thing was that as soon as the B words had been uttered, Miss Withersby stopped calling Darcy, "Miss Harris" and began using her first name. I was, of course, still Mr. Norton, even after I rather graciously informed her that my Christian name was John, that my friends called me Jack, and that I would be honored if she would do the same. She simply smiled, reached over Darcy and patted my hand, but in further conversation, declined to avail herself of this privilege.

The antique grandfather clock in the hallway chimed five when we began to stand and make our farewells. That is, I began to stand. Darcy remained seated and the two of them went on for another five minutes about God knows what.

I stood there awhile, pretending to listen, then looked out the window at the woods and lawn and shrubbery. Alonzo silently appeared and began discreetly removing the tea service. Darcy and Miss Withersby began to rise, then thought of something that they both just *had* to say and sat back down again, this time thankfully perched on the edge of the sofa as if in preparation for a quick ascent the second time around.

I paced casually over to the grand piano and began to look through all the Victorian clutter and bric-a-brac that adorned the polished ebony top of the old Steinway. And there it was. Set amid a gaggle of mostly nineteenth century family photographs, was that picture of all those young people in the old speedboat. I remembered seeing it earlier and picked it up to have a closer look.

Two things in the old photograph immediately caught my eye: The speedboat wasn't just the garden variety runabout as I had remembered from my first look. It was a mahogany planked, triple cockpit GarWood. And the man behind the wheel? I looked more closely. The man behind the wheel was Sidney Reilly, looking almost exactly as he had looked two weeks ago on the Chesapeake Bay.

I didn't tell Darcy about the picture until we were almost back at her parents' house. We came out of the building and headed for the car talking non-stop about what a sweet old dear Miss Withersby was, and how elegant the apartment, and Alonzo the perfect butler and on and on. Miss Withersby had evidently felt that Darcy was ideally suited to accompany her car shopping for her niece and had set a date for doing so. I did not seem to have been included. We swung out into the still frantic rush hour traffic on Connecticut and headed north for Darcy's.

By the time we pulled up at the door of her parents' house, I had told her about the picture. We had already laughed about my fantasies of Art and the mysterious spies; and of course all that had gone by the board last evening when we had seen the blonde girl entering the rooming house. It was all just Art the Spook delicately tightroping between a waning extra-marital affair and Linda, his new-found love.

Of course, Darcy laughed and wanted to know if the Vargas girl were sitting on his lap or perhaps it was Miss Withersby. Then, she realized that it was troubling me and became concerned.

"Sweetheart, it's a forty-year-old picture of a boat like the one we saw. That's all."

"What about the clothes they were wearing in the boat we saw? What about that bathing dress on the Vargas girl?"

"It was a lark. She was just dressing the part with that old boat."

"*Why*, for heaven's sakes?"

"Who knows why? Why do people give masquerade balls?"

"Actually, I've never understood that one either."

"Because it's silly and fun and harmless make-believe, these people are bored, Jack."

"What about the man, then? What about Reilly?"

"Jack, in all those old pictures the men always look more or less the same with their hair slicked down and parted in the middle and all wearing the same black swim suits with shoulder straps. Come on. How long do you think that picture has been sitting on Miss Withersby's piano?"

I answered without hesitation. "Since she moved in."

Darcy leaned over and kissed my cheek, breathing a loud sigh of relief. "That's right, my love. That's absolutely right."

CHAPTER EIGHT

S ome years ago, Darcy's father had purchased an enormous tract of wilderness land in the mountains of West Virginia. When I asked him why he had bought so much, he said it was because it was so damn cheap. At $5.00 an acre, I could not disagree.

Recently, the Harris family had selected a suitable building site on one of the remote peaks. A bulldozer had cut a logging trail four miles through the woods from the nearest county road. A rough sled was bolted together and dragged behind the dozer with all the building materials necessary to construct a weekend retreat. Local carpenters had recently finished the work. The family quickly formed the habit of loading up the camping gear every Friday to make the two-hour pilgrimage to the weekend hideaway. Of course, Darcy was dying to show the place to me.

An early start was anticipated by the family for the upcoming weekend, but with my uneven track record at the Arlington Yellow Cab Company, taking off Friday was simply tempting fate, the dispatcher and Neil. In short, if I missed work Friday, I might not have gainful employment the following Monday. Mr. and Mrs. Harris and Darcy's 15-year-old brother, Sam, would go ahead. Darcy would loyally wait for me to pick her up at home after work.

I called the dispatcher promptly at 4:00 pm and announced that I was quitting for the day. Before five, I was already in my room, changing out of the taxi driver's uniform and packing like mad. The cabin had been described to me as rustic, which, in the Harrises' terminology meant sleeping bags on the floor. I decided to forego pajamas and robe and just sleep in my clothes. Also, since the temperatures were said to fall quite sharply at night in the West Virginia mountains, I included a pair of Levis to supplement the usual weekend Bermudas and added a couple of wool sweaters and a nylon sailing jacket, lovingly purchased from Abercrombie & Fitch.

I opened the top drawer to my bureau and started throwing a stream of essential weekend items into the open duffel bag. Two fresh packs of Winstons were followed by a handful of foil-wrapped condoms from a newly purchased box. I gazed thoughtfully at the little packages and, after some pride and reflection, added a second handful. Socks, underwear and some other odds and ends, including a large pocket knife were tossed into the bag, and I closed the top drawer and snatched up the duffel.

At the last moment, I remembered that my Zippo lighter needed recharging and went back and rummaged hastily through the top drawer searching for the can of lighter fluid. In about 30 seconds, I realized that it wasn't there.

This was exceedingly peculiar. I did not smoke during the daylight hours, preferring to light up after the dinner meal or with drinks in the evening. Consequently, my smoking paraphernalia was always kept in one place. I carried cigarettes and lighter with me in the breast pocket of my shirt when I went out at night and they were always on my bed table when I left for the day. Now, since Darcy had come into my life, they remained neatly stowed away in my top bureau drawer with the rest of the carton.

Two nights earlier, it had taken zip, zip, zip and a lot of smacking the thing into my palm to make it light instead of the one zip that normally did it.

Last evening, Darcy had bought a new can of Ronson lighter fluid at Higger's Drugs. While she was making this innocuous purchase, I had been slowly dying of shame and embarrassment back at the Pharmacy counter, trying to think of a convincing lie about why I wanted to purchase a box of condoms.

"My older married brother asked me to pick up a box of prophylactics for him. I have no idea what brand he likes," I whispered, smiling nervously at Dr. Higger and desperately hoping no one else in the store had heard the remark.

Higger's was a neighborhood drugstore and the Harrises were regulars. Darcy purchased the lighter fluid while exchanging pleasantries with a female clerk at the front of the store and walked out to the car, alone. Dr. Higger quietly handed me a box of Trojans, discreetly hidden in a small paper bag. I hurriedly thrust a five dollar bill at him and pretended to be fascinated by a large, prominent rack of assorted moleskin foot patches while he got me my change.

The new, unopened can of lighter fluid had been in my bureau that morning. I had to turn it on its side to get the creaky old drawer to close. Now it was gone. Someone had been in my room earlier today. I was pretty sure it had not been Darcy. I wondered about Art and the Vamp, but there was nothing I could do about it now. I pushed the little mystery from my mind, closed up the bag and left.

Darcy was more or less ready when I arrived. We folded the rear seat down in the VW and hurriedly piled in all our collective stuff. I had completely forgotten about the missing lighter fluid by the time I reached Darcy's house, and with the excitement of the two us going on a great adventure, I didn't think of it again until much later.

That night we traveled west through Maryland and West Virginia hamlets and villages of ever diminishing size as we progressed from federal to state and finally to county road. As usual, I hadn't the slightest idea where I was going and Darcy acted as navigator, holding an ESSO road map on her lap and constantly making decisions about turns and things.

When in each other's company, neither Darcy nor I was ever at a loss for words. I loved to tell her stories of American history and the Southern mountains, and she loved to listen and to talk to me of people and their inner workings. It turned out that Darcy was a people person. She had been fascinated all her life by people of every stripe and she was filled with insights about them and the way they wove their personal little dramas into the larger whole.

And not just about people. Upon our first meeting, I had taken both her and Linda for a pair of lightweight wastrels, but that was just the life into which Darcy had been born and her completely rational adjustment to it. Beneath the apparently superficial, upper middle class veneer, she exhibited a sensitivity and appreciation of everything around her to a degree that was frequently moving and, at times, truly astonishing. These things came gradually to light in bits and pieces as we headed west. We talked and laughed and pulled back the big sunroof and drank in the warm summer evening, bursting in the pleasure of each other's company.

It was almost dark when we passed the turnoff the first time and black as pitch when we finally turned around and discovered it ten minutes later. The two-lane county blacktop wound its way bewilderingly up a steep grade. Somewhere near the summit, there was a deep gash in the earth and a spur road off the narrow shoulder. A few feet beyond a raw opening in the tree line, ten feet of heavy logging chain with a white sign stretched across the opening.

Private Property No Trespassing

Darcy had a key to the 'gate' and performed the honors in the headlights of the VW. In thirty seconds, we were on the final leg of the journey.

This leg proved to be long and bumpy and very slow. The road had been created by the double transit of a bulldozer pulling a heavy sled loaded with lumber and building materials. Very little backing and filling had been attempted, except in the most impassable spots. The dozer had simply chugged along winding its way gradually up the hill to the summit, bypassing any obstacle too large to fall in its path. Subsequent entry by the trucks of construction crews had smoothed off the rough edges somewhat, but it was still the type of road that was tailor made for a mule.

We wound up hollows, along ridges, down through swales and three times right through the rocks and small boulders of a trickling creek. The VW had no trouble negotiating any of this. The little car was fitted with heavily cleated mud and snow tires and was almost as nimble as a Jeep and a lot more comfortable. But it was slow. We idled along at a walking pace, the generator needle frequently swaying back into the discharge range.

We didn't care. The altitude was such that we were bringing in an AM station from Pittsburgh with crystal clarity, and we laughed and chattered and enjoyed the bounces and turns as the yellow headlights bore down the mud trace and lit up the fringes of the black woods.

We saw the lights of the cabin and heard the Harrises' golden retriever, Cyril, barking about thirty minutes after we dropped the chain across the entrance of the property. We parked in the little clearing below the house next to the family's Chrysler station wagon. It occurred to me that getting up the trail in that barge must have been a noisy and amazing trip.

The house wasn't really a house at all, but an octagon set on a large raised platform with a broad deck completely circling it. It appeared to be made entirely of California redwood and was bolted

81

and concreted with great structural steel beams into a rock promontory. It was too dark to see, but I was assured that the building looked out over wooded valleys and blue mountain ranges stretching fifty miles into the distance.

There were no windows. Approximately half of each of the eight exterior walls was made of heavy redwood panels and designed to slide back on rollers, almost completely opening up the entire main floor of the house.

A great stone fireplace was the center piece. Long box-like benches were arrayed along the permanent portions of the walls and a few chairs and a low table were scattered about in front of the big fireplace. The towering cathedral ceiling was supported by enormous beams held together at strategic points by massive steel plates and bolts. There were ladder-like stairs leading up to a bedroom-sized loft with open railing. That was all of it, lit softly by the glow of three or four Coleman lanterns.

No interior walls, no bathroom so far as I could make out. No nothing except a king sized room with a helluva view: an extremely impressive structure for seasonal use. It sort of reminded me of the big shelter houses that had been built in the wonderful state parks of Kentucky in the nineteen thirties, with the added feature of rolled back walls. Neat. But where did we go to the bathroom and where did we take a shower? And how did we turn on the lights when we wanted to read at night?

No one else seemed to concern himself with these questions, and we happily unloaded the car and piled our gear in the great room next to all the boxes of food, ice chests, and mountains of duffel.

Happy hour had been merrily under way for some time before we arrived and I was given a beer and a tour around the deck with Mr. Harris. He clutched a gin and tonic in one hand and gently waved an additional Coleman lantern in the other as we made the tour. Of course, you couldn't really see anything except what a large deck it was. It seemed to be located quite high off the ground, and there was the sense of looking down into the tops of trees in the blackness just beyond the yellow fringe of Coleman light.

The Harris family recounted their travel adventures of the afternoon. Darcy and I, in turn, told them of ours. More getting acquainted tours ensued and Darcy showed me where the outhouse was located at the end of a steeply winding black trail about fifty yards from the cabin. Sam and Cyril took me down to the "shower," leading the way through the darkness with flashlight and .22 rifle. It turned out to be a small pool in the nearby creek where Sam and Cyril planned to return after dinner to gig for frogs. Back in the cabin, we all trooped around near the fireplace and got in each other's way trying to be helpful about fixing dinner.

Sam bounced around all over the place fetching this and that and being helpful. He was a handsome, happy athletic kid in perpetual high spirits. Just like Darcy, I thought. He joined the adults in conversation, played with the dog, told funny stories about his friends and shared his plans for frog gigging in the creek that evening. He was first to stake out his territory in a far end of the room with his sleeping bag, his dog and his .22 rifle. I liked Sam a lot.

The fire eventually burned low enough for thick steaks to be pressed between wire grill affairs with long metal handles and thrust on top of the coals. On the way to the property, ears of sweet corn had been purchased at a farm below and were about to be introduced into water that had been struggling toward the boiling point on the little Coleman stove for the past two hours.

It was approaching ten o'clock when we sat in a semi-circle at the edge of the great fireplace and ate our long anticipated meal. Mrs. Harris and Darcy had somehow managed to come up with a tossed salad to go with the steak and corn, and we ate hungrily at the end of the long day.

Along about the third ear of sweet corn, slathered in butter and coated with salt, I decided that I loved this family. I loved Darcy, but I loved her family, too; and I would take them to my heart. They were happy people. They were completely at ease with themselves and delighted in the company of each other. All of them were extremely bright and led interesting, purposeful and successful lives. They were the least neurotic people I'd ever met. They were genuinely kind and considerate of everybody. They were not in the least complaisant or passive; but, at the same time, they were reaching for nothing. They were sensible, solidly-rooted citizens who enormously enjoyed being who they were and who carried a social consciousness as one simple Christian duty, along with a lot of others. I truely liked them.

We emptied our plates and sorted what went to compost and what went to Cyril. The dishes were rinsed and put in a plastic tub for washing in the creek the following morn. We did our various chores, each taking responsibility for some little aspect of things without anyone ever asking for help or giving orders or directions.

Then we broke out the bedding which had been stowed away in the long, box-like benches. Air mattresses were inflated and sleeping bags with dozen of blankets and pillows were piled near the great fireplace. The elder Harrises lugged theirs up the steps to the loft, then came back down and joined the rest of us and we sat and lounged and drank. Like all good Washingtonians, we talked of the just-completed Berlin Wall and Khruschev, Castro and Kennedy until well after midnight.

We were all wonderfully tired and deliciously drunk, except for Sam and Cyril. There was no thought of Hanky Panky as Darcy and I arranged our air mattresses in front of the dying fire. We simply kissed each other longingly and collapsed into our respective sleeping bags. The woodland sounds of the summer night proceeded in concert without us. At some point, Sam and Cyril returned and stumbled into ice chests and boxes in the general area of the room reserved for the galley. The moon was late in rising and a velvet starry blanket provided the only mantle of illumination to wrap the world for miles around.

Saturday, or at least the first eight hours of it, was devoted to work. Mrs. Harris and Darcy cleaned, made the beds and tidied up the cabin. This began shortly after breakfast and seemed to run up toward noon. They washed the dishes from breakfast and the previous evening's meal. They folded everything back into the long boxes. They "straightened." What exactly it was that they straightened was never clear to me.

Sam was pressed into service to tote water from the creek from time to time. The little Coleman stove hissed and whirred incessantly all morning as Darcy and her mother discovered an apparently endless number of new objects that required a fresh introduction to hot soapy water. I managed to stroll through the room once or twice during all this activity and began merrily whistling the tune from Snow White and the Seven Dwarfs. This bit of effrontery promptly earned me a soapy wet dishrag dramatically hurled at the back of my neck.

Mr. Harris had all sorts of little projects, which included some sort of sanitary improvement to the pit privy, the creation of a series of little steps leading off the deck at various points and, of course, the cutting of brush. This last was the central fallback activity of the place and seemed to me likely to be without end, since the Harrises owned about three thousand acres of the stuff. When one ran short of creativity and could think of nothing else to do, there was always cutting brush.

The idea was really to prune and selectively clear the area on the promontory to the rear of the house for future scenic paths and byways as well as to completely clear a large plot for a kitchen garden of some kind. Chainsaw, wheelbarrow, pruning shears and brush hooks were the implements employed for the greater endeavor, while hoe and spade and mattock were the tools of creating a garden worthy of the Harrises.

No one mentioned the need for irrigation or where you were supposed to hook up the hose after the land was cleared and fertilized and all the little seeds had been lovingly inserted and covered with new earth.

The week before, Darcy and I had seen a Japanese film called *The Island*. In the movie, a family living on a barren, inhospitable island was required to row a boat several miles to the mainland and back about four times a day. The sole object of this backbreaking endeavor was to fill water barrels from a drainage ditch so that a garden plot about the size of the one that Mr. Harris had just roped off could be irrigated. The effort put forth by the father and mother to obtain water for their garden was agonizing to watch.

The little creek for washing dishes wasn't anything like the distance rowed by the Japanese couple, but it seemed to me that more thought might have been devoted to this end of the project before all the heavy work began. The Harrises, however, were never ones to waste time worrying about incidentals.

No assignments were made. One just picked up and did whatever struck his fancy. Sam mainly worked with his father on his many and varied little home improvement projects, then, like everybody else, turned to general brush cutting as his default position.

My fancy was struck by the garden plot, since it seemed the only one of the current projects limited enough in scope to have some chance of being realized in the immediate future. Faced with the choice of cutting all the brush on a West Virginia mountain top or digging out a simple garden plot with neatly defined lines and borders, it wasn't a hard choice.

James E. Haley

So I toiled in the 'garden' until noon: slashing with the murderous brush hook, ripping out the defiant little roots of trees and weeds with spade and mattock and carting the slash over to add to a number of other growing piles which Sam was amassing.

As both sun and temperature rose, I put aside my shirt and lay at the unyielding stuff, hacking and pulling, foot by foot, until the dust and sweat and broiling heat covered my face and head and upper body and slowly painted its way down into my jeans and the soles of my feet.

From time to time throughout the morning Darcy would tear herself away from the domestic duties to bring me a cold bottle of beer. We'd stand and look at the miserable little piece of denuded forest and I'd point out the borders and comment about this or that recalcitrant root or shrub.

Resting on the long dirty handle of the hoe, gingerly feeling the latest blister to arise on my torn hands, I said, "Someday, Maw, all this'll belong to the Young'uns."

"Yes Paw, I 'spect little Jeter and Cheryl June uh'l be rah't proud uh this lan' some day." said Darcy gravely.

"Oh, not little Cheryl June, Maw. I've noticed she's right sweet on that thar' Kallikack boy liv's down the holler, or is that boy a Jute?"

"Hit don't make no difference, Paw. Hit's all in the family."

We carried on in this fashion until Mr. Harris happened by and asked what the joke was.

After lunch there was more hoeing, cutting, pulling and carrying but the roast beef sandwiches washed down with three more ice cold bottles of Heineken's tended to subdue the pace set before the noon hour. We wound down about three o'clock and everyone trooped off to the creek for a dip in the little swimming hole.

Later, dressed in clean clothes and sitting out on the deck absorbing the majestic view, we guzzled delicious gin and tonics and nibbled on wonderful little _h'ors d'oeuvres_ that Darcy's mother seemed to produce by magic from an immunerable supply of tiny Tupper Ware containers.

The evening's entree turned out to be chicken and frog's legs grilled on the embers of the log fire. The gin and the day's vigorous activities had taken their toll and the evening closed down a lot earlier than it had the previous night.

On Sunday morning, everyone was up and bustling shortly after 7:00 am. I was somewhat surprised when the elder Harrises and Sam began packing up and loading the station wagon soon after breakfast. Mr. Harris mentioned something about a deadline and a writing assignment. I viewed this bit of intelligence as a definite letdown and the thoughts of an abbreviated weekend left me feeling a little depressed. Mrs. Harris glanced in my direction and saw my downcast face.

"Jack, there's no reason for you and Darcy to leave when we do. You kids enjoy the day and come back this evening." It was, of course, simply the best idea I'd heard all weekend.

At some point during the packing and cleaning up, Sam and Cyril disappeared for a time. A few minutes later, we all looked up with a start when frantic barking and the crack of a .22 rifle shattered the morning stillness. As the sound of the shot echoed away, Cyril's barking could still be heard down near the creek. This was not something to upset the Harris equanimity and, apart from the initial collective flinch at the sound of the shot, we all went right back to doing whatever it was that we were doing. This had happened before.

On the previous afternoon after work and our swim, Sam had slipped away to take his rifle back down to the creek and plink at cans. He had been thoroughly trained in firearm safety and was the grounded, sensible kind of kid who simply wouldn't do anything foolish or dangerous. Consequently, no one gave his disappearance a second thought. Then the shooting began. After about thirty shots had been fired and conversation on the deck was having to zigzag between them, Mr. Harris had gotten up, walked around to the side of the cabin and called a halt to the fusillade.

Now this morning, with the sound of a single shot and the resumption of barking, we hardly commented. In three more minutes, the sound of running footsteps pounded the deck. Sam and Cyril loped into the cabin with a four foot long rattlesnake draped over a long stick. Sam recounted the tale with great flair and flourish.

It seemed the serpent had been sunning itself on a large rock at an integral bend of the trail down by the swimming hole. Cyril bounded up and barked furiously. The snake buzzed, coiled and was preparing to strike when Sam dragged the dog off. With a scissors-hold around Cyril's lunging body, Sam had blasted the rattler's head from a distance of about ten feet.

The trophy was dutifully measured and extensively photographed with Sam and Cyril. Its rattle severed for a souvenir, the beast was flung over the railing of the deck and landed in the woods about a hundred feet below the promontory.

At some point during the hub-bub engendered by the dead rattlesnake, Mr. Harris insisted that Sam leave the rifle for Darcy and me in case any of the beast's relatives showed up seeking vengeance.

Eventually, the Harrises got under way with Sam and Cyril crammed in among the various gear. After much backing and turning, the big Chrysler slowly worked its way up out of the little parking area and disappeared over the first rise, audibly dragging and scraping its long, low body over the primitive trail with each bounce. Darcy quickly disappeared into the cabin to do her Snow White impersonation and 'Paw' headed back to the garden plot to hack and to hoe. As on the previous day, Darcy came out to the designated plot from time to time with a beer and good cheer.

Eventually, her Snow White duties successfully completed, she appeared with heavy gloves and brush hook and made determinedly for the remaining stands of thick foliage which ringed the little clearing. We worked mightily for the next two hours, dirty, sweaty and broiled by the merciless sun.

Darcy eventually said something about lunch and making sandwiches and disappeared for half an hour. When she returned, she was carrying a wicker picnic hamper a rolled-up towel and Sam's rifle.

"Lunch. Down at the old swimmin' hole," she said, looking at me with that deliciously wicked smile.

I sank the cutting blade of the mattock hard into the root that had been tormenting me for the past fifteen minutes and pulled off my sneakers and filthy sweat socks. Grinning at Darcy, I shucked out of my Levis and undershorts, leaving the grimy little pile in the freshly turned dirt. Darcy, her hands still full of gun and hamper, leaned upward on tiptoe and softly planted a long slow kiss on my sweaty lips. I stood there in the buzzing heat, naked and unmoving.

She giggled and took a hesitant step backward, looking me over carefully.

"You Tarzan, me Jane."

"No. Me Tarzan, you Jane."

Darcy laughed. "Tarzan very dirty. Tarzan need bath." She said, scolding.

"Jane need bath, too." I said. "Tarzan wash Jane." I moved toward her with outstretched arms, but she shied away.

"Noooo," she squealed, wriggling her nose. "Tarzan smell like jungle goat. Tarzan wash first, then wash Jane." She started off down the trail to the swimming hole, skipping and swinging the picnic hamper. About ten feet down the trail, she stopped, turned with that wonderful impish smile, and stuck her tongue out at me; then scampered off down the trail without another word. I loved my wonderful Darcy.

"Tarzan race Jane," I thumped my chest and yelled. "Last one in be rotten banana."

Darcy's trill of laughter echoed below me. I left the forlorn little pile of clothing where it had fallen and loped off after her, my bare feet gingerly padding through the hot brown dust of the trail.

The swimming hole was shaded with thick forest and ringed with enormous boulders on both sides of the little creek. Below the pool, water cascaded on down the rocky streambed in a small water-fall created by the twigs and limbs and rotting logs of an ancient beaver dam. A low, flat limestone shelf protruded out of the water at the bottom of the trail, and I launched myself from the middle of it with a long, yodeling jungle yell. I smacked into the center of the pool and fetched up immediately on the far side. As I brushed the water out of my hair and eyes, Darcy was setting down the picnic stuff and beginning to remove her clothes.

We stayed by the pool all afternoon. We made love in the shallow water. We ate tuna sandwiches and drank beer on the sloping rock. We explored the wondrous secrets of each other's bodies and made love again and swam and slept in the pleasant, drowsy heat of the afternoon.

In our timeless reverie, time nevertheless wriggled free and asserted itself; and we both recognized it and reluctantly knew what it meant. Time. Time to end this dreamily blissful and joyous afternoon. Time to withdraw from this Eden paradise. Time to walk back up the hot, dusty trail. Time to begin the task of putting stuff away and closing up camp. Time to begin loading the car and the long twilight trip back to the City. Time.

As we ascended the trail, I carried the picnic stuff and rifle. Darcy was just ahead of me. She saw the discarded clothes in the garden plot before I did.

"Jack! Look!" She turned back to me while pointing at the garments on the ground. They were no longer as I had left them. I had simply stepped out of shorts and Levis in one motion and dropped them piled one inside the other. The grimy white boxers were now wadded in a ball lying some six feet away. The Levis were not heaped, accordion like, where I had stepped out of them, but were spread wide and twisted, several feet away.

"Shit. Probably a feral cat or dog," I said.

I set down the basket and rifle and began to collect the strewn clothing. I picked up the twisted Levis and felt the pockets. They were empty.

A chill passed over me and an uneasy tingling sensation began in my lower abdomen. I plunged my hand deep into the tight little pockets. Nothing. My big Case pocket knife and a ten dollar bill were gone.

I refused to believe it, of course. I cast around quickly, frantically searching the ground where the clothes had been. Stuff can spill out of pockets when the pants are dragged about by the legs. Easy to do. Done it lots of times. But not a wet-with-sweat, sticky, folded ten-dollar bill. Not a five-inch pocket knife jammed hard into the bottom of a tight pocket. Not those things. I stood there naked on the dusty ground, and looked at my sweet Darcy love. That awful, tingling sensation fluttered in my belly. My heart began to pound.

"Jack, What is it?" She said.

"Somebody's been here. While we were down at the creek."

Darcy looked toward the cabin with its eight wide-open doors.

CHAPTER NINE

S he was half way to the cabin steps when I called out.
"Darcy, hold it. Wait up."
She turned as I crammed my legs into the Levis. I picked up Sam's rifle where I had laid it on the picnic basket and pumped a live round into the chamber of the little Winchester. Barefoot and fumbling with buttons, I raced past Darcy and was up the three steps to the cabin deck before she moved again.

"Jack," she called. "Don't." There was a sharp frightened edge on her voice. I stopped and looked back at her but she made no further sound or move. I slowly advanced into the cavernous room, rifle raised as if I were on a skeet range and about to yell "Pull!"

The place looked empty. I peeked up into the loft and carefully circled the deck before telling Darcy that everything was okay. She came up on deck, and the two of us reentered the cabin together.

Most of the camping gear had been packed up or stored away by The Harrises'. Darcy had done her usual magic cleanup while I was working in the garden plot, and the place was almost as pristine as a military barracks. Then we saw the duffel.

The bags had been turned inside-out and their contents strewn in a wide circle. We knelt and starting going through the spilled gear. I saw immediately that my leather shaving kit had been opened and its contents dumped as well. Darcy's cosmetics case was upside down, and weird little jars and bottles were lying all over the floor. We looked quickly, urgently through the pile of belongings trying to remember what had been there.

A leather belt and my few articles of extra clothing and sweaters had not been taken. My flashlight. The carton of Winstons still two-thirds full. Most of the condoms were still there, spilled from my shaving kit, and I knew that the remaining three were wrapped in a paper towel in the bottom of the wicker picnic hamper along with their discarded foil wrappers.

I looked at Darcy who was doing a similar inventory.

"Anything missing?"

She shook her head while continuing to sort and organize.

"No. I don't think so. I just can't be sure."

Suddenly, the uneasy tingling in my belly took a leap and spread right around both hips to my spine. "The car!"

I picked up the rifle and ran for the VW.

Behind me, Darcy cried out, "Jack. Is the car all right?"

I yanked open the driver's door and stared over at the glove compartment, my heart going like a triphammer. The cubicle was closed and I leaned down into the seat and quickly stabbed the button on the little door.

Oh, God. The brown wallet was there. It was lying there, along with my checkbook, undisturbed. It remained neatly sandwiched between ESSO road maps, about twenty or so church keys, and a stack of filling station invoices. My heart kept pounding. I could feel the rush of blood in my ears as I noted that the keys were in the ignition where I'd left them two nights ago. Thank you, God. Thank You.

Drained of emotion, I reached over for the wallet and examined its contents. Nothing seemed to have been touched, including three twenty dollar bills. I twisted around in the seat and looked for signs of entry. When packing for the trip, we had pulled down the rear seat to convert the passenger space into a storage bay. Darcy's purse had fallen over. The spill had probably occurred during the ride in to the cabin on the night we arrived. A billfold, keys, coins and lipstick were scattered on the little cave-like floor. The billfold was still snapped shut.

Relief! The VW bug sat there silently in the afternoon heat, faithfully waiting for me, just as it had a thousand times before. Nothing was stolen. Nothing was damaged. We were all right. We were all right.

The tingling in belly and spine gradually diminished. The heart rate subsided to somewhere near normal levels. But I couldn't control my hands. My fingers were trembling, and I couldn't make them stop. I heard Darcy coming toward the car asking again if it were okay. I got out of the driver's seat and grasped the little rifle hard with both trembling hands.

"It's okay. Nothing's missing. I don't think they got into the car.

"Thank God," said Darcy.

"I just did. Several times."

She leaned against me, and we held each other for a moment. Almost at once, my hands stopped trembling, and a deep anger began to build. I was overcome with a feeling of sick revulsion at the thought of strangers entering our private sanctuary and pawing through our personal things. The feeling of utter violation, of contamination, rose up in me. I realized suddenly with a feeling of black despair that those who had been here had touched with their dirty alien fingers the things that my sweet Darcy wore next to her skin. And I had been helpless, unable to prevent it.

After we talked about it, Darcy said, "But Jack darling, you weren't here. Neither of us was."

I hugged her to me and kissed the top of her head. "I know that. I know it. It's just how it feels, inside."

We stood for a long moment, not speaking, just holding each other. Then we walked back to the cabin and sat on the steps.

"Who do you think it was?" Darcy asked.

"Just kids probably. Some of the good ole boys down the holler, I expect."

Darcy was silent for a while, then she said, "It wasn't just some kids, Jack."

I looked at her in surprise, waiting for an explanation.

"I looked at the stuff in your duffel, just now."

"And?"

"There's almost a full carton of cigarettes that they didn't touch."

I waited, not speaking.

"Also," said Darcy, her voice very quiet and serious. "None of those prophylactic things are missing. I counted them before we went to the swimming hole."

The queasy tingling between belly and lower spine washed over me again like a wave. I tried to smile and be funny.

"Obviously, what we have here is a clean living youth who has taken a vow of celibacy."

Darcy didn't laugh.

"Jack, I'm frightened."

The fluttery belly shrank away and the smoldering anger surged back up. I hugged Darcy close and whispered reassurances which had returned with the anger.

"Let's get packed up and get out of here. We're almost ready to go except for locking the doors. We'll stop down at the village and give the Sheriff a call. It's just petty vandalism, but it's going to really upset your parents."

Darcy put her hand on my arm. "Jack. Whoever was here was *searching* our stuff, not stealing it."

"He did more than search my goddam pockets."

"Taking that knife and the ten-dollar bill didn't mean anything, Jack. He was looking for something in our stuff. I know he was. What about all the money he just ignored in your wallet and my billfold?"

"He didn't get into the car, Darcy. Nothing was taken."

"Jack." She was desperately trying to keep back the tears. "Somebody *was* in the car. I came out this morning when Mom and Dad were packing and put my purse down behind the front seat out of the way. Somebody pulled it out this afternoon and opened it."

I tried to think, to get a starting point that would make some sense and account for what had happened. I had an awful feeling that Darcy was right. That someone had been looking for something and had not invaded our lives just to steal from us. Our belongings had been openly, contemptuously rifled and nothing of value had been taken except one small bill and a pocket knife. Why? My wallet and Darcy's billfold had apparently not even been examined.

"Somebody's idea of a joke. Just curious about the city folks. Didn't want to do anything that would land him in big trouble with the law. Lifting ten bucks and a pocket knife isn't enough to draw much flack from the local gendarmes. Figures we won't be sore enough to report him, that's all."

Darcy held on to my arm and looked into my eyes with her serious ones. "Then why the hell didn't he lift *just* one or two packs of cigarettes or take *just* one or two of your rubbers? Why Jack? Tell me why." She was almost crying now.

I looked at my sweet Darcy love, and I couldn't tell her why. Anxiety began to build, and I said nothing and stared down at my dusty bare feet. "I don't *know* why, but there's always a very logical explanation to these things." I stood up. "I'll go get my shoes and stuff."

I headed immediately for the spot where my discarded shorts and shoes lay on the freshly turned earth. As I reached down to retrieve the wadded boxers, that awful queasy tingle started in the base of my

94

spine and spread upward through my scrotum. There, next to the grimy shorts was a shoeprint.

Of course, there were lots of shoeprints on the broken ground. There were Darcy's small dainty ones all over the place. My enormous ones were there too, and they looked just like gigantic versions of Darcy's because both of us had worn Sperry TopSiders right up until the moment when I had discarded mine in order to play Tarzan.

The shoeprint that I saw next to the sweat and dirt-smeared shorts had not been made by a Sperry TopSider. Nor had it been made by a work boot or an old Army shoe nor by the hand-me-downs of a juvenile prankster. This was the crisp, sharp delicate impression of a man's expensive dress shoe.

I crouched there, looking carefully at the strange shoeprint, then started looking for more. They were everywhere. It was amazing that we hadn't noticed them before. The tracks led up and down the trail to the swimming hole. They were overlain now in the hot brown dust by our own prints; but they were there, going right down that trail and ending just to the side of it in a clump of foliage not ten feet from the rock shelf where we had made love all afternoon.

The man in the city shoes had watched us. The degenerate piece of filth had stood there silently, maybe for hours, and just watched Darcy and me. He'd watched us do everything. Heard us say things to each other that belonged to no one else in the world. Seen every part of us that there was to see. He'd seen my Darcy love. I choked back the tears of rage. He'd seen and heard everything that we felt. That we were.

I stood there shaking with anger looking around desperately for something to smash. I would kill him. I would execute him. I would snuff out his life without warning.

The tears came on and I wept, heaving with each ragged sob. I felt so unclean. Smeared with filth and disgust and totally violated for both of us. We had been so deliriously happy, in innocent joyous discovery all afternoon; and, all afternoon, a stranger had been raping us.

I wiped my eyes and went down and washed my face in the little pool. It had been our little pool, now it was something else. I went quickly back up the hill, feelings of deep sadness and smoldering hatred roiling within me. Telling Darcy about the shoeprint could wait until we were well out on the highway. Maybe even a lot longer than that.

She was busily putting bags and stuff into the rear compartment of the Bug when I returned. I stood on the little rise for a moment, watching her, loving her, seeing her be Darcy. My throat tightened and the angry tears began to well up.

"Goddammit!" I coughed and cleared my throat and spat and swore about the damn bugs that were beginning to gather in the late afternoon stillness.

Darcy turned quickly at the commotion. "Jack, darling, where did you go? I was worried." The concern was plain in her voice.

"Just a look around," I hedged.

"See anything?"

"I think there were some footprints where he went through my pants, but they were pretty much smudged over by our own."

"What did they look like?"

"You couldn't really tell much," I said, and felt a terrible sense of betrayal and separation between us. We were still being violated by this man and I hated him beyond all feeling.

In the afternoon sunshine, two men sit at a table in a Parisian sidewalk cafe. A folded copy of Le Monde lies on the table between them. For a few minutes, they sip their Dubonnet and do not speak. Finally, the silence is broken by the Young Man of Good Breeding.

He speaks with a soft urgency. There is fear and revulsion in his voice. "All right, you have it. What else do you want from me?"

The fat man watches him, heavily lidded eyes unblinking, the jowly face impassive.

"You are nervous about something, my young friend? You wish to leave? An assignation, perhaps?" He casually nods toward a stylish young woman who is passing on the Boulevard.

"You have what you want from me. Mr. Zhakharov. Please. There's no further need for us to meet like this or to be seen together." The Young Man nervously adjusts his tie, tugging at his high stiff collar.

The fat man smiles with the corners of his mouth, and his carefully clipped goatee moves a little. The heavy-lidded eyes remain impassive.

He slowly lifts the glass of Dubonnet. "You seem to be forgetting our little arrangement."

"I'm not forgetting anything, Mr. Zhakharov. I just can't keep on this way. I simply can't."

The fat man chuckles softly. *"You simply can't,"* he repeats mockingly. *"And your young lady? Cannot she simply keep on this way?"*

The Young Man of Good Breeding sighs heavily and lowers his gaze to the folded newspaper.

The fat man speaks in a swift hoarse whisper. There is cruelty in his voice. *"You will continue to supply me with what I want when I want."* He smiles, evilly. *"And you know why, do you not?"*

The Young Man nods resignedly, his eyes never leaving the newspaper.

The fat man continues: *"Your young lady is very beautiful. It would be a terrible pity if your priorities became confused. A terrible pity."*

The Young Man of Good Breeding stares across the table, hopelessly, and nods again.

The fat man slowly rises from the table and reaches for his hat and cane. He casually lifts the folded copy of Le Monde and puts it into the pocket of his tailored overcoat. Slowly adjusting the homberg on his large head, he moves away from the circle of tables and merges into the moving crowd on Le Boulevard St. Germain.

Sitting in a car in a narrow alleyway, Sidney Reilly sees the fat man leave the table. Reilly pulls the black Citroen over onto a tiny sidewalk, cuts the engine and swiftly crosses the great Boulevard, pushing and jostling his way along the crowded thoroughfare. He rapidly approaches the fat man who has just paused to study a shop front window. Reilly walks briskly along, sidestepping, using his hands, slightly nodding and smiling to avoid passersby. He inserts a gloved hand into his overcoat pocket and withdraws it quickly just as he nudges the shoulder of the fat man in a small collision. A nod. A murmured apology and Sidney Reilly continues down Le Boulevard St. Germain. He quickly inserts the folded copy of Le Monde into his overcoat pocket.

The fat man wheels instantly at the brushing encounter. His searching eyes are filled with terror. His mouth gapes wide in a long, shrill intake of breath. His walking stick clatters to the pavement. He takes a faltering step and flings up both hands to his heaving chest, his face contorted in agony. As darkness closes over him, he looks

frantically through the crowd at the disappearing back of Sidney Reilly,
then collapses onto the busy sidewalk.

The sun had sunk below the West Virginia peaks, but the long summer twilight was still with us when I finished locking all the cabin's doors. The little back cubby of the VW had been snugly packed with duffel, cases, cooler and ice chest when, at last, we climbed in and slammed the doors. I depressed the clutch and twisted the key in the ignition. Absolutely nothing happened.

"What the hell," I said, and the tingling, pukey feeling rose instantly in my lower belly.

Darcy said nothing as I twisted the silent key again and again.

"Battery."

"He cut the wires?" asked Darcy.

"No." I shook my head. "I don't know yet." The sick tingling growing by the second.

I popped the beetle's hood and looked carefully into the shallow little compartment. I had no idea what constituted an ignition wire and what did not. All the connections that projected through the firewall seemed in good shape, pretty much like new. I walked quickly to the rear of the car and opened the engine compartment. I stared for a long moment, uncomprehending, at the little mechanical marvel. What wires I could see looked perfectly all right. Actually, everything about the engine looked perfectly all right.

The battery," I repeated. "It's under the back seat."

Almost frantically, we pulled gear out of the rear compartment and opened up the seats. Under the rear seat bottom, on the passenger side of the little car, sat the 6-volt battery, almost certainly being viewed by human eyes for the first time since leaving the dealer's showroom, twelve months earlier. All connections were shiny and tight and the whole thing had a look of pristine newness to it. I checked the water level. All cells were full. I got back into the driver's seat and turned the ignition key once more. The ammeter on the instrument panel was hard over against the discharge peg. I pulled on the headlight knob. There were no headlights. Shit. Shit. Shit. Shit.

Instantly, I knew exactly what had happened. On Friday night, we had driven in over the bulldozed trace that was Charles Harris's idea of a proper wilderness driveway. Radio blaring, headlights blazing and the little car moving too slowly for the generator to keep the battery charged. We had arrived at the cabin with a dead battery. The Volkswagen had sat there all weekend beside the cabin and the Harrises' big Chrysler with a fucking dead battery. Norton, you're a total IDIOT!

"Can we push-start it?" asked Darcy.

I nodded glumly, then reached over and released the hand brake. "We can try, but there's no room here to get a run."

But we did try. We tried valiantly for half an hour until dusk began to settle in earnest on the cabin and the four miles of woods between us and the county road.

The car had been parked at the bottom of a small depression which steepened rapidly on all sides. We could push the beetle only a few feet in either direction before it rolled back to the bottom again. Darcy took the wheel and popped the clutch when I yelled to do so. Each time there was only a sudden lurch as we ground immediately to a stop and no saving sound from the little air-cooled engine.

Darcy got out and came around the rear where I was leaning on the car and trying hard to catch my breath.

I shook my head. "It's no good. We're going to have to walk out of here and the sooner we get started, the better."

We opened a single sliding door to the cabin, unearthed one of the Coleman lanterns from its locker and filled it with white gas. After a final look around we closed the house again and locked up the dead beetle with all our stuff inside. I took Darcy's hand in mine, and we set off carrying the rifle and my flashlight, the unlit Coleman lantern swinging noisily from its wire handle.

Hansel and Gretel, wide eyed and walking hand in hand, move deeper and deeper into the darkening forest. Sitting on a nearby tree stump, Sidney Reilly quietly observes the passing spectacle. A rueful expression plays across his thin lips.

We figured that it would take about an hour to reach the county road at the best pace we could muster in the dark and on the uneven terrain. Then, at least another hour to get down to the village, call in a report to the Harrises and find some kind soul with a truck and jumper cables to take us back up to the cabin.

Darkness overtook us in the first thirty minutes. After we had stumbled and almost fallen a half-dozen times over stream bed rocks, I called a halt. It was clearly stupid to keep rushing ahead in pitch blackness, completely unable to see the trail ahead.

We sat down on a fallen tree and pumped up and lit the Coleman. It immediately hissed its reassuring signature sound and threw out a brilliant circle of white light about ten feet in all directions.

Darcy had one TopSider off and was massaging a toe. I reached down and gently lifted her foot and brushed my lips along the velvet skin, kissing each of the polished nails. "Piggy, piggy, piggy," I smiled at her. "Now all the little piggies are better."

Darcy laughed softly and kissed my hand and held it against her cheek. "I love you, Jack Norton."

I nodded, smiling at her beautiful face in the light of the lantern. "I love you, Darcy Harris."

We quickly reassembled ourselves and continued on along the logging trace, walking easier now with the ring of bright light. We had been at it nearly a full hour, and I had been saying that we were almost to the highway for half of it when the sharp sound of breaking branches cracked about thirty yards off to our left. We stopped dead in our tracks.

For a moment, neither of us dared speak. The noise had suddenly stopped.

"A deer?" said Darcy.

"Shhhh. Maybe." I set the lantern on the ground just ahead of us and cocked the .22, lifting it to my shoulder with the flashlight sighted along the barrel. Both of us stepped back away from the Coleman's glow. When the noise to our left resumed, I aimed the rifle and hit the flashlight button sending a brilliant white spot into the pitch black woods.

Thirty yards away, a small yellow white fireball erupted out of a thicket of branches. Simultaneously, a shattering roar like a close-by lightning stroke filled our whole world. At the sound, we both instinctively crouched in the trail. A shower of stinging dirt and rocks bit into my legs with the second roaring explosion from the dense woods. Somehow, the flashlight had gotten switched off. I grabbed Darcy by the arm and flung her ahead of me over the berm of the dozer trail and into the woods. We ran at a crouch, pushing unseen branches from our faces and falling repeatedly in the deep-packed carpet of leaves. I held onto Darcy, and we didn't stop until we had run right into a large boulder. We groped and crawled our way around it and lay flat in the dead leaves, not breathing.

We listened and lay there for another five minutes. No more gunshots. No sounds of bodies crashing in the brush. Nothing. I raised up on one elbow.

"Jack!" There was pure terror in Darcy's voice. "Please don't move. Don't move at all."

I could see the glow cast by the Coleman where it still sat on the trail. The lantern itself was beyond my view. In order to see it, I would have to leave our shelter.

Darcy pulled at my arm. Her grip was desperate. She hissed, "Jack, please."

As silently as possible, I settled down beside her, gripping the rifle and flashlight, trying in vain to peer into the blackness which lay between ourselves and the glowing Coleman.

I began to understand our situation. No one could possibly find us without using some sort of light. Also, no one could approach us without making noise. This would get him shot; or at least, shot at. Ergo, we were safe so long as we didn't move, shine a light or make a noise. Darcy was absolutely right.

Had she not spoken, I would have attacked. Not out of bravery but out of a primitive, automatic sense of survival. I would have gotten close enough to the Coleman to see whoever might have walked up to it. I would have shot him from ambush as many times as the little rifle would fire. I lay back down beside Darcy and the first fear came flooding in. I suddenly realized that, had I acted, I might well have gotten us both killed. There was very likely more than one person out there in the dark. Also, I had no idea what had just been fired at us, but I knew it wasn't a .22 rifle. It was a grownup's gun. No question about it.

We lay huddled in the safe blackness all night. At some point during the long hours, we both dozed. I awoke suddenly to find Darcy shaking me. The light from the Coleman was no longer visible. We waited and stared off into the blackness straining our ears for the slightest sound, again not daring to breathe. Fifteen minutes passed, then an hour. There were no sounds.

"It just ran out of fuel," I finally whispered.

"How do you know he's not still out there?"

"I don't. We're safe here 'til daylight though."

"What about daylight," Darcy asked.

"I don't know. We'll see."

Daylight came and we waited for another hour without moving or making a sound in the bed of leaves behind our boulder. Finally, I raised my head and said, "I don't think anybody's out there."

Darcy looked me in the eyes and I could tell that she was thinking the same thing.

"The road isn't all that far. We don't go anywhere near the trail or the lantern. I've been working it out half the night," I whispered. We cut over the ridge in back of us and head down into the valley on the far side of the mountain. We can hit route 122 somewhere down by the river."

"By the river! Jack, that miles and miles from here. It would take all day to walk that far."

Again, Darcy was probably right. During the weekend, Charles Harris had showed me a big U.S.G.S. map which adorned one of the cabin's little walls. The map was actually several taped together and covered all of the 3000 acres of Harris holdings. I had realized then that, apart from the little county road we had ridden in on, the nearest highway was route 122, at least 5 or 6 miles down in the valley. We could easily see the river which flowed beside it from the cabin deck. It was a big river, but it looked small when viewed from the promontory.

Leaving our close surroundings and taking off for parts unknown was probably not really necessary. Whoever had fired those shots at us was probably no longer around; but, of course, maybe he was. Taking off quietly in the opposite direction was the only sensible thing to do.

Moving like Cherokee Indians, we silently crept off a hundred feet or so and watched our backtrail for a full five minutes. We repeated this maneuver another dozen times until we were certain we weren't being followed. At the ridgetop, we rested half an hour, then plunged down the reverse slope, moving quickly now, no longer afraid of someone coming up behind us. It was just noon when we stumbled out of the woods and onto state route 122. We resumed walking and in twenty minutes a farmer in a Studebaker pickup stopped and gave us a lift.

A deputy sheriff in a four-wheel drive Jeep station wagon took us back to the property where the chain was still locked across the trail.

Darcy unlocked the chain, and we drove through. Almost immediately, we came upon the empty Coleman lantern sitting in the middle of the trail. It was just as we had left it, about one quarter of a mile inside the property. The deputy and I trekked all around the area. We walked to the spot where I thought the shots had come from. We looked in the trail itself for signs of the bullet which had sprayed my legs with dirt and gravel. We went over to the place behind the boulder where Darcy and I had spent the most unforgettable night of our lives. There were no signs of anything. Nothing at all.

Back at the cabin, the VW started right up as soon as the jumper cables from the Jeep were attached. We had told the deputy all about our gear being rifled and the stolen knife and ten dollar bill. In the light of day and with a deputy sheriff standing there, it all sounded a little silly; and, of course, there was no hard evidence of anything.

Deputy Otis Perkins suggested that it was a local prowler, and that he'd just tried to scare us off with the shots after we flashed a light on him. He took down a description of the knife and promised to keep a close eye on the property. We let him go ahead of us and followed him out to the county road. I got out and locked the chain gate, thanked him and waved goodbye.

As we started down the road, Darcy said, "Jack, you forgot to mention the tracks."

"What tracks," I said, knowing exactly what tracks.

"You know, the footprints where you took off your clothes."

"Oh, they wouldn't have been any help. We'd walked all over them and messed them up."

We rode along in silence for several moments. Darcy made no comment. "Besides," I added, "There are all kinds of footprints around the cabin: family, carpenters, delivery trucks, everything." Darcy nodded with a faint, hopeful smile and said nothing.

We settled down for the two-hour ride back to the District. We were both still badly shaken and somewhat in shock. We had talked the thing out on our plunge down the far side of the mountain and were exhausted after the frantic trek and the sleepless night. Darcy's head nodded on my shoulder and the subject of footprints didn't come up again.

CHAPTER TEN

When they awakened that morning and discovered that Darcy had not been in her room all night, the Harrises were worried and confused. As the hours passed, worry gave way to anxiety and dread. As noon approached, Mrs. Harris was on the phone to her husband at least three times.

"They're all right, Sylvia," he reassurred her. "They just lost track of time and decided to spend the night."

"Why haven't they called? Darcy would have called."

"I agree. It's extremely irresponsible."

"What if there's been an accident?" She continued.

"Jack's a very capable young man. Besides, we would have heard if anything had happened to them on the road."

"Charles, I *know* something is wrong. I think we should go back up there, now."

"Sylvia, just hold on. They'll call as soon as they can. They're not children any more."

"They *are* children. They're just babies. Both of them."

But she waited and busied herself and paced the rooms of the big house and watched the street for any signs of the Volkswagen. Shortly after noon, just as she was about to place a second call to the West Virginia Highway Patrol, the call came and her life was restored to her.

We were met at curbside where we recounted the whole story, suitably edited for parental ears. We were brought in and questioned and sent to shower and clean up and given food and sustenance after the manner of the prodigal son. By the time we had finished eating a hastily-prepared early evening breakfast, Charles Harris arrived home from the Hill, and we had to tell the whole story all over again.

The Harrises were overwrought with fear and worry and relief. Darcy's father had been on the phone to West Virginia and the

Sheriff's office since we had first called in and had insisted that further investigation into the incident be carried out.

One of their locals had broken into his house and had stolen property. Moreover, he had fired a shot at us when we discovered him in the process of leaving. He wanted something done about it, and Charles Harris wasn't a man to be put off by casual assurances from the local cops. The Sheriff promised to send a regular patrol out to the place and to round up all the usual suspects. Mr. Harris informed them that when next he visited his weekend retreat, he would bring his own protection in the form of a 12-gauge shotgun and plenty of ammunition. I think they were a little surprised that he hadn't done that already.

At any rate, this was the story that finally satisfied everyone and that crystallized and became fact.

"So, it was one of the damned squirrel shooters or bootleggers sniffing around and you kids startled him with that flashlight on the rifle. Sheriff said they have an idea who it might have been. I'll bet he ran all the way to the next county. If he ever comes back, he's going to have some explaining to do." Charles Harris chuckled at his neat little summation and Mrs. Harris smiled weakly.

"Oh Charles, they might have been shot or even killed." She looked at Darcy and the tears welled in her eyes.

"He wasn't a killer, Sylvia. Just one of those closed-mouthed, inbred mountain types who's always getting hassled by the law for this or that minor infraction. He thought the kids were going to expose him, or maybe even take a shot at him with that little gun."

By the time we were all talked out, I was almost able to believe the tale. It all made perfect sense. Except for the shoe prints which I could never mention. I could never let Darcy know that this man had watched us all afternoon. I could not puncture the Harrises' reality about the incident. They had worked themselves around to believing that the new problem at their weekend Shangri-La was of the same order of magnitude as pesky bears occasionally raiding the garbage dump. As far as their weekend retreat *per se* was concerned, it probably was. I very much doubted that the man from the city who had stalked us and searched our belongings would ever visit the camp again.

And, of course, there was always the chance that I was wrong. The shoes which made the prints might well have come from Sears and Roebuck or J.C. Penny; but, somehow, as much as I wanted to believe that, I knew that they hadn't. A local man might buy such shoes to wear to church, or to town on Saturday, but he wouldn't wear them in the woods. He'd have on his old clodhoppers for that. This man had followed us all the way from Washington. I could feel it, and it brought back that queasy, tingling feeling in my gut.

By nine o'clock, Darcy and I were falling asleep on the sofa. Mrs. Harris insisted that I spend the night; and, though I feebly protested, the rest of the family urged me to stay. As I was bringing in stuff from the car, Mrs. Harris stopped me at the front stairway and put her hand on my face in a motherly gesture.

"Thank you, Jack. Thank you for bringing Darcy home to us." She kissed my cheek and patted my shoulder as I headed upstairs for one of the guest bedrooms.

The next morning, Darcy awoke to hear me already up and using the hall bathroom. It was early and the house was quiet. By the time I had showered and dressed, smells of coffee and toast were emanating from the kitchen below. She was there pouring coffee, barefoot in her white summer nightgown and pink robe, and her eyes lit up when I entered the room.

There was little time for talk. I was running late and had to stop by my room at Miss Withersby's Hall for Celebate Gentlemen to get my uniform before heading over to Arlington. I had placed a call to the dispatcher yesterday afternoon just after we had called Darcy's parents. I had plead car trouble. Overnight trip to West Virginia. Dead Battery. A plausible line since it was mostly true.

"Okay 41. Not comin' in today." The dispatcher repeated the words slowly as if taking them down as he had the last time I was out. This time there was added emphasis on the word: *today,* as in: 'for the second time'.

"You bin actin' peculiar lately, 41. You ain't got yourseff a little nooky hid up in them mountains, now have you?" This was followed by an ugly snigger.

I said nothing.

"What's that, 41? I didn't hear you real good."

"No!" I said loudly into the receiver.

"No!" He laughed hoarsely. "Well, what about the livestock, 41? You the kind of boy that likes the livestock? I hear they got some real friendly sheep in those parts." This was followed by a cackle of obscene laughter.

"You ignorant, degenerate redneck turd," I said, as soon as I had slammed down the receiver.

The day was fairly rocky after that. The dispatcher evidently decided that it would do me good to experience firsthand the detritus of society; and, consequently, he gave me fares to be picked up at cheap bars in the early afternoon. These nearly always turned out to be hopeless alcoholics who wanted to go to the White House to make their counsel and wisdom available to the President. There were a number of these, all variations on the same theme.

As suicides in San Francisco seemed to be naturally drawn to the Golden Gate Bridge, so drunks in Arlington seeking death by a more painful means seemed to be naturally drawn to the White House. One of these was a Southern Highlander from the Appalachian Mountains of Kentucky who had nobly served his country in World War II.

I picked him up that afternoon at a bar which had no name. The dispatcher simply gave out the address, knowing that the place was a dive and enjoying his little joke on the "college boy" who liked five-dollar words.

"Have a nice ride, 41. Give my regards to the President," the radio squawked off to his cackling laughter. I hadn't the foggiest idea of what he was talking about.

I pulled up at the entrance of a place with painted-over windows and a neon sign that just said **BAR**. The street address was indifferently scrawled on the weathered brick wall. I waited a few minutes to see who might appear without my having to leave the cab and enter the place. As usual, my luck held, so after a while I got out of the cab and pushed through the battered doors into the den of iniquity.

Inside, it was dark and smelled primarily of beer and sour mash bourbon. Added to this rather delightful combination were the odors of unwashed bodies, kitchen grease and vomit. I went over to the bar and asked the man standing behind it which of his patrons had called a Yellow Cab. He proceeded to interrogate one of the men seated in front of him, and there ensued a flourish of incoherent exchanges.

He spoke to the gentleman, sounding somewhat like the dispatcher. "Yuh call uh goddam cab?"

"Huhh?"

"Yuh call uh goddam cab?"

"Huhhhh?"

"Uh cab, goddammit."

"Cab?"

"Uh cab! Yuh call uh goddam cab?"

"I don't want no goddam cab."

"Then why th' hell didja call one."

"I don't need to call no goddam cab."

"Yuh called a goddam cab."

"I reckon I can call a goddam cab, if I want to."

"Well. He's here."

"Huh?"

"He's here. Th' goddam cab is here."

"I don't want no goddam cab."

"Yuh called him."

"I can drive my own goddam self."

"Huh? You caint drive shit."

"I'm gonna drive my ownself home."

"You caint drive shit. Th' cab's here fur yuh."

"I don't need no cab."

"His name is Sizemore," I said, trying to be helpful and to bring new light to the debate.

"Yur name's Sizemore, ain't it? said the bartender, accusingly.

"Huh?"

"Yur name's Sizemore?"

"Hell, no. I ain't no Sizemore. I can drive my own self in no goddam cab." This went on, repeated with subtle variations on the recurring theme until another of what I took to be one of the regular patrons sitting at the far end of the bar attempted to dismount from the stool and fell off onto the floor.

A few heads slowly turned, but nobody moved to help the man who was trying to get up. I went over and began helping him to his feet. He smelled horrible and was as light as a feather. His body did not appear to be substantial enough to support his large head which kept wagging this way and that, as if threatening to fall off his shoulders. The large head was deeply creased and lined and reddened by booze. It looked as if it had worn out at least three previous bodies. I was trying to get him rearranged on the barstool when he started mumbling and moaning.

"Sizemore. Corpuhl Bingham Sizemore reportin' fur duty."

He put his head down on the bar and mumbled this military salutation two or three times before I thought I understood what he was saying.

"Are you Mr. Sizemore?"

"Huh?"

"Did you call a goddam cab," I asked, trying to cut right to the chase by using the local argot.

"Hell, yes. I called a goddam cab." he mumbled belligerantly. "Corpuhl Bingham Sizemore, reportin' fur duty."

"Git him the hell outta here," yelled the bartender, his pointless exchange with the first patron now apparently forgotten.

It took another five minutes of wheedling and cajoling and threatening to get Corporal Bingham Sizemore off the stool again and headed out the door to the 'goddam' cab. The very act of drawing breath in close proximity to Mr. Sizemore required an act of considerable courage. Slowly drawing in air through a small open corner of my mouth on his windward side, I held him up with one hand as we shuffled unsteadily out the door and across the filthy sidewalk. I quickly opened the rear door of the cab, pushing him gently in the direction of the back seat. For some reason, the vision of taking a cat to the vet popped into my mind.

"Fuck *that* shit!" he yelled out suddenly and slammed the door, almost catching my fingers in it. He wrenched free of my faltering grasp, opened the front door and was in the passenger seat before I could stop him.

Deciding to let him enjoy a small victory, I walked around to the driver's side and got in.

"Where to, Mr. Sizemore?"

"Huh?"

"Where do you live?"

"I live with my daughter."

"Where does your daughter live?"

His head dropped to his chest. We sat in silence. I repeated the question, pronouncing each syllable slowly and loudly as if speaking to a foreigner. Not a peep from Mr. Sizemore. We sat there for a few moments with him stinking up the cab and me wondering what I was going to do with him. Finally, with head bowed and eyes closed, he spoke.

"I wanna go to th' goddam White House. Wanna talk to Ike."

I hoped the dispatcher was enjoying his little joke, but I knew that whatever else might happen, I was not, definitely not, going to call in and tell him that I was taking this fare to the White House.

"Where does your daughter live, Mr. Sizemore?"

"Huh?"

I repeated the question.

"She lives with her goddam boyfriend."

"Where is that?"

"How th' hell do I know?" He began making sobbing noises and his shoulders heaved with emotion.

"Take it easy, Mr. Sizemore. You have to tell me where you live."

"Take me to the goddam White House."

"I can't do that and you know it." I said, angrily. It was high time for a dose of reality.

"Why the hell not?" he snarled. "You think I ain't got no money?" He struggled in his seat and brought a wad of bills out of his pocket. "Here, Goddammit. You take it all." He flung the wad, about the size of a baseball, into my lap."

I picked up the roll and tried to stuff it into his shirt pocket, but it was too big to fit. "I can't take your money, Mr. Sizemore," I pleaded.

"My money's no goddam good? He got up close and breathed into my face, his bloodshot eyes trying desperately to focus. "My money's no goddam good?"

I gently pushed him back down in his seat. "Your money is fine. I just can't take it, and I can't take you to the White House."

He started to heave and weep again, and I sat and said nothing.

"I was Ike's driver in the war," he suddenly blurted out.

That would be news to Kaye Summersby, I thought.

"I was Ike's driver an' I fit them goddam Germans." The thought of his glorious past was too much to bear, and he broke down upon confessing this and was wracked with more heaves and sobs.

"I thought Ike had a woman driver. A WREN."

The sobs and heaves stopped abruptly, and he sat up at atttention. "Ike had womurn drivers." He affirmed. "Ike had anykinda goddam drivers he wanted." He sat, looking carefully at me, his head slowly weaving to see how I would respond to this profound revelation. I just nodded.

He struggled up and suddenly shouted. "But I was his driver! And he done give me a medal, by god!" His voice broke and he repeated, softly, "he done give me a goddam medal."

We sat in silence broken only by the soft intermittent sobbing. Finally, he turned in the seat and looked at me through bleary, reddened eyes.

"Honey, how old air yu?" he asked, using that peculiar, gentle term of endearment commonly employed between grown men of his mountain background to bridge the generations.

"I'm 21 years old," I said.

"Huh?"

"I'm 21 years old."

He peered searchingly into my face and the tears welled again in his eyes. "Oh Lordy, Lordy. Twenty-one years old. Oh, Lordy, Lordy," he moaned. His trembling hand gripped my shoulder. "I fit them goddam Germans. I fit 'em. I did."

"I know," I answered softly. "I know you did. And you got a medal from Ike."

He put both hands down into his dirty, pee-stained lap twisting the roll of money over and over, weeping softly and nodding quietly to himself.

After a bit, I explained that Ike didn't live in the White House anymore; and he nodded knowingly and kept twisting the roll of bills.

A dirty piece of paper had fallen out of his pocket when he had produced the roll, and I picked it up and handed it toward him. He didn't seem to notice. I glanced at the writing. Scrawled in pencil was the name, Mabel Sizemore and below that the address: 1453 Duluth St., Alexandria, Virginia.

I called the dispatcher on the radio and told him where I was going. Bingham Sizemore sat quietly weeping, his head slowly shaking and eyes squinted tightly shut, all the way out to Alexandria. He did not speak to me again, but now and again would sigh and groan deeply, "Oh Lordy, Lordy."

Darcy's white Corvair was parked across the street from the rooming house when I arrived that evening. The horrors of the weekend were still powerfully with us, and each sought desperately to relieve the tension and anxiety in the soft, life-giving safety of the other's body.

Our clothes made two small piles, side by side, where we had been standing, just inside the door. The hot, airless little room was in deep shadow as we rolled and tossed frantically on the narrow bed. There was a fumbling, convulsive, last moment search for one of the little foil packages and the bed table with open drawer went over with a crash.

On the wall at the head of the bed came two quick thumps and a muffled voice.

"Hey, Jack. Okay in there?"

I couldn't answer, and for, several moments, there were only the sounds of violent breathing and the movement of the bed. Then, that quick, double knock repeated on the wooden door.

"Jack? You all right?"

I quickly left Darcy and slipped the latch on the door, bringing it open about three inches. Art Baldwin was standing in the hallway, apparently still in the process of tying his tie.

"I'm fine, Art. Thanks."

"Oh. Uh, sorry old man. Sorry," he mumbled and nodded, and backed his way down the hallway still tying his tie.

I came quietly back down to Darcy, and our legs automatically entertwined and we held each other closely. After a time, lying in the semi-darkness, we heard the sounds of clump-clump-clump punctuated by the opening and shutting of the street door.

We had dinner that night, as we often did, at the Hot Shoppe near the Shoreham Hotel, the romance of the dining experience somehow enhanced by close proximity to that elegant establishment. Darcy had mostly regained her perpetually ebullient spirit and was dying to tell me all about her forthcoming excursion with Miss Withersby. Earlier in the day, the *Grande Dame* had called and the two of them had scheduled a second trip to Manhattan Motors. As I suspected would be the case, I had not been invited.

I carefully spelled out in detail all the acceptable choices which she and Miss Withersby might consider. I cast my vote by proxy in the direction of something along the lines of the Sunbeam Alpine or, perhaps, one of the new model, MG roadsters. Darcy listened to all the names, carefully repeating some of them to ensure that my proxy would be successfully cast.

After dinner, we dropped down to DuPont Circle and took P Street back to Georgetown. During the evening, we had not really spoken of the recent unpleasantness. Both of us were still very much frightened by the events of Sunday night. We took refuge in the edited and sanitized story that the Harrises, with some relief, had accepted as Gospel. But they hadn't been there and we had. Then, there was the shoeprint. My private rotten little secret festering like a sore with its implications and continuing to create a tiny, sickening separation between me and my Darcy love.

When we reached the rooming house, there was a bottle of Chateau Latour Rothchild 1958, sitting in front of the door to my room. The little white attached card said only, 'Enjoy in good health, Art.'

"Oh. What a sweet guy," said Darcy.

I smiled, observing the label. "This is *very* nice. Art can be so damn decent when he feels like it."

Inside the room, I rummaged through the top drawer for a corkscrew.

"We should save it, for a special occasion," Darcy crooned.

"This *is* a special occasion," I countered cunningly, pushing aside the socks in my top drawer. Then I saw it, lieing right there alongside the cigarettes and the box of condoms.

"Darcy?" I said, slowly.

"Yes, my Lord." She assumed her pussycat smile.

"Do you remember buying that can of lighter fluid the other night in Higger's drugstore?"

"Yes, Master." She continued, rubbing her fingernails up and down my back. "While you were making great sacrifice and enduring the tortures of the damned back at the perscription counter, all for me."

"Well, its here, in my drawer."

"Yes, Lord." She encircled my waist and laid her cheek tenderly against my back.

I turned, holding her beautiful slender hands and looking into her upturned face. "Darcy love, this can wasn't in my drawer last Friday afternoon."

"Of course it was. I put it there, myself. Let me see." She moved quickly around me and pulled open the little drawer for a better look.

"There. That's *exactly* where I put it. It hasn't moved an inch." She smiled up at me.

"Darcy love," I explained patiently. "I tore that drawer completely apart Friday afternoon before we left, looking for that damned can.

You know how compulsive I am when I misplace something. It simply wasn't there. So help me, it wasn't."

We stood there a moment without speaking. Then Darcy brightened and said something about Art and his having borrowed and returned the can. But I was thinking of a shoeprint and of the upended duffel bags with their contents strewn all over the cabin floor.

CHAPTER ELEVEN

It was dinner at Darcy's house the next evening. Creamed herring on Triscuits and gin & tonics were being served on the patio when I let myself in the front door and shouted hello. Darcy wasn't home yet. Sam was up in his room engaged in teenage practices. The senior Harrises and Cyril welcomed me warmly while Sylvia trundled between patio and kitchen for refills and to check on dinner.

Charles and I sat and chatted, recounting portions of the harrowing Night on Bald Mountain. He had spoken again with the Sheriff but nothing had turned up yet. And nothing would, I thought. Nothing ever would.

The man with the city shoes had been in my room last Friday. He had taken the can of Ronsonol. He had followed us up to the cabin. He had searched our things, my things, for something he hadn't found when he filched the lighter fluid. Then yesterday, to my total bafflement, he had entered my room again and replaced the unopened can.

"Hi! I'm home," trilled Darcy. She came, breathlessly, through the French doors and out onto the patio looking deliciously radiant in a flowered print summer frock and white, leather sandals. I rose immediately, drinking in her golden tanned shoulders and her painted, bare toes. She stooped beside her father's chair to confer a quick kiss, and, to my intense embarrassment, quickly rose to take both my hands in hers and kissed me full on the mouth.

"Yum yum, creamed herring." She flashed her impish grin.

"Well, did you get it?" I asked, my ears burning with the open display of intimacy.

"Get what," she teased.

"Darcy."

"Yes. We got it."

"Well?"

"Well what?" She gaily crossed to the little table and started scooping ice cubes into a glass. Charles Harris chuckled.

"What kind of car did you buy," I pleaded.

"Guess."

"Darcy!"

She put down the glass and took my hand, heading for the house. "Come and see."

"It's here? You drove it home?" She laughed, nodding vigorously.

We came down the brick-lined walk to the street at a half run. Sitting a few car lengths away from the house was a dark green Jaguar XK-E roadster. It was simply the most beautiful, the most elegant mechanical creation that I had ever seen. It sat there gleaming, its wire wheels sparkling in the afternoon sunlight. The long-awaited E-Type from Jaguar had just been introduced to the showrooms of New York and San Francisco. I had never seen one before.

"There has to be a waiting list a mile long," I stammered. "How did you ever manage it?"

"A personal check for $6485.00 drawn on the Riggs bank is extremely persuasive," laughed Darcy.

"Sixty-five hundred dollars! Wow!" I gasped, shaking my head in disbelief. I didn't think Miss Withersby had *that* kind of money."

"You thought she was subsisting on a small pension?"

"No, but, my God! Sixty-five hundred smackers for a present? She could have bought the Morgan and had enough left over for a new Cadillac."

"Yes." Darcy yawned, patting her lips.

"Do you know what this is?"

Darcy nodded, "A *very* nice car."

"It's a *gran prix* racing car made street legal with bumpers, a top and roll up windows. It'll do a hundred and fifty miles an hour. It's no car for a young girl."

"But it's perfect for the superior male." She gestured grandly toward me while coquetishly turning her head and making a little bow.

"Darcy, what have you done?"

She clapped her hands. "I've gotten you a set of new wheels for the summer. Miss Withersby wants us to break it in before presenting it to Priscilla in the fall."

"Us? Break it in? It doesn't need breaking in. It needs to be driven."

"And you shall drive it, Sir John."

I stood there, helplessly staring at the Jaguar and shaking my head in disbelief. "Miss Withersby thinks all automobiles must be properly broken in by a man who understands such things before they're fit to be driven by a lady. Her father told her that fifty years ago, and her father was always right about everything."

"Why doesn't she have Alonzo do it? He's a professional driver."

"Oh, Alonzo only knows about regular cars. These little foreign things are a mystery to him. So I volunteered your services. Miss Withersby is very impressed with you."

"Oh, Darcy. Thank you. Thank you."

"Your servant, my Lord." She made another little bow.

"But it's not right," I moaned. "Giving an E-Type to Priscilla is like giving a jet fighter to a child."

"Nonsense. It's a perfect pussycat. It drives like a dream. It will be ideal for Priscilla."

"Good God," I said.

I got back to Miss Withersby's answer to the Barbizon Hotel for Women early the following evening and was pleasantly surprised to hear saxophone music emanating from Art's open door. Darcy was picking me up in the Jag at six o'clock, and I quickly poked my head into Art's room to say hello and thank him for the wine before dashing into the shower. There was still twenty minutes to kill after I finished dressing, and I walked back down the hall and rapped on the door casing. Art was half into his Brooks Brothers suit and busily putting papers into his slim leather attaché case.

"Jack, old man. Sorry about the other night. Damned embarrassing."

"No harm done. The wine was really *very* nice. You didn't need to do that, you know."

"Forget it. How was your weekend?"

I gave him the sanitized, edited version.

"My God. That's awful. Do you think they'll catch the guy?"

"Art, I don't think it was a hillbilly. I don't want to upset Darcy and the Harrises any more than they are already, but I think our prowler was

117

from here. From the District." I told him about the footprints, omitting all references to the swimming hole.

Art listened carefully and then began shaking his head. "But that just doesn't make any sense at all. Why on earth would someone follow you all the way out there and paw through your stuff? I mean, my God, this guy was wearing street shoes, for crying out loud. That's not so bizarre. These people don't have your wardrobe selection, you know."

"That argues to my point," I said. "If the guy can afford only one pair of shoes, why woud he have street shoes?" "If he has two pairs, and one is his 'going to town shoes,' why would he wear them out in the woods? I know the shoeprints weren't from a local. They just weren't."

"Were any pictures taken? Plaster casts?"

"Sheriff dusted the car for fingerprints."

"He didn't notice the shoeprints?"

"Not really. I didn't say anything about them."

"So you took no photographs of the shoeprints?"

"Me? Oh, come on. With what? When. What's the point, anyway?"

"The point is, Jack, that there are people who can probably identify the make of shoe from a good photograph."

"You're kidding. People? You mean J. Edgar's boys?"

"And others," Art replied, not smiling.

"Art, if I were to get you a photograph of one of the shoeprints, could you have someone identify it for me?"

He was silent for a moment, watching me carefully.

"You serious?"

I nodded slowly.

"Sure."

"Well, we'll just see then." I patted my shirt pocket. "Say, can I bum a smoke?"

Art nodded toward his dresser. "Top bureau drawer."

I opened the bureau which was much like my own; and there, beside several packs of Winston cigarettes, was a blue and yellow can of Ronsonol. I took one of the cigarette packs, broke it open and patted my shirt pocket, again. Art reached over on the little bed table and picked up the lighter, snicked it and held the flame to my cigarette. It was a gold Ronson costing about fifty times the price of my Zippo, but they used the same fuel.

A fast series of horn blasts stopped the conversation cold. I grabbed Art and pulled him toward the door. "You gotta see this for yourself," I grinned.

We stood and ogled and talked and salivated over the Jaguar with Darcy for about ten minutes. Art reluctantly begged off to finish dressing for work, and Darcy and I vanished down O street, the electrifying sexy moan of the Jaguar's engine reverberating off the fronts of the ancient brick and limestone houses.

I spent a significant portion of the following morning, more or less, considering Art Baldwin's offer of shoeprint identification. On my lunch break, I stopped at a People's Drugstore and purchased one of the new Kodak Instamatic cameras complete with flashbulbs and film for about $8.00.

The clock had already passed one a.m. when I put Darcy into the Jaguar down the street from the rooming house and kissed her goodnight.

"Good night, my Lord and Master," she whispered, grinning devilishly at me and bringing my outstretched hands to her lips.

A flood of self-loathing swept over me at my deception.

"You've got a busy day tomorrow." I said.

Darcy had taken on daily volunteer work with a summer class of kids at Sidwell Friends' School and had scheduled two sets of tennis with Linda Townsend for the next afternoon. After my shift was over, I was joining the girls, and we were all expected at the Harrises for dinner. Only tomorrow, I was not going to be hacking fares from pillar to post in Arlington. I was going to West Virginia to get evidence.

Since this meant another day absent from work, I had endured the painful task of informing the dispatcher that afternoon. I deftly produced Excuse #243-c (dental appointment), fed it into the dispatcher's fetid brain and hung on the phone for his reaction.

All he said was, "Gotta keep them pearly whites shined up for that little gal, eh 41?"

One day last week, Darcy had driven me to work and word had spread like the discovery of nuggets on the American River. So I said, yes, that was about it, and the dreaded exchange was over.

Now, over the next two hours, I got as much sleep as possible which wasn't much; and, shortly after three a.m., I dressed in my Yellow Cab suit, got into the VW and headed west. When I finally pulled up in front of the chained-off trail the sun had been up for half an hour and my bladder was bursting with coffee.

I relieved myself by the side of the car and quickly changed out of the cab suit. Pulling on a pair of old khakis and topsiders, I checked my watch and loped off down the trail swinging the little Instamatic from a cord on my wrist. In 48 minutes, the cabin hove into view.

To my immense relief, the tracks were still there. In many places, they had been overlaid with the heavy boots of the Sheriff's deputies. Nearer the creek, small animal tracks were everywhere, but a number of the city shoeprints had remained untouched.

I photographed them extensively. Immersed in the warm smell of pine needles and powdery dust, I pointed and snapped and the metallic sounds of the little camera punctuated the buzzing drone of forest insects.

I walked some distance upstream from the swimming hole where white water cascaded over small boulders and washed the sticky heat from my face and arms and drank from the little stream. On the way up the hill to the cabin, I snuffed out the alien shoeprints with my feet, scuffing and tearing at the dusty earth.

I saw the Sheriff's Jeep parked just behind the VW just as I came over the last rise.

Deputy Otis Perkins and I greeted each other like old pals, and he immediately wanted to know if we'd had any further trouble. I said that we hadn't.

"Looks like you're getting an early start on the weekend," He nodded at the Instamatic. "Nice little camera. What kinda pitchers, you takin'?"

"Oh, just some shots of the garden plot and the house. I promised my girl." It was the first time I'd ever referred to Darcy as 'my girl.'

"Uh huh. I see. What brings you up in these parts in the middle of the week?"

I had half expected to run into him after Charles Harris's input to his boss. Accordingly, I was prepared with a convincing lie.

"Keys," I said, holding up a small leather case. "I knew right away that they must have fallen out of my pockets when I changed into my trunks to go swimming the other afternoon."

Deputy Perkins nodded. "Uh huh. Funny we didn't see 'em when we had a look around Monday morning."

"I changed in the outhouse."

"Yeah, we checked the outhouse pretty good. People always droppin' things outta their hip pockets when they go to the can."

Oh what a tangled web we weave when first we practice to deceive.

The deputy grinned and said, "Say cabbage without smilin'."

"What?" My heart thumped and the blood began to rush to my ears.

"Say cabbage without smilin,' son. That's what my mamma used to tell me when she caught me in a fib."

"My mother used to say that, too."

"Yeah, them muh-thers. You just can't fool 'em. First place we checked in that shithouse, son, was the floor in front of the crapper. There warn't no keycase layin' there." With the last utterance his voice changed sharply, became hard and I half expected him to say, "Draw!" or "Hands up!" or something.

"Cabbage," I said grimly, looking him straight in the eye.

He burst out laughing. "It don't make no difference to me. The boss has got to keep Mr. Harris and all them bigshots happy; but I think I know what really happened."

I felt a wave of dizziness and that awful tingling feeling was solid from scrotum to throat.

"You all right, son? You look a little green around the gills."

"Just what do you think happened?" I asked.

"Oh, not too much. I think you wuz jist havin' so much fun with that little gal that you forgot to go home when you should have. That's all."

"That's not true," I said, angrily. "You saw the dead battery in our car."

"Yeah. I used to run out of gas on dates a lot, myself," He drawled, grinning right in my face.

"Listen . . . ."

"Like I said, it don't make no never mind to me. You see we didn't find no strange prints on that there little car of yourn, but no harm done. Nobody got hurt. Th' bigshots are all congratulatin' theirselves about how they got things under control now. Takin' decisive action, they call it. They ain't done nuthin', but they all got a lot of good PR out of it, you know?"

"Somebody *was* here. He stole my knife and money right out of my pants."

"Son, maybe what you ought to do next time you take that little gal out, is keep your pants *on*. That way, won't nobody be able to steal from you."

I turned abruptly and walked over to the VW, unlocking the door. Fucking hick deputy. He stood there on the broken ground watching me with his shit-eating grin, then opened the door to the Jeep. I took a large swallow of pride and slammed the door to the VW. I raised my hand and walked back to the Jeep.

"Listen Otis. I do want to thank you for everything you did for us the other day. I'd really appreciate it if you didn't say anything to anybody about me being up here today. It would mean a lot to me and my girl." Jack, you gutless wonder!

"No problem, son. I understand these things. I wuz young once, myself." He laughed. "Gotta stay on Mamma and Daddy's good side. Like I said, it don't mean nuthin' to me." He winked, suddenly pointed his index finger at my face and shouted, "Say cabbage!"

I said cabbage, and we both broke out with wild laughter and bonhomie.

He reached out the window and playfully slapped me on the shoulder. "Ya'll take care now, you heah?"

I mumbled thanks and waved, as he backed the Jeep onto the county road and pulled away.

I bypassed Miss Withersby's Hall for Unwed Delinquent Young Males and made straight for Darcy's house with a quick stop at Higger's Drugstore to drop off my film for developing. By the time I arrived, the Harrises and Linda Townsend were partaking of cocktails and *hor's d'oeuvres* on the patio.

Linda had secured tickets for *Brigadoon* which was playing in a live performance at the Arena Stage. After an early dinner, the three of us wedged ourselves four abreast into the little cockpit of the Jaguar and motored the short distance to the little outdoor theatre.

A significant portion of the cocktail and dinner conversation had centered around the events of the previous weekend, and I had to keep on my toes to properly juggle the story and to give all the right answers.

I knew, without having to be told, that Darcy and Linda had talked all afternoon. It would have been a forlorn hope to imagine that Linda knew no more of what had actually transpired last Sunday afternoon than did Darcy's parents. My dread proved justified on the ride to the theatre when Linda blurted out,

"Gosh, what a creep. What if he were watching you?".

I felt Darcy stiffen beside me, but no one said anything more; and, in ten minutes, we were seated stage-side at the Arena.

For two hours or so we were transported back in time to the ancient Scottish Highlands. It was terribly romantic, and Darcy and Linda couldn't get enough of it. I liked it too. As a sort of combination Shangri-La/Rip Van Winkle tale, it carried with it the appeal of a secret and cozy safehaven hidden perfectly away in a time long past.

As we were leaving the amphitheater it was impossible not to notice the relatively few people who had worn evening dress. Among them, about a dozen steps ahead of us as we made our way out with the crowd, was a stunningly dressed platinum blonde.

"Straight out of Hollywood," I whispered to Darcy and Linda.

"Jack, Shhhh. People can hear," said Darcy.

The blonde was encased in a sheer white silk evening gown into which she appeared to have been poured. Her hair was dressed beautifully and she wore elbow length gloves. There was even what looked like a diamond necklace around her long, naked throat. But the gown, which reached from ankles to about half way up her torso, was almost obscene.

I leaned down to Darcy. "She doesn't have on any panties. She's not wearing anything *at all* under that gown."

"Jack darling, please be quiet. They're going to hear," Darcy hissed.

"I'm shocked! Shocked!" I said with mounting umbrage.

Several people ahead of us laughed, turned and looked back. As did the man on whose arm the blonde was hanging.

Sidney Reilly!

Now, I really was shocked. It was the couple from Middleburg. The couple from the speedboat. I urgently whispered to the girls.

"That's them!"

"That's whom, love?"

"Reilly and the Vamp," I blurted.

Linda was totally confused. "Who?"

"It's the people from the speedboat," Darcy said.

"Ohhh," said Linda. "It *is.*" She put her hand to her mouth.

We had reached the street curb in front of the theater by this time. The line of impossibly shiny limousines which always attended social events in the nation's capital was dutifully present and began receiving their charges from among the formally dressed patrons.

Reilly and the Vamp waited their turn at curbside and were received by an antique Rolls-Royce with diplomatic plates. The old car made the others in the line appear somehow cheap and ready-made. The old Rolls conferred instant chachet to its passengers in the same way as did Miss Withersby's Packard V12. It also instantly occurred to me they were of almost exactly the same vintage.

"That car's from the British Embassy!" squealed Darcy as the stately limousine ghosted away from the curb.

"I'll be damned," I stammered. "So Arthur Thayer Baldwin IV has diplomatic connections. As they say down home, Art's cutting in tall timber." As soon as I had muttered this inanity, I realized that I was standing next to Linda Townsend. Darcy had realized it even sooner and had pinched me, very hard.

"Oh," I said. "Uh, I . . . ."

"It's okay. They're not seeing each other. Art's broken off diplomatic relations." Linda smiled at me. "You're so sweet, Jack. Always thinking of other people's feelings."

"Bullshit." I said.

Linda and Darcy looked at each other and frowned grimly, then repeated, in unison: "Bullshit!" A middle-aged couple in front of us turned abruptly around and stared angrily, horrified at the three of us.

We beat a hasty retreat, laughing down the darkened street to the waiting maw of the wonderful E-Type.

CHAPTER TWELVE

The following evening, Darcy and I planned to see *Dr. Strangelove*, currently showing at the DuPont Theatre. We would take pot luck at the Harrises, then run down Connecticut to catch the eight o'clock showing. I arrived at the rooming house about five thirty and checked for mail in the little box on the front stoop. The name on the metal mailbox read: John R. Norton, 1435 O St. N.W. apt. B.

I fitted the little key into the lock and the front of the mailbox swung open. There was the usual weekly letter from my mother, and a large manila envelope with no postmark or writing of any kind. I closed the box and walked into the darkened hallway, quickly opening the letter from Mother to find the check. I would deal later with the Epistle to St. John.

Inside my room, I sat down on the edge of the bed and pried open the heavy manila envelope. There were photographs of Darcy and me. For a moment, I sat there stunned.

The sickening fear that had coursed through my bowels the previous weekend rose up massively within me, now intermixed with a horrible black feeling of eternal doom. There were scores of photographs, 81/2 x 11 glossies, and they recorded every aspect of every act committed by my Darcy love and me throughout the long afternoon by the swimming hole.

Dully, I half-thumbed through the pile. Behind the last picture was a sheet of white paper. I pulled it out as if in a trance. Typed in small, neat letters were the words:

You have new masters now. Do nothing. You will be contacted.

I sat there staring at the words for a full five minutes. Then, slowly, it began to all make perfect sense. Art Baldwin. The only real spy I knew was my so-called friend down the hall. The only person who knew my whereabouts last weekend was my so-called friend down the hall. The person who had been in my room fiddling with the can of Ronsonoil was my so-called friend down the hall. The only person who could have followed me from here to West Virginia and photographed the two of us together was my so-called friend down the hall. He had asked for photographs of the shoeprints, shoeprints that he had made, shoeprints that he would undoubtedly identify as coming from the shoes of a total stranger.

The rotten bastard. Art was a spy, a voyeur and a sadistic pervert. God damn him! Why was he doing this? I could not imagine, but I was prepared to wager that the prints in those photographs would exactly match a pair of dress shoes in his closet next door. I knew it and I would prove it. I would confront him with the evidence. I would get the negatives of the pictures that lay in my lap. I would beat the living shit out of Arthur Thayer Baldwin IV.

I stowed the package under my mattress, then showered, dressed and left the building feeling a horrible, deep anger and an imminent sense of impending doom.

The sudden electric click sounded loud in the belly of the B-52, and Slim Pickens dropped slowly away riding 25 megatons of hydrogen bomb right down into the Soviet heartland.

"Yeeeeeee Haaah!"

The crowd in the theater roared with hysterical laughter. Waving the big Stetson hat from side-to-side and straddling the huge cylinder, the only sounds the eerie moan of the wind and the lonely haunting cry that signaled a doomed mankind, Major "King" Cong fearlessly rode the monster into eternity.

"Yeeeee Haaah! Yeeeee Haaah!" Again, again and again. The long, plaintive yell dying away ever more faintly until, at last, silently disappearing forever into the landscape. And the screen went brilliant white. The audience roared.

Darcy squeezed my arm, laughing and looked up at me. She saw the glistening tears on my cheek.

"Jack? Sweetheart, what is it? You're crying." Her joyous expression had turned instantly to one of concern.

I wiped my eyes and smiled at her.

"Oh, Baby. It's just a movie."

"I know," I laughed. "It brought tears to my eyes."

She looked up at me, not being entirely sure in the dimly lighted theater. "My funny wonderful Jack," She said, and held me close as I wiped my eyes and cleared my throat.

We stopped at the Hot Shoppe for a late night ice cream something or other and talked of the upcoming weekend. The Harrises were again bound for West Virginia, but Darcy had volunteered to help organize a benefit at Sidwell Friends' School on Saturday morning and would stay behind. I thought this was the best news I'd heard all week.

I delivered my Darcy love safely home before midnight for the first time since we'd met. We tip-toed down to the garage and sat in the Jaguar, and smelled and licked and petted it, and listened to the Stromburg-Carlson radio in the dark. Then I smelled and licked and petted Darcy until the garage light popped on and the voice of Charles Harris sounded from the head of the steps.

"Darcy? Jack? What the hell are you kids doing down there?"

"Necking!" cried Darcy, as I frantically zipped up my pants and fumbled with the buttons of my shirt.

"It's late, "came the reply with more than a trace of annoyance.

"I'll see you tomorrow afternoon as soon as I get off work." I whispered.

"We can stay here tomorrow night.".

I squeezed her tightly in the moon-lit shadows and inhaled the perfect aroma of Darcy Harris and the Connally hides, the latter painstakingly hand-sewn by British craftsmen. "Ummm. I know," I breathed. "I know."

At the rooming house, in the wee hours before falling asleep, I got up and tried to slip the latch on the door to my room using a bunch of oil company credit cards. It didn't work, and I went to sleep turning fitfully on the horrible little package pressed beneath the mattress. Until sleep finally came, I lay there and wondered how I was going to get into the room of my so-called friend down the hall.

Friday was a particularly frustrating day. I had three fares in a row that I couldn't find in a reasonable length of time and the dispatcher never let up.

"You not there yet, 41? Boy, what is the *matter* with you? I'm gonna getcha one of them seeing eye dogs. Look at yur map, 41. Piedmont runs right up the hill at the top of Chestnut. Are you *blind*?

"Chestnut's not on my map."

"Well, dammit. Go up 31st then."

Oh, of course, I thought. Thirty-first. How silly of me. When you don't have a Chestnut, just take 31st. Simple.

Finally, a little past noon as I was heading for a cabstand, the radio squawked and the dispatcher said, "Where you at, 41?"

I told him and he gave me an address clear out at Tyson's Corner.

"Garfinkel's, in front of the main entrance. Somebody asked for you, special, 41. You gettin' to be real popular these days."

I knew not only how to get to Tyson's Corner but was familiar with Garfinkel's department store as well, having shopped out there in the new suburban complex with Darcy.

In twenty minutes, I pulled up in front of the impressive marble facade. Art Baldwin opened the door of the cab and jumped right into the front seat.

"Art!" I smiled and laughed, feeling and sounding exactly like Uriah Heep.

"Jack, old man. Popped in here to pick up some underwear and stuff on the lunch hour. Had a friend run me over, and it just occurred to me to give you a call to run me back."

I'd much rather run you over, I thought, as I said, "Great, glad you called."

During the ride over to Langley, we talked, strangely enough, about him and Linda. I wasn't even sure he was seeing her on a regular basis. Linda hadn't revealed very much, at least to me, the night she had gone with Darcy and me to the Arena Stage. I was mulling this over and not really listening to Art going on and on when I realized that he was suggesting another double date for the upcoming Sunday. Sailing, no less.

"Hey, sounds great to me. Let me see what Darcy wants to do."

"Oh sure," He said affably, "We'll let the girls decide."

I told him that I'd ask Darcy to give Linda a call the next day, and that I was sure that the two of them would work something out for Sunday. In fact, I was going to make damned certain that Darcy and I came nowhere near Art Baldwin, Sunday or any other day. I didn't want the rotten son-of-a-bitch to ever lay eyes on her again.

We pulled up at the guardhouse at the entrance to the Bureau of Roads. Art showed his pass to the uniformed officer, and we were waved through. As we circled the drive in front of the massive brick edifice, Art suddenly turned in the seat.

"By the way, did you ever do anything about those shoeprints?"

I had been waiting for this. "No. The more I thought about it, the dumber it seemed. He was probably just a local moonshiner who was afraid that we'd stumble onto his still."

Art thanked me for coming out, said he was looking forward to the Sunday outing and gave me a twenty dollar bill. The fare was $4.35.

"Keep the change," he said and went briskly through the big glass doors.

I drove out to the highway, carefully folding the twenty to quarter size. Then I tore the bill into as many tiny strips as I could manage and threw each one out the window.

Darcy picked me up at the rooming house that evening. We drove toward Chevy Chase in the late Friday afternoon rush-hour traffic. The E-Type responded like a rocket sled in a shattering series of lunges as I threaded her around the milling mob. We had decided to leave my VW parked near the rooming house for various reasons, not least of all, the neighbors.

We drove up the scenic little winding alleyway that ran off Rock Creek Parkway right into the rear of the Harris property and the quiet sanctity of the garage. I pulled the big door down behind us. When I turned, Darcy was standing beside the Jaguar, holding my duffel bag.

"Let's not go out tonight," Her impish grin running up the corners of her soft lips.

I nodded, smiling. "A quiet evening at home with Lord and Lady Norton-Harris."

"We could play chess or backgammon." Darcy offered.

"You could catch up on your letter writing, and I could finish reading that chapter of Gibbon. Perhaps, put in some time with my stamp collection, or my etchings. Have I shown you my etchings, my dear?"

"It's been so long," crooned Darcy. Sounds wonderful."

We linked arms, both smiling hugely and skipped up the stairs to the house.

The sun broke through the windows of the guest room the following morning as I gradually floated up to the surface of the waking world. I instantly sensed the warm, sweet smelling, incredible naked softness of my still-sleeping Darcy love, lying full-length against my body and was filled with such joy as I had never experienced in all my twenty-one years upon the earth.

I brushed her cheek with my lips and disengaged as quietly and gently as possible. A little uncertainly, I padded to the bathroom with two of the five empty foil packages that were littering the carpet, sticking to the soles of my feet.

Oh God, the bathroom! We had started there last night. The stubble on my chin had proved to be an irritant to Darcy, and she insisted on giving me a shave. This she did while perched securely on my lap as I lay back in the tub filled with frothy white bubbles. It will never get any better than this, Norton, I thought. Never.

By the time I got out of the shower, I could smell breakfast and hear dishes clatter down in the kitchen. Darcy was a veritable whirlwind, flying around the room, frying eggs and corn beef hash while simultaneously attending to the buttering of English muffins, the setting of the table and the pouring of coffee.

I opened the front door and retrieved the *Washington Post* from the side yard hedge, then joined Darcy in the little sun-lit breakfast room just off the kitchen.

"Oh boy, corned beef hash! You're going to make me fat."

Darcy shook her head and poured cream in her coffee. "You Tarzan. Tarzan no fat. Tarzan strong, like ape."

"Don't start that. There isn't time this morning. When do you have to be at Friends'?"

"Ten o'clock, which is just," She glanced at the wall clock, "thirty minutes from now and I haven't even showered or anything." She was off in a flash with a captive English muffin, and I sat and read the *Post* and ate my corned beef hash and eggs all by myself.

I used the morning to good advantage. Darcy had taken the Jaguar over to The Friends' School, so I fired up her Corvair and drove to the hardware store just down from Higger's Drugs. I stopped by the drugstore to confirm what I already knew: my shoeprint pictures would not be back from Kodak until the following Tuesday. I then walked down the street to the little neighborhood hardware store with its racks of brooms and mops, lawnmowers and galvanized trash barrels sitting out on the sidewalk. In five minutes I had purchased a complete, do-it-yourself shoeprint kit.

Darcy was back home by early afternoon. We put on swimsuits under old clothes and went down to the Key Bridge boat dock and rented a canoe. We pushed off against the current and struck out upriver in the direction of Great Falls. Somewhere in the vicinity of the Three Sisters, a tall rock outcropping in mid-river, I brought up the subject of double-dating with Art and Linda on Sunday.

"I'd just rather we spent time alone." I said.

Darcy kept on paddling. "You just want to make me your love slave." She pouted.

"Me! Why, you shameless wench," I shouted, sending a paddle full of Potomac River cascading toward the bow of the little craft.

She went on. "I know you too well, Sir John. You want to keep me locked away in your castle tower, the key to my chastity belt on a golden chain, safely nestled against your manly chest."

I snorted. "I'm totally convinced that those things never worked."

Darcy laughed. "Aye, you'd be known,' Squire." We paddled a few more strokes. I remained silent. "Why not?"

"Vaseline," I said. Two resourceful lovers would have found ways to get around them. The human anatomy is very supple."

"They didn't have any Vaseline."

"Goose grease, then. Necessity is the mother of conception."

We pulled over to the river's edge in the area of shallow riffles above The Three Sisters and swam and played and talked of 'cabbages and kings' until we had just half an hour to get the canoe back downstream by the five o'clock deadline.

That night we drove down to the Tidal Basin off 14th St. and dined on beer and steamed clams served in a huge, old-fashioned coffee pot of the kind cowboys used over open campfires.

I had been deeply dreading having to tell Darcy about Art and the shoeprints, but after purchasing the do-it-yourself shoeprint kit that morning in the hardware, I realized that I couldn't properly handle the job alone. Besides, she had a right to know.

Sitting in the restaurant overlooking the yacht club and the boats moored in their slips, I told her of my suspicions and divulged my plan omitting, entirely, any mention of the tracks down to the swimming hole and the horror in the brown manila envelope.

"But why would Art do something like that?"

"I have no idea, but he was the only person in Washington who knew where we were."

"You don't think he saw us, do you?"

I shook my head quickly. "Art's a fundamentally decent sort."

"But the gunshots."

"He was afraid we'd see *him* and he just panicked. It got out of hand."

Darcy nodded, slowly. "I think you're probably right, but why bother going into his room and taking pictures of his shoes? He just did something that started out as a prank, and he got in over his head. He didn't actually hurt anybody. He's probably terribly embarrassed about the whole thing."

I dug my fork into the white tablecloth. "I need to be sure, that's all."

Darcy was watching me closely. "There's something else, isn't there.".

I looked down at the snowy covering and doodled on it with the tines of my fork. "I think he might have watched us."

"Oh Jack. Why?" The pain in her face resummoned the gut wrenching fear when I'd seen the pictures, the sense of doom. "Why do you think that?" She said, depending on me, pitifully counting on me for the answers.

I told her about the tracks down to the swimming hole. Darcy put both hands to her face.

"If it was Art, we can't see him again."

"I know." She shook her head sadly. "God. Poor Art. I just can't picture him doing anything like that. You know? I mean, he might take off his clothes and join us, but I just can't see him hiding in the bushes taking secret pictures. What?" She stopped. "Why are you looking at me that way?"

"Take off his clothes and join us? Why Darcy Harris. You think the strangest thoughts, for a nice girl."

Darcy leaned across the table and whispered something in my ear, then rearranged herself in her chair. We both burst out laughing.

When dinner was over, we fired up the Jag and drove around the Tidal Basin, past the Lincoln Memorial and on up Rock Creek Parkway. Darcy snuggled down beside me in the leather seats.

"You know, it's weird," she began, "but, somehow, I don't mind too much if it had been a total stranger." She laughed. "We didn't do anything wrong and you could almost hope he found us instructive. But I could just never, ever face him if he turned out to be someone we know, like Art Baldwin."

I nodded silently, but my Darcy love didn't know about those horrors in the manila envelope. She couldn't know and had never dreamed of having to face, not a total stranger who had gotten a secret eyeful, but parents, friends and family who might be given copies of those evil pictures.

Art Baldwin would be a dead man were he to do such a thing. I would kill him in a cold-blooded instant and without remorse. He would vanish from the earth and never be heard from again. But, first, I had to have proof.

CHAPTER THIRTEEN

When we got back to the Harrises, Darcy called Linda and begged off the double date for the next day. The excuse given was that I had been looking forward to a real workout for the Jaguar along the Blue Ridge Parkway, and Sunday was the day we had picked.

Linda seemed delighted by the opportunity to have Art all to herself but dutifully maintained the fiction that he had been counting on us going and would be dreadfully disappointed. I fervently hoped and prayed that Art Baldwin would live out his miserable life in a perpetual state of dreadful disappointment.

Later that evening, we made popcorn and watched a play on *Hallmark Hall of Fame* down in the den. Following the classic scenario of the peasants breaking into the manor house, I uncorked a bottle of Old Rarity single malt scotch from the liquor cabinet of Charles Harris. By the time The Stars Spangled Banner began to play on the TV set, I was sloppily, happily drunk and had to be helped up the stairs to bed.

We stayed in bed and fooled around, and breakfasted and read the Sunday *New York Times* until noon. I wanted to be certain that Art and Linda had not gotten a late start and that they were well on their way to Annapolis before we began our clandestine activities.

Although Art was almost as bad a car nut as I, he kept his immaculate '57 Ford convertible almost permanently parked on O street and hardly ever drove it anywhere. When going to work, he simply walked out to Wisconsin and hopped a streetcar down to M street where some sort of government bus took people across the river to various civilian and military installations. We cruised down O street at 1:00pm, and I saw immediately that the convertible was gone.

I found a safe parking spot for the Jag about a block from the rooming house. Retrieving my duffel bag from the boot, Darcy and I headed straight for Miss Withersby's Hall of Shame.

Snow is beginning to fall on London streets and the gas lamps in the monolithic German Embassy cast a yellow glow upon the glistening pavement. In an anteroom, the German ambassador turns away from his valet and waits. The manservant lifts the long heavy evening cloak, pulling the satin lining onto his master's shoulders and quickly steps in front of him to adjust the collar. A silk opera hat and gloves are waiting on a small table beside a silver knobbed ebony cane and the valet deftly hands them to the ambassador. He watches approvingly as the white kid gloves are worked onto the chubby fingers.

"Will there be anything else, Your Excellency?"

"No, thank you, Schmidt. I shall return at eleven."

The valet nods slightly and there is a faint clicking of heels. He withdraws a step, crosses quickly to the door and opens it for the Ambassador, bowing again.

As soon as he is alone, Sidney Reilly walks quietly back through the rooms of the Ambassador's private apartment. He enters a bedroom, momentarily pausing before looking quickly about and closing the door after him. From the wall safe behind a small Brueghel oil, he deftly extracts a thick sheaf of papers. Reilly removes his valet's jacket and seats himself in the Ambassador's great chair before the hearth with its crackling coal fire. He selects a Monte Christo from the nearby humidor. Slowly and deliberately, he begins to read:

Blohm & Voss, Shipbuilders:
Projections for Armament and Weapons Systems of Capitol Ships

<u>Top Secret</u>

My earlier failed attempts with the credit cards had convinced me that there was no way I could break into Art's room without doing all sorts of damage to his door. However, upon waking the following morning, the solution was as clear as a bottle of gin. The windows! The two hot little airless rooms that Art and I occupied received ventilation only from a pair of small windows, set in the same wall, and facing an enclosed setback between Miss Withersby's rooming house and the building adjacent to it. A high board fence closed off the alleyway at each end; and both windows, his as well as mine, were never closed in summer, the only grace against the murderous heat.

Darcy and I planned the caper right down to the last detail, leaving nothing to chance. The complexity of the scheme was daunting. I would slip out my window, crawl back in Art's and open the door for Darcy who would be waiting in the hallway.

The do-it-yourself shoeprint kit consisted of a square 14-inch baking pan into which a couple of pounds of dampened garden sand had been spread. After opening the door to Art's room, I ran past Darcy into my own room, unzipped the duffel and pulled out the pan and a paper grocery bag containing sand gleaned from the Harrises' garden shed.

I sent Darcy out to the hallway near the front door to give warning, should the need arise, while I set about spreading out the grainy stuff in a smooth layer. A quick wave of the pan under the shower head across the way and I was almost set. I took a paint-stirring stick and kneaded and mixed the dampened sand and smoothed it out evenly in the pan. Picking up my Instamatic with its little package of flashbulbs, I returned next door.

Sitting in three neat rows on the floor of Art's closet, were nine pairs of extremely nice leather shoes. Except for color, most of them appeared to be identical. All were highly polished and contained wooden shoe trees. They gave the distinct impression that, while some were older than others, none had been worn more than a few times.

Anyone seeing the shoes in *my* closet could have instantly established a time of ownership chart based solely on the index of wear. When my Weejuns became scuffed, battered and ratty looking, leather cracked and seams failing, I bought another pair, while hanging onto the older ones to wear on weekends or for just knocking about.

The shoes of Arthur Thayer Baldwin IV apparently did not become scuffed, battered or ratty looking. They just aged like fine wine. I picked up one of a pair of sober black Oxfords of the type that Harold Macmillan probably wore. The label embossed in the elegant leather lining read *Church's English Shoes*. I quickly checked the others. They were all of the same manufacture. Besides the leather streetware, there were a pair of rubber overshoes and a pair of canvas TopSiders. I knew that Art also had leather TopSiders and that he was probably wearing them right now.

"Why can't you just take pictures of the shoe soles themselves instead of having to make prints in a sandbox?" asked Darcy, who had silently tip-toed up behind me. I jumped half way into the closet, almost toppling the sand-filled pan.

"God Damn, Darcy! You scared the hell out of me." I closed my eyes and held my hand to my chest which was pounding so loudly I could hear it. "I almost had a heart attack. Love, go back out in the hallway and keep a watch on the street. Please."

"But why not?" she persisted, heading for the bedroom door.

"Not the same," I whispered. "I have to compare tracks with tracks, not tracks with soles." I wasn't totally certain of the accuracy of this last statement, but I sort of expected it to be the case. Indentations would have to be compared with indentations. Right? Right. I certainly hoped so as the procedure I had adopted was amounting to a great deal of trouble.

One by one, I set each pair firmly and gently into the sand, made a faithful imprint and snapped a picture, the flash from the little Instamatic lighting up the dim bedroom with each click of the camera. After each impression, I carefully wiped the bottom of the shoe with a cotton cloth and replaced it in its row. The work went fast. Screeding out the sand for each new impression and wiping down each shoe took only a little longer than snapping the photograph, and in less than twenty minutes, I was finished.

I had touched nothing else in Art's room and had worn rubber dishwashing gloves despite their awkwardness. After locking the door, I carried the sand pan and the Instamatic with a pocketful of little spent flashbulbs back to my room. The Shoeprint kit went back into a tightly-wrapped Safeway bag. I bundled the whole thing into my duffel, and we were out the front door and down the street to the waiting E-Type in a wink and a nod.

Before leaving the Harrises that morning, Darcy had washed and ironed the sheets and made up the bed in the guest room. In fact, she had done everything but place a mint on the pillow to remove any possible signs of the wanton debauchery that had taken place during the weekend.

When we arrived back at the house that evening, just as dusk was settling in, the family was home from West Virginia and reported that all was well.

I finished out the role of film shooting pictures of Darcy, Sam and Cyril playing fetch in the Harrises front yard and took it over to

Higger's Drugs; then, as the Civil War generals were fond of saying, I began awaiting developments.

Darcy and I settled back into our little semi-domestic routine of interrupted nights and drives across town in the wee hours. Linda had called to gossip about their respective weekends. Though the sailing had been as much fun as always, she and Art hadn't exactly hit it off in any intimate way. Linda had almost immediately taken refuge in her hyper-enthusiastic Beautiful/Sportsy mode, while Art had become more old school tie until he sounded like a fairly good imitation of William F. Buckley, Jr.

It made me wonder about Art. Linda was as luscious and desirable as a sun-ripened peach, as well as having the hots for Art. They seemed to make an ideal couple; but, apparently, Art had made no moves in that direction when he'd had the perfect opportunity. According to Darcy, neither of them had ever mentioned Art's connection to the strange couple in the old speedboat.

Then on Tuesday evening, something happened that caused great puzzlement; but which shed new light on the chilly temperature of the Art and Linda thing.

Darcy and I were dozing peacefully in my room after our most recent exertions when I suddenly heard the sounds of clip-clip-clip out in the hallway. I lay in the dark, listening until I heard Art's door open and close. A few minutes later, the shower went on across the hall.

The Baby Ben on the bed table indicated a few minutes past ten p.m.. I planted a long slow kiss on the lips of my sleeping Darcy love.

"Ummm. Hi," she responded, dreamily.

"Somebody's taking a shower in the bathroom." I whispered.

She rose up on her elbows, and we listened together in the darkness.

"Is it the Vamp?"

"Uh huh. Clip-clip-clip, and all that." I answered, smiling.

"No wonder he's been cool to Linda. And she thought they had broken up, 'severed diplomatic ties.'"

"Art hasn't said anything at all to Linda."

"Jack?"

"Ummmm?"

"When do they see each other? She just shows up here occasionally when he's working and takes a shower, sleeps in his bed. Then what?

"I suspect their paths cross for that crucial fifteen minutes or so as soon as he gets home in the morning."

"That's so weird," said Darcy. "When was the last time she was here?"

"I don't know. Long time. Art probably pencils her in for the first Tuesday in every month." We hugged and giggled together.

"She's going to hear us. The shower's turned off."

We lay still, holding our breaths until we heard the door to Art's room gently close and the latch snap shut.

The next thing I knew, Darcy was nibbling at my neck and making little noises and leaning across the bed on my chest.

"Jack, Jack?" She said, softly.

"Ummm?"

"It's time for me to go."

"I *hate* it when you have to go. I much prefer it when you come."

"So do I," She whispered, lowering her head to my chest and giving me a little bite.

But we both knew that she did; and, after a few more minutes of procrastination, I turned on the bedlamp and sat dully on the side of the bed rubbing my eyes. The sound of clip-clip-clip echoed rapidly through the hallway and we heard the front door open.

Darcy popped to her knees on the other side of the little bed, laughing. "Well, It is *definitely* time for every non-male to flee from Withersby Hall." She jumped up and started looking for her clothes.

As I threaded my legs back through the boxer shorts which I'd so recently dropped beside the bed, a woman's scream pierced the entire neighborhood like the sudden blast from a Maserati air horn.

Darcy and I stared at each other, wide-eyed and silent. The scream came again.

"Jack! Do something!" Darcy stood transfixed in the middle of the little bedroom, clutching a blouse to hide herself.

I looked around for a weapon. Nothing. Then saw my six-cell Ray-O-Vac Sportsman standing up on the bed table. I grabbed the big flashlight and flung open the bedroom door. The scream sounded again, and I felt the stark terror like an electric shock.

The front door to the building was standing ajar, and the blonde woman was being dragged across the sidewalk by a large man. At the curb was a long, black Cadillac car. The front and rear passenger doors were flung wide, but no light shone from the cavernous interior. The car had no lights showing. The Vamp was struggling like a tigress with the thug. She flailed and pulled away from him as they fell against the side of the long black car. Her handbag suddenly bridged a space which opened between them, and I yelled at the top of my lungs.

"Hey!"

The big man turned toward me, and I threw the flashlight as hard as I could. It whirred, end over end, past his head striking the curved roof of the Cadillac just above the rear door and shattering all over the sidewalk. The man reacted like Dracula seeing the Sign of the Cross, throwing his hands up in front of his face and lurching away.

Across the street, a light came on and somebody yelled, "What's going on out there?" The blonde lunged toward the man, striking downward toward his upraised arms and chest. He suddenly clutched his left arm and cried out.

"*Procthtytka!*".

She hesitated at the sound of his voice. He backed away and scrambled into the front seat of the car. The rear door slammed shut and, with a squeal of tires, the Cadillac shot away from the curb.

The blonde took several steps backward then looked up at me standing on the little brick stoop. She turned quickly and started walking away.

"Wait!" I shouted, then realized that I was standing out on the street in my underwear and quickly ducked back inside the doorway. She turned the corner at Wisconsin Ave. and was gone.

I ran back to the bedroom where Darcy was rapidly pulling on her clothes.

"Man in a car. Attacked her. They're gone." I said, pulling on my khakis and a tee shirt and stuffing my feet into Weejuns.

I quickly ran back out to the curb and picked up the battered and broken flashlight. A siren sounded on Wisconsin and the reflection of a flashing red light lit up the intersection.

The Metropolitan Police stayed long enough to take down a brief statement from me and the four or five people across the street who had heard the commotion and called them. During the questioning, Darcy slipped out and stood with the little crowd of onlookers. We took no obvious notice of each other. She volunteered nothing and the police asked her no questions.

I explained what I had seen and done. This was largely corroborated by a man across the street who had reacted in much the same way. As far as anyone knew, a young woman had been walking along O street, presumably on her way home, when a car had appeared and an altercation had taken place. The young woman was the only apparently injured party; and, since she had vanished, nothing much could be done about the matter. Probably a case of domestic violence. A fight with her boyfriend. A general description of the car was given to the police, and they thanked us and left.

I walked Darcy down the street to the Jaguar, both of us beginning to tremble badly.

"What does *procthtytka* mean?" I asked.

Darcy shook her head. "I don't know."

That's what he said when she hit him. *"procthtytka!"*

"Maybe that's her name," said Darcy.

There was no mention of the incident in the following afternoon's edition of the *Evening Star*. A barbecue with the neighbors was planned that evening at the Harrises, and we grilled hamburgers on the patio and filled our glasses continually from a big steel keg of Hamm's beer, set in a barrel of ice.

It was a wonderful variation on the usual Washington cocktail party. Soon everyone, including Sam who kept sneaking drinks from the keg, was delightfully happy. The neighbors and guests were made up of judges, lawyers, professors, upper-level bureaucrats, and a French family from the diplomatic corps. The air cracked with the latest expression of the Soviet menace in Berlin, that worrisome problem in Cuba, and the goings-on at Camelot.

Late in the evening, one of the neighbors, a district judge named Samuel Goldstein, picked up a golf club from somewhere and performed a hilarious, impromptu skit concerning the 'Cherman Method' of playing golf. This occurred around midnight out on the Harrises' front lawn and at least a dozen adults and half-grown children screamed and rolled on the ground as Judge Goldstein carefully lectured us on the correct Cherman Method of putting, dealing properly with one's caddie, selecting the correct irons and so forth.

Finally, the laughter and tears wound down and people staggered off down the street in the dark, giggling on the way to their homes. The Harrises and I stumbled back into the living room and collapsed on the sofa and chairs. We sat there drunkenly dazed, breathing hard for half a minute and then broke out in another wild spasm of hysterical laughter.

Eventually, we went returned to the patio to finish what was left of the keg of Hamm's. All hands made some confused muddled efforts toward cleaning up and putting stuff away. Sylvia Harris was afraid for me to drive home, and I was directed to take the guest room for what remained of the night.

I rose early and quietly fixed myself coffee and got out of the house before anyone else stirred. I stopped by the rooming house for a change of uniform and ran into Art Baldwin as he was coming home from work.

"You missed all the excitement, the other night," I said.

"What?"

"A woman was attacked and almost abducted, right here before my very eyes."

"Oh?" He looked at me with renewed interest, waiting for the story.

I told him exactly what I'd told the police, saying nothing about the Vamp's connection to the rooming house. If she wanted to tell him that, she could do it herself. As far as Art knew from what I told him, a Jane Doe who had been walking home suddenly screamed when she was attacked by two men in a car in front of our rooming house. I came out, yelled and threw my light and everybody ran away. Then the police and people from across the street showed up. End of story.

"Were they Black?" asked Art.

"The street was sure as hell black. I really couldn't see anybody very well till the lights came on and the cops arrived."

He nodded, musing. "Boyfriend?"

"Maybe. She was sure going after him tooth and nail."

"There goes the neighborhood," said Art. He pushed on up the steps and entered the hallway.

I called after him, "Oh, by the way, do you know what the word *Procthtytka* means?"

Art turned and stepped back across the threshold, a quizzical look on his face. "Yes, as it happens, I do."

I waited, expectantly. "Yeah?"

"It means 'whore' in Russian."

CHAPTER FOURTEEN

The list of daily assignments for my Darcy bug included calling Higger's Drugs each morning to see if the prints had arrived, as well as seeking out and procuring little amenities to make our life together less oppressive in the tiny sweatbox at Miss Withersby's. Among the latter were another reading lamp and a portable electric fan for which I rose up and called her Blessed. Without prompting from me, she added lots of thick, fleecy towels, exotic shampoos, soaps, and mysterious, scented oils and balms to keep our ripe young bodies from becoming overly ripe in the fetid little room.

Darcy was happy in her work. She went gaily about Georgetown in the sexy green Jaguar with top down and honey-gold hair flying. Along the sidewalks, every male head instantly turned and oceans of deep, lustful, never-to-be-fulfilled longing were unleashed as she made her little excursions to this smart shop or that.

The nesting instinct was becoming evident in many ways. Darcy decided we should budget my money, live within our means and economize. We would be sensible. We would be responsible and adult. Ever mindful of Miss Withersby's prohibition, we would clandestinely prepare *haute cuisine* on the little hotplate in the room instead of constantly indulging in expensive restaurant fare.

Accordingly, my Darcy love flew away to Carl's Caterers, just below Chevy Chase Circle on Connecticut Ave. Carl's was the nicest little grocery in the District with the most helpful clerks you could possibly imagine, all of whom knew Darcy by name. There, personally assisted by Carl himself, she ordered up a cornucopia of gustatory delights, omitting not a single one of my favorites or hers.

Beautiful wooden delivery crates stamped with Carl's logo and wrapped in heavy cellophane were filled with this ambrosia and lovingly placed in the boot of the Jaguar. Carl and his respectful underlings stood smiling gratefully in the little parking lot behind the building as Darcy waved and the E-Type moaned away down the street. That evening, Lord and Lady Norton-Harris dined at home.

When I arrived at the rooming house, exhausted from a hard day's hacking for Arlington Yellow Cab, Darcy met me at the door with a dry martini, ice-cold in a tall stemmed glass. Sitting in the only open space remaining in the tiny chamber were two of Carl's wooden delivery boxes, upended and covered with linen to serve as a table. Cutlery and china settings were bathed in the soft light of a single silver candlestick which I was certain had come from the mantelpiece in Sylvia Harris's parlor.

I quickly showered and dressed while Darcy fiddled with some little baked dainties that she had spread onto a cookie sheet and set on the electric hot plate.

We seated ourselves on the worn carpet, Japanese style, next to the improvised dining table. From an ice-filled Styrofoam cooler Darcy produced little servings of quail's eggs in aspic while I expertly opened a bottle of very good California champagne. This was followed by a pink salmon mousse with cold asparagus perfectly complimented by a chilled bottle of white Bordeaux.

We cleansed our palates with a simple green salad seasoned to perfection with an astringent vinaigrette dressing. Finally, as I carefully uncorked Art's bottle of Chateau Latour, Darcy unveiled *la piece de resistance*, a chocolate-and-strawberry torte which, according to everybody, was a particular *specialite* of Carl's. A cheese plate, embellished with slices of melon and apple completed the repast.

I sighed contentedly and gazed across the little table at my Darcy love. My wonderful, wonderful Darcy. I almost shed tears of joy each time I beheld her.

"How much did all this cost?" I asked without a care in the world.

"I don't know, Love. I just charged it." She replied a little tipsily.

"To whom?"

"To youm, that's whom." Darcy laughed her wonderful laugh.

I looked at her and loved her and laughed too. "But, Sweetheart, I don't have an account at Carl's."

Darcy nodded her head. "You do now."

"What did you tell him?"

"I just said to charge it to Mr. John R. Norton of 1435 O St. N. W."

"And he *did* that?"

"Of course. Mom has an account there. Carl knows us."

"Darcy love, we can't afford an account at Carl's Caterers." She looked at me, a hint of disappointment beginning to show. "It's like having an account at Tiffany's."

Darcy smiled at this and I could see the wheels turning. I had just planted a dangerous new thought in that beautiful head.

I scrambled up from the banquet table and got my checkbook from the bureau drawer. I signed the first two checks, left them in place and handed the whole thing to Darcy.

"First thing tomorrow, go over to Carl's and pay for all this stuff. Make sure you write down the amount in the register. If the pictures are back at Higger's, write another check to cover whatever they cost. Okay?" I could see my paltry little checking account at First Arlington National falling below single digits.

This outpouring of domesticity and talk of charge accounts and checkbooks inevitably led to other things. Darcy and I had never spoken formally of marriage in the time we had been together. During the weekend spent at the Harrises, in a particularly tender moment after making love, she had apparently discovered my ears for the first time, and, not unexpectedly, decreed them, beautiful. This led to a speculative discussion on how our children would look and which body parts, in particular, would be inherited.

"They'll all be blue-eyed, blond-haired, fat little roly poleys," said Darcy with blissful confidence. "And they'll have your ears."

"And your belly-button," I had countered, delicately kissing my almost favorite spot on her delicious anatomy.

This evening, however, we got quickly right down into practical stuff.

"We're going to be awfully poor, you know, until I get to be a professor. We'll both be pushing thirty, too."

"How much does a history professor at Harvard make?"

I laughed. "Post doctoral fellows are not offered professorships at Harvard."

"I know," she persisted, "but how much?"

"I don't know, but not nearly as much as your father makes."

Darcy wrinkled her nose. "Daddy's not rich."

"He's a long way from poor."

We went on with this idyllic discussion, never speaking of marriage, but completely engrossed in the economics of living, of house-buying and child-rearing. We both had known for some time that we were going to spend the rest of our lives together. The wedding was taken for granted. The question posed by the economic consideration of making our way in the world at a time when my highest earning potential was on the order of twenty dollars a day tended to focus the mind, wonderfully.

The next day after school, Darcy performed her mission to Carl's Caterers. The balance of the afternoon was then spent nursing the E-Type through its 500-mile oil change and tune-up at Manhattan Motors.

The pictures had still not arrived and we made do for dinner with imported tins of smoked baby clams and *pate de fois Gras*, followed by beluga caviar spread with Carl's own wonderful cream cheese before going off to see *On The Beach* at the Georgetown Theatre. Both of us found the film so depressing that we went across the street to my room and lay, fully clothed, in each other's arms for about two hours before I took Darcy home for the night.

When I arrived at the rooming house the next afternoon, I found Darcy sitting on the little bed, arranging photographs. Both sets of snapshots were spread out neatly on the rumpled sheet.

"They all look the same. You can't see any detail." she said, with more than a trace of disappointment.

Indeed, they did all look the same. Just a bunch of footprints with no distinguishing characteristics. I had worried about not having had the presence of mind to insert a ruler or some object of known size by the tracks in the dust but that didn't seem to be the problem. The fine, crisp detail which had been immediately evident to the naked eye was simply missing from the little 3 x 5 pictures. I picked up several, finally selecting what appeared to be the most sharply focused and held it up beside one of the pairs of tracks from Art's shoes.

"They look about the same, if you adjust for distance from the camera," I said. "Damn."

We examined each of the little pictures, comparing sets with the single shots taken at the West Virginia camp until I finally tossed them all back onto the bed.

"We need a good magnifying glass."

"Mom has one in her desk. It belonged to my grandfather."

We gathered up the pile of pictures, faithfully locked the building as I had been instructed by Miss Withersby and headed for Chesterfield Street. In her mother's little secretary in the downstairs hall, Darcy discovered the big round glass with its long metal handle hiding on top of some stamp albums in the bottom drawer.

We took the snapshots up to her room and spread them out on the flowered quilt which covered her little white bed. The differences in the shoe prints practically leapt out at us. I felt as if I'd just received a blow in the stomach.

"They're not the same at all," I said. "Even the shape of the sole is different. Look."

Under the rigorous stare of the magnifying glass, the marked differences in the two sets of prints were readily apparent. The prints from Art's shoes were longer and much more narrow. Also, in the tracks from the West Virginia camp a sort of oval logo appeared, which had apparently been embossed in the instep leather of the sole, just beyond the heel. Encircling the logo was some sort of lettering which was impossible to make out, even with the aid of the glass.

"I looked up at Darcy and slowly shook my head. "Art Baldwin wasn't at the camp that weekend. He didn't watch us at the swimming hole."

"Oh, thank God," breathed Darcy, and I could see the awful strain physically lift from her countenance. But it didn't lift from *my* countenance. I was, of course, relieved that Art was not involved in the sickening business, but *someone* had sent that manila envelope. Someone had been there snapping away all afternoon, the click of the camera muffled by the burbling little stream. Someone had sent me a note that read: **You have new masters now**.

As long as I had remained convinced of Art's involvement in the photo session, I had sneered at the cryptic message. I'd teach the smug bastard about new masters. Now, at the thought of the message, a trembling, queasy chill ran up through my belly. Who the hell had sent that note? And what did it mean?

We heard Sylvia Harris returning from a shopping trip to Safeway. I went down quickly to help bring groceries in from the station wagon while Darcy packed away the photographs. Our provisions from Carl's Caterers were beginning to run low, and when Mrs. Harris asked if we were interested in staying for dinner, we declined only once or twice before enthusiastically accepting the invitation.

Darcy delivered me back to the rooming house quite late after our evening at the Harrises. I went to bed immediately and lay there in the sweltering darkness listening to Darcy's little electric fan and feeling the warm air on my naked body. As I tossed and rolled, unable to sleep, I thought, and I worried.

I had to find out who sent that note. Much more importantly, I had to find out who took those photographs and how to procure the negatives. God! They might have been made by any fucking slimeball pervert, and he might start mailing them out to people just to cause pain and grief. The note had said, **You have New Masters.** What the hell did that mean? I didn't have any *old* masters, let alone *new* ones.

Do Nothing. You Will be Contacted. So far, I hadn't even thought twice about the damned note, except as some sort of little joke of Art's. So, I had very much done **Nothing**; and, as far as I knew, I had not been **Contacted**. I suddenly got up and slipped on my robe. I hadn't checked the mailbox in about two days. Outside on the little brick stoop, I fitted the key into the slotted container. Nothing. I came inside and lay back down on the damp sheets.

The tiny bistro in a small lane just off the Wilhelmstrasse is packed with an early evening crowd. At a miniature table near the rear corner of the shadowy room sits The Young Man of Good Breeding, nursing a stein of dark lager. He nervously removes a silver case from his jacket and lights a cigarette from the softly glowing candle pot on the table. A strange voice is heard, just behind him. "Haben sie ein zigaret?" The Young Man turns suddenly, almost knocking over the candle pot.

Sidney Reilly steps carefully around the Young Man and seats himself, quickly removing his scarf and homberg hat. Reilly smiles, looking directly into the eyes of the Young Man. "Steady old boy, we don't want to cause a scene."

"What the hell. Who are you? This table is taken." The Young Man looks around angrily. "I'll call the waiter, if you don't leave."

"Oh, I shouldn't do that, old chap. Were you expecting someone else?" Reilly carefully removes his gloves and places both hands on the table. "Rosebud, perhaps?"

At the mention of the word, the Young Man goes pale in the flickering light.

"What did you say?" he gasps.

Reilly nods slightly toward the surrounding tables and smiles evenly at The Young Man. "Oh come. Let's not repeat it for the benefit of the good burghers, shall we?"

The Young Man reaches hastily for his hat and starts to rise. "I'm leaving," he hisses.

Sidney Reilly continues to smile, his gaze never leaving the face of The Young Man. "I am sorry to hear that. Your friends at Whitehall will be quite upset."

The Young Man sags in his chair. "Who are you? What the hell do you want from me?"

"A friend, old boy. A friend to whom you will now pay close attention." Reilly speaks with quiet authority, the smile never leaving his lips. "Are you with me?"

"You can go straight to hell," The Young Man hisses in a savage whisper. "I'll have no part of you or the people you work for."

"Afraid you really have no choice, old boy. You have new masters now."

I awoke bathed in sweat, a blinding headache pounding my temples. The thing had gotten out of hand. It had gone from being some sort of sick practical joke between Art and me to a mortal threat to Darcy involving blackmail and strangers unknown. I had to talk about this with someone. Had to get more thinking, get help on it. I had no idea what was going on.

I got up and took three aspirin, then showered until all the hot water was used up. As I came out of the bathroom, the door to Art Baldwin's door was just closing.

I dressed quickly, leaving the door to my room ajar. In a few minutes, Art stuck his head in the door on his way to the bathroom.

"Hi." I said, cheerily, feeling only anxiety. "Talk to you a minute?"

"Sure. Be right back." He stepped across the hall and closed the bathroom door.

I retrieved the snapshots that I'd taken up at the camp and, after a moment's hesitation, picked up the mattress and extracted the typed note from the manila envelope before replacing the package with the photographs.

"I'm afraid I owe you an apology and an explanation," I said to Art when he returned.

Art laughed, apparently genuinely puzzled. "About last weekend? Don't be silly. You guys want your time alone."

"Art. It's not about the weekend."

"Oh?" The suddenly guarded tone appeared abruptly, then was gone. "Confess all, my son. Tell Father Art everything. You'll be the soul beneficiary." He laughed.

I handed him the little snapshots of the shoeprints.

"I thought you decided to drop this business."

"I lied."

Art studied my face for a moment and then leafed through the pictures. "Can't tell much from these," he said. "Need to enhance them somewhat."

"Art. Whoever wore those shoes is trying to blackmail Darcy and me. Me, really."

I told him about the swimming hole and about the pictures in the manila envelope.

"Can I see them?"

"No. You'll just have to take my word about them."

He nodded.

I pulled out the sheet of paper and handed it to him. "This came with them."

He read it quickly. "A joke?"

"Ha. Ha. Funny joke."

"Yeah, right. Listen, Jack. Let me take these shoeprint things to work this evening. There are some people I'd like to have take a look at them."

I nodded, feeling as if a weight had been lifted. "I was hoping you'd say that. Thank you, Art. Thank you very much."

He nodded, thoughtfully. "In the meantime, let me know immediately if the guy makes contact."

"I will. I certainly will, but what *kind* of contact would he make?"

"Another note in the mailbox, probably demanding money. That's a crime, you know. J. Edgar's boys would be very interested in it."

"Those pictures, Art. Darcy doesn't know about them. I couldn't risk her being exposed to them, involved with the cops and all."

Art shook his head dismissively, "The FBI is very discreet in matters like this, Jack. Anyway, there is probably no reason for Darcy to be involved at all. If he demands a ransom, they'll set up their own surveillance and nab him. Darcy simply isn't a part of it. What you have to remember is that if that creep doesn't get what he wants from you, or maybe, even if he does, he might just send a set of prints to Charles Harris. Wouldn't that just do it? Wouldn't that be cute?" He smiled at me without a trace of humor.

I quickly excused myself, walked across the hall to the bathroom and vomited into the open toilet bowl.

CHAPTER FIFTEEN

The next morning I went numbly through the anxiety-ridden tedium that comprised my average day at the Arlington Yellow Cab Company having relatively few foul-ups and periods of getting lost. The dispatcher seemed to have other things or other drivers on his mind; or, perhaps, it was just that rarest of birds, a slow day.

In any case, I found myself and my trusty Checker parked on a series of cabstands during the morning rush and throughout parts of the long afternoon. I tried very hard to keep my mind off the blackmailer, but it was just impossible. *Rise and Fall* was let rise and fall a dozen times in my lap as my mind drifted back to those ugly pictures and the note that came with them.

I was unable to rid myself of the image of Charles Harris being handed a stack of mail by his secretary. The plain brown manila envelope on top would be marked "Personal".

He would seat himself at his desk as he began the process of peeling back the label. He would see with a shock more profound than any he had ever experienced his little Darcy, his sweet blonde kitten, the light of his life, his first born, his baby. And he would also see the cruel, loathsome creature who was wound about her like the Serpent in the Garden, corrupting and violating, melting her will, enticing her slowly to the abandonment of all decency and to the lust of ecstatic madness. This naked, slithering creature insinuating himself into every orifice, contaminating that innocent sweet body with spit and blood and sweat and semen and the very soul of evil desire. This crawling thing that he had taken into his home, to his bosom, and offered succor. This vile creature to whom he had extended the hand of friendship, accorded trust, respect, and, even, affection. Me. Jack Norton. XLI.

He would forgive Darcy, in time; but it would break his heart and he would lose his baby girl forever. He would not forgive the Creature.

Plain and simple. Even after the first sickening waves of anger and disgust had passed, even after he had told himself that these two young people were simply deeply in love and destined to marry, he would never really find a place in his heart for the Creature who had thrust the brutal evidence of his baby's womanhood right into his face.

I told and retold myself the part about him eventually understanding that Darcy and I were just two people in love, doing what people in love do. But, after a moment or two of feeling a little better about it, the image of the Serpent would reappear and that tingling, queasy feeling would return to my belly.

Of course, there were variations on this theme.

Sylvia Harris opening the package. Part I. Aaaand Action!

Oh God! Oh God! Each time I tried to conjure up the face of Darcy's mother gazing in horror at the spectacle, the screen went blank. Oh God!

The Reverend Dr. Playfair of the First Presbyterian Church of Chevy Chase who had baptized Darcy and Sam as infants and who counted the Harris family among his congregation. Oh dear, oh dear. We might have been married in his church. What now? Sin! Sin and Eternal Damnation! God might forgive us. The Presbyterians never would. What was the Calvinist version of excommunication? Stoning, perhaps.

Then there were the gentle, scholarly Quakers at Sidwell Friend's School, colleagues at Darcy's place of work. They would quietly consider the matter in their individual consciences.

I began to feel a little better with that thought and let out a half-sigh of relief.

They would silently pray and think upon it; and, eventually, they would silently consider those gentle slim fingers and the musical sound of her laughter as she suffered the little children to come unto her. And they would also silently consider where those hands and those lips had been on a certain sultry afternoon. Oh God! They would drive her from the schoolyard, banish her from their midst! She would receive no

153

further sustenance from them; although I was hard put to think of any that she was receiving now.

I tormented myself in this fashion until five o'clock, then drove back to Glebe Road and checked out for the day.

When I slogged up the steps to the rooming house, weary with the heat and the emotional exhaustion of self-flagellation, my Darcy was waiting with martini in hand. I came quickly inside lest we be seen together by unfriendly eyes. Arm in arm, we walked back to the room. The sizzle and aroma of grilled cheese sandwiches was radiating out of a frying pan on the hot plate, and the little fan was doing its best with the attendant greasy cloud.

Darcy loved grilled cheese sandwiches. Also, since paying the bill at Carl's, she had sobered to the somewhat austere economic realities of our present and, for a long time to come, future circumstances.

I sank into the old overstuffed armchair with the bottom sagging and the arms threadbare.

"Woman of the house," I cried abruptly. "Fetch me slippers."

"Aoww, that's my good Jack," Darcy purred as Eliza Doolittle. "Th' 'ole bleedin' day, poundin' 'is beat, 'e is, all to keep a shift on me back and bread on table."

She sat on the floor and laid her head against my knees.

"Jack love?"

I stroked her long, golden hair and whispered, "My wonderful Darcy."

"I found the pictures under the mattress."

The shock came as a silent, numbing deadness. "Oh Baby." I gripped her to me. "I'm so sorry. I'll get the negatives. So help me. If its the last thing I do, I'll get them. No one will ever see those pictures." We held each other tightly for a long moment. Finally, Darcy spoke, her cheek against my knee.

"I like them, Jack. It's just us, together. That's all." She spoke softly and her eyes did not meet my own.

I looked down at my Darcy and, in that moment, felt a weird mixture of tremendous anger and pride and knew that I loved her beyond all being. Tears welled and my throat clutched tight. I nodded, silently, thankfully.

The problem remained, of course, that no one else in the world would see those pictures in the light of love's innocent benevolence. Dark images of the Serpent, the Beast, began to re-emerge.

In the darkness, an angry, howling mob storms down the middle of Wisconsin Avenue on its way to Miss Withersby's rooming house. The stench of boiling tar and wet chicken feathers rises above the deep, ugly roar of angry voices. Firelight from smoldering torches dances off the tynes of upraised pitchforks. Behind the rooming house, hidden among filthy garbage cans in a narrow alleyway, the naked Beast sniffs the night air and cringes in terror as the surging mob draws nearer.

With some effort, I dismissed these abhorrent images from my mind. After all, it wasn't Jack Norton who would suffer most from those pictures. I should merely be hated for the rest of my life. It was Darcy who would be subject to the day-to-day heartbreak and shame. Our lives, as we had known them, were at an end.

We would elope. Sail to Europe on the Queen Mary. Paris was still cheap enough for an expatriot couple to live. I would complete my studies in european history at the Sorbonne while Darcy made a proper home for us in a simple loft on La Rive Gauche. Like Ernest Hemingway forty years earlier, I would sit on a park bench in Le Jardin de Tuilleries gently rocking the pram which cradled our sleeping firstborn while enticing unwary pigeons within my deadly grasp. My little family would never starve. I would see to that. And anyway, my mother would probably continue to send the weekly check. Mothers can always be counted on.

Darcy and I really didn't really flesh out this plan verbally as the better part of wisdom seemed to be to keep it to myself. Hold it in reserve, so to speak. Finally, I got up, showered and dressed and feasted on Darcy's wonderful grilled cheese sandwiches. After dinner, we drove up to Chevy Chase and saw *To Catch A Thief.*

It was after midnight when Darcy dropped me back at the rooming house. As I let myself in, the mailbox key caught my eye on the keyring, and I opened the little box. There was a single letter in a legal sized envelope with no return address. My name and address were typed in the usual place.

I kicked off my Weejuns and popped a bottle of beer from the ice chest before falling into the sagging chair and opening the letter. A single, folded sheet of paper read, **I still need a light. Don't be so rash as to disappoint me for a second time.**

I jumped across the little room and heaved the mattress back to retrieve the manila envelope. Side by side, the two notes appeared to be identical. Typed on the same machine. The question was, what the fuck did they mean? If this were a ransom note asking for money, we weren't at all on the same wavelength. "Leave the ten G's in the hollow tree, Louie" was the kind of thing I had been expecting.

I lay in the darkness thinking about the man who needed more light and had been disappointed once. Disappointed how? Maybe, he didn't get enough light the first time. When was the first time?

I thought of the light that I had thrown at the Vamp's attacker. He had almost gotten a light, right between the eyes. Could that be it? Hell no. It wasn't a random attack.

It was someone she knew. A scorned lover pissed off because she had been caught sleeping with Art. And *Procthtytka*? The Russian word for whore? Well, she probably *was* Russian. She certainly looked Russian: a member of the displaced Aristocracy, decadently flitting around Monte Carlo and the French Riviera? It was Russian they were speaking on the speedboat that day. I'd bet anything it was. I was dead tired. After quickly rinsing off under the little shower, I half toweled off and fell across the bed with the light still on.

I was still sleeping the next morning when two fast knocks sounded on the bedroom door followed by a single hard one. Art Baldwin. I got up, put on my robe and let him in.

He shook his head as he handed me the little package of snapshots. "Couldn't tell anything from these. Not enough detail."

"What about the logo and the lettering?" The disappointment was clear in my voice.

Art almost flinched. "Logo?"

"Yeah. Darcy and I looked at them with a hand lens and you could see that much at least, and some lettering like a brand name around it."

"Art nodded quickly. "Oh that." He shook his head dismissively. "Too fuzzy. You just couldn't make anything of it."

"Damn. That's so weird. You could almost see it with the hand lens. I would have sworn you'd be able to read the lettering with something like a jeweler's loupe."

"No." Art snapped. "You can't. The resolution's no good. The picture just breaks up."

"God. That's disappointing. I was so sure."

"Listen Jack, and this is very important. When he contacts you again, let me know immediately."

"Well, that's easy," I said. I went over to the bureau and got the second note.

Art ran his eyes over the lines and made no comment, staring at the white page.

"So," I said. "What the hell do you think it means?" **'I still need a light'**? "It doesn't make any sense at all."

Art's eyes were still on the paper. "I don't know," he mumbled quickly. "Probably just a crank"

"A crank!" I shouted. "Are you insane? This guy follows us all the way to West Virginia, rummages through our stuff, watches us all afternoon, takes pictures, and sends two weird notes. The son-of-a-bitch has violated us. He isn't just a harmless nut. He *wants* something from me, and I don't know what the hell it is."

"Take it easy, Jack." Art's voice was quavering. There was something close to panic in his eyes.

"Easy? How can I take it easy? I shouted. "If I don't give this slimy cocksucker a light, he's going to ruin my girl's life.

And suddenly I saw it. 'Gimmie a light.' 'Can I bum a light?' 'Do you have a light?' 'Can I get a light from you'? Lighter fluid. Not only in my drawer, but in Art's as well.

"The Ronsonol." I said, suddenly.

Art stared at me, the nervous hand and eye movements arrested for a moment. "What?"

"The can of Ronsonol. Somebody came into my room last week and took my brand new can of Ronsonol. When we got back from West Virginia, it had been replaced. Darcy thought you'd borrowed it and then brought it back. I didn't think any more about it, but you have your own can. It was this guy. He was right here in my goddamn room."

"In your room?" Art laughed weakly but the hollow quaver betrayed his extreme nervousness and preoccupation. He didn't really seem to be listening to what I was saying.

"He was after the damn lighter fluid."

"Don't be silly, Jack. This isn't some James Bond thing. This guy wants money, or maybe he wants more pictures."

I whirled on him in complete shock. "What?"

"Maybe he wants an encore performance, this time with whips and chains for your new masters."

"What?" I stammered, incredulously.

"Jack. I hate to leave you like this without resolving anything; but I can't talk now. Early appointment this morning that I can't put off." He backed out the door. "We'll get together tonight and work something out. Okay?" My bedroom door closed and he was gone.

More pictures? An encore performance? He watched us again but there wasn't enough light? He still needed light? Was that what he was saying? Where the hell could he have watched us without enough light. Here? No way. It would be exactly like taking pictures in a darkened freight elevator. In the guest room at the Harrises? A second story room and the drapes were pulled. The bathroom was even more private and inaccessible. I ran over the possibilities again and again, and I was absolutely convinced that no one had ever eavesdropped on us except at the swimming hole. Art was nuts.

Whips and chains? Bullshit! The note hadn't said, 'I needed more light the first time.' It had read, 'I still need *a* light.' The Ronsonol. Art didn't get it, but it was the Ronsonol.

I went over to the bureau and opened the top drawer. There beside the fresh carton of Winstons and the sorely depleted box of condoms was the blue and yellow can. I picked it up and shook it. Nearly full. I took the can and walked out into the hallway. The door to Art's room was closed and I knocked and waited. He wasn't there.

I went slowly back to my room and sat down on the bed. After a few moments, I shrugged out of the bathrobe and put on a pair of khaki shorts, an old tee shirt and my Topsiders. I walked quickly to the street door. It was still before seven and the din on Wisconsin had not built to the standard roar of rush hour traffic. No one was visible on the tree-lined street.

Coming back, I latched the door to my room and crossed immediately to the open window. It was about a five foot drop to the concrete alleyway. I was out and up through Art's in about ten seconds. As always, the room was neat as a pin, making my own look like a storage locker by comparison. As on board a small boat, there was a place for everything and everything in its place.

I went immediately to the bureau and pulled open the top drawer. The can of Ronsonol was right there in the same place where I had seen it a few days before. I picked it up and shook it. Almost full, just like mine. I fished into the pockets of my shorts and pulled out my own can. Setting them, side by side on the bureau top, hefting the two of them, squirting a little of the lighter fluid out into my fingers and smelling it, all left me with a single, indelible impression. They were identical and totally unremarkable. Shit! Back to square one. I placed the can back in its spot and closed the door. Five minutes later, I was standing in the shower, every morbid thought on the subject leading quickly to a dead end.

During the noon break, Darcy met me with a picnic hamper of chicken salad sandwiches made with her own beautiful sweet hands. I parked the cab and we drove in the Jaguar down to the park-like river embankment near the Pentagon and spread out a blanket on the green lawn. I told her about the second note and the disappointing snapshot news from Art and the Ronsonol business. I told her about Art's suggestion as to the true meaning of the second note.

"Whips and Chains?" She giggled in astonishment.

"I think its Art's secret fantasy. The note didn't imply anything like that."

I sprawled out on the blanket and put my head in Darcy's lap. "What do you do when I say, "I need a light."

"I wonder what you've done with your Zippo."

"That's right!" I confirmed. "But that isn't what he said. He wrote, 'I *still* need a light.' Now, what do you do?"

Darcy looked off across the river, thinking for a moment. "I flick your Zippo again."

"Why?"

"Because it didn't light the first time, I guess."

Zippos always light. "'Why Zip Zip Zip when one Zip does it?'"

"Not when they run out of fluid," said Darcy, quietly.

"Ah Hah! Exactly. Not when they run out of fluid. This guy wants lighter fluid. He broke into the room and took it. But something wasn't right about it. He followed us to West Virginia looking for it. He didn't find it there. He returned the can when he got back. There's something not right about the can, don't you see."

"Jack my love?"

I looked up into her gorgeous face, waiting.

"If this creep wanted lighter fluid, why didn't he just go to Higger's Drugs like we did and buy a can?"

I nodded my head slowly. "I know. I know. It comes right down to that, every time I go through the scenario. Why doesn't he just buy a can of Ronsonol at any drugstore?"

We remained silent for a moment, then Darcy said, "Art was sure that the shoeprint photos were no good?"

I sighed. "That's what he said. He seemed positive."

"Why don't we have a look for ourselves?"

"How? What do you mean?"

"There's a dissecting microscope in the biology lab at Friends' School. It's not like a regular microscope where you can see cell structure or bacteria magnified a hundred times. It just lets you see organ detail clearly when you're dissecting a frog or something."

"I know what a dissecting microscope is," I said, impatiently. "Are you allowed to use it?"

"I don't see why not. I've seen it sitting there on a shelf. The lab isn't being used during summer. We'd have to get a key from somebody to get in. That shouldn't be too difficult."

"When?"

"Why not in the morning?"

"What'll you tell them? Why do you need to use the dissecting microscope, for God's sake?"

"I want a closer look at the patterns on some rocks we picked up at our place in West Virginia."

"Do you have any?"

Darcy grinned. "Sam does. He's always picking things up and putting them in his mouth."

"I'll meet you at Friends' at nine o'clock."

"What about work?"

"I'll call in late."

We wrapped up the picnic stuff and Darcy took me back to my cab. "See you tonight, Love." she called. Darcy and the Jaguar split off over Key Bridge for the District while I descended back into the pit, to toil in the vineyard of the Arlington Yellow Cab Company.

The Harrises were dining out that evening and they asked us to join them. I stopped by the rooming house to shower and change into my ubiquitous Brooks Brothers travel suit. I was somewhat surprised to find no evidence of Art, who was usually preparing to leave for work at that hour.

We all met at the Harris home and traveled downtown in the big Chrysler station wagon. Sam was off on some overnight adventure with his pals. The remaining four of us made an evening of it with dinner at the National Press Club followed by live entertainment by a young comic named Jonathan Winters. He had appeared from time to time on the Ed Sullivan Show and was fast becoming extremely popular. I thought he was the funniest man I had ever seen.

CHAPTER SIXTEEN

The following morning at the rooming house dawned a bit sooner than I was prepared to receive it. The dinner and show at the Press Club the previous evening had put us quite late getting back to the Harrises'. By the time Darcy and I did our thing and parted company, the wee hours were already making good progress.

I called the dispatcher to offer excuse #381-b (car won't start) and then showered and shaved as fast as possible. As I was leaving, I noticed again that there was no sign of Art. At this hour, I should have bumped into him on the steps. Oh well. Perhaps he had suddenly flown off on a secret mission, helping put down the Communist rebels in some unimportant little Central American dictatorship.

When I turned in at Sidwell Friends', there were lots of little kids running to and fro on the playground and the dark green Jaguar was neatly ensconced in a parking slot. I found Darcy in one of the empty classrooms talking to a very nice lady who was introduced to me as Mary Anderson, and who was, apparently, more or less in charge of the summer's goings on.

"Well Darcy, you probably know more about this instrument than I," she said, smiling, motioning toward the large, gray dissecting microscope sitting on a bench behind us. "I know that you have to plug it in to get the light to come on, but I'm afraid that I'm completely at sea after that."

We thanked her and murmured grateful and polite things, and Darcy set her little plastic bag of Sam's rocks on the bench by the microscope.

"Do you know how to operate it?" Darcy asked, after we had privately kissed good morning.

"Yeah, I think so. I've never used a dissecting scope before, but the principle has to be the same as for any other. Place the specimen on the moveable stage, aim the light source which is on top rather than underneath the specimen and focus with the low power objective. Two X in this case. Move the stage to the area you want to study and switch over to the Hi power objective, 10 x, it looks like. You can't illuminate large, gross objects from the underside in order to focus light upwards into the objective and the eyepiece. This is really only a crude cousin to a real microscope, sort of a great big pair of close up binoculars."

Darcy opened the packet of photos. "Isn't that just what we need?"

"Yes. I think maybe it is."

I took one of the shoeprint photos from the packet and placed it on the microscope stage. When I set the Lo Power objective and focused down on the print, the oval logo jumped into the upper right hand corner of the field. I centered it and set the Hi Power objective. At first, it was like looking at the surface of the moon, until I centered the logo again and focused sharply. And there it was. The oval logo contained some sort of picture which looked very much like a flowering plant, a rosebush maybe. Around the outer rim of the oval were six or seven strange symbols which looked like a mix of letters of the Greek and Roman alphabets.

I showed them to Darcy. "Can you draw them, the way they look?"

Using the white back of the photograph packet, Darcy carefully drew the logo and the surrounding symbols.

"Weird," she said. "Are they Greek?"

"I don't know. There's one that sort of looks like the Greek letter pi, but it could be an 'm' just as well."

"Ohhh! Jack. They're backwards. The shoeprint makes them backwards like a rubber ink stamp."

"Ah," I sighed. "Of course, we need a mirror."

Darcy grabbed her shoulder bag off the lab bench and began digging through it A playing card sized mirror popped out of the leather lining of the purse, and she held it up triumphantly.

"Great!"

We locked the classroom, located Mary Anderson and thanked her with Darcy enthusiastically describing the geologic strata laid down in her rock samples. Ten minutes later, I was pulling volumes of the Encyclopedia Britannica off bookcase shelves in the living room of the Harrises' house.

In less than an hour we had the answer. About half the symbols were too degraded to match up to any sort of lettering system, just little melted squiggles in the dust; but a few of them, one or two, were indisputably from the Cyrillic alphabet. There was definitely a word on the sole of the shoe; and the word, whatever it said, was a Russian word. The blackmailer wore Russian shoes.

"Art knows about this," I said. "He lied to me."

"You thought he was lying before. We thought he'd made the prints himself."

"Darcy love, if we could see this much, I can guarantee you that Art not only knows that they're Russian shoes, he knows the brand and the name of the store where they were purchased, probably GUM. He was lying through his perfect teeth."

"The man in the street the other night. He spoke Russian."

"He knew the word for 'whore'."

"You think he made these tracks?"

"I think a Russian made these tracks, and a Russian sent those notes. The man in the street was probably a Russian."

"But, Love, the man in the street was probably a jilted boyfriend, just as we thought."

"Then why the hell is he after me and not Art?"

Darcy slowly shook her head.

"We just need to think this whole thing through, slowly, step by step. There's something missing from the puzzle."

"Maybe Art can supply the missing pieces," said Darcy.

"I'm sure he could, but I don't think he's going to do it willingly. He was more upset when he gave me back these pictures than I was. He knows he's deeply involved in this and it has him scared. I have a feeling that he hasn't even been back to his room since yesterday morning."

"Poor Art," said Darcy.

"Poor Art, my foot. Somehow, this whole thing is because of Art. I can just feel it."

"Jack. We know that Art didn't make these prints. We know that he didn't follow us to West Virginia and make those pictures. We know he didn't send those notes. We know he didn't even borrow your can of lighter fluid. He has a can of his own."

"I know. I went back in his room yesterday morning and compared the two. They're identical, might even have come out of the same shipment lot." I was out of ideas and we sat in the rising heat of the summer day, doing and saying nothing.

Darcy lay back on the big sofa. "It's so hot." Then she jumped up, beaming. "Let's drive out to Difficult Run and go skinny dipping."

"You remember what happened the last time we went skinny dipping?"

She threw her arms around me and we enjoyed a long, intoxicating kiss. "I remember," she smiled.

We took the Jaguar and stopped by the rooming house so I could change out of my cab driver suit. I quickly slipped into tee shirt and khaki shorts and opened the top bureau drawer to retrieve a couple of the little foil packages, just in case. The can of Ronsonol lay quietly in its place. I picked it up and tossed it to Darcy.

"So why would that asshole 'still need a light' from me?"

"Oh, Love, I don't know. I'm just weary thinking about it." She turned the can of lighter fluid over in her beautiful slim hand. "Are you absolutely sure it wasn't here that Friday afternoon?"

I swung around, looking terribly aggrieved. "Darcy."

"Well, you could have missed it. You *were* in an awful hurry."

"Sweetheart. I did everything but turn the goddam drawer upside down. It was *not* here. It was *gone*."

"You don't have to swear at me."

I bent down to the chair and pressed my cheek to hers. "I'm sorry. It's all just so damned frustrating."

"I know." She tapped down the side of the can with the manicured nail of her long, index finger: tunk, tunk, tunk, Tink She looked quickly down at the little can and repeated the last tap. Tink. Tink, Tink, Tink.

"Jack? Listen." She repeated the little scale running from the top, down the metal surface to the very bottom. The dull tunk tunk sounds were replaced on the last two taps by the sounds of Tink, Tink.

"There's no fluid in the bottom of this can."

"Let me see." I tapped the can from top to bottom. A hollow, metallic sound emanated from the bottom inch of the container.

I dug my fingernails between the walls of the container, squeezed and pulled at the metal bottom. It came away easily in my hand like the little top on a can of paprika. I turned the bottom up and looked straight into a small empty compartment."

"But, that's impossible," I stammered. "You picked this can right off the shelf at Higger's. There were half a dozen others lined up in the same row."

I sat down on the bed across from Darcy holding both pieces of the little can. Darcy looked at me, helplessly. We sat in silence.

Suddenly, I had it. "This isn't my can," I shouted.

"Oh Jack, Love." Tears were brimming in her eyes.

"No. Wait. Listen. That's the can from Art's room. I mixed them up by mistake when I took mine over there yesterday morning to compare them. I know I did. I set them both, side by side, on the bureau to compare them and then just put one of them back without thinking. They were identical, so it didn't matter."

I went on fast, the thoughts coming out in a rush. "The blackmailer went to my room by mistake that Friday afternoon. He found my can, the normal one, in the top drawer of my bureau with the cigarettes, just like Art keeps his. He thought he had the right place. He totally goofed up, just like I did yesterday morning. He thought it was *this* can; and, of course, it wasn't.

"When he discovered it was the wrong can, he figured Art was holding out on him; and he followed us to West Virginia and tossed our stuff still hoping to find it. Then he went down to the creek and took those pictures to give him a threat to hold over Art's head."

"But, Jack. He took pictures of *us*, not Art." The anguish in her voice flooded across the little room.

I looked at Darcy, nodding, "He's confused John R. Norton with Arthur Thayer Baldwin IV. He's got Art and me mixed up."

"What's supposed to be in that little compartment? What does he want from Art, from you?"

"Art's been putting stuff in that can of lighter fluid. Leaving it there for people to get."

"What stuff." Darcy wailed. "What kind of stuff is he leaving for people?"

"Spy stuff. Government secrets. Art's a spy."

Darcy looked bewildered. "What on earth are you going to do?"

"I have no idea. This has something to do with the government, with the C.I.A. This is Art's thing, not ours. I'm going to have to talk to him, get it straightened out before somebody gets seriously hurt." The image of the thugs in the Cadillac came readily to mind.

There was nothing much more to say, and we sort of looked helplessly at each other and began to gather up picnic and swim gear.

We threw towels, blanket and goodies into the boot of the Jaguar, folded the top and swung out onto O Street. As we slowed for a stop at the first intersection, I automatically glanced in the rearview. A long, black Cadillac car left its parking place a half block down from the rooming house and pulled rapidly out onto the street. The intersection was clear. I gunned the E-Type and we shot down toward M Street leaving twin trails of black rubber painted on the cobblestones.

Darcy looked over at me and laughed. "Ride 'em, Cowboy."

We slid down fast onto M Street, downshifting into second and powering hard past the turn for Key Bridge and Rosslyn. Flashing up onto Chain Bridge Road, I put the spurs to the Jaguar and wound the tach past 5000 in each gear until the big Smith's speedometer was quivering at a steady 80 miles per hour.

"Jack," Darcy squealed. "We're going to get arrested."

"Not unless they set up a roadblock," I yelled over the roaring slipstream.

For the next twenty minutes, I did my best Sterling Moss imitation, coaxing the big cat into the realm of its supreme competency.

It had been born of the awesome C-Type grand prix racer, three times winner of *Le 24 heures de Le Mans* and a world champion. Now, it settled into its own on the little two-lane strip of country road and its race-bred engine wailed its banshee's shriek through the sparsely settled forest land. Like an Olympic downhill skier, we power-drifted through the turns with the marvelous engine spooling up in long, high-pitched howls on the narrow straight-aways. The big white speedometer repeatedly rolled up over 130 mph before violent braking dragged it down to catapult through the oncoming curves. We were buckled in with aircraft-type lap belts cinched tight. I paid grim attention to the work at hand and Darcy screamed and laughed like a kid on a rollercoaster.

We came over the little stone bridge and flashed by the turn-off to Difficult Run at ninety miles an hour and I let her run on for another mile before hitting the big Girling Disc brakes and bringing her down into a squealing U-turn. We drove slowly back to the turn-off, the

Jaguar purring as smoothly as a Rolls. I did not expect to see the black Cadillac, and we did not.

We pulled off the road at the turn, ran up into the trees and switched off the ignition. For ten minutes we sat in the afternoon heat, the cicadas buzzing and the Jaguar making hot, plinking noises. The roadway out beyond our little cave-like parking hole was silent.

We raised the top and locked the car and started down the quarter mile path to the little waterfall and pool where generations of kids from the Northern Virginia countryside had come to swim and frolic.

I told Darcy about seeing the black Cadillac behind us, and she pooh-poohed the notion and teased me about just wanting an excuse to play boy racer with the Jag.

"How many black Cadillac sedans do you think there are in Washington?" She asked.

"Probably about ten thousand. Every bureaucrat above a GS-12 seems to have one complete with government driver."

"Case closed," said Darcy.

We came down along the little stream to the three-foot high waterfall that surged over a pile of granite boulders. The place was completely deserted, as I thought it might be on a week day afternoon. We spread the blanket and towels and I quickly peeled off my Topsiders and dropped my clothes in a little heap.

I turned to wait for Darcy. In a race to beat me into the water, she had shed her outer clothes and bra and was wriggling out of her blue silk bikini panties. She glanced up at me, laughing and pulling the wispy fabric down her smooth, tanned legs. I stood on the boulder above the pool, stretching and reveling in our open nakedness.

"Jack?" Darcy said suddenly, holding the crumpled panties in both hands. "I just realized why that man thinks you're Art Baldwin."

I chuckled. "What do you mean? The dumb bastard just got our rooms mixed up."

Darcy shook her head. "No, it's more than that. You look alike, you and Art."

"What?"

"You look alike. You're both very tall, 6'3"and you're both perfect mesomorphs."

I squinted and shook my head.

"You're mesomorphs, you have wide shoulders, long legs and torsos . . ."

"Darcy, I *know* what a mesomorph is. Art and I don't look any more alike than any other two guys."

"No. Jack, that day we were all naked on the boat. I watched you two standing together. With the sun at your backs, I couldn't tell one from the other. Linda couldn't either. We talked about it. Your hair is the same, your coloring is the same. You're almost exactly the same size. You could be brothers. On a city street, fifty yards away, even I would have a hard time telling who was who."

"I don't think so, Love. Art is a rich, New England Yankee upper class twit, and I'm certainly not."

Darcy grinned. "Well, you're not rich, and you're certainly not a damn Yankee."

"Why, thank you, Scarlet."

"Jack, that guy didn't just get in your room by mistake. He's taken pictures of you from every conceivable angle. He's seen you coming and going lots of times. He saw you throw a flashlight at him the other night. He thinks you *are* Art Baldwin."

"What are you saying, Love?"

"I'm saying that Art doesn't know this guy. They've never met face to face. Art's been leaving stuff in the Ronsonol can for somebody else to pick up. Now this guy wants to get it, instead of whoever was getting it before."

"Who? Who the hell was getting it before this creep?"

"Who shows up at Art's place from time to time when he's not there?"

We looked at each other and spoke simultaneously, "The Vamp!"

"Jack, he *was* the man in the street the other night. That wasn't just a domestic argument. He wanted whatever she had picked up in that little can in Art's drawer."

I nodded slowly. Darcy was making perfect sense.

She went on. "Now you've got the little can in your room and he's demanding that you put some stuff in it and leave it for him to pick up, or else."

"What's the 'or else'?"

"Or else he'll mail sets of photographs to my family and everyone he can think of."

I shook my head. "I don't think we have to worry about that any more. It just isn't a credible threat once we know what's going on and what he wants. If he sends out the pictures, he instantly loses all chance that I'll provide him with more stuff in the can. He knows that he'd never get anything again. It might just possibly work, as a threat, with somebody like Art. I mean he's legitimately involved and has a very sensitive reputation to protect on a lot of different levels; but its an empty threat. Once it's used, it's the end of the game for our Russian friend. He eliminates his hoped-for source, for no benefit to anyone. I say, screw him. We simply go on about our lives. As a matter of fact," I broke into a huge smile, "I just had the most wonderful idea."

Darcy looked at me, expectantly. "What?"

"I'm going to leave 'Boris' a little message," I giggled, wickedly.

Chapter Seventeen

We drank beer and swam, frolicked, sunned and behaved ourselves for the next two hours. The experience at the swimming hole in West Virginia was constantly on our minds, and Difficult Run too public a place, at the best of times, to warrant any hanky-panky.

At one point, we saw a flash of white in the distance, back along the footpath, and Darcy was into her shorts and pullover before I could even blink.

"Jack! Somebody's coming."

I flipped over onto my stomach and scanned the trail. "It's only a couple. A guy and a girl." I said.

She whacked me across the rear end with the flat of her hand. "Put your pants on, now." There was fire in her voice, and I hastily retrieved my khakis and struggled into them while lying flat on the blanket.

The couple was about eighteen or nineteen, and they said, "Hi," as they went by our boulder and found their own about twenty yards upstream. They spread their blanket and dropped their towels and then just sat there talking.

"They didn't bring any suits, and now they can't go in the water with *us* here," I laughed.

"Neither can we," said Darcy with more than a trace of annoyance.

So the four of us sat there for a while and the two kids got up and waded in the shallows. Each party kept casting glances at the other, hoping they were going to pack it in and leave, so the remaining couple could get naked. Finally, we caved.

"Let's go," said Darcy. "We've had our swim. Let's give them some privacy."

The return trip to Georgetown was entirely uneventful and took about twice as long as the trip out had taken. We were hot and sticky again when we got to my room. We squeezed into the little bathroom and indulged in a long, highly erotic shower made all the more titillating when I had to break off and run naked across the hall to fetch one of those little foil packages from the pocket of my discarded shorts.

Later in the room, I took the can of Ronsonol with the false bottom from the bureau drawer and wrote a note in ink on a small square of one of the printed notes that had been left for me.

Fuck you, Ivan, You Barbarian Stalinist Peasant. Get Your Own Light.

"Jack, are you sure about this?" Darcy watched with concern as I printed out the little note.

"Absolutely. This slimeball needs a good kick in the teeth."

"But what about the can? Art is sure to notice that it's been switched sooner or later."

"Let him. Maybe it'll scare the shit out of him enough so that he'll stop sending secret messages to people." I turned around and looked up at Darcy. "This isn't a training exercise he's involved in. He's been passing secrets to somebody who shouldn't have them. We could call the FBI and get him fired and maybe jailed; or, he'll find that the can has been changed on him, probably guess it was me, and back completely away from what he's been doing."

"I hope so," nodded Darcy. "That way he's not publicly embarrassed and he can just stop it."

"Right. He'll figure out, sooner or later, that we know what he's been up to; but, so what?"

On the bottom of the little note, I drew a crude clenched fist with the middle finger extended and folded it into the false bottom of the can. I carried the container over to my bureau and deposited it in the top drawer, next to the condoms and cigarettes.

"What if he comes calling at night while you're sleeping?"

"I don't think so. He's come at least twice before that we know of, and that was in the daytime when nobody was here to interfere with him."

Our venture into domesticity in terms of dining at home had waned somewhat after I had seen the bill from Carl's, and we dined at a Hot Shoppe that evening and spent some time browsing through the record shop on Du Pont Circle before calling it a night and driving Darcy back to her parent's house. By a little past midnight, I was back in my room and snug in the arms of Morphious.

I dreamed of my Darcy lying on the blanket by the swimming hole. I swam round and round in the delicious cool water and teased her to join me; but she just laughed that wonderful laugh and lay there on her side, her beautiful naked blonde body stretched out full length, her delicate slim fingers caressing a little pile of colored stones that were lying on the blanket.

I swam over to the little waterfall and heaved myself up on the rock shelf. The delightfully cool water cascaded over my neck and shoulders and down both sides of my body, tickling my spine and sending pounding, throbbing pulses into my groin.

"Darcy Love," I called, and the waterfall lost its chill. I was reclining in a great white tub, torrents of warm water spilling forth from the wide spout between my propped-up feet.

I raised my arms along both sides and lay back to look for my Darcy; and as the tub slowly filled, I watched the warm clear liquid crawl up the cool marble surface until it reached the spot where I was sitting. As it closed over my upper thighs and buttocks, the sensual warmth spread through me and I swelled and throbbed and burned.

I burned! I rolled on the sweat-soaked sheet and reached down my back, gingerly probing between my sprawling legs. Sunburn? A tiny wet stream sprayed over my forearm. Convulsively I jerked upright and peered into the darkness.

I shouted, "Who's there?" peering frantically into the blackened room.

"Do not cry out," whispered an alien female voice.

I grabbed for the top sheet which had fallen off on the floor and dragged it over the side of the bed onto my lap.

The dark form at the foot of the bed sniggered, "You think I am interested in your body?"

My heart was almost pounding out of my chest. "What the hell?" I finally managed. "What did you pour on me?" I squirmed on the bed sending daggers of burning fire up between my legs and the cheeks of my buttocks. The overpowering smell of lighter fluid was everywhere.

"Your little note was very childish," she said. "You have been playing with fire, John Norton. You know what happens to little boys who play with fire, don't you?"

"What do you want?" I screamed.

"They get burned. Or, if not, they surely get their bottoms warmed, so they will never play with fire again."

To my horror, I heard the characteristic metallic clank of my Zippo lighter and a flame sprang out of the darkness.

I hugged the crumpled sheet around me. "Hey! No! Don't! Please! Don't! Put that lighter out. I'll do anything you want. Just put it out."

She stood quietly by the foot of the bed, the smoky flame of the Zippo casting dancing shadows on her face. "You have mixed into something that does not concern you. Leave it alone, John Norton. Leave it completely alone." She tossed the empty can of Ronsonol at my feet.

"No, don't," I yelled and scrambled hard for the head of the bed. The Zippo snapped off and clattered to the floor, leaving the room in darkness.

Instantly, the door opened and shut and she was gone, the sound of clip-clip-clip echoing in the corridor.

I hit the switch on the bedlamp, threw aside the sheet and examined myself. Red chafe spots were darkly visible on both my inner thighs, and my buttocks felt the same. I crossed quickly to the bathroom and turned on the shower.

After ten minutes of cold water and soap, and another ten of crouching with my legs apart in the tub applying some of Darcy's stash of soothing unguents, I patted myself dry and dusted off the stricken area with Johnson's Baby Powder.

I limped back across the hall to the fume-filled room, the affected body parts quietly glowing and feeling as if they had been subjected to two hours with a sunlamp at close range.

I turned on the bedroom light and hobbled over to the bureau. The fake Ronsonol can was gone. I glanced at the reeking bed where my own can lay empty and discarded.

My rear-end was too uncomfortable to contemplate sitting all day long in a hot cab. I called the dispatcher and offered up excuse # 622-k (I'm sick) employing a tone and demeanor that had worked like a charm with my mother when I was 12 years old and a math quiz was ominously looming up at me.

I rolled the bedclothes into a ball and threw them into the VW for a trip to the Laundromat. The mattress still stank of lighter fluid, and I planned for an aerosol spray air freshener of some sort.

I didn't bother doing anything about the lock on my door. Changing it wouldn't make any difference except maybe to piss the intruder off so he (or she) would do something unspeakably heinous to me after gaining entry anyway. My bottom hurt and I was badly frightened and depressed and I needed my Darcy love.

Darcy was tied up at Friends' School all morning so I bought some sprays to absorb the odor of lighter fluid and then sat and waited for the washing to finish in a Laundromat on the other side of Key Bridge.

While I was waiting, I got a copy of the *Washington Post* out of a nearby machine and tried to keep abreast of the President's foreign policy. He didn't seem to be doing very well. Additional evidence for this seemed to lie in another article that appeared in the lower right hand corner of page 6. *Clandestine Buildup of Russian Advisors in Cuba in Wake of Bay of Pigs Disaster*. I poured over these and other matters of historical moment until the dryer turned off, then carried the still fragrant sheets and stuff back out to the VW.

The lighter fluid smell vanished from the room and mostly from the mattress as soon as the aerosol began to hiss and was replaced with a nauseating, cheap candy aroma which was much worse than the Ronsonol.

A second trip to People's Drugs brought back something that smelled like lemons; in fact, intermingled with the first air freshener, the room smelled like a whole lemon grove had somehow been squeezed into the restroom at a Greyhound bus station.

I couldn't stand to stay in the room any longer. I had to get away and think about this very serious, now terrible situation. I needed to lie on my stomach on a cool green lawn with my head in my Darcy's lap and feel her hands on my face and hair and hear her voice.

But what was I to do except carry out the instructions of The Vamp? The memory of her standing with the lighted Zippo beside my naked, Ronsonol-soaked body was too traumatizing to bear contemplation. Just *leave it alone*. Period. That woman was as cold and vicious as an angry rattler. If there *were* a next time, she'd kill me. I didn't doubt it for a moment.

And what about the Russian guy in the Cadillac? So far, he had been civilized enough to just send ominous notes, even after I almost brained him with a flashlight. Maybe next time, when there was no little false-bottom can waiting for him in my drawer, he wouldn't be so polite.

At noon I met Darcy at Friends' School. We dropped the VW at her house and rode the Jaguar up into Rock Creek Park to the small green field where people walked their dogs and had obedience training classes. Maybe that's what I needed. I could see myself in collar and leash with The Vamp in black leather and three inch heels cracking a little whip and shouting, "Heel, Capitalist Running Dog!"

We walked out into the little meadow and stopped under a grove of big shade trees. I lay down slowly on the green lawn and put my head in Darcy's lap and told her of the horrors of the previous night.

She went through the gamut of emotions from rage and weeping impotent sympathy to abject fear and back to rage. Finally, she just encircled my head with her arms and said nothing.

"I just can't live like this," I said. "I'm not sure I can even go back to my room and get a night's sleep."

"You've got to call the police."

"And tell them what? They'd just laugh at me."

"The FBI?"

"Same thing. They'd think I was a nut."

"No," said Darcy. "Not if you told them that your neighbor down the hall worked for the CIA, and you had evidence that he's been passing government secrets to a foreign power."

"What evidence?"

"The fake lighter fluid can."

I laughed, in spite of myself. "Darcy love, that's not evidence. It's just something you can buy in a novelty shop. You squeeze the can and a bunch of coiled-up snakes jumps out at you. They'd haul me in to St. Elizabeth's for psychiatric observation if they took me seriously at all. They might question Art. He'd deny everything. The can would turn up missing. And that woman would know it was I who stirred up the whole thing. I'd probably die in a mysterious rooming house fire."

Darcy sat on the cool green grass, silently stroking my hair and rubbing my shoulders. Suddenly, her hands stopped moving and she spoke. "What if we had real evidence?"

"Like what?"

"Like whatever Art puts into the bottom of that can."

"I don't have *his* can anymore, Love; and the contents of the other one were poured all over *my* can."

She groaned in sympathy. "Your poor bottom. Does it still burn?"

"Not much," I groaned and twisted my head in her soft lap.

She patted me thoughtfully. "I bet I know where the fake can is."

I turned again and looked up at her. "You think it's back in Art's drawer?"

"It has to be. That's where they make the exchange. I know that blonde woman put it right back in Art's drawer."

"She probably told Art about me finding out about it, and they've set up a whole new system, by now."

"I just don't think she did," said Darcy. "You said Art is very, very skittish about the whole thing. I don't think she wants to run the risk of upsetting him, having him back out and close off the information source completely. I don't think she wants the apple cart upset. Otherwise, why did she confront you at all? Why not just arrange with Art to have another spot for the 'drop' and forget all about the Ronsonol can?"

I looked up at her and nodded. "Right. Come to think of it, why did she just give me a warning last night instead of starting a fire and killing me in it? That would have simplified matters and tied up all the loose ends."

"Do you think they'd actually *kill* anybody?"

I nodded. "If it's important enough. It's happened before, lots of times."

We stayed in the meadow for several hours. Darcy chattered non-stop, as she always did, and I listened and made comments and snoozed in her lovely lap. By the time we got up to go, we had formulated something like a plan.

The first priority was the security of my room. I could never again close my eyes in that room at night without paralyzing fear of being awakened by monsters. Not the childhood monsters who lived under the bed and in the closet; but real monsters who opened my door and walked in when I was sleeping and poured things on me, or worse. Maybe next time it wouldn't be something as innocuous as lighter fluid. Concentrated sulfuric acid. In my face. An icepick. In my eyeballs. Balls? A straight razor! Shut the fuck up, Jack. Good Lord!

At some point during my discussion with Darcy, I remembered the iron bar that people in New York apartments fit into little sockets at the doorknob and in the floor. A three-foot long angle brace is erected that cannot be moved from the outside. Once inside the apartment with the bar set in place, nothing can force entry of that door short of a battering ram.

I would construct my own 'bar' and sockets with 2x4s and sixteen penny nails. Without such a device, I would no longer consider spending another night in that room.

There would be no plan, of course, if Darcy were not correct in her assumption that the business between Art and the blonde woman would continue as usual.

If the fake can of Ronsonol had not been replaced in Art's drawer, then I would be able to do nothing but give Miss Withersby my notice. I'd have to pack my bags and seek other lodgings, leaving the mystery to work itself out and hope that a very angry Russian with a package of compromising photographs would only shake his fist and say, "Drat!" instead of hunting me down and murdering me.

I considered the possibility of just leaving a letter in my mailbox addressed to IGOR. Upon opening it as he fled down the silent street in the dead of night, he would read the following: Dear Stalinist Thug: You make big mistake. Me not CIA. Me Yellow CAB. Me no have SECRET in little can. HONEST. Sincerely, John R. Norton, American Citizen.

Of course, the frightening truth was that there just wasn't much of anything I could do about the Russian. He'd hardly be willing to take my word that I was the wrong man. If he searched my room again and found nothing, what could he really do? He'd already tried to blackmail me with Darcy. He must realize that wouldn't work. And then a new thought occurred to me. Darcy. He could try a more direct approach on Darcy to get control of me. Physical threats? Kidnapping, even? I had no idea what to do about it, and I couldn't get the sick feeling of worry out of my mind.

I appropriated some scrap lumber and nails and some of the tools in Charles Harris's woodworking shop in the garage to construct my angle bar lock. After making several cuts in the wood, I borrowed a sack full of sixteen penny nails and a hammer and we went back to the rooming house.

It was an hour past the time Art normally left for work, if he had been home at all. Darcy stood guard in the hall, and I shimmied through the alleyway windows. Inside Art's room, I carefully opened the bureau drawer. The can of Ronsonol was sitting right were it belonged. I picked it up and pried off the false bottom. Empty.

Back in my own room, I marked the spot where the 2x4 piece of pine made a forty-five degree angle between the closed door and the floor, and nailed a foot-long cleat right down through the old carpet, the flooring and deep into the underlying floor joists. Miss Withersby would have a fit if she saw this, but she wasn't going to see it. With the bar slipped into place between doorknob and floor cleat, the door was secure.

But not the window. The window, like the one in Art's room, opened out onto the little alleyway between buildings. The alley was walled off at both ends with a six—foot-high board fence. It wouldn't take much for a determined Russian, or a blonde Vamp for that matter, to climb the fence and be at the window before you could say Leon Trotsky. I could clearly see the shadow of the pickax creeping across the bedroom wall as the cloaked figure came in stealthily through the open window. If I tried to sleep in the little airless room with the window closed, I'd be just as dead by morning as if a Soviet death squad had paid a visit during the night. The thing had to stay open. Accordingly, I cut the remaining old sash cord and rigged a fiendishly clever deadfall using a single thin stick tied to a piece of fine wire gleaned from a spool of the stuff in Charles Harris's workshop.

Never one to leave well enough alone, I took the empties from the last two six packs of Heinekens and smashed them up using Charles' hammer. I spread these jagged pieces on the sill, and, at last, felt fairly secure that I could sleep without fear of being awakened by the barrel of a gun twisting slowly in my left nostril or a dagger at my balls.

The room felt contaminated. Not only from the pervasive, cloying odor, but from the new fortifications and the knowledge that others had invaded it with impunity, rendering it a hostile, alien place. Over the past weeks, it had been our little home. In some strange way, both of us had grown to love it because it had served as the primary setting for our life together. Now, neither of us could bear to sit down in the little space. Our place of sanctuary had vanished.

CHAPTER EIGHTEEN

"You're going to crawl through broken glass and sneak in Art's window every evening after he leaves for work until you find something in the can. Is that it?" said Darcy, suddenly giving me her concerned look.

"Of course, what else is there to do?"

Darcy shook her head and sighed. "I don't know, Love. It's just that when we were talking about it this afternoon, it seemed so simple. Now that we're actually here, it doesn't. It sounds extremely dangerous to me."

"You think I'm gonna cut myself on the beer bottles?" I laughed.

Darcy shook her head and her face was twisted. "I just realized how very dangerous all this is." She put her head against my shoulder. "Jack, I can't think about anything happening to you."

I put my arms around her and we stood in the little bedroom and appraised my craftsmanship and rocked each other. "Nothing is going to happen to me," I said. "I'll make absolutely sure he's gone before I go in. It only takes ten seconds to be in and out. Nothing is going to happen." I shrugged, "Anyway, worst case is that Art catches me in his room stealing a pack of cigarettes. Big deal."

She leaned hard against my shirt front, the honey blonde of her hair contrasting sharply with the Madras collage of bleeding pinks and greens. "Art's been taught to kill with his hands." Darcy said quietly. "He's like Richard Burton in *The Spy Who Came In From The Cold*. He's trained to use wooden match boxes as deadly weapons."

I burst out laughing. "He doesn't have any matches, wooden or otherwise. He'll have to stab me in the eye with the little spout on the lighter fluid can."

Darcy didn't laugh. She looked up at me for reassurance. "How long before he puts something in the can?"

"I haven't the foggiest. Tonight, tomorrow, maybe a week. Who knows? I haven't even seen him in nearly three days, and the Vamp's only paid two visits in the last week."

"You think he leaves something for her every time she shows up?"

I shook my head rapidly, "Huh-uh, I think she comes on a regular schedule and checks the can. He leaves something whenever he has it."

"How do you know that?" asked Darcy.

"I don't *know* it, Love. It's just that she wasn't concerned about having lost anything from the can last night. She didn't say, 'all right, you took something that belongs to me and replaced it with a silly note. Hand it over.' She just wanted me to stay the hell out of their drop box. Period. 'Leave it alone' is what she said."

"God. What a creature," said Darcy.

"So, each evening, I check the drop. When he finally puts the stuff in it, I take it out and run, not walk, to the nearest FBI office. Meanwhile, nobody will be able to creep up on me at night."

"What if they throw a bomb through the open window?"

I burst out laughing. "Darcy, *please!*"

"Well, you don't know."

"This isn't a bomb-throwing type situation, Sweetheart. You only throw bombs if you want to assassinate Arch Dukes and spread terror. You have to be an anarchist to do it. These people are True Believers, Stalinist thugs. They don't want anyone to ever suspect they were even here."

"Russian peasants used to always throw bombs."

"I know, but only at the Czar."

We theorized about totalitarian regimes and the similarity of their methods, whether politically left or right, until the depressing little room got to be too much to take. The Jaguar waited at the curb, and it was off to Darcy's house, stopping briefly at Higger's Drugs to buy a bottle of "sunburn" lotion and some cigarettes. I picked up another can of Ronsonol to replace the one that had been dumped all over me.

The senior Harrises were out on the perpetual Washington cocktail circuit and we fixed ourselves sandwiches from leftovers. Sam was rapidly developing a strong interest in track and field events and we gabbed about this with him as we ate.

I disappeared into the bathroom during a discussion about long distance running and applied liberal amounts of the "sunburn" lotion to my crotch and posterior. Reeking of cocoa butter, I joined Darcy and Sam and the three of us proceeded to spend the evening together, mostly watching television with Sam periodically asking, "What's that smell?"

Charles and Sylvia Harris arrived home about nine and looked in on us in the den.

Charles Harris sniffed the air, suspiciously.

"Is somebody baking a cake?"

At about midnight, Darcy walked me out to the car.

"Why don't you take Sam's rifle with you?" My greater reluctance than usual to return to the little room was palpable.

I shook my head. "I don't want to ask him. Too many questions. Your parents would find out and worry."

"But," I said, snapping my fingers, "that golf club that Judge Goldstein had the other night would be just the ticket. I think it's in the hall closet."

"Daddy carries that with him sometimes when he takes Cyril out for a walk at night," said Darcy. "How about a baseball bat?"

"Perfect," I smiled. "Three feet of stout hickory."

I entered the nauseatingly hot little chamber carrying the Louisville Slugger and the package from Higger's. I had parked the VW just down the street and waited and watched in the dark for five minutes before locking the car and making for number **1435.**

All sense of privacy had vanished from the little room during the previous night and I hurriedly pulled on my pajama bottoms in spite of the heat. I set the 2x4 angle brace against the door and propped the baseball bat against the wall near the head of the bed. Remembering Jimmy Stewart in *Rear Window*, I loaded the Instamatic with a fresh flash bulb and set it on the night stand before turning off the lamp.

The shaft from a pale moon streams past the balcony and through the open French doors of the silent bedroom. Transparent draperies billow slightly in the night breeze as a tall, silent figure crosses the threshold. The large chamber with its high ornate ceilings and heavy crown moldings is darkly cast in feeble light and undulating shadow. The intruder stands quietly for a moment, silhouetted against the open doors. A large canopied bed stands imperiously at the far end of the long room. The intruder deftly removes a small leather case from the breast pocket of his coat and pads soundlessly across the heavy Persian carpet. The linen bed curtains move gently in the night air, but there is no sound from the great bed. The intruder pauses at its head. He quietly opens the leather case and the moonlight's gentle caress reveals the glittering chrome and polished glass of a large hypodermic syringe. Positioned next to the syringe, resting benignly on a pillow of satin, lies the scalpel. The intruder reaches forward and slowly draws back the bed curtains. The smiling face of Sidney Reilly confronts him at eye level. A sharp intake of breath. Frantically, the intruder's gloved fingers fumble with the case, spilling the scalpel and syringe onto the coverlet.

"Were those intended for me, old boy?" says Reilly, glancing at the hideous implements. "Surely not."

The sudden explosion of the Luger fills the room with light and sound like a stroke of lightning and the intruder flies backward through the bed curtains, hands clutching at his torn throat.

Toward dawn, through sheer exhaustion, I finally dropped off to a dreamless sleep and awoke an hour later to the sounds of clump-clump-clump in the corridor. I got up and wearily showered and shaved and anointed my rear-end with soothing lotion, making it to the Arlington Yellow Cab Company just before the starting shift at eight o'clock.

During my lunch break, I called Darcy at home and recounted my unhappy night in the rooming house. We chatted for a while and planned our evening together, a free Watergate Concert by the National Symphony Orchestra on the barge moored down by Memorial Bridge.

Art Baldwin was not in his room when I arrived after work. Without bothering to further consider the consequences, should something go awry, I plunged ahead. I carefully removed the deadfall from the open window after propping it up with a piece of 2x4, then whipped my desk chair through the opening, carefully avoiding the broken beer bottles, and set it quietly on the walk below. In another five seconds, I was standing in front of Art's bureau. I gingerly opened the top drawer and picked up the Ronsonol can. It was as empty as a politician's promises.

That night, we double dated with Linda Townsend and a very pleasant and uninteresting Navy Ensign named Philip Ward. The four of us sat together on the concrete steps leading down to the river's edge and listened to two hours of Mozart from the Symphony barge. It was cool on the water and, overhead, a million stars twinkled in a glittering tapestry.

I had left my car at Darcy's and Linda and Phil had picked us up in his convertible. In the back seat on the way home, I fell asleep twice on Darcy's shoulder.

Linda turned in the front seat after I popped awake at a stoplight whispering and babbling incoherently. "Jack, I know we're not boring you, so you must be driving yourself to an early grave with that taxicab."

I yawned. "I've got to get more sleep, that's all."

The couple in the front seat made the worst inference, of course, and laughed, heartily. "Darcy!" Linda squealed. "It's *your* fault."

"Both our faults," I said. "Not enough hours in the day."

We said our good byes at Darcy's and the two of us went inside for coffee.

"Linda could do a lot better for herself." I said, pouring cold water into the percolator.

"Oh, she will. Just wait," said Darcy. "She's just looking carefully for a future admiral."

"We're not at war and not likely to be. Guys my age will be pushing retirement before they make admiral, or even captain."

"Linda will do okay. She'll find Mr. Right and be a beautiful, dutiful Navy wife with about five kids."

"Phil's a total bore. He doesn't have an opinion on anything, except that the communists are the enemy of mankind."

Darcy poked me, playfully. "Well, he's right about that." She rose on tip-toe and kissed my lips. "You're dead on your feet, aren't you, Love?"

I nodded slowly and sighed. "I'm sorry to be such a negative, depressing shit."

Darcy put her face against my chest. "You're not a negative, depressing shit. I'm never depressed when we're together."

"Me neither," I said, and all my thoughts rushed back to darkened rooms and cryptic notes and photographs. The smell of lighter fluid flashed, for an instant, in my brain.

The second night in my fortress, I was so tired that I went to bed forgetting to put the bar in front of the door. I half roused during the night, recalled that I was totally safe, and immediately sank back into dreamland. In the morning, when I saw the bar leaning against the wall instead of in its rightful place barring the door, I was sure that I had been invaded.

The weekend was upon us again. I desperately needed to get away from the depressing rooming house and be with my Darcy love. Charles and Sylvia Harris were planning a trip to the shore to a house that some family friends had taken at Rehobeth Beach. The couple had a son Sam's age and had taken the boys with them when they left Washington mid-week. The home front was clear for Darcy and me, and I intended to make the most of it.

Accordingly, I hastily showered and packed my bags as soon as I got back to the rooming house that evening, tossing extra cigarettes, my dwindling supply of condoms and the new can of lighter fluid into my bag before preparing for my cat burglar foray into Art's room.

As I was maneuvering the desk chair through the open window, a noise from next door stopped me in mid-swing. Somebody was already in Art's room. I put the chair back down on the floor and waited and listened. I could hear the bands of a radio being searched and, finally, the strains of classical music coming from WGBH. What the hell? Art should have already caught his bus to work.

I nervously paced around the room for a bit, then opened the door and walked out into the hallway. The door to Art's room was open and I looked in. He was there, casually dressed and fiddling through a stack of phonograph records in a little cabinet beside his bureau.

"Hey, Jack. How've you been?"

"All right," I said. "Starting the weekend early?"

Art frowned and shook his head. "Don't I wish. I've got the late shift and most of tomorrow as well."

"Are we at war, yet?"

He laughed. "Not as far as I know."

"President seems to have been sending Khruschev the wrong messages. Understand the Maximum Leader to our south has been seeking advice from lots and lots of his little Russian comrades."

Art's eyes widened and he looked up at me sharply. "Oh?"

"It's plastered all over the *Post*, Art. Hardly a state secret."

His face softened. "Oh, I know. Mostly Republican blathering. They're not going to let him forget the Bay of Pigs."

"The public hasn't forgotten it, either." I said; nor the CIA who had apparently bungled the whole operation, I didn't say. The administration-sponsored invasion had cost the lives of fifteen hundred men when President Kennedy had broken a promise and refused to supply vital air support to the operation.

"No. I suppose not," said Art. He quickly replaced the albums and rose to his feet. "What do you and Miss Darcy have planned for the weekend?"

"Going to run away where nobody can find us for at least two days," I grinned. "How about you?"

"Taking Linda to dinner and a movie tomorrow night."

"Ah ha," I said, non-committally. Linda should stick to recent Naval Academy graduates, I thought. Anyone who got close to Art Baldwin was going to regret it.

We said 'have a nice weekend' to each other, and I went back to my room, collected my stuff and left.

There was no way I was going to hang around half the night. The chance that this, of all nights, would be the moment of the big exchange, was too remote to interest me. I most definitely had other plans and I hadn't planned to be there for Saturday night, anyway. Things could just wait until Sunday evening. I badly, sorely needed my Darcy.

We cut rapidly through what was left of the rush hour traffic and headed east, out into the Maryland's Prince George's' county on highway 50. Darcy hopped up on the seat, folding her knees beneath her.

"Jack love, secrets are fun for a while, but I've been waiting all day. Where are we going?"

I had told her to pack for a grand evening of dining and dancing. Beyond that rather tantalizing hint, I had said nothing of our destination except that we were not spending the weekend at the Harrises. There was always the chance that Sylvia Harris would call the house during the weekend just to make sure her little Darcy hadn't been kidnapped by a white slave ring. She would know we were together, but by the time we returned, it would no longer matter.

I looked over in the seat at my wonderful Darcy, looked lovingly into those sparkling, dancing eyes with their deep intelligence and profound gentleness. "I've made reservations for us at The Shorebird Lodge in Annapolis," I said.

She squealed. "Ohhhh. I know all about it from Linda. It's the most posh hotel between here and New York. Jack, Did you really? You didn't, did you?"

I smiled smugly and nodded. "I did."

"Will they let us in? How do they know we're married?"

I laughed. "We're not married, are we?"

Darcy hit me in the shoulder. "You know what I mean. How did you do it?"

"I just made reservations this morning for Mr. & Mrs. John R. Norton of Washington, D.C."

"What if they want to see our marriage license?" She gripped my arm. "Oh Jack, I'd just die."

I leaned over and kissed her hair. "This isn't a cheap tourist court. They wouldn't dream of asking."

"Are you sure?"

"I'm sure," I said softly.

Darkness was falling when we drove through the gates and up the winding drive to the lodge. As the white clapboard, three story mansion came into view, it was obvious that the term 'lodge' was a gross misnomer. The place had originally been a summer resort hotel, dating from the 1890's. It was set high on a bulge in the shoreline which projected out into the bay and done up in a sort of genteel southern naval fashion with blue awnings and anchors. French doors opened onto private balconies on the upper floors and onto wide sweeping verandahs on the first level. The whole place was shaded by enormous elms and maples.

Beyond the vast lawns was a private beach and the bay. The hotel was sited so that each room offered a slightly different offshore view. We parked the Jaguar on the crushed shell driveway in front of the main entrance and climbed the broad staircase up to the ground floor. In the lobby, I gave the desk clerk our names.

We were both nervous as cats. Darcy had put her Bryn Mawyr ring on her left hand and turned it around. As we had entered the grounds, she had taken my arm and said, "Jack, have you ever done this before?"

"What? Checked into a hotel?"

She pinched my shoulder. "With a girl?"

"Not really."

She leaned quickly across the seat and gave me a fast, furious kiss on the cheek. "I'm glad. If it's too awful, we can just turn around and walk out, can't we?"

"Sweetheart, it's going to be all right, I promise."

"What if they just laugh at us? What if they tell us to leave at once or they'll call our parents?"

"Darcy love, they would never do that."

But I wasn't so sure. I could well imagine hearing the desk clerk saying something about Maryland law requiring proof of marriage followed by the worst period of absolute silence since the Big Bang, with all sorts of elderly, highly respectable married people looking up from the chairs and sofas in the lobby with shock and disapproval registering on their faces.

"If you'll just sign the register, Mr. Norton, I'll have someone take care of your luggage."

I could feel Darcy tense beside me and my hand was shaking as I put the long old-fashioned fountain pen to the creamy dry parchment of the ledger. I signed us in with a flourish, nodding in the middle of it to hear the clerk ask if I would be paying by check.

"We're putting you in room number **324**," he said, handing the key to an approaching bell captain. "It has a lovely view."

He went on explaining about the dining room hours, and the pool, and the stables, and cabanas as well as check cashing privileges, and just signing for everything while we were "guests of the hotel." I gave the keys to the Jaguar to the middle-aged bell captain wearing a navy uniform with brass buttons and anchors for epaulets. He thanked us and disappeared in the direction of the main entrance. The desk clerk also vanished into a small office behind the registration desk area. In a moment, a nattily dressed assistant clerk suddenly appeared behind us as if by magic, introduced himself as Robert and politely asked us to follow him. We rode up on the ancient elevator nervously making small talk about the heat and the prospects for a clear weekend.

We entered a large room with flowered wallpaper trimmed in blue and white and furnished in the tasteful hotel style of the 1940s with that ubiquitous nautical flourish that apparently was the hallmark of the place.

Robert, as we were already willing to think of him, went around the room turning on lights and opening the French doors which led out to a private balcony. He showed us where the bathroom was and freely dispensed information concerning room service and the choice poolside cabanas. Finally, he bade us a pleasant stay and urged us to ask for him by name if there were any little thing our hearts desired.

He was so friendly and self possessed in his bearing that I wasn't certain about tipping him. The subject of money would have been so crass under the circumstances. Nevertheless, when he hesitated for just a fraction of a second at the door, I nervously thrust a brand new fifty cent piece into his hand. That morning I'd picked up a handful of the heavy coins at the cab company just so I'd have them ready for tipping.

We barely had time to walk out on the balcony and see the lighted view of the lawn and gardens when there was a knock at the door. I went numb. They're on to us, I thought. They've made some telephone calls and found out the truth. I looked silently at Darcy and went to the door. The bell captain simply pushed the big iron baggage cart through the open doorway and began depositing luggage on racks set in an alcove. I stood there, feeling for another fifty cent piece in my pocket while he lined up the bags and carefully arranged the hangered items in the closet. Finally, as he handed me the keys to the Jaguar, I pulled out one of the coins and murmured our thanks. When he was gone, Darcy grabbed me by both hands and whirled me around the room until we collapsed on the big double bed.

"Oh Jack. This is so wonderful! I've never been so nervous in all my life. What if they mistook us for somebody else and they come back and get us tonight?"

I cackled with nervous laughter. "Nonsense. They're stuck with us now."

Darcy pulled me off the big bed to go exploring. We walked into the enormous bathroom with its pale blue tile floor. There, past the mirrored sink and vanity were what appeared to be two toilets, side by side. I was staring at the only bidet that I had ever seen in my life.

"Ohhhh," squealed Darcy, as if she had just been presented with a large box of chocolates. "Look, Jack."

I was speechless for a moment. "It's one of those French things," I said.

"It's a bidet," cooed Darcy.

"I know what it's called."

"Every hotel in Paris has a bidet," said Darcy as if in a dream. She had traveled to Europe on the Queen Mary the previous summer after graduation and could never stop talking about French culture.

I walked over for a closer look. "What exactly, do you do with it?" I asked.

"Jaack!"

"Do we both get to sit on it, or in it, or whatever you do?"

"It's for girls, not boys," Darcy replied primly, taking my arm and leading me back into the bedroom.

"Can I watch?"

This last question got me a soft knee in the groin and a very definite No.

We laid out our finery for dinner in the hotel restaurant and then got preoccupied with each other in the shower, and, a little later, on the big double bed.

By the time our hunger shifted to food, the dining room had closed. Undaunted, we sent down for hamburgers and fries and ate them in bed watching *The Twilight Zone*. Finally, as jet fighters and the American Flag finally appeared on the screen with a voice-over reading a schmaltzy poem and Sousa music floating in the background, we snuggled close and kissed and held each other tight.

When the sun reappeared and the picture on the television set popped back on with a test pattern followed by the delights of Howdy Doody, Clarabelle and Buffalo Bob, we were still lying face to face with arms and legs intertwined. I gently extricated myself, turned off the TV and made a trip to the bathroom, pausing to look closely at the bidet. Then I returned to the bedroom and crawled quietly in behind my Darcy, and we curled up like two spoons for another hour.

We felt wonderful! We got up and showered and had coffee on the little balcony. The day was clear and hot and bright, with a steady breeze off the Bay. We went down to the Verandah Grill for brunch and then sought out the advice and services of Robert. He had just arrived on duty and we inquired about obtaining a sailboat from the hotel fleet.

An instant phone call and a 21' Olsen Sloop was reserved and waiting for us at the hotel dock, a delightful half-mile walk across the grounds. Robert strongly recommended that we allow the hotel restaurant to prepare a light luncheon repast to accompany us on our voyage; it was suitably boxed and waiting for us when we started off for the afternoon's sail.

The Olsen was a trim little day-sailor with a small trunk cabin. For us, she was the perfect vessel. We stowed the picnic hamper below and hoisted sails. We had wind! Lots and lots of it. A fresh breeze was coming straight out of the Bay, and we reefed the mainsail and beat into it on a close reach for two hours. The little sloop heeled hard over and fairly danced over the three foot chop and the rolling swells. It was an afternoon of constant tacking, jumping frantically from side to side in the little cockpit, pulling like crazy on jib sheets, dodging the boom, all the while going to windward, like a runaway horse. In ten minutes, the spray had wet us down. In two hours, we were sopping wet.

We had set off at noon and by two o'clock we had taken enough of the pounding, the violent motion and the solid sheets of spray that broke over us with every wave.

"Let's come about," shouted Darcy. "Please?"

We came about, and the world changed.

As soon as we let the jib and mainsail all the way out, the violent slamming softened to a gentle rise and fall. The wind and spray in our faces ceased altogether; and the boat sailed almost upright for the first time since leaving port.

We were famished and broke out the light repast of lobster salad and cold artichoke hearts. This simple provender was joyfully washed down, not with rum, but with a very decent Johannesburg Riesling. We returned to the hotel just before five. Bone tired, sun burned, sopping wet and salt encrusted, we were happier than we'd ever been in our lives.

We peeled out of our wet soggy clothes in the big bathroom and took a long, delicious shower. I wrapped a towel around my middle and returned to the bedroom. Just for a moment, I thought, and gently lowered myself down across the freshly made bed.

The sun had disappeared when I jerked awake. Darcy was lying beside me, completely zonked. The clock radio on the bed table showed a little after seven-thirty, and I kissed her awake and frantically began to dress.

"We're going to miss dinner if we don't get a move on."

Darcy was up like a shot and into the maddeningly sexy white silk sheath that she had worn to Miss Withersby's for tea. She piled her long golden tresses up on her head the way I liked; and, after a few minor adjustments from her makeup case, she was ready. I made do with my trusty Brooks Brothers travel suit and off we went.

When we'd returned from the sail, I had asked Robert to make a reservation for us for eight o'clock. In the dining room, we were expected and immediately shown to a table on the terrace.

We were not especially hungry after the sumptuous mid-afternoon lunch and made do with salads and rather small side orders of crab cakes and other delicacies from the endless bounty of the Chesapeake Bay. Later, we danced to the slow romantic music of the little orchestra which played throughout the evening in a corner of the dining room.

After the third dance, I called the waiter to our table for a bottle of champagne.

"Jack? Are you sure we can afford all this?" Darcy was not one to concern herself in the least about money; but she had seen the pitiful condition of my checking account and suddenly realized that the day of reckoning would soon be at hand.

"It's okay, I'll just put it on the room," I said.

"But what's the room being put on?" she asked.

I laughed, "It's all right. I've already paid Miss Withersby for this month. I'll be wiped out till Tuesday or Wednesday, then I'll be solvent again."

"I want to help."

"Not this time. This is my treat."

"But Love, it's costing you all the money you work so hard for. I could pay for half."

"Next time."

"Why not this time?"

I took both her slim graceful hands in mine and gently kissed the fingers and the palms that I loved. "Because this time, I want to ask you to be my wife."

She looked at me, smiling and knowing that this time would never come again. Her dazzling blue eyes began to fill with tears and still she did not speak.

I held her hands to my face. "Darcy, will you marry me? Please?"

She nodded slowly and the tears spilled onto her cheek. "Entreat me not to leave thee nor to keep from following after thee; for, whither thou goest, I will go and whither thou lodgest, I will lodge, and thy people will be my people and thy God, my God."

My throat tightened up like a vise. I wanted to scream to the heavens with joy and I could not utter a word without weeping. So, I rose from my chair and went round the table to my Darcy love and lifted her up and kissed her passionately right in front of God and the whole restaurant.

We drank the champagne and danced far into the night until we were both fairly drunk. Nobody else remained in the restaurant, and the orchestra wanted to pack it in and go home.

Neither of us wanted the evening to end so I suggested a walk on the beach. We took our shoes off and ran for half a mile through the gentle Bay surf, finally collapsing on the sand. After a while, we walked back slowly, beginning to feel the alcohol and the sheer physical and emotional exhaustion of the most wonderful day of our lives. We left the shore and padded up through the thick lawn to the winding driveway and crossed to the front steps. In the line of parked cars beside the hotel was a long black Cadillac car.

"Oh, God." I whispered.

Darcy caught the fear in my voice. "Jack?"

"That Russian is here."

"What?

"There's his car." I nodded at the black Cadillac.

"Oh Love, that could be anybody's car."

I shook my head quickly. "Anybody's car doesn't have a big fresh dent just above the rear door like that one does."

CHAPTER NINETEEN

"What does he look like?" Darcy asked, glancing at the entrance of the hotel.

"I'm not sure I'd know him if he walked up to us right this minute."

We glanced at the entrance and into the lobby beyond. The driveway, as well as the portion of the grounds that we could see, was completely deserted.

"Let's get inside, quick." I took Darcy by the arm, and we trotted up the steps and into the hotel lobby.

The place had about half the lights turned off and was as vacant as you would expect the lobby of a resort hotel to be at one a.m. The light from the front desk drew us like moths. We walked quickly in that direction, our shoes clicking hollowly on the terra cotta floor. As we approached the desk, Robert came briskly out of a small office in the rear.

"Ahh. Mr. & Mrs. Norton. Have you had a wonderful evening? How was the sailing this afternoon? Plenty of wind, eh?"

Oddly (it was, after all, the middle of the night), he went on and on like this apparently happy to be doing his job as gracious host to paying guests, but also probably just glad to have someone to talk to in the middle of the night. We smiled and nodded and thanked him for all his little kindnesses. Then I asked if we'd had any messages.

I had traveled and stayed in hotels on trips with my parents almost all my life and I had never had occasion to ask the desk clerk if there were any messages. How could there possibly be any messages if you were stopping for a few nights in a strange city where no one knew you? Anyway, people in Hitchcock films, Cary Grant especially, always asked the desk clerk if there were any messages when they couldn't think of anything else to do, so I did the same.

"Let me check, Sir." Robert smiled, made his little bow, and turned to the shelf of pigeon holes behind him.

"Ah! So you do." He deftly plucked a small white envelope out of the box labeled **324** and handed it to me with a flourish.

Startled, I looked searchingly at Darcy and opened the sealed envelope.

You are in great danger. Place the lighter fluid can in the hotel safe immediately.

I handed the note to Darcy and turned back to Robert.

"Could I put something in the hotel safe? Now? Tonight?"

"Certainly, Mr. Norton. Do you have the item with you?"

Darcy was rapidly glancing from the note to me with a look of fear and total confusion. "It's in our room. I'll bring it down in a few minutes if that's all right."

"Of course, Sir." I thanked him and took Darcy by the elbow as we started for the elevators.

"Jack. What is it? What does this mean? Who sent this?"

"I don't know. Let's just get up to the room."

I turned the key and opened the door to suite **324** slowly, then hit the light switch and looked into the room.

We went in and I quickly double locked the door and hooked the chain. Darcy stood in the middle of the bedroom, holding the note, uncomprehending. I stepped over to my open duffel and pawed through it until I found the can of Ronsonol. I picked it up and shook it. It was almost full. Last night, after we had eaten hamburgers and fries, I had used it to fill my Zippo which was taking about six zips to light a cigarette.

I slowly turned the little can over in my hands, holding it upside down, then squeezed the sides and pulled quickly. The oval metal bottom came off in my left hand. The little cavity was stuffed with Kleenex. Without speaking, I turned toward Darcy.

There was a sudden intake of breath. "You brought Art's can!"

"No! I told you. He was in his room when I was there. I couldn't wait for him to leave. I wasn't going back to look at the can until tomorrow night. Darcy, look!"

I pulled out the little wad of Kleenex and uncrumpled it. Inside was a small shiny steel disk that looked almost exactly like one of the bobbins on my mother's Singer sewing machine.

"What is it?" Darcy was staring at the little disk with eyes as big as saucers.

"I think it's microfilm. I think it's our evidence."

"But how did you get it? How did it get here in your bag?"

"I put it there. I put it in the bag when I packed yesterday."

"What? Jack, I don't understand." Darcy's voice began to break.

"It's Art," I said. "The son of a bitch has been using *my* room for a drop the whole time. Probably even with the previous tenant. He didn't leave this film in his own room for the blonde girl. He's never left anything for her in his own room. He had a key to my room for her to use. She came to visit him or at least to his room on a regular basis."

It all began to make some sort of weird sense and I went on with a rush. "When he had something to pass to her, he planted the can in my drawer and she picked it up there. She's probably been in my room a dozen times." Instantly, I thought back to the night when I had 'locked myself out' and had crouched naked in the hallway behind a plastic shower curtain.

"But why put it in *your* room? Why go to the trouble or risk somebody finding it?"

"Because he wanted to make sure that it was *never* left in *his* room, not even for a minute. He was away every night. His room wasn't occupied. The chances that it might be searched were just too great. Maybe even his own bosses search his room routinely. Who knows with these spy types."

What are you going to do with it?" asked Darcy."

"I'm putting it right into the hotel safe," I said, stuffing the little package back into the false bottom. "I don't know who sent that note, but it sounds like good advice to me. "I'll sock it away. We'll get a good night's sleep and tomorrow morning we'll go to the nearest pay phone and call the FBI."

"Why not call them right now, tonight?"

"Because I have a very strong feeling that we shouldn't call from the hotel. Everything goes through that old switchboard downstairs. I'd just rather be out in the open daylight when we place a call to the cops and then have to wait till they get here."

"Me, too. I think," said Darcy.

I put the can of Ronsonol in my coat pocket and kissed Darcy quickly on the lips.

"Lock everything while I'm gone. If anybody knocks on the door, call the front desk immediately. Don't answer the door. I'll be back in five minutes."

Darcy looked at me in total astonishment. "Wait a minute, Jack. What are you doing? I'm not going to stay here by myself." She looked searchingly into my eyes. "What if something happened to you?" A sob and the tears came. She whispered, "What if something happened and you didn't come back?"

"Nothing is going to happen, and I'll be back in five minutes," I whispered back. Both of us seemed to sense that someone might be listening. Darcy began to hug herself and weep softly. Shit.

I crossed over to the telephone and called the front desk. "Robert, this is Mr. Norton in **324**. I hate to ask this of you at this time of night, but could you possibly come up to our room for a moment?"

I replaced the phone in its cradle and went over to Darcy who was still standing in the center of the room, making little sobbing sounds. "He'll be right up, Love. I'm not going anywhere. It's going to be all right."

I reached into the bureau drawer and took out some of the hotel stationery and a long envelope. I wrote my name and Washington address along with the hotel room number on the envelope, wrapped the can in the stationery and sealed the whole package. I hung my coat and tie in the closet, took off my shoes and fished a couple of one dollar bills out of my wallet before slipping into my pajamas.

Darcy went into the bathroom and closed the door. I walked over to the little balcony and looked out just as the soft knock sounded.

"Yes?"

"It's Robert, Mr. Norton."

I opened the door and gave him the envelope with the bills folded against it.

"I really apologize for asking you to come up here like this," I said. "This package really needs to go into the safe right away, but when we got up to the room, we were just too pooped to go back down again."

Robert smiled and shook his head vigorously. "I'm more than happy to do it, Mr. Norton. But I'm afraid that you *will* need to come down and sign it in. Hotel policy. I'm awfully sorry. Could it wait until morning?"

"No," I said. "It really does need to be put away tonight. If you'll just wait a moment, I'll come with you."

"Certainly, Sir. I'm terribly sorry to put you to all this trouble but the hotel insists that every item is personally signed in by its owner. Otherwise . . . ."

"No. It's all right. I should have realized. I'll just be a moment."

I knocked on the bathroom door and told Darcy.

"I'm going too, Jack." The determination in her voice was as clear as the moon-lit night sky beyond the balcony, and I nodded and went to get my robe and TopSiders.

I tried to make casual small talk with Robert about our afternoon sail, but it was all but impossible. I kept forgetting what I was saying and looking around furtively at every doorway and cross corridor we passed. While we stood and waited for the old elevator to rise to our level, I prepared myself for a Soviet agent to be standing there when the big doors silently parted, a long slim dagger clenched in his fist. Darcy held onto me with a deathgrip round my arm and only smiled and nodded at Robert at every lull in the dialogue. When the doors opened again, the lobby was still half-lit, shadowy and completely deserted.

We crossed the foyer to the reservation desk and Robert disappeared into the little office for a moment and came back carrying a ledger of some kind.

"If you'll just fill this deposit slip out and sign at the bottom, Mr. Norton."

I quickly filled out the spaces and wrote one thousand dollars on the line for **value of item to be deposited.** Then I signed my name and the time and date, and Robert did the same on the line beneath it.

We thanked him and I gave him the two bills. He apologized over and over about the necessity for observing such strict rules which he completely understood were a nuisance and an irritating bother for people like us.

We started back for the bank of elevators. Darcy, who hadn't released my arm the whole time, whispered up to me.

"Jack, do you think we could just sit down here in the lobby till it gets light?"

"No. We're going to be just fine in about two minutes, in our own little bed."

"That note said you were in great danger."

"Melodrama. We've followed his advice. We've gotten rid of The McGuffin. We'll be all right."

She pulled on my arm as we reached the open elevator door. "The what? What did we get rid of?"

I smiled. "The McGuffin."

"Jack, please."

"The McGuffin is the little gizmo in all Hitchcock films that absolutely everybody wants, and is willing to kill for."

Darcy yanked my arm. "Don't tease about this, okay."

"I'm sorry, Love." I patted her and pushed the button marked **"3"**.

I thought the trip back down the silent, third floor corridor would never end. By the time we reached **324**, we were both trembling badly, and my heartbeat could be seen as well as heard through the terrycloth robe. I double-locked and chained the door with the same frantic motion that a child uses when wildly leaping up into his bed, so something underneath won't grab his foot.

Sleep was impossible. We kept all the lights turned on and held each other close and talked and talked, stopping every few minutes to listen for scratching noises at the door.

"But who sent the note?" asked Darcy for the tenth time.

"I just don't know, Love. I'll find out from Robert in the morning."

"He doesn't come on duty till almost noon. We have to check out before then."

"Maybe we'll be here then. We'll just have to see what the FBI says."

Darcy snuggled closer. "Do you think that Russian left it."

"He certainly left the others, but I can't imagine he'd want me to put that microfilm in the hotel safe where he can't get at it. What good does that do him?"

"Well, his car is certainly here. So he's here."

"He may be here, but it doesn't make any sense that he'd leave a note like that."

"It's not coincidence that he's here, Jack; and leaving notes is his style."

I sat up suddenly. "It could be Art."

"What?"

I nodded, explaining. "If Art and his blonde girlfriend found that the can was missing, they would have immediately realized what had happened. Just thought I'd taken it with me for the weekend the way I did to West Virginia. Except that this time, it was the real thing, and the microfilm was in it. They'd try to get it back, quietly."

"Why not just wait till we got back?"

"I don't know."

"And anyway," Darcy continued, "Art would never openly reveal his part in this to you with a note. He just wouldn't."

"I suppose," I said, and nodded off to an uneasy oblivion.

The sun was flooding in through the open French doors when I slowly regained partial consciousness. Darcy was still peacefully sleeping, sprawled half on top of me with her head in the little hollow of my neck and her sweet, small hand lying on my chest.

I lay quietly, listened to the steady breathing, felt her soft warmth and inhaled the wonderful aroma of her body. I worshipped her and she had said, yes! She was going to be my wife! I loved and adored her beyond all reason. Now, she was going to be all mine, for all time. But the ecstasy of this realization was short-lived as I realized what had intruded upon us at the pinnacle of the happiest day and night of our lives. This evil thing that had forced its way into the new life we were making and threatened its very continuance.

I had to think and act sensibly in order to quickly end this thing, and to keep Darcy and me well clear of any physical danger while doing so. Art Baldwin had managed to outsmart himself. He had cleverly used my room as a drop for a long time. I suspected he had used the previous tenant in the same way. I remembered getting the initial impression of a hasty departure by the previous tenant that day I had been shown the room by Miss Withersby. I'd almost bet anything that the previous tenant had been surprised by the Vamp or had caught her or Art in his room. As soon as he was onto them, he'd just bolted.

Of course, it wouldn't have been a can of Ronsonol then, just some convenient object that the tenant possessed and which was subsequently duplicated by the blonde woman and her comrades. The blonde might well be on the outs with the male comrades now, but I had no doubt that they all worked for the same side and were part of the same faction.

And for reasons unknown, at some point quite recently, the blonde woman and the others had simply had a falling-out and were quarreling over whatever it was that Art was providing them. Because of this internal dispute and the subsequent actions of the blonde woman, I had been tipped off about the Ronsonol can. They had given the whole thing away, which was not only very stupid, it was very hard to understand.

The more I thought about it, the more difficulty I had in understanding why the blonde woman did not simply eliminate me that night, instead of merely scaring the bejeezus out of me and giving me a sore behind. She had given the whole show away and had banked that I would remain too frightened to ever breathe a word to anyone about the operation. That really didn't make a lot of sense given the high stakes of Cold War espionage. Now, they all realized that I had made another feckless mistake ("Where you at, 41?"), unwittingly taking the precious 'drop' with me when I left for the weekend and their response was to kindly ask me to put it away for safe keeping. Why were they being so nice to me? Why hadn't they simply come to the room and taken the thing? There was clearly a piece of the puzzle that was missing, but that call to the FBI was long overdue. Once I turned the microfilm over to them, the whole thing would be theirs to figure out, and my Darcy love and I would be free. I looked down at her sleeping face and kissed it softly.

I began the task of nibbling Darcy awake, and she began the task of moving slowly and arching and sensuously stretching and exploring with her hands; and, before you knew it, we were both wide awake. An hour or so later, we got out of the shower and started to dress.

Room service arrived with English muffins and coffee, and we paused long enough to dash out onto the balcony and break our fasts of the last ten hours or so. It was almost eleven-thirty when we finally bolted from our little sanctuary. We unlocked the door, cautiously peered in both directions, and flew down the hall in a half-run to the elevator. Twenty or thirty people were milling, sitting and going to-and-fro in the lobby. We approached the front desk and asked a tall man with white hair for the whereabouts of Robert.

"Robert usually begins his shift at eleven, Sir, but . . . ," he looked around at the wall clock, "he hasn't come in yet, this morning. I expect him at any moment. Would you like me to call you when he arrives? Ah, Mr. and Mrs. Norton in **324**, isn't it?"

I nodded automatically at the Mr. and Mrs. Norton query, and he said, fine, where would we be? I heard myself saying that we would be having lunch in the Terrace Grill. We thanked him and walked away.

"Jack, why did you do that? We should be in the car right this minute heading for the nearest deserted pay phone to call the FBI."

"What's a deserted pay phone?"

"Jaack, cut it out. You know what I'm talking about."

"I'm sorry, Love. I just automatically said yes when he asked if we were Mr. and Mrs. Norton, and then I felt silly when I realized what he was really talking about, so I said we'd just have lunch."

"It's almost noon. Don't we need to check out?"

"We'll just get a quick sandwich, come back and see Robert and then check out and call the FBI."

"We should call the FBI *before* we check out, Jack. We shouldn't touch that package in the hotel safe."

"They'll probably charge us for another day if we haven't left by noon."

"I don't care," said Darcy angrily. "We've spent this much, I'd rather spend another fifty dollars and be sure that we'll both be able to attend a certain wedding which is going to take place in about three months."

"I wouldn't miss it for the world," I said and gave her a peck on the cheek. "Okay, you're right, as usual. We act as if nothing has happened. We see Robert and then stroll out to the car and then drive like hell to one of your deserted phone booths. We'll place a call to the FBI and we'll follow their instructions to the letter. Happy?"

"Happ*ier*," Darcy said, but I still think we should be on our way now. These people want to hurt us."

We ordered BLTs and iced tea and were just wolfing them down when I happened to glance out across the lawn, which abutted on a stand of woods between the hotel and the riding stables. I signaled with my eyes and said, "Quick, look!"

Darcy turned quickly in her chair. A tall woman with short-cropped platinum blond hair was striding deliberately along the path toward the stand of trees. She was dressed in boots and riding habit and was swinging a riding crop. A black bowler hat was in her other hand.

"It's her! It's the same outfit she was wearing at Middleburg! She sent the note last night. She would have been the first one to know exactly why the Ronsonol can was missing." I got up from my chair.

"What are you doing?" stammered Darcy.

"I'm going to talk to her. I'm going to confront her right here and now. You finish your sandwich, and I won't be a minute."

"Nooo!" shouted Darcy. People at several tables turned abruptly. I flinched at the outburst. "I'm not staying here alone, Jack Norton. If you're going to talk to that woman, I'm going too."

CHAPTER TWENTY

I was seething with anger. I hurried back inside and signed for the lunch, then rejoined Darcy who had walked over to the verandah railing and watched the blonde woman disappear down the path into the woods. The mere act of attending quickly to details tended to calm and settle me, but each time I thought of the woman and what she and Art had put me through, explosive rage welled up again. I threw down a fifty-cent tip for the waitress and we left the open porch by the outside stairway.

Darcy was wearing sandals which were really only thin leather soles held to the bottoms of her feet by long laces, but she easily kept pace at a half run along the winding old brick walkway. About a hundred yards beyond the hotel, the path changed to ground sea shells, and Darcy quickly called a halt to rid herself of the hard little kernels that were scooped up by the open toes of her sandals.

Holding onto my arm and standing on one foot while wiggling the other, she said, "What are you going to say to her?"

"I'm going to tell her to get the hell out of my life. Goddamn her soul. How dare she follow us here and make threats and try to frighten us and spoil everything. I'm going to do a little threatening of my own." We started to run again, and the thick beech woods closed in quickly around us.

"With what?" gasped Darcy, holding onto her bouncing shoulder bag with one hand and grabbing onto mine tightly with the other.

"The damn microfilm is locked in the hotel safe where she and her buddies can't get at it. It's going to stay there until the feds and I open it together. There's nothing in the world that she can do about it now. I'm giving her a ten-minute head start before I call the FBI. I'm ending this nightmare right now. She and Brother Art are going to be sent away for a long, long time, and I couldn't be happier." I snarled.

"Jack, let's not follow her," Darcy pleaded. "Let's turn around right now and go back and call the FBI. I can't run or even walk in this stuff."

"Go back to the lawn and wait for me, Darcy. You're in no danger. I just want to see her face for one minute," I said, flushed with rage. "I just want to look that vicious bitch in the eye. Let *her* be scared for a change. I want to see *her* run like a goddamn rabbit. Let *her* know what it feels like to have a goddamn 24-hour anxiety attack. Goddamn her rotten soul!"

She shook her head, pleading. "Jack, please don't go. Come back with me, now." I turned quickly and hugged her to me. "I'll only be a minute or two, Love. Wait at the bench at the edge of the woods. Please, Darcy." And I turned and left my Darcy Love and ran.

Another half mile and my breathing was coming in heavy, ragged gasps. There was no one on the trail through the woods, but I wasn't surprised. I had talked to Robert about coming out to the stables, and he had recommended the scenic route.

"Most people just drive or walk around by the road. It's a lot quicker but not nearly as romantic."

Now I ran madly down the romantic route for another hundred yards. My chest was pumping like a bellows, and I prayed that the stable wasn't much farther. I staggered over the next little rise and saw the two of them standing together, just off the trail.

The blonde looked up first, then the man in the blue blazer turned and stared, his face an appalling mask of shock. Robert! Then I saw, gripped tightly in her hand, the cream-colored envelope with the blue piping.

Robert saw my eyes and looked desperately for an escape route, then thought better of it and raised his hands in a placating fashion.

He smiled, "Now, Mr. Norton . . . ."

I came straight at him and hit him in the side of the head as hard as I could. He was thrown back against the blonde by the force of the blow, then stumbled over into a large beech tree and lost his footing, rolling over and over in a deep pile of dry leaves. The blonde woman took several steps backward. I was on top of Robert before he stopped moving, dragging him to his feet and slamming him again and again.

The woman cried out. "Stop! Stop it!"

I grabbed Robert by his blue blazer and lifted him off his feet in a wide, half circle swinging him head first into the beech tree. There was a sound like a sack of grain hitting a concrete floor, and Robert bounced off the tree and collapsed again in the pile of leaves. He made no sound, and he didn't move.

The blonde woman had backed up a few more steps and stood stock-still, her head going from me to Robert and back again. She made no move in his direction. The whole encounter had taken about four seconds.

I turned on her, "You fucking bitch. I want that envelope."

She backed up another step and clenched the package tightly. Her voice was taut with fear. "Don't be foolish. If you take this, you'll be dead in five minutes. Your friend as well. It is absolutely vital that this document not fall into their hands."

"Bullshit!" I spat. "Whose hands is it in right now?" There was a faint moaning sound from Robert.

"I am not at all what you think." She said, evenly. "The man who attacked me the other night is here, at the hotel. If he should get this, your country will be in great danger. Please! I appeal to you. Take your friend and leave this place."

"Gimmie the fuckin' envelope!" I screamed.

No one spoke or moved. Robert continued to make garbled moaning sounds. My breathing was so tortured that I bent over slightly and rested my hands on my knees, my eyes never leaving the blonde woman. The heavy, labored breathing had put a stitch in my side and my stomach was swirling with nausea. Neither of us moved an inch.

Suddenly, there sounded a smack like an over-ripe plum thrown against a tree. The blonde woman gave a little cry and hopped backwards, falling as if from a diving board. I lunged forward on one knee and crawled through the dry leaves to the fallen woman. Her mouth and eyes were wide-open, fixed and staring. She was not breathing.

I heard a branch snap in the distance behind me and snatched up the envelope where it had fallen beside her. I dived forward and launched myself down a little hillock just beyond where she lay. I rolled over and over through the dry beech leaves and hit the bottom of the little gully running hard.

Oceans of adrenaline flooded my body and I ran like a wild man, zig zagging through the trees and foliage, tearing my legs and arms with briars but not feeling them or anything else. I broke out of the woods onto the wide lawn about fifty yards below the trail.

Darcy was standing by the white wrought-iron bench and saw me immediately. She started off in a bare-footed run, with her sandals and shoulder bag flying wildly in her hand. We met half way and ran together for the driveway and the car.

I had the keys in my hand, and we were in the Jaguar and fishtailing down the long winding drive before either of us spoke.

"It was Robert," I began, speaking in gasps. "He was there with her in the woods. He gave her the package from the safe. Someone killed her right in front of me."

Darcy looked at me in absolute horror. "Killed the woman?"

"Yes! Someone shot her as we were standing there. One second she was talking, then she just fell over backwards like a rag doll. She just said, "Oh!" and fell right down."

Darcy's face was frozen in a grimace, mouth and eyes wide. "She was *dead*?"

My breathing slowed and I managed to nod. "I'm positive. Her face had no life in it, like a dead dog on the highway."

Darcy burst out crying, and we spun off the crushed shell driveway onto the county road at almost fifty miles an hour.

"What happened to Robert?" She asked, through sobs.

"I beat the hell out of him. He was out cold on the ground."

She grabbed my arm fiercely with both hands. "Tell me what happened, Jack. Tell me the whole thing so I can understand it. Please."

I recounted the whole thing for her from the point we had parted on the trail. Darcy's face was streaked with tears, and she heard the story, clutching me tightly and nodding her head swiftly at each new revelation.

She spoke frantically, "I knew we shouldn't have followed her. I just had a feeling. You could have been killed instantly! Just gone, like she was!" She broke into tears again and then caught her breath. "We have to call someone. We have to call the police or the FBI. We have to get help for them."

"She's already dead."

"You don't know that. She could be alive. What about Robert? Jack, you witnessed a shooting. We have to call for help. We should have told them at the hotel. We have to let them know."

I turned on her angrily, "If we'd gone back into that hotel, we both might be dead by now. Don't you know that? I can't tell who's involved in this. Anybody could be. That Russian is at the hotel, and there's probably somebody with him. The blonde woman said we'd both be dead in five minutes if she gave me this envelope." I wrenched it out of my pocket and threw it in Darcy's lap. "All I could think of was to get away from there as fast as possible."

I negotiated a fast left turn, straightened the car and looked over at Darcy. She was staring at the dashboard in front of her and seemed about ready to scream. "Oh Baby, I'm so sorry. I didn't mean to yell at you. You're right, as usual. You're absolutely right. I just couldn't think of anything but getting us away from there."

The E-Type screamed by a country store with gas pumps, and I could see a phone booth at the roadside. I glanced in the rearview and slammed the brakes, bringing the car down onto the shoulder of the little two lane road.

"We'll call them from back there." Darcy tried to smile and just nodded.

I had to ask information for the number of *The Shorebird*. The phone was answered on the second ring by the switchboard operator, a pathetically drab little woman about fifty years old. I had seen her, several times, sitting at her station off to one side of the front desk and could not help but note that she bore a striking physical resemblance to Olive Oyl.

I asked to speak to the manager, and she wanted to know who was calling. A good five seconds of silence ensued.

"Hello, Sir. Are you still there?"

I assumed my most obnoxious *nouveau riche* manner and shouted at her. "Young woman, this is an emergency! I am a guest at this hotel and I want to speak to the manager. Now!"

"One moment please."

There was a short pause and the soft dulcet tones of the hotel manager came over the line. "This is Mr. Henderson. May I help you?"

"There's been an accident in the woods by the stables. A woman has been killed. Robert Briggs is there too. He's been hurt."

"An accident, sir? Robert Briggs?"

"Someone killed one of your guests. A girl. She was shot dead. Robert is there with her. He needs help, immediately. First-aid."

"May I have your name, Sir."

And, automatically, I heard myself saying, "Mr. Norton in **324**."

"And may I ask where you're calling from, Mr. Norton?"

"We've left the hotel. Our lives are in danger!"

"We'll call the stables, immediately, Mr. Norton." A sense of urgency had come into his voice.

"They're not at the stables. They're in the woods near the stables just off the gravel path.

"I'll send out someone from the stables right away, Sir. If you'll just give me a number where you . . . ."

I slammed down the phone and ran back to the car.

"I really screwed up."

Darcy looked up at me. "What did they say?"

"They're sending someone out to the woods."

"Oh, Thank God," breathed Darcy.

"I gave the hotel manager my name."

"Well, of course."

"Darcy, when they find that woman and Robert, they'll come after us. Robert is sure to point the finger at me as soon as he comes around . . . ." I stopped in mid-sentence. "What if they killed him, too?"

"What?"

"Whoever shot the girl was right behind me. He might have shot Robert, too."

"Jack, you don't know . . ."

"There could be two dead bodies lying there. I'm the only name they have. They'll send the police after us. They'll have to."

"Call him back and explain. You were just a by-bystander."

"Robert knows I wasn't just a by-bystander. I beat the hell out of him."

"We can't just run away, Jack. Daddy will get Judge Goldstein to help us."

"I'm not afraid of the cops. They're not going to shoot us. "It's the *killer* I don't know about. What about *him*? *We're* carrying something that he's willing to kill *us* for."

"But if we go back . . . ."

"If we go back, he could shoot us as we drove in the gate. We have to find out what's going on before we go back, before we let anybody know where we are."

"The FBI? Tell them about the microfilm."

"Sweetheart, I just don't know. We need to think. I'm scared as hell I'll do something stupid and get us both killed."

We were driving west through pasture land and small farm country. The Jaguar kept a steady 75 miles an hour. I realized that my left hand was throbbing badly and becoming painfully stiff. I looked down at my hands. Dried blood and torn flesh was all over the backs of both of them. Darcy saw them too.

"Oh God! Jack Your hands."

"I banged them up on Robert's head." I tried to flex my left hand and winced sharply. "I think I might have broken a knuckle or something."

"We have to stop. Get some ice. Some water. Something to put on them. The skin's hanging off. Jack, you have to go to an emergency room." She looked at my arms and upper legs. "You're all scratched and torn. Jack, please."

I laid my mangled right hand on her knee. "Darcy Love, just calm down. We both have to calm down, or we're really going to hurt ourselves. These are just briar scratches on my legs and arms. They sting, but that's all. We'll stop at the next little store and get some ice and Band-Aids. Merthiolate or something to put on my knuckles. We can't be showing up at some emergency room."

"But if your hand is broken?"

"I'm not sure. I'm not sure about anything right now, Love. I just know we have to get to a safe place for a while before I do something really stupid and makes things worse."

Five miles on, an AMOCO sign hanging from a pole by the side of the road caught my eye. I braked fast and swerved the Jaguar onto the gravel siding. We drove past the pumps and pulled in front of the little store. My left hand was swelling. Both hands burned like fire. I stayed in the car.

"I won't be a minute, Love." Darcy swung out of the cockpit and disappeared into the shaded interior. I sat and tried to flex my fingers. Both hands began to feel like burning stumps. Several cars passed on the highway. Bugs buzzed and droned in the afternoon heat. I closed my eyes and tried to tell myself that the pain in my hands was only a rhythmic throbbing which didn't really hurt.

I was having some success with this approach when a middle-aged mechanic working on a '57 Chevy put his tools down, wiped his greasy hands on a filthy rag and walked over to the car.

He smiled and nodded. I nodded back, the throbbing immediately starting to get even with me for attempting to scorn it.

"How you doin?" he asked.

"Hi." I said, and looked longingly into the store for my Darcy.

"Whatta you call that? Thunderbird? Or is it one of them Eyetalian cars?"

"It's the new Jaguar."

"Don't look like no Jaguar I've ever seen."

"It's the new E-Type. Just came out."

"That shore is sumthin'." He said admiringly. "What'll she do?"

"About one hundred and fifty."

"Lord have mercy. A hundred and fifty! Well," he turned and started back to the Chevy as Darcy opened the passenger door, "You shore are havin' yoreself a time. Howdy," he nodded to Darcy.

Darcy smiled at him and I said 'see you later' and pushed the starter button, and we went out on the road, fast. Darcy set a grocery bag on the floor at her feet.

"I got ice, Band-Aids, cotton, aspirin and a bottle of hydrogen peroxide." She opened up her little first aid items on the cockpit floor and cleaned off each of my hands with the disinfectant. I put the bag of ice down between my legs and held each hand in it repeatedly for as long as I could stand it.

We kept going, heading west. The knuckles of my left hand hurt like bloody hell despite the ice bath. I could flex my fingers with the greatest of difficulty, but the hand had swollen and the skin was tight as a drum. Darcy kept asking to see me move my fingers every few minutes. Finally, we both concluded that no bones were broken.

"What does it feel like?" Darcy asked.

"Like I smashed it into a rock. Oh God, Darcy. It hurts so bad that I'm starting to get sick."

"Let me drive. Pull over up here right now."

I drove on for a mile or so before the pain in my hands triggered responses in my stomach and wave after wave of green nausea swept over me. I saw a wide spot and pulled over. I slipped over into the passenger seat while Darcy got out and ran around to the driver's door. A Maryland State Trooper cruised by in a gray and white Dodge Coronet with a big light on top.

He came by us from the opposite direction at about 45 miles per hour and kept right on going with hardly a glance in our direction. The pain and nausea vanished momentarily, and I watched him disappear in the rear view as my heart bounced madly. Darcy put the car in gear and pulled out onto the highway.

"He didn't pay any attention. He's not looking for us," I said.

"Maybe he hasn't heard anything," said Darcy.

"It's been over an hour. If the people at the hotel have found the bodies, you can bet your life that an all-points bulletin has gone out for our arrest."

"We should call the hotel."

I nodded. "We will, but right now I'm so sick. I just have to lie here and not move for a little bit."

Darcy looked anxiously from the road to my hands. "The swelling doesn't seem to be getting any worse."

It was true. The icebath was doing its work, closing down the capillaries to prevent the inflammatory reaction from becoming full blown. Massive pounding pain, however, was not so easily blocked. It flared out from below each wrist and the sick trembling weakness swelled up from belly to throat. I was sweating freely and wolfed down a small handful of the aspirin tablets.

"Oh God. Jack. You look awful. You're in so much pain! We need to get you to a doctor."

"No Sawbones," I murmured, in my best Humphrey Bogart imitation. "It'll pass. My hands are just going to be very sore for a few days. There's nothing else a doctor could do except maybe give me codeine or maybe a shot of morphine. I just need to get somewhere and lie down."

"We could be at the cabin in about two hours."

"I know. I've been thinking about that." I nodded.

"What about calling the hotel?"

"We'll call as soon as we cross the state line."

We stopped at a roadside diner just beyond the Maryland line and made the call. The horrible green sickness had slackened and then come back in ever fainter waves. By the time we stopped, it was almost just a ghastly memory. The pain in my hands was at a manageable level unless I tried to move them or touch something.

Olive Oyl answered on the second ring, as usual.

"This is Mr. Norton. May I speak to the manager, please?"

"Oh yes, Mr. Norton. Mr. Henderson has been trying to reach you. Just a moment, please." Her voice was as calm as a millpond.

"Mr. Norton? This is Adam Henderson." His voice was as calm as a *frozen* millpond.

"Yes, Mr. Henderson. I was concerned about that matter at the stables. In the woods."

"Mr. Norton, You've had your little joke. I must say I think it was in *very* questionable taste. You managed to badly frighten not only me but a number of our staff. High spirits among young people is one thing, but shouting fire in a theatre is *not* protected by the First Amendment, you know.

"I don't understand," I stammered. "What do you mean?"

"Mr. Norton, your room is still occupied." The patronizing tone was bristling with annoyance. "Do you and Mrs. Norton wish to extend your stay with us, or shall I have your things packed and sent on to you?"

"No, no," I said quickly. "We'd very much like to stay over another night and perhaps through Tuesday. Is Robert there now.

"Robert?" The indignant note became more pronounced.

"Robert Briggs," I persisted.

"Mr. Briggs is at home in bed where he has been since last Friday. I spoke with him personally just after you came to the desk and a second time after your *prankster* call. He knows of no altercation behind the stables and is suffering no injury except a slow recovery from apparent food poisoning." Adam Henderson sighed, audibly, "Mr. Norton, I really don't know what you saw in the woods behind the stables today. Some young people scuffling perhaps. You most certainly did not see Mr. Briggs."

I was stunned. I simply didn't know what to say or think. There was a blank spot in the conversation and finally I said, "Since Friday? But he checked us in on Friday."

"I'm afraid not. That would have been—let me see—Mr. Soames."
A note of condescending amusement in his voice.

A note of extreme irritation flared into mine. "And I suppose it was
Mr. Soames we saw at the desk late last evening, and who came to our
room, and who deposited a package in the hotel safe for us."

Mr. Henderson lost none of his poise and equanimity. "And what
time was that Sir? If you remember?"

"It was last night, just past midnight. I signed the receipt for the
hotel safe at 12:35am, and Robert countersigned."

"Just a moment, Sir, if you please." He spoke to someone. There
was about a minute of nothing, then I could hear the phone being
picked up. "Mr. Norton, I'm afraid there is no record whatsoever of
your having made any deposit in our safe at any time. I just personally
checked the contents of the safe against the deposit slips. There are no
unaccounted-for items."

Of course there were no unaccounted-for items. My unaccounted-for
item was presently sitting on the floor of the Jaguar, not ten feet away.
But the deposit book?

"Mr. Henderson, I know this sounds silly when the item is not
physically present in your safe, but I *did* sign the deposit book last
evening. My signature and the entry *have* to be there."

"And what time would that have been, sir?"

I shouted: "At 12:35! I've already told you!"

"Yes. Quite right, You have indeed;" the breezy condescension
was instantly gone, replaced by pure venom over a thin coating of ice,
"but, you see Mr. Norton, that is just one more piece of the continuing
problem that we seem to be having with you."

"What the hell are you talking about?"

"I am talking, young sir, about the indisputable fact that the hotel
switchboard and the registration desk close down every evening at
midnight and do not re-open until five am. I am further saying, sir, that
you did not make a deposit to the hotel safe at Twelve Thirty Five this
morning, for the simple reason that there was no one on duty at that
hour."

"I see," I said in a somewhat subdued voice, and this time, I really
did see.

Mr. Henderson sensed his victory and my defeat at the same instant
and decided on an outreach of diplomatic magnanimity. "Mr. Norton, I

understand that you and Mrs. Norton had quite a late evening, dancing and dining." Not to say, *drinking*, which he didn't. "I'm sure you must have *intended* to make the deposit and just forgot to do it."

"Yes," I said. "That's probably what happened. I want to apologize, Mr. Henderson, for the bother I've been."

"That isn't necessary, sir. It's quite all right. An evening of perhaps a little too much celebration . . . . Happens to us all at one time or another. If you'll just bring the item for safekeeping to the front deck when you come in, we'll be happy to deposit it for you."

I thanked him, hung up and got back into the car.

I recounted the exchange for Darcy. "The Robert Briggs we saw was an impostor. We've never even met the real Robert Briggs. He suddenly became ill before we arrived. There are no problems at the hotel. Everything is dandy and normal. They're expecting us back later in the evening to stay over another few days. No body or bodies were found in the woods. No female guests are missing. Nothing was ever put into the hotel safe. Henderson thinks I got drunk out of my mind last night and imagined or just made the whole thing up."

Darcy listened with disbelief, shaking her head slowly. "How did they know we were coming? To the Shorebird, I mean?"

"My fault. I made a reservation from the phone at the rooming house on Friday morning. The vamp had it tapped and when the microfilm was not in my drawer where Art had put it, she knew I'd inadvertently taken it with us to the hotel."

"But the killer. How did he know we'd be here?"

"I can't imagine, Love." I shook my head and groaned softly. My hands were a continuous massive ache and the energy and the repeated adrenaline rushes had taken their toll as well. I was beginning to feel very tired. "He probably just followed the Vamp. Or, maybe, he just followed us. No way to tell."

Darcy leaned over and put her face against my cheek. She placed her cool hand against my forehead. "Your color looks better and you're not wringing wet the way you were. You're awfully tired though, aren't you Baby?"

I closed my eyes and nodded.

"I need to call the folks. Won't be a minute."

"Darcy, I don't think it's a good idea to tell your parents or anyone where we are right now."

"I'm going to tell them the wonderful news." she beamed.

I looked over and smiled weakly at her. "I'm sorry this horrible mess has spoiled everything."

"It hasn't spoiled anything, Silly. Tomorrow morning we are going to walk into a police station with this microfilm and not leave until the FBI comes. Then the whole thing will be over." She kissed me again and opened the driver's door.

While Darcy made her call, I fervently prayed the whole thing would be over, but I was frightened in a way I had never before experienced. It had been a wrenching, horrible, terrifying day for Darcy. The worst day of her life since we had spotted the Cadillac in the driveway, just past midnight. But she had not seen that woman's face. She had not looked into those staring eyes. Those windows to the Soul. She had not seen that the Soul was no longer there.

CHAPTER TWENTY ONE

There were squeals and peals from a highly animated and enthusiastic Darcy as she fairly danced in the phone booth during the conversation with Sylvia Harris. Had we not been on the run from an international murderer, who might well appear and kill us both before Darcy could end the conversation, I should have been giddy with happiness.

As it was, Darcy eventually waved at me and said, "Jack, come say hello, quick."

As I opened the car door and painfully struggled out, I planned my speech.

Hello Mrs. Harris. I've just had sexual intercourse with your daughter, and I'm going to do it again, over and over.

What Sylvia Harris actually said when I got on the phone was, "Oh Jack, I just want you to know how happy Charles and I are for you and for Darcy. We think you both have made the right choice."

I muttered profuse thank you's and other inanities, feeling so embarrassed that I could hear my own voice echoing back in my ears. Sylvia said something about Darcy and me being sure to call *my* mother and something about a Christmas wedding and everyone staying at their house. I have absolutely no memory of what I said.

The thought of calling my mother and saying:

I've just had sexual intercourse with this strange girl that you don't know, and I'm going to do it again, over and over.

was not particularly appealing, and I decided to put it off to a more propitious time.

"Didn't they want to know where we were and when you were coming home?" I asked.

Darcy laughed, shaking her head. "Mom was too thrilled with the news to even ask. She'll wonder about that in ten minutes or so."

The respite with Sylvia Harris had given us both a badly needed emotional bridge, as well as reassurance that there was still a normal world out there with parents and friends, family and weddings and normal life. Now we had to re-awaken to our own nightmarish predicament and act intelligently so as to overcome it and return to that normal world which we had so briefly re-entered by telephone.

"We're less than an hour now from the cabin," I said. "It's Sunday evening and even gas stations are closing down out here in the country. If we call the FBI now, we'd just have to wait until morning to see them. I'm not at all sure that they would take us seriously until they've actually looked at the microfilm. I mean telling them about Art and the blonde woman and the murder and what happened at the hotel this morning will just make us look like kids pulling a hoax or crying wolf or something. They'll call the hotel to verify our story, and Henderson will tell them I was drunk and imagined the whole thing." I took Darcy's hands gently in my own, gritting my teeth a little from the movement. "For the time being we're safe," I said. "There's no way the killer can know where we are. Our calls to the hotel couldn't have been traced to the roadside pay phones, even if they were trying to trace them. Let's lie low at the cabin tonight. Your father said the Sheriff has a regular patrol keeping an eye on the place now. Nobody's going to bother us there. We'll be completely safe. In the morning, we can go down to the Sheriff's office and make them listen to us and call in the FBI."

"We won't be able to drive in with this car," Darcy said.

"I know. We'll park inside the gate and walk."

Darcy's worried look matched her voice. "Oh God. The last time we walked that trail."

"That was different," I said, quickly. "They knew we were there and that we were alone."

"We're going to be there again, and we're still going to be alone."

"You know what I mean," I said quietly. "If you're not going to feel safe there, we'll go to a tourist court."

Darcy shook her head. "No. If they're looking for us, for that film, that's the kind of place they'd go to first. They'd check every place on the highway, looking for the Jaguar."

"Darcy, they have no idea what highway we're even on. They . . ."

"Jack, if you were the killer or killers, and you wanted to get that film, what would you do?"

I thought for a moment. "I'd stake out the hotel, the rooming house, your house, anyplace we might turn up; but, mostly, I'd just wait to collect it all at the rooming house, as usual. Look Love, they know our story about the murder at the hotel won't be believed. They've seen to that, buried the bodies, have an alibi with Robert Briggs and so on. But, most of all, they think that this film originated with me instead of Art. It would never occur to them in a hundred years that I'd be so insane as to turn it in to the authorities. They'll just wait till I go home and deal with me there. They've eliminated their competition. Who am I going to sell the stuff to but them? They're the only game in town."

"Jack, we don't really know *anything*." Darcy burst out. "We have no idea what those people are thinking. We have no idea who they think you are. They know you have that film, and they want it badly. We don't even know what's on the bloody film that's so important. They just killed a person, maybe two, to get it. *That's* what we know and that's *all* we know. We won't be out of danger until we turn this film over to the FBI, and the killers *know* we've turned it over to the FBI."

For some reason, a picture of poor old Bingham Sizemore flashed in my mind. 'I want to go to the White House' he'd said, but I wouldn't take him there. Nobody would take him there. No one would take him seriously.

"Darcy?" I said. "Why don't you give Linda a call? Find out if she saw Art on Saturday night."

She looked at me with alarm. "Why?"

"I'm just very curious to know if anything happened at the rooming house or with Art after the can was discovered missing from my room."

"Jack, Art wouldn't tell Linda anything about all that, especially if something had happened."

"She'd know if he broke his date with her."

Darcy got out of the car immediately and walked quickly to the phone booth. When Linda came on the line, there were a few muted words and then squealing and pealing of the type that had occurred with Sylvia Harris.

"Linda says congratulations and she loves you like a brother," Darcy shouted from the little kiosk.

I grinned and held up both hands, clasped together in a victory wave.

They chattered on excitedly and with characteristic enthusiasm for five minutes. I kept overhearing snatches of the conversation which mostly had to do with when I had proposed and how and all that, and, of course, the Christmas wedding. I began to feel vaguely like the Christmas turkey.

Finally, I called to Darcy and, when she turned, pointed to my wristwatch. She nodded, and they both apparently calmed down and talked quietly for another minute. When Darcy came back to the car, she was smiling and shaking her head.

"What?" I asked.

"Art took her out to an evening of dinner and dancing."

"No kidding," I said. "And that's it?"

"That's it," said Darcy, "except that he asked her about where we had gone."

I scoffed. "Like he didn't know."

"Linda doesn't think he had a clue, and he didn't exactly ask her if she knew just so he'd know the place. It wasn't like that. He just asked because he couldn't imagine that I hadn't told her before we left. When he found out that Linda really didn't know, it became sort of a game, a parody of a secret romantic scenario. Like the place you'd drag me off to for our assignation would be a truck stop motor court with blinking neon signs and pink plaster flamingoes on the lawn. The sign would say Kitty's Kozy Kabins and things like, Taxi Drivers Welcome, and the place would have a row of half-buried truck tires painted white to form a border around each individual love nest. Then they both laughed at that and Linda said *The Greenbriar* or *The Homestead* were more your style. And Art made some crack about showing up at The Homestead wearing a Yellow Cab uniform, and that was it."

"So Art not only didn't have a clue, he didn't particularly care where we were?"

"That's what Linda thought. They both just joked about it and hoped we'd have a good time."

"Yeah. He hopes I have a good time while he plants his dirty secrets in my bureau drawer. So let's just think about something here for a minute. Art had changed the can and planted the microfilm before I got back to the room on Friday afternoon. We leave for the weekend and Art leaves for work? No. It just couldn't have happened that way.

"The blonde would have come in as usual about midnight, discovered the can was gone and that would have been that. We would never have met Robert. Nobody would have showed up at the hotel. Nothing would have happened until I got back to my room on Sunday night. So, obviously, it couldn't have been like that.

"Art must have checked my room *again* after I left, because I had just told him that we were going away for the weekend, and he suspected that I might take the Ronsonol with me like the last time, which I did. He checked his phone tap, probably a voice operated tape recorder in the hall closet, found where we were going and informed the Vamp. She must have sent Robert to intercept us when we checked in at nine o'clock or whatever it was.

"Art knew exactly where we were all weekend, Love. He joked with Linda and made references to *The Greenbriar*, but it was *The Shorebird* that he was thinking of. The only thing he doesn't have a clue about, is that we know *his* part in all this. He still thinks he's squeaky clean. I'll bet he doesn't even know about the woman being killed."

Darcy listened thoughtfully, then took one of my aching hands in hers and gently kissed it.

"Jack, love, Why didn't Art simply wait until we got back tonight to make the switch? We didn't know it was his can. We would have come right back home and the Vamp could have picked it up tonight for all Art knew. What was so important that he had to upset the apple cart and send that woman after you. Why was the Russian willing to risk getting caught at the hotel for murdering her. What's so important and urgent on that microfilm that it can't wait even two days?"

"Who knows? State secrets? War plans? God, Darcy, I don't know. Something that's happening now? Some diplomatic crisis? Cuba. Berlin. Could be anything."

"Jack, I'm just saying that if it's so important that it can't keep for two days when they would be almost certain of getting it just by waiting, they'll kill us right away to get it now. Tonight. It's not a matter of them thinking you're Art. They won't care if you are or not. You're just the guy who has what they want. It's not a matter of them waiting back at the rooming house to resume business as usual. This thing is urgent for them. They're going to come after us for it. Right now. I can feel it. We need to be someplace hidden, someplace safe until it gets light in the morning."

"The cabin," I said.

Darcy nodded. "The cabin." She pressed the starter button and the Jaguar roared to life.

The evening light was fading when we pulled in front of the chained-off trail. I noticed that a second lock had been fastened to the post on the opposite end of the chain and it carried the stamp of the county sheriff. Two official-looking

NO TRESPASSING
Sheriff's Department

signs hung from the chain on metal staples.

"Sheriff has his own key, now," said Darcy. "I guess that's good. It probably means that he occasionally drives in to the cabin and looks around."

"It probably means, Love, that Deputy Otis Perkins has a nice cool place to sleep on sunny afternoons."

I unlocked the chain and waved her through, then pulled it taut around the hickory snag and snapped the padlock. Darcy drove the Jaguar just out of sight from the county road, up and off the trail into a clump of laurel and quickly cut the engine. I followed a short way behind. The car was very difficult to see from only a few yards distance.

We traveled light with nothing but the paper bag of first aid equipment and a second, half melted bag of ice, knowing that the cabin was stocked with some canned goods and several gallon jugs of water for emergency use.

It was still just light enough to make out the lock on the big sliding doors when we came up the steps and onto the deck. In another ten minutes, the Coleman stove and lanterns were hissing reassuringly, and pork and beans larded with little chunks of Vienna sausage bubbled merrily in the pot.

While dinner was heating, Darcy cleaned and re-bandaged my hands. The swelling seemed to be under control and the massive throbbing had subsided to the level of a low ragged idle. They were sore as hell to the touch.

We broke out the air mattresses and blankets and zipped the sleeping bags together to form a sort of wrap over, robe-like affair out on the front deck. I found one of the evil looking brush hooks and laid it within easy reach.

Darcy took the pot off the Coleman, set it on a hot-plate in the middle of the bed and fed both of us using a big serving spoon. When we had finished, she took it away, poured some water into the pot and extinguished the two lanterns. She lay down beside me, and we kissed and held each other gently. In about thirty seconds, we were both fast asleep.

Darcy moved violently against me, and we both cried out at the same time. I jerked upright, staring. Blinding light everywhere. I tried to shield my eyes with my arm. Darcy was screaming my name, and I frantically reached out for her.

A voice cut through the blinding whiteness.

"Silence! If you make the slightest move, you will be shot! You are in no danger if you follow orders." The disembodied voice came from beyond the white light. Darcy shrieked again and moved against me.

"Who is it?" I shouted.

"You will be silent! You will remain perfectly still, or I will shoot you. Do you understand? I will not say this a third time. You are in no danger if you do exactly as I tell you." The voice stopped for a moment and the only sound in the room was our own frightened breathing. "You will not speak. You will listen. Do you understand this?"

I put my hand in front of my face to shield my eyes from the blinding light and nodded my head.

We lay there, totally exposed, not daring to move. We could hear footsteps around us but the voice was silent. I heard a scraping noise beside me on the deck and then realized that someone had slid the brush hook out away from the bed.

I could hear the sound of clothing being moved and loose change jingle in the pockets of my discarded shorts. I knew they had found it. There was the quick tearing of paper, then the false bottom of the

Ronsonol can popping off with a soft sucking sound. The voice made a tired, exasperated sigh.

"Mr. Norton, please, this game of hide-and-seek is quite unnecessary, as you surely know. Where is it, please?"

"What happens to us when I give it to you?"

There was a note of surprise in the voice. "Happens to you? Nothing happens to you. You will continue as before."

"Continue? Continue what?"

"Come now, Mr. Norton. As you know, we have already wasted a great deal of time. The woman, Gregovnia, will come to you no more. Your arrangement was with her alone. We understand that. Now, she has been replaced. That is all."

The voice paused, then continued. "It does not look as if you have been particularly inconvenienced by her absence."

It had been too hot for the sleeping bag robe. Darcy squeezed herself as close to me as possible on the open bed.

There was an audible smirk from somewhere in the room as the voice resumed. "Please, you will continue as before. It is quite simple, yes? We belong to the same club, do we not? Or perhaps we have been misinformed?"

"It's in a Band-Aid can under the front steps of the deck," I said, quickly.

The voice spoke to someone in a hoarse whisper and the light dimmed a bit. Footsteps sounded along the deck to the front steps. Then there was silence.

Darcy and I lay completely still, our arms tightly around each other, my left arm and hand shielding our eyes from the worst of the light. A minute ticked by, then two. The sound of footsteps returning.

The voice spoke: "Thank you, Mr. Norton. You will be contacted. We will need a great deal from you in the next weeks, you understand?"

I nodded, squinting into the light.

Suddenly, there was a double click; and we were left blinking in pitch darkness. The sounds of footsteps receded along the deck and were gone. We lay there, not moving, holding each other tightly. Then soft weeping and the uncontrollable trembling began.

CHAPTER TWENTY-TWO

We lay trembling in the darkness, holding each other tightly, and Darcy began to cry. I had seen Darcy break into tears several times recently when some piece of shocking news was revealed to her; but never had I heard her break down and pour out the wracking sobs of the heart broken, the terrified and the hopeless. I reached down and covered us with the sleeping bag robe and held and rocked her for a long, long time in the blackness.

At some point during the endless night, she put her hand on my lips. "Jack?"

"Yes, Love?"

"I don't want us ever to see those people again. I want it to end. I want them out of our life forever."

I kissed the palm of her hand and nodded, vigorously. "I've just quit the spy business. Whatever Art does with them is his own affair. I'll have no further part in it."

She swallowed hard. "No police. No FBI. No climbing into other people's windows. No microfilm. Okay."

"Okay," I said. "No nothing. For me, it's over."

"What about the 'drop' in your room?"

"As long as they don't come in and bother me when I'm at home, I just don't care."

We finally drifted off to a troubled sleep and awoke almost immediately as the sun peeked over the distant ridges and lit up the deck and cabin.

We visited the outhouse and went down to the creek for a quick bath before packing everything back into the long wall bench box and locking the cabin doors. I found the Ronsonol can sitting upright in the middle of the floor about ten feet away from where our mattress had lain and quickly stuffed it into my pocket without saying anything to Darcy.

The hike back to the road took the usual forty-five minutes, and we were tremendously relieved to see that the Jaguar was waiting, apparently undisturbed. About sixty seconds later, we were on the pavement and didn't stop until we entered the little village four miles down the county road. I called the dispatcher and offered the car trouble excuse.

"Yew need to do sumpin' 'bout that car, 41. I thought them German wondercars wasn't sposed to break down."

"It breaks down about the same as a Ford. Just costs less to fix, is all."

"Yeah? Well, 41, if I wuz you, I'd git it fixed on my own time. Them long weekends ain't lookin' too good. Neil was asking 'bout you the other day."

At the mention of Neil, I felt as if I'd been struck with a curare dart. After a long moment of silence, I stammered "Well, thanks, Sarge. I appreciate you telling me. I'll make sure this is the last time."

"Awright, 41." and he hung up without another word.

'Get it fixed on my own time?' It was *all* on my own time. It wasn't as if I was taking paid leave to get my car fixed. When I didn't work, I didn't get paid.

I left the phone booth and ranted a bit to Darcy about the niggardly attitude of the Arlington Yellow Cab Company wanting me to get my car fixed at night or on weekends until she quietly pointed out that my car was practically new and there wasn't anything wrong with it anyway.

We decided to return home by way of Annapolis and The Shorebird. A heady sense of invulnerability had suffused us in a weird way since the midnight visit by the KGB or whoever they were. Lying there naked on the deck floor, trembling with anger and fear, we had simply resolved that we were no longer a part of this thing. The strange foreigners, the secret messages, Art and his fellow spies, even the killing at the hotel which apparently no one but us believed had even occurred, all that was behind us now. We were no longer a part of it, and, knowing that, we had given ourselves a sense of detached omnipotence. The phrase 'living in a fool's paradise' didn't even cross my mind at the time.

We pulled onto the seashell drive just before eleven a.m. feeling perfectly at ease. Opting to skip a potential scene at the front desk with Mr. Henderson, we made straight for the bank of elevators and were opening the door to **324** in about two minutes. The bed had been made. Fresh towels were in the bathroom. All our things neatly placed in an orderly row in the little alcove. We walked around the room and looked through our bags. There was no evidence that anyone other than Housekeeping had been in the place.

There was no reason to linger. We closed up the suitcases and called the front desk. In about ten minutes, the bell captain knocked and silently shuffled into the room pushing his heavy iron baggage cart.

We crossed the lobby to the front desk, dreading a confrontation with Mr. Henderson, only to find a small, white haired gentleman who smiled and asked if he could be of assistance.

"Mr. and Mrs. Norton. Checking out of **324**," I said.

At the mention of my name, he paused and looked strangely at us, then walked over to a bank of file cards, drew out the one for **324**, and began making out our bill.

As I was writing the check, I said, "Oh, I wonder if you could tell me if Robert Briggs has come in yet this morning?"

He looked at both Darcy and me and said very evenly, "Yes, Mr. Norton. I am Robert Briggs. How can I help you?"

We both turned red and I couldn't quite get my breath for a moment. Then I smiled and said, "I'm awfully sorry about what happened yesterday, Mr. Briggs. I was celebrating a little too hard and I mistook someone else for you. I don't quite know how it happened."

Robert nodded and laughed along with me to ease the tension and said that there had been no problem, and that I certainly shouldn't feel that I needed to apologize. We then thanked each other three or four times, and he hoped we would return often to The Shorebird. By this time, the bell captain had come back to the desk with my car keys. I tipped him and we headed for the door.

It was early afternoon when we finally pulled up in front of the Harrises's place on Chesterfield Street. Sylvia Harris met us at the door with all the joy and enthusiasm of a mother receiving what was rightfully hers. For the next two hours, we sat in the big living room and recounted a highly edited version of our weekend adventures and the talk centered on the upcoming wedding and where and what kind and who would be invited. Since last evening, Sylvia had been on the phone to Linda and Darcy's other friends, family members and relatives of all dimensions and descriptions. Now, celebratory drinks were served, and a call to my mother was placed with all the attendant hullabaloo that went with it. She and Sylvia took thirty or forty minutes, to the delight of AT&T, to become acquainted; and, after that, there were more calls to relatives and plans for showers and receptions.

Both Darcy and her mother conducted a non-stop telephone marathon for most of the afternoon; and, when I had the opportunity, I took Darcy aside and said that I needed to get over to my room for a while to change and clean up. Dinner at the Harrises was the order of the evening, and she let me go without protest, with the idea of having me back in an hour.

I took the VW which had been parked in front of the house since Friday and worked my way across town in the afternoon rush. It was just after five p.m. when I found a parking place on O Street and carried my bags to **1435**.

My room was apparently as I had left it. The door to Art's was open. Saxophone music rolled out into the hall. I removed the can of Ronsonol from my duffel and went directly next door.

"Jack! How was the weekend?" Art was as jovial and disarming as always. "Manage to find a hiding place that was sufficiently anonymous?" He was half dressed for work and in the process of buttoning his shirt.

I took the can, still in two pieces, and tossed it on his bed. He was watching through the mirror with his back to me and heard and saw the object land on the tightly spread blanket.

"What's that?" His stare never left the mirror.

"If you ever put this fucking thing in my room again or use my room for a 'drop' in any way whatsoever, I'll take whatever you leave and give it to the FBI. Do you understand that, Art? It's very clear and very simple. I don't want to talk to you. I don't want to hear what you have to say. I don't need excuses or bullshit. I simply need to know if you understand me."

He was completely silent for a long moment. As I was speaking, his fingers had stopped to linger absently at his top shirt button. "I understand," he said.

"Good." I turned, went back to my room and closed the door. I sat in the semi-darkness for half an hour waiting for him to leave. When I finally heard the familiar clump-clump-clump and the close of the street door, I got up and went to the bathroom.

Dinner at the Harrises was a happy affair in which we covered all topics having to do with Darcy and Jack from six or seven generations before they had been born to a time in the future when their grandchildren might be contemplating retirement.

I had not bothered to reveal much, in particular, to the Harris family concerning my own background, preferring to let them draw any inferences they liked based on their day-to-day observations. Now, however, I sensed a metamorphosis occurring at the dinner table. Questions concerning all things Norton which had been, heretofore, of merely passing curiosity, were examined and debated with a fervor that in ages past had been reserved only for the search for the source of the Nile or the question of Original Sin.

I played my part well by supplying endless streams of vignettes ranging from amusing childhood anecdotes to old family stories and national legends in which some ancestor or other had enjoyed a peripheral role. The Harrises matched these, story for story, until with evident relief, the entire assemblage seemed comfortably assured that we all belonged to the same tribe.

Having satisfied themselves that their daughter was not marrying beneath her, Charles and Sylvia aimed a series of gentle queries in the direction of future plans, further education, a life's work and that sort of thing. By the time we had finished dessert, introductions to faculty members in the history departments of Princeton and Yale had been mentioned by Charles, and intentions to promptly acquire graduate school catalogues had been promised by me.

It was almost midnight when congratulatory good-byes were said, and heart-felt kisses and handshakes were administered. Darcy and I went out and sat in my car before I left for the rooming house.

I told her what I had done with Art.

"And that's all he said? 'I understand.'"

"That was it. Not another peep. No apology. No lies. No explanation. Nada."

Darcy was plainly worried. She shook her head. "I don't understand. "What's going to happen now? What if that man comes to your room looking for more microfilm?"

"He won't find it. I'll leave a note in my drawer saying that the source has permanently dried up. What can he do? He's counting on a willing participant, not someone who has to be forced or threatened. He thinks we're on the same side."

We said our own good-byes taking more time and with rather more passion than was shown with the elder Harrises.

The first in a series of August storms had rolled into the Washington metropolitan area during the early evening. Now thunder rumbled in the distance, and a steady rain began to fall just as Darcy shut the door to the VW and I pulled out, bound for Georgetown and 1435 O St.

By the time I found my usual parking spot about half a block from the rooming house, the rain was coming down in torrents. I slammed the door locked and ran the fifty yards or so, splashing along the darkened sidewalk through inch-deep puddles, and was thoroughly soaked by the time I bounded up the steps and managed to unlock the street door. There was no sign of activity in the building. I immediately checked the top bureau drawer.

The note I had left was still sitting atop the carton of Winstons addressed To Whom It May Concern. I unfolded it and read the words for the tenth time since writing them that afternoon. **There will be no more information. The source has completely dried up as a result of occurrences of the past weekend**.

I replaced the note and closed the drawer. My wet clothes were quickly thrown atop the desk chair. I toweled off in the bathroom, set the bar against the door and was asleep in five minutes.

For the next three days, it rained pretty much off and on continually. This was considered a great boon by the cabbies, as business essentially doubled, though with most of the trips of very short duration with low profits and meager tips. The pace was hectic and calls were backed up at Arlington Yellow Cab. For the first time since I had started driving, I did not spend a single moment sitting on a cab stand blissfully reading *Rise and Fall*.

Each night when I returned to the room, I approached the bureau drawer with an anxiety level just under hysterical, but the note remained undisturbed. As far as I could determine, no one had attempted to enter my room.

There was no indication of Art Baldwin either. I had not laid eyes on him since our confrontation on Monday night. Darcy and I ruminated over the probability of his immanent withdrawal. Had I been in his shoes, I should have packed up and found new digs; but his room remained locked and silent and the name on the mailbox was still in place.

Darcy and I began to receive a host of invitations to parties and dinners. With the notable exception of Miss Withersby, these were all friends of Darcy's, some of whom I knew slightly, and some of whom had seemed to come out of the woodwork as soon as word of her betrothal had spread.

The betrothal had also changed my life in a number of other ways besides a blossoming social life. There were applications to various graduate schools to be completed. In the happy event that any of these august academic institutions were willing to accept me as a student, short term living accommodations in the Washington area, which didn't require a year's lease, had to be secured. Meanwhile, of course, plans for the wedding in December went forward on a twenty-four hour basis. As might have been expected, Darcy and her mother were only too eager to attend to the lion's share of these arduous duties, and I was only too glad to let them.

Two or three times a week, the voice of the dispatcher would come growling over the cab radio to the effect that my 'wife' had phoned and wanted me to call home immediately. I made lame attempts to correct this misidentification the first few times it happened. The dispatcher, however, seemed to have solidly formed some bizarre image of me as a young, hen-pecked husband. He was so enamored of this thought that I automatically fell into the role in hopes of currying favor and creating a sort of bond between us. Such a bond had been utterly impossible so long as I was perceived merely as a rich, feckless college boy, whose frivolous summer lark snatched bread from the mouths of honest working men. With my engagement or 'marriage' to Darcy, my status had changed from playboy to working stiff, doing what I could to put that same bread on my new family's table. Different kettle of fish altogether.

These urgent phone calls from Darcy were always to describe the 'cutest little apartment' that was only five minutes from Chesterfield Street and rented for only $120.00/month and which I simply had to come and see. Darcy and Sylvia usually arranged to go and see these little gems at 4:00 pm, or just about an hour or so before I normally finished my shift.

Any hope of a bond with the dispatcher was severely deflated by these requests to leave work early; and since I didn't relish the prospects of starting my forthcoming marriage as an unemployment statistic, I generally declined and made arrangements to view the place at a more convenient hour.

On a late afternoon in September, as I was rushing to comply with one of Darcy's apartment-viewing requests, I had just showered and changed and was charging out the front door when I met Art Baldwin coming up the front steps.

I was, by this time, grudgingly prepared to smile and say hello, since the issue between us had apparently receded into the background or, at least, had been sufficiently buried by the frenetic activity preceding a marriage to Darcy Harris to convey the *impression* of having receded. I opened my mouth and started to speak. Art fixed his eyes on the street door and walked right past me as if I hadn't existed.

Fine, I thought. That's just fine and dandy. Turd.

During the next few weeks, we saw each other twice in the hallway as we were plying back and forth to the bathroom. As far as Art was concerned, I might as well have been a ghost.

The note in my bureau drawer remained undisturbed; and, in time, another can of Ronsonol was added to the detritus. Eventually, the message was buried under a collection of mismatched socks, underwear and loose condoms. I gradually thought less and less of the great spy mystery and even fantasies of Sidney Reilly shrank to a vague memory. The nervous anxiety that had, for so long, accompanied my evening arrivals at the rooming house began to dissipate and finally went away.

The image of the dead girl, however, did not go away. On late evenings when I was driving home alone I found myself thinking of her, lying on her back with staring eyes and open mouth. Once, when a light shone from beneath Art's door, I lay awake half the night listening against our common wall for signs of activity. Wondering who, if anyone, had taken her place. But nothing ever came of it, and the sounds of clip-clip-clip were no longer heard in the darkened corridor of Withersby Hall.

Miss Withersby, herself, was thrilled and enchanted by news of the impending nuptials. She created a minor debacle by secretly calling the Dean of the Washington Cathedral and seeking his consent to stage the ceremony in that imposing edifice. This act of kindness and generosity precipitated a flurry of embarrassing phone calls, awkward apologies, hurt feelings, and the public confession that neither of us was Episcopalian. This last, to Miss Withersby's mind, was not a relevant condition. The Presbyterian creed, being also that of the Church of Scotland was, at least for her, close enough.

Fall came early that year. All of Georgetown was cosseted in rich shades of gold and red and brown. The rows of maples along O Street were a brilliant yellow and, for the first time since I had arrived, the nights were downright chilly. A jacket was needed upon starting out to work each morning.

Darcy and I had managed to put about three thousand miles on the Jaguar throughout the summer and even by the most conservative standards of Miss Withersby's late father, the car had been properly broken in. The birthday of her grand-niece was but three days off; and, before returning the magnificent beast to its rightful owner, we decided on a last fling along the Blue Ridge Parkway while the foliage was still in full glory. We packed Sylvia's picnic hamper which had come from Abercrombie & Fitch at about the same time that Darcy and I were born. This wicker contraption was equipped with vacuum flasks, leather straps for this and that, collapsible silver cups and enough plates, cutlery and flatware to capture the complete attention of six rich sybarites for an entire day. We filled it with wine, cheese, vichyssoise, deviled eggs, stuffed grape leaves, and wonderful little tongue sandwiches that Darcy had stayed up past midnight to prepare the evening before.

It was a perfect fall afternoon, sunny, with the temperature in the mid-sixties. We put the top down and motored sedately through a continuous blaze of color. The speed limit on the Parkway was only 45 mph, and we were content to idle along in the Jaguar in a rolling line of light traffic, all of which, like ourselves, had come for the dazzling foliage.

Eventually, we spotted a grassy knoll high above the roadway. We pulled over and climbed the thirty feet or so of steep bank to discover a convenient picnic spot with brilliantly splendid vistas equal to any of the crowded Scenic View areas which dotted the Parkway. We spread an ancient Hudson's Bay blanket on the grass, kicked off our shoes and laid into the picnic hamper, starting with the cold *creme de vichyssoise* and working our way slowly through the other delectables.

Two days before, I had received an extremely polite, albeit a somewhat circumspect, letter from the Princeton office of admissions which was enclosed with their graduate school catalogue. This had buoyed our hopes and precipitated endless speculation as we began to feel, for the first time, that acceptance into graduate school and the subsequent move to Princeton the following year might actually become a reality.

Darcy thought automatically in enormous, wonderful, enthusiastic dreams. She wanted me to be a world famous professor who would pen great volumes of American History. She wanted to live in a big house surrounded by beautiful gardens and acres of lawns and woods. She wanted to create the perfect home. She wanted us to have five children. She wanted me to stay with her all the time and never leave.

I grinned. "If I stay with you all the time and never leave, I won't get to be a famous professor. Nobody will hire a teacher who doesn't come to class."

"You could show up on occasional Wednesday afternoons to give seminars." She twinkled with a new thought. "You could be like Nero Wolfe and never leave your brownstone mansion. We could just stay in bed all day long."

"Nero Wolfe is a big fat detective, not a handsome young professor; and I've given up the detective business, remember?"

Darcy immediately dropped the teasing banter. "What do you suppose Art is doing now that his woman friend is dead?"

"You know what interesting and detailed conversations he and I have enjoyed the last few times we happened to bump into each other."

"I know, but do you think he's still slipping microfilm to those people?"

I nodded. "I suppose he is. You don't just stop doing it because something happens or you get bored. The people who do that sort of thing believe in the cause. They keep doing it all their lives or until they're caught."

"How do you know that? About Art, I mean."

"The usual thing. Because he's a true believer. Because Marxism is a religion for him. Because of guilt about his family's money. It's nothing new. I mean, look at all the people your parents know who were communists in the thirties, before they received a much needed dose of reality by Stalin's cozying up to Hitler. Now, they're all highly respected academics, journalists, government leaders. I don't think they're so different from Art."

"But you haven't talked to him about any of that?"

"Of course not. He knows I'm too conservative. We always kept to the safe subjects: cars, boats and women."

Darcy grinned her sly little smile. "Your favorite subjects, but not in that order."

"Boats, cars and women," I corrected and was immediately hit on the cheek with a dollop of filling from one of the delicious deviled eggs.

The high intellectual plane of our discussion abruptly halted amid a mad scramble for more deviled eggs. In an instant, a rolling, grappling food-squashing contest ensued, peals of laughter being gradually suffused with moans of pleasure as we set about removing egg from each other's faces delicately using only our lips and tongues.

Overhead, enormous white cumulus balls had been steadily coalescing for most of the afternoon. Now a solid bank of fluffy clouds rose high above the mountains and a pale gray veil gradually darkened the brilliant azure blue. The wind picked up as the temperature dropped and, in the far distance, thunder rumbled ominously. The first few quarter-sized drops had wet the white linen table cloth when we pried ourselves apart and rapidly began our retreat down the hill to the still-open Jaguar. We stowed our gear, quickly raised the top and were on our way. The rain caught us in earnest before we had traveled a mile and stayed with us all the way back to Washington.

An elderly couple, cousins of Sylvia, who were considered by the family to be fairly important, were scheduled to come for dinner that evening. I left Darcy and the Jaguar and took the VW back over to Georgetown to shower and change into my ubiquitous travel suit that I might gain much favor in their eyes.

The storm had maintained its ferocity. With the glare from the streetlamps and headlights from other cars blinding me, I had to circle the block at O Street before I found a spot that I had missed on the first go-around. As I backed into the tight little space, a tall figure on crutches and a cast on one foot hobbled across the street in front of my headlight beams and came pumping fast along the sidewalk to my passenger door. Art Baldwin.

He rapped hard on the window. In the downpour, I leaned over and unlocked the door without thinking. He opened it wide and tossed in his crutches. I said nothing as he awkwardly levered himself into the little car. He slammed the door and brushed the water from his face.

"Jack, I really need your help," he said.

CHAPTER TWENTY-THREE

"Well!" I said. "It hobbles. It jumps into my car. It talks. It even asks for help. And here, all this time, I thought I was being 'cut'. Isn't that what you and your friends call it, Art, when you decide somebody you know doesn't exist anymore? Being cut?"

Art shut his eyes tightly and shook his head. "Oh hell, Jack, listen . . . ."

"I listened before, Art. I listened to everything you had to say. We both did a lot of listening to each other." I slowly shook my head. "I even thought you were my friend. I certainly treated you like a friend, and then I find out that all along and right from the start you've been treating me like a piece of shit." The words brought the anger roiling to the surface and I laid into him with a vengeance.

"Because of what you did, Darcy and I have been put through hell. We were almost killed. You're an amoral, unprincipled son of a bitch. Just get the hell out of my car," I shouted.

"Jack, I know what you think of me, and . . . ."

"Good! Now, get out." I reached across him and opened the passenger door.

Art grabbed my arm and slammed the door shut. "Will you just wait a fucking minute?" He looked frantically up and down the rainswept street. "We can't sit here in the car like this. I'll explain everything, but we have to get out of here right now, Jack. I'm not kidding."

"What the hell are you talking about?"

"There are people after me!" He screamed.

I didn't say anything and Art sat trembling, staring at the floor of the car.

I shook my head. "No dice, Art. Not this time. If somebody's after you, just get out of my car and go your own way. I don't want anybody after *me*, ever again."

He breathed a long sigh and inhaled deeply. "Jack, there is no time right now. There's something extremely urgent that I have to do. Now. Tonight. I'll explain it later."

"I have something extremely urgent to do tonight, too," I said. "If you're going to sit here in my car, just lock up when you leave." I turned off the ignition and killed the wipers and headlights and started to open the door. Art swiveled quickly in his seat, and I felt a sudden sharp jolt in my right rib cage.

I couldn't really see his face in the darkness, but the tone of his voice changed instantly. "I'll shoot you right here. I'm deadly serious. Start the engine and let's get the hell out of here."

"Do you have a gun? I squawked. What the hell *is* that?" The hard object prodded me again as I heard the signature click of a pistol hammer being pulled back and cocked.

"Goddammit! What the hell are you doing?" I flung myself involuntarily back against the door trying to get away from the thing. "Shit! Art! Watch it! Point that away from me! I'll listen to you! Just point that thing at the floor!"

Since childhood I had been carefully trained in the safe handling of pistols and sporting weapons. I had enjoyed shooting and hunting all my life and had never come even remotely close to having an accident, because I treated loaded guns with a respect essentially equal to that accorded the Almighty. I regarded a loaded and cocked pistol inside a car with the same sheer terror as a land mine or a bottle of nitroglycerin.

"Drive. Right now." He pushed the pistol barrel into my ribs.

I tried hard to speak calmly. "Art. I'll drive. But point that thing some other direction. I just can't function this way." I felt the pressure of the gun barrel ease, and Art's hand moved back toward his lap. "Is the safety on?"

"I'll worry about the bloody safety. You just drive. I mean it. Now!" I twisted the key, pulled the lights and catapulted out of the narrow slot. The windshield was a translucent mass of running water. Art reached over and pulled the wiper switch.

"Where?" I said, angrily.

"Head for P Street, up around 19th or 20th."

We came onto Wisconsin and ran the block up to P before making a right turn toward the city. Traffic was heavy for a stormy Sunday evening. We pounded along with visibility only to the fuzzy ends of the VW's low beams, splashing through puddles and little lakes while trying to weave in and out of a moving phalanx of heavy American cars.

We didn't speak for the first two or three blocks. When we passed some buildings belonging to George Washington University, Art said, "Turn right in the next alley way."

I did as I was ordered, and we rode between two large buildings sending up spouts of water on both sides of the car. Art gestured and we slowed just in front of a steel entry door which fronted onto the alleyway. Beside the door was a heavy drain pipe which descended from the roof gutter system.

Art rolled down his window and aimed a small flashlight beam at the downspout. For perhaps two seconds he seemed to be searching up and down the pipe. Suddenly, he doused the light and furiously cranked up the window.

"Go! Go! Go!" He shouted.

I hit the gas, expecting a hail of bullets through the back window, and we shot on down the flooded alley and out onto 21st St.

"Where?" I said.

"Take Massachusetts, go north."

We rounded the corner in front of the Fairfax Hotel with the traffic light showing green and, in less than a minute, had pretty much submerged ourselves in the flow of traffic along Embassy Row.

Art was highly agitated. He glanced constantly over his shoulder, peering into the shiny darkness and the surrounding blaze of anonymous headlights. He watched the cars in front of us and never stopped moving and jerking about when we came to a halt at a red light.

You couldn't really see anything more than shiny black shapes and glistening headlight beams. I could hardly see well enough to drive.

"Nobody can see us, Art. We'll be lucky not to have an accident. Why don't you calm down and put that pistol away?"

His voice carried a note of fatalism that belied his frenetic behavior. "Just drive. All you need to do right now is drive." He chuckled wearily. "Feel up to an evening's sail, Jack?"

"A sail? Jesus Christ, Art, people are expecting me to show up. I have a dinner engagement with my future in-laws. I need to call Darcy,

239

tell her I'll be a few minutes late. I *cannot* drive you all over town tonight. You said we were just going to talk."

"That's right. Talk. We'll just sit on the boat and talk."

By now we were almost up to Chevy Chase and Art waved his hand at an ESSO sign. "Pull over there. There's a phone on the other side."

We drove onto the wide concrete slab of the service station, brilliantly lit in the driving downpour with half a dozen overhead arc lights situated on tall poles around the facility. We went past the two phone booths on the far side of the slab and Art made me keep going until we were out of the direct glare of the lights and half-sheltered in the darkness.

I jumped out of the car and Art rolled down the passenger window. "Tell her you'll see her tomorrow."

"Tomorrow? I'll damn well see her tonight."

It's going to be late," he said with the same resigned air. "If you don't want her to worry, tell her you'll see her tomorrow. And Jack, don't do anything stupid. I'm sorry about the gun, okay. I'll deliver you safely back to your Darcy but not just yet."

He may have been sorry about the gun, but if he hadn't had it, I would have pulled him out of the car and beaten him half to death with one of his crutches.

I dialed the number and Sam answered on the third ring.

"Harris residence. This is Sam."

"Sam, it's me. Could you put Darcy on, please?"

Sam was his usual enthusiastic and ebullient self. "Oh, hi, Jack. Sure thing. She's doing something medieval to her face. Just for you." He dropped the phone and I heard him calling Darcy's name.

She was as chipper as always. "What's up, Love? It's turning cold." She laughed. "You're going to freeze to death in that summer suit. We should have gone to Lewis & Thomas Saltz yesterday and gotten you a new one."

I took a breath and spoke quietly into the receiver. "Darcy, I can't come to dinner. I'm with Art, and he's insisting that I drive him someplace tonight. He says it's extremely urgent."

She was silent for a moment. "Where does he want you to take him?"

"I don't know. He said something about going up to the boat and talking."

"Tonight? In this weather? That's insane!"

"I know, but that's what he said. I think he just wants to go somewhere that's snug and private and where he feels safe. I've got to go. I'll be all right. I'll come by as soon as I've gotten rid of him. Love you."

"Jack!"

I heard her whisper, 'love you too,' as I put down the receiver.

I adroitly puddle-jumped from phone booth to Volkswagen and quickly slammed the door shut. In the darkness of the car, Art Baldwin said, "Let's go," and we pulled back out onto the street.

"Turn here," he said, motioning at the next intersection. "Run over Military Road and then on to 16th St. and pick up East-West Highway. We'll get highway 50 from there."

"Art, this is nuts. Let's just pull off on a quiet side street and we'll talk. We don't need to drive all the way to Annapolis."

"I have to make a delivery. Now. Tonight. It won't wait. We're probably being followed right now."

I involuntarily glanced in the rearview at the mass of shining headlights. "Are you crazy? Nobody could follow anyone on a night like this."

We left Massachusetts and were running down a residential side street lined with small apartment buildings. Art pointed at the break in the line of cars along the street. "Pull into that next drive. Quick!"

I pulled into the delivery entrance of an apartment building and braked to a stop.

"What the hell is going on?"

"Kill the engine. We're getting out." I saw him brandish the small black object in his right hand.

"Art, I'm really not dressed for this," I protested, indicating the light windbreaker, which was my only covering.

His voice was a hoarse whisper. "Get out of the fucking car."

We both got out and stood by the front bumper in the black, pouring rain. It was exactly like standing under the shower head at Miss Withersby's after all the hot water had been used up. Cold water plastered my hair and surged right down my back and legs into my Weejuns. I hugged the jacket around me to keep from shivering.

Art snapped on the flashlight and waved it at the car's front bumper. "You'll have to do this, Jack. I think there's something attached to the underside. A small box. You'll have to take the light and look for it." He thrust the flashlight toward me in the driving rain.

"Oh, for Christ's sake, Art. Get under the car? Are you serious? I might as well dive in the river."

"Goddamnit, I can't argue with you. There isn't time." He pushed the light into my hands and waved the pistol. "Get under there."

Recalling Winston Churchill's comment that being shot at concentrates the mind, wonderfully, I reached for the front bumper and swung down onto the concrete driveway. It was running with ice cold water, and my first sensation was of a torrent of wet running past my belt and down into the back of my pants between my buttocks. God damn Art Baldwin!

I poked my head under the nose of the VW, slipped sideways and stared up into the floorpan, streams of muddy crud dripping steadily into my face and open eyes. I squinted up through the cascade of muck and saw it at once: a box the size of a transistor radio was stuck to the metal bottom of the car. A green light on one end was rapidly winking at me.

I reached up and yanked at it. It came away easily in my hand, like pulling a steel ball off a horseshoe magnet.

I rolled out from under the VW and handed the thing up to Art as I struggled to my feet. Without a word, he turned and made three limps to the car door. Before I could get in, he had levered himself into the seat and slammed the door.

When I joined him in the dry cocoon of the VW, he was holding the little box up in his hand, green light blinking.

"Drive!" he said.

I started the car and we drove.

When we got to 15th St., Art simply said, "Turn south."

We ran down the longest street in the District in the pounding rain. The traffic had markedly diminished as it always did during any sort of storm in the Washington area. Snow or rain, the city sort of ground to a stop against any serious challenge from the elements. Now with a heavy fall rainstorm those who didn't have to be abroad on an early Sunday evening elected to stay off the streets, making easier the drive toward the 14th Street Bridge and the Potomac River.

The parking lot at the Watergate Restaurant was about half-full of cars belonging to the hardier souls among the weekend dinner crowd who were not put off by the rain. We cruised through the lot until Art spotted a Volkswagen which looked like the twin to mine and called a halt. He handed me the blinking box.

"Put it under the front end, just where it was on this car."

"What the hell is the matter with your leg, anyhow?"

"Popped an Achilles tendon playing touch football. Now put it under the Goddamn car."

I started to argue; but, in fact, it seemed like a pretty clever idea. "Another casualty of Camelot," I said, and jumped out once again into the maelstrom and planted the thing between the front wheels of an unsuspecting stranger's Beetle. I was as wet as if I *had* been swimming in the river and had begun to chill rapidly.

I ran back to the waiting car and jumped in out of the rain, though there was no longer any part of me that wasn't soaked through. "I've got to get into some dry clothes, Art. I'm freezing."

He began to rapidly twist the little white knob nestled between the front seats. "We'll turn on the heater. You'll be dry as toast by the time we get to the boat."

The poplin windbreaker was wrapped around me like a wet sheet. The shirt beneath just as bad. I wriggled out of them and pulled off my Weejuns and socks and sat there shirtless and barefoot. The puny heater from the little air-cooled engine blew luke warm air on my ankles.

"Now what?" I asked, feeling annoyed, miserable and ridiculous.

"Head north for Annapolis again."

I nodded and put the car in gear.

It struck me then as quite odd that I had not the slightest fear of Art Baldwin. I greatly feared the accidental discharge of the pistol he carried, but not of any harm he might try to inflict on me.

He came across as depressed and morose. He was in his own private hell, and it was with a sense of observing a drama that I sat next to him in the pounding storm and pondered his next move. He didn't seem to know exactly who had put the radio receiver under my car. But I did.

The same people who had been at the hotel. The same people who had been to the cabin. The same people for whom Art had been supplying microfilm. The same people who had invaded the privacy of my room for months. That they had apparently had a disagreement and fallen to squabbling among themselves with one of their own shot dead did not surprise me in the least. That they badly wanted Art's latest message to them on an urgent basis was no surprise either.

The only thing that was puzzling was why contact between Art and themselves now seemed to have taken such a turn for the worse. On the theory that if you don't ask, you won't know, I popped the $64 question.

He nodded wearily, not bothering to be evasive or deny any of it. "All the drops were closed down this afternoon. The one in your room and the two backups, the last of which you saw."

"What do you mean, 'closed down?' You were just shining your light on a downspout."

"It was marked, 'keep off, don't approach.' They've all been compromised."

I had read of such things and had no doubt that John LeCarre had gotten it right, but sitting there hearing Art talk about it brought a new tremor of anxiety to go with all the other tremors that I was beginning to violently experience.

Art looked over at me in the darkness. "Your teeth are chattering." It was simply an observation, or maybe the sound of clack-clack-clack was beginning to annoy him.

"Nuh-no sh-shit."

"I'd let you wear my raincoat, but it's all I have." He said it without humor, as an afterthought.

"Thanks," I said. "don't give it a thought. I'll be warm as toast in about an hour."

We drove on back up never-ending 15th Street timing all the lights at a precise 30 miles per hour, and I pressed on with him.

"So what does it mean that they've all been compromised? Compromised by whom?"

During the last ten minutes or so Art had lapsed into a low state of despondency, his voice monotonal. "The people in my shop. Who did you think?"

"The CIA? The CIA is after you?"

There was no answer.

That thought had never really occurred to me, but when he said it, I felt a surge of elation. The whole thing would be over quickly now. Whatever Art had been passing to the Soviets would be stopped forever. It would all come to an end this night. Darcy and I would be plagued no more by people with guns waking us up as we lay naked in our bed.

I let out a long sigh of relief. "Art, let's drive over to Langley right now and you can give yourself up." The phrase 'come in from the cold' occurred to me, but I immediately banished it.

He laughed a long, hollow, humorless laugh which, toward the end as it ran down sounded almost as if he were weeping. "Jack, old man. You're perfect. You're just perfect. You really have no idea, do you?"

Quick anger flared and I said, "No, Art. I have no idea. Why don't you enlighten me?"

"Do you know what's been happening in Cuba since the Bay of Pigs?"

"Only what I read in the Post."

"That's right," he said. "The Post is full of tantalizing little stories about the buildup of Russian advisors and what else those Russian ships might be bringing into Havana harbor." He leaned over close to my ear, and I wondered exactly where the pistol was. "They're probably going to put missiles on the island, Jack."

"What? What kind of missiles?"

"They're going to do it so that the United States can never again attack them."

"What kind of missiles?" I repeated.

"No one knows. At this point, it's just speculation. Probably intermediate range."

"Intermediate to what?"

"They'd be able to reach most cities in the eastern part of the country."

The transitory quiver of anxiety leapt back into my belly like a bolt of lightning.

"How sure are you about all this?"

"It's a matter of reading history, old man. That's your subject, isn't it? We have missiles in Turkey, England, Germany, all over the world. The Sov's have them installed in their eastern satellites. Cuba is their first western satellite, and it's already been attacked once by the United States. Kennedy has publicly said that Castro will not stand. What would you do if you were in their shoes?"

"The American public won't stand for this." I said, angrily. "Nuclear warheads aimed at us from only 90 miles away? There'd be no warning time at all, no defense. It would be intolerable."

"Intolerable for you, maybe. Not so intolerable for the millions of Cubans who have a chance for a decent life for the first time."

"Decent life? It's a fucking police state. No freedom of the press, no freedom of speech, assembly, right on down the line."

"Those freedoms aren't worth very much, Jack, if you're an ignorant peasant dying of illness and starvation."

"Cut the crap. Nobody on Cuba ever starved to death."

"Jack, *Batista* ran the police state. He was totally corrupt. He stole millions for himself and his family. He worked for the Mafia. That's who *really* ran Cuba. Now, after three years, when the revolution that Castro has given the people is just now starting to pay off, Uncle Sam comes in and launches an invasion and is getting ready to do it again."

"You've bought the whole Marxist line, haven't you?"

"Jack, those people have free education, free medical care, full employment, pride and self respect for the first time and hope for the future in a real country, not just some Mafia-controlled playpen for rich foreigners."

I nodded vigorously. "A Worker's Paradise, eh. Listen Art, I'm not going to debate Marxism with you. We've seen what it always becomes. Russia, China, Korea: all police states of the most brutal and repressive kind. The point is that the U.S. will not permit this little tin pot Stalin to aim nuclear missiles at us. That ought to be crystal clear, even to the Soviets."

"It's going to happen, gradually."

"Isn't that sort of like getting pregnant, gradually?"

"No, Jack. It isn't. People need to talk and to understand what's going on while historical change occurs. The people responsible for the defense of Cuba need to know what the United States government is thinking in response to their build-up."

"That's no mystery. Nobody likes it worth a damn. And we're certainly not going to tolerate having missiles aimed at us."

"I'm not talking about the public discussion. I'm talking about what the administration is saying privately, what the Kennedy brothers are planning to do about things. As long as the Cuban defense people know how each step is likely to be received in Washington, there'll be no sudden fast moves with disastrous consequences for us all."

"But Art, we have diplomatic channels. We talk all the time to the Russians. The Soviet Ambassador is the social lion of Washington."

"Of course we talk to the Russians. It's what we don't talk to them about that our friends in Cuba are most interested in."

"Horseshit! our 'friends in Cuba' are nothing but a Soviet stooge and a bunch of puppets. We're not worrying about a little half-assed Latin American country that's had one dictator after another for the last 400 years being any kind of a threat to us. We happen to be locked in a cold war with the Soviets, in case you've forgotten. The stakes aren't about a bunch of Cubans, Art. The stakes are about world civilization."

"Oh God, Jack. What a speech. Did you hear it at the Rotary Club meeting in the charming little southern village where you grew up? How quaint!"

"Fuck you."

"Oh, fuck me. How delightful. How articulate. Look Jack, you're a decent, intelligent chap. Why don't you educate yourself to what's really going on in the world instead of mouthing dogma you heard as a child?"

"Art, what is really going on right now, it seems to me, is that you're in a shitload of trouble and you've humbled yourself and asked for my help. Is that right? At gunpoint, but you've asked for it."

Art said nothing, and the wipers crawled endlessly across the windshield to the sounds of drumming rain and the liquid hiss of the tires on the glistening street.

CHAPTER TWENTY-FOUR

Nearly 45 minutes had passsed since we reversed our course near the Potomac Tidal Basin. We had traveled back up15th St. and were now out on Route 50 headed for Annapolis. The air in the car was cold and damp, and it was a constant effort just to keep the windows defogged. I was shivering uncontrollably and my feet and upper body felt like fish in an ice chest.

"Art, I've got to have a cup of coffee."

The VW heater produced about as much warm air as Darcy did when she blew gently in my ear. I hadn't eaten since mid-day and I was sitting shirtless and barefoot, wrapped from waist to ankle in sopping wet pants.

"I could use a cheeseburger, too," I said.

"Fine with me," he said, as if arousing from a stupor. First we have to find a drive-in. I think there's one just outside of Bowie, if it's still open in this storm."

The rain had gotten worse, if anything. Usually, rainstorms at this time of year hit with a fury and then settled down to steady rain or drizzle; but this was a big system with high winds coming up from the south, and the main body was a long time in reaching us.

The weather had not, however, caused the Prince George's Drive-in to bow to its ferocity. The big neon sign, plainly visible a half-mile down the highway, swung back and forth with each violent gust of wind as we drove under it and ground to a stop beneath the metal awnings. Three or four cars were parked in a semicircle around the place and lights blazed brightly within.

As I cut the engine, a girl ran out of the building clutching her order pad in one hand while trying desperately to keep her Jackie hair-do covered with the billowing plastic hood of a transparent rain parka. She wore what appeared to be a red highschool marching band uniform, with very short skirt and white tasseled boots. Traveling the few feet from the drive-in to our car required a genuinely majorette effort with extraordinary jumps, steps and little hops reminiscent of the gravity-defying skirt of Marilyn Monroe atop a sidewalk grating. I glanced over at Art who was watching the performance as attentively as I.

"Maybe we should order each item individually," I said, smiling. Art didn't respond. I rolled the window half way down, grinned and made the obligitory inane comments about the weather. The girl stood there with one hand on her head, squirming against the gale as the plastic parka and little skirt flapped above her waist. I ordered coffee, fries and a double cheeseburger.

Art said, "Nothing for me."

We sat waiting for the order while Art withdrew more and more. He just sat there staring at the dashboard, not speaking, with an expression of hopeless despair.

"You should at least have some coffee," I said.

He shook his head and said absently, "I'm fine. We need to get moving. Where is that girl?" He rubbed the fogged up windshield and peered toward the lighted restaurant.

The food and drink arrived to an even more virtuoso performance than had the initial entry. I thanked her for her efforts under such conditions, added a quarter to the dollar bill for the food and told her to keep the change.

Art insisted that I eat on the go and we pulled back out onto the highway that was, increasingly, ours alone. The VW was being blown almost from lane to lane by the heavy gusts, and I warmed up my lap with spilled coffee as Art gamely balanced the little cardboard carton of fries and burger on his knees. I strained my eyes ahead, sawing the wheel against surprise gusts of wind and trying to see what couldn't be seen past the beating wipers.

"Shit, Art. This crazy. The damn boat is going to be bouncing like a cork in her slip. We won't even be able to board her."

The figure beside me didn't respond initially, then a moment later: "We'll be all right. Just keep driving."

"Why are we even going to the boat? You said all the drops have been compromised. Why do you have to do anything now? We could just go back to the rooming house. You could call your people."

Your people, I thought. Good God. Now I'm sounding just like one of them. One of whom? Who talks that way? Madison Avenue types. Horseshit artists? Phonies.

Art continued to stare and said nothing.

"Well? What about it? Can we drive over to your office?"

"Shut up, Jack," he said softly. "Just shut the fuck up."

By the time we reached Annapolis and crossed the Severn River bridge, I could hardly see the road in front of me. The little windshield wipers valiantly tried to keep up with the deluge, but they might as well have been operating under water.

We ran down the little winding lane leading to the yacht harbor. Just beyond the street lamps in the parking lot, we could see the horizontal blue and white forms tossing in tempo with the wind and waves.

I figured that the wind must be blowing about 35 knots, with gusts quite a bit higher. The parking lot was mostly deserted except for the few live-aboards whose vehicles hadn't moved since the last time we were there. We drove down the rows of floating wooden walkways which extended for a quarter of a mile up the little creek inlet.

"Which one is yours?" I asked, unable to remember or recognize anything familiar.

"Keep going. It's almost to the end."

We drove quickly past the heaving rows of slips, and I could see the end of the lot coming up. A single car was parked at the far corner. The silhouette of the E-type Jaguar was absolutely unmistakable. Darcy!

I pulled in close to the Jaguar and opened my door. As quick as a striking snake, Art brought the pistol up to my right nipple and pressed hard.

"Don't get any cute ideas about taking off and leaving me sitting here. You wouldn't even get the engine started."

I stared coldly back at him, then opened the door and got out into the driving rain. Art stepped out the other side, retrieved his crutches and hobbled out onto the floating dock to his boat's slip. I was in the Jaguar's cockpit in an instant.

We kissed and held each other in the darkness before Darcy spoke. "Where's your shirt?" She wiped the water off my shoulders. "Jack, you're ringing wet. What happened?"

I put my fingers gently on her lips. "He's been passing American Intelligence about Cuba to the Russians. The CIA is onto him. They're looking for him right now."

Darcy listened, rapidly nodding her head. "I knew something had to be terribly wrong. He's very dangerous. I could feel it when you were on the phone. I can feel it even more right now." She continued to squeegee the water off my head and arms. "Oh, Jack. You're freezing. Where is your shirt? The blanket is still in the trunk."

"I'm all right. I'll be okay when I get dry."

Art was standing on his boat's slip about thirty feet away. He started back toward the parking lot. We watched him as he approached.

"Lets just get out of here now and leave him." Darcy reached for the Jag's ignition key.

I reached over and covered her hand. "Don't. He has a gun."

"What?"

"I think he'll shoot the car, engine or tires, if we try to pull out and leave him."

"I knew it! I knew he had a gun or something. He's going to kill someone, Jack."

Art came around to the passenger side and rapped on the window. I opened the door a crack.

"Check under the rear of the car." He gestured with the pistol and for the first time I could see that it was a Colt .45 government automatic.

"He thinks there may be a bug under the car," I explained to Darcy. "They put one under the VW."

"What kind of bug?" called Darcy, but I had slammed the door and was crouching in the gravel parking lot.

Art produced his pocket flashlight, and I rolled bareback down into the wet slurry of gravel and peered up between the two big chromed mufflers of the Jaguar. There it was. Just like the other one. Same winking green light. I pulled it off and rolled out from under the car.

"Son of a Bitch!" Art roared. He grabbed the thing from me and flung it in a long arc out over the tossing boats. It was immediately swallowed by the rain swept blackness of the harbor. Art looked back down the empty parking lot, squinting into the teeth of the storm. He spun around quickly, yelling into my face. "God damn you! She's led them right here. We have to go *now*. There's nothing else to do."

I shouted straight back at him. "What are you talking about?"

Art pointed the pistol at the tossing sailboat. "We're taking her out right now."

"In this storm?" I yelled. "Hell no!"

"Why do you think I brought you along ?" He giggled insanely. "Because you're my 'friend'? Because we're 'buddies'?" There was another cackle of laughter. "Maybe to get the benefit of your cracker barrel political wisdom?" He chuckled a moment, shaking his head at his private joke. Then his wild eyes searched the heavens and he raised the pistol into the pouring rain as if having an epiphany. "Ah! Ah! I see it now. For your sophisticated wit and intellect! For your astute counsel." He stared straight into my face from no more than a few inches away and continued to giggle.

I was certain then that he'd lost his mind. I thought of grabbing for the pistol. I thought of the lunging clash of our two bodies. I thought of a shattering explosion and a sudden burst of white light. I thought of oblivion. I thought of Darcy. I stared right back at him, not daring to move, trying to be nothing.

The giggles subsided, his face becoming cinched down and mean. He nodded slowly and jabbed the heavy pistol into my chest. He took a deep breath and screamed, "I brought you along, you fucking idiot, because I can't crew the boat with this bad leg!" He held onto his crutches, the gun prodding my chest to emphasize each word. I shut my eyes, hearing only the last part, feeling the sudden rush of salvation.

Somehow, I managed to nod, even smile. "All right," I said. "Okay. I'll help you." Art stood watching me for a moment, then the pressure of the pistol barrel slackened and the gun dropped to his side. He looked away, toward the Jaguar, then out at the tossing sloop. When he spoke, his voice was composed.

"I'm sorry, Jack, about all this." He waved the pistol away toward the parking lot gravel. "Let's just get going before it gets worse."

A sudden noise instantly lost in the roar of the storm, a car door, and Darcy was around the Jaguar and standing beside me, trying to shield me with her billowing raincoat. I put an arm around her and felt the intensity of the storm afresh. I turned back to Art, shaking my head.

"This is just plain fucking crazy, Art. We won't even be able to get out of the estuary."

"We'll motor out with the Seagull. Let's get aboard," he shouted in what seemed to be a more or less rational voice.

I shook my head. "Not enough power. We'll just get blown aground." I decided to push gently against the apparent newly dredged up window of sanity. "Let's all go to a tavern. Have some chowder. Wait a bit till it lets up."

With a quick, sliding motion, he brought the pistol up under my throat and I recoiled as the barrel leaned hard against my adam's apple. Darcy clutched my arm and gave a smothered cry. "I'll keep us from running aground," he nodded. "You just steer the fucking course I give you."

I put my hand up and backed away, nodding my head. Darcy didn't seem to even be breathing. Art's window of sanity, had it ever existed, had splintered and dropped out of frame with the upward thrust of the .45. I tried to speak normally, tried to appeal to the looney without stepping on a land mine. "Art, I'll do what you want but this is stupid. The boat won't take it."

"Bullshit," he spat. "This is no hurricane. She was built for weather like this. Just shut the fuck up and get moving, NOW!" he screamed.

I turned and bent my head down to Darcy who had no idea what was going on.

"He wants to take the boat out, Love. I have to go with him."

She put her hand on my face, and I heard the catch in her voice. "I'm coming too, Jack?"

"Darcy." I shook my head. "No, ..."

From behind me, Art thundered, "You're *both* going. I need all the time I can buy without leaving more signposts along the way. If your darling fiancee hadn't been so stupid as to drive all the way up here, we could have sat out the storm in the harbor and then gone in the morning. But not now. Not now! Move it, Goddamn you!"

I felt the now familiar prod of the pistol barrel in my right kidney and moved instantly, pulling Darcy along with me. The three of us bounced uncertainly along the floating dock to the slip where Art's little sloop was trying to tear her cleats out of the deck. He tossed me the keys to the cabin. Down below, out of the driving rain and wind, I stripped off my wet pants and shorts and toweled dry as best I could. There were foul weather suits stowed in the hanging lockers. The three of us clamored into the rubber outfits. There were no shoes aboard that would fit me. The leather soles of my Weejuns were treacherous as hell on the wet deck and I left them on the cockpit sole, moving around as best I could on numbed feet.

The Seagull was mounted on a little bracket, outboard of the stern. Fortunately, the gas tank was topped off as filling it in this weather would have been all but impossible. I wound the starter rope around the flywheel and pulled only about ten times before she started with a sputtering gargle. Against the shrieking wind, I manually reversed the powerhead on the primitive little engine and opened the throttle all the way. The sloop immediately responded by backing against her decklines.

Darcy clawed her way forward in the darkness to cast off the bow and springlines. Art sat in the cockpit next to me and loosed the stern. We backed fast out into the channel.

To my surprise and considerable relief, except for getting used to the semidarkness, there was no immediate difficulty in the harbor channel. The water was choppy with wind enough to throw up lots of spray, but the sloop shrugged it off as a normal condition. The part that concerned me was that this normal condition was occurring far up the creek in the sheltered harbor channel instead of out on the open Bay.

In another few minutes, we swung out of the buoyed harbor channel into the river itself. The sound of the wind immediately rose a couple of octaves, and the boat pitched violently for the first time. Darcy stumbled down onto the cockpit thwart beside me, holding two kapok vests and lifeline harnesses.

"Jack, It seems awfully rough," she yelled, grabbing quickly for a hand-hold. "Put these on, right now."

The change was instantaneous. The water around the boat was whipped up like a caldron. Waves were at about five feet, but you couldn't see them coming, and there was no pattern to them anyway. Then the wind began to shriek through the wire rigging. The sloop rolled and pitched like an insane metronome. Each time we were hit by a big comber head-on, the little ship would bury her bow, shudder to a stop and the Seagull would cavitate madly, revving clear out of the water. There was not much real danger, except for falling overboard, but steering the boat was increasingly difficult; and, increasingly, I couldn't see.

Art sat wedged forward in the cockpit, next to the cabin door and the compass binnacle. We set running and cabin lights and two shielded lanterns low down in the cockpit. He crouched there, across from Darcy and me, like death itself, calling out compass headings and keeping his pistol tucked up inside the sleeve of his foul weather jacket.

There was, of course, no moon or stars; but despite the heavy rain, we could see enough of the lights along the shore to have some sense of where we were. The trouble was that we couldn't see anything that was *immediately* around us. We simply could not see the waves coming, and got smacked amidships or astern almost as often as we took them over the bow. Beyond that, the boat began to pitch and roll so violently as to make it nearly impossible to control. The Seagull might as well have been bolted to a 50 gallon test drum on shore. Beyond producing some muted noise and a boiling wake, its effect on our forward progress was open to conjecture. "Row well and live, XLI."

I yelled out above the wind. "Art, we need to put up a bit of sail to steady us. I can't steer like this. The motor's not giving me any control at all."

"Let Darcy steer." he shouted. "You go forward and raise the jib."

I yelled back at him. "We're *both* going to have to go forward. The jib is going to have to be reefed down a hell of a lot and I can't do it alone."

Art scooted down the cockpit bench toward Darcy and me, clipping and unclipping his lifeline to the steel railing that ran all the way around the ship. As long as he didn't have to stand using the crutches, he appeared to be as mobile as I was.

The wind was coming off the Bay now about 15 degrees off the bow and I was doing everything possible to maintain that heading, trying to take most of the waves head-on. The thrust of the Seagull was essentially negligible.

Art came up hard against me on the seat as the sloop rolled and righted herself viciously. I clung to the rudder, yelled directly into his ear and wondered about where the pistol was pointed. "If you can hold just enough way on her to keep her pointed straight, I think we'll be able to get the jib in position."

He nodded and shoved me away from the rudder. Darcy and I began the trek to the forward deck, never moving without at least one hand on a stay or the life rail and with both life lines securely snapped. We managed to pull the jib through the forward sail locker hatch, feeling that every downward plunge of the sloop might bring green water over the bow, filling the cabin and carrying us right on down. We dragged the big sail up on the madly pitching deck and managed to wrap it around the forestay enough times to reduce its size by almost half. Darcy led the sheets back through the blocks to the cockpit, and I ran our new storm jib up the mast and cleated it off. The sail was still large as a bedspread despite the reefing, and I thought it would tear itself apart. Darcy and Art sheeted in hard on the leeward side and the sail came taut and flattened with the wind.

Immediately, the little boat heeled to a steady angle and held it without whipping back and forth. Our speed had been practically nothing, and the violent pitching subsided as well. For a moment, we were almost stationery. I quickly worked my way back to the cockpit, took the tiller from Art and found, to my immense relief, that I could finally hold a compass course. I cut the Seagull and with only the little reefed storm jib flying, we started out across the Bay.

From our wake, when I could see it, I judged our speed to be maybe four or five knots. The boat now rose to the crest of each wave easily maintaining its stability all the while. But steering her was not easy. With the reefed jib set and no main to counteract the wind's force, the little sloop constantly wanted to fall off, away from the wind. I had to keep the tiller hard over to correct this tendency and after an hour of doing so, my arms began to cramp.

The weather had slowly and steadily improved from about the time we had reached the Bay itself. The wind speed had slackened to perhaps 15-20 knots and the rain came now in short squalls and sometimes stopped altogether for brief periods. According to Art's sailing directions, we were running down and across the Bay headed for a small group of islands off the Eastern Shore.

"I think you should raise the main," he shouted. "She'll sail a lot better. Wind's not so bad now. I've sailed in this sort of thing dozens of times."

So the crew raised the main, with two reefs in it, while Captain Art held fast to the tiller and his pistol. When I took over the steering again, it was almost pleasant, very lively sailing. The tiller had eased enormously and our speed had increased to more than six knots. Most importantly of all, the little ship was fully under control and in her rightful element. We sliced hard through a trough and rose up the side of an enormous swell, the boat suddenly heeling and the lee rail running under before she righted herself. Darcy grabbed onto me and actually squealed with laughter. We looked at each other and grinned madly.

I had never experienced sailing like this, and, of course, we had our dear friend Art to thank for this wonderfully stimulating experience. I actually might have caught some of Darcy's infectious enthusiasm had it not been for the fact that I was freezing cold, and my bare feet were now completely numb. I gave Darcy the tiller and told Art I was going below.

"I've got to do something about my feet. I can't feel them any more"

In the locker beneath the settee, I found a pair of thick woolen socks which Art had not bothered to mention. The soaked Weejuns lay on the cabin sole. I crammed them on over the dry socks, preferring, at this juncture, to risk a fall with the slick soles than the pain of frost bite and amputation.

By the time I made my way on deck again, the rain had stopped altogether and a few stars could be seen as the clouds began to part overhead. The little sloop ran like a racehorse, completely at home in the rough seas and what was now a force 4 or 5 breeze.

I felt a tremendous sense of relief as I made my way along the cockpit to my Darcy love, watching her steer the ship like a veteran single-hander and seeing the obvious pleasure she found in each moment. The exhilaration of the night sail into a winter storm and our apparent (at least for now) triumph over it, buoyed us considerably and for the moment relegated the immediate nightmare of our personal involvment in the Cold War, i.e., Art and his pistol, to a very small back burner. At least until I saw him, at the other end of the cockpit, crouched down against the cabin bulkhead. He seemed a shrunken figure, ill somehow or in pain. Maybe he was just trying to sleep. I couldn't tell if his eyes were open or not. He seemed to pay no attention to me or Darcy or anything at all.

For the past hour we had been steering a south-easterly course, running about two miles off shore. As I settled myself beside Darcy, I saw the wink of a buoy off our port bow about three miles ahead. Art saw it too.

"Make for that buoy," he shouted, and we changed course and trimmed sails accordingly.

In less than 45 minutes we had passed the winking, mile buoy and Art came aft and took the tiller for the first time all night. He set us on a westerly heading and in a few minutes I could see lights from the shore in the far distance.

CHAPTER TWENTY-FIVE

I should probably have missed the narrow inlet, even in daylight. It was a quietly flowing tidal creek, no more than about one hundred feet across. There was enough moon and starlight now between the parting clouds for us to see outlines and silhouettes as we came inshore. Art signaled for me to start the Seagull. When I did, he sent Darcy and me forward to drop the sails.

On the shore, pasture land was interlaced with stands of dark trees. We motored into a little inlet and I could see we were in horse country. The hills sloped gently upward from the banks on either side delineated by the signature flat rail fences. For the past hour, the sky had steadily brightened and visibility from the stars and a new moon was adequate to steer by.

We rounded a slow sweeping bend, and I could see the lights from a great house about a mile beyond the rolling pasture land. At about half that distance along the narrow inlet, a light suddenly flashed at the water's edge. Art altered course slightly. As we approached it, I could see a sort of pier or jetty projecting out into the stream and the silhouette of a boat tied up alongside.

We came abreast the jetty and Art turned hard to starboard and brought the sloop smartly alongside. I cut the motor, went forward and made the bow fast to a wooden piling.

"Someone will be down in a moment," Art said. "We'll wait." He gestured toward Darcy and me with the pistol. "Get below and don't make a sound. Turn off the cabin light. As far as these people are concerned, I'm here alone."

These People? What people. Your people calling my people. Oh shit. Big Ugly Russian People, in all likelihood.

I took Darcy's arm, and we went forward and down through the little companion way into the tiny enclosure. We sat on the bunk, and I switched off the overhead lamp. I clamped my fingers very gently over

259

Darcy's sweet lips and determined that neither of us would breathe for the next 10 or 15 minutes.

After a moment or two, the glare of headlights was reflected through the cabin port. I heard the sound of tires on gravel. A car door opened and closed softly, and the hollow sound of footsteps echoed along the pier.

The voice was English and male. There was a civilized, chiding tone to the words which barely managed to conceal their underlying displeasure.

"You shouldn't have come, old boy. You know the rules. You were warned off."

Art spoke rapidly. "I had no choice. My own people are on to me. I was followed to the marina."

His people, I thought. I'll bet *these* people aren't in the least pleased with *his* people.

The voice was easy. Gentle and almost teasing. "All the more reason why you should have stayed away. Too many people out on a stormy night."

Ah, here was a man who understood the 'people' thing. I decided that I liked him.

Art broke in. "I have the stuff from yesterday's meeting. It's absolutely dynamite." He thrust his hand into the bib pocket of his foul weather pants.

The Englishman on the pier chuckled softly. "Afraid we can't use it now, old man. It'll have been contaminated, you know. You should have been the first to see that."

Art snapped angrily, "What are you talking about, Victor? I've thrown away everything to get this to you."

"I'm afraid that's true." The voice continued, evenly. "They've been on to you for days now, old boy. The stuff's gone sour." His voice softened. "Go home, Baldwin. It's finished."

Art's voice burst out with that crazy roar as it had back in the yacht club parking lot. "Go home? You know I can't do that. I've paid my dues, Victor. You have to help *me* now."

"I help you, old boy? And just how could *I* help *you*?"

"Cut it out, Victor!" Art was screaming. "I need asylum. You have contacts in Moscow, in Havana. You have diplomatic immunity."

The voice continued, as smooth as James Mason on castor oil. "But I'm a *British* diplomat, old boy. Had you forgotten?"

"What the hell are you talking about? I know you're British."

The even, soothing voice continued: "I'm merely saying that the only people in Moscow who know me would like very much to see me in a basement cell in the Lubianka prison. They're certainly not very likely to seriously entertain requests for asylum that come from me."

"What?" The sheer rage in Art's voice was palpable. What is this shit, Victor?" He paused and I heard only the sound of heavy breathing from the cockpit of the boat. When he began again, the voice quavered, not really getting it. "You're known everywhere. The Ambassador respects you. Gregovnia said . . . . !"

I held my breath and craned my neck to hear the soft response. "Yes, I'm sure she did, old boy, and we received much for which Her Majesty's Government is terribly grateful, but I'm really in no position to offer you shelter in the *Eastern* bloc. Not my bailiwick, you know."

"But Gregovnia . . . ?" Art repeated.,

A sudden coldness flashed up through the smooth flow of words. "Is no longer with us, I'm very sorry to say."

The Englishman paused and now I could hear his breathing. After a moment, he continued gently, evenly. "Her entire family were starved and worked to death in the Gulag. Were you aware of that, Baldwin? Or did she perhaps neglect to whisper that little fact among the sweet nothings the two of you exchanged? And now, of course, she too, is dead. Murdered by the KGB as a result of your feckless incompetence. Even if I were in a position to assist you, old boy, I believe I'd decline the honor." The softness left the voice instantly. "Gregovnia was a particular friend of mine."

"Dead?" Art laughed. "What do you mean, she's dead? We both know she's traveling in the south of France. Look, Victor, I know she was very pleased with the stuff. She told me. The Ambassador said . . . ." His sentence drifted off and we listened hard in the silence. Then he screamed out, "Victor, I got everything for her, for you . . . ."

The voice on the dock remained calm and soothing. "And it *was* very much appreciated, I assure you. The Cousins give us quite a lot up front, but we really do prefer having our own backchannel in these matters. Reinforces the Special Relationship, you know."

"What are you talking about? I know she saw the Ambassador."

The Englishman chuckled ruefully, "I'm afraid she saw a great many people."

"But the Soviet Ambassador? He got the stuff directly."

"Yes. I believe His Excellency did see one of your little notes." There was bitterness in the voice. "The one Gregovnia died for."

There was another long silence, and I couldn't tell what was going on.

Then I heard an incredulous Art say, "You're telling me you're MI-6? That's just not possible."

The Englishman laughed softly. "Oh come now, old man. You didn't really want to give those *other* people all those juicy little secrets? Did you? So much better to keep them in the family."

An anguished cry erupted from the stern of the boat. "You bastard! God damn your soul!"

I heard the sound of crutches dropping to the deck and the rubbery flapping of a foul weather parka.

The Englishman barely raised his voice but it easily cut through the night like the soft, whirring buzz of a Diamondback Rattler, sharp and cold as naked steel spread on the wings of death.

"Drop the gun."

The silence stretched on and on, unbearably. Then I heard the sound of a heavy object clattering to the deck.

The Englishman spoke again, his quiet tone like oil spread on troubled waters. "Go home, Baldwin. Go home. There's nothing for you here. There never was."

"God damn you. What do I do?" Art screamed.

"Do?" There was a short harsh laugh. "Why you could do the right thing, old boy. Your family and all."

A ghastly vision of Art poking his pistol into his open mouth flurried through my mind. Another period of silence followed during which I could hear labored breathing coming, presumably, from Art.

The Englishman went on. "Still, I don't imagine the Cousins will be too hard on you if you choose to make a fuss. One hundred million pounds commands a great deal of respect and tolerance these days." He laughed softly in the darkness.

"It was you." The rage seemed to have gone from his voice and it was flat with defeat. "You put them onto me."

The icy hardness returned to the Englishman's voice. "You had let the whole operation get out of hand, old boy. Amateur spies, KGB goons running amok, Gregovnia . . . ." His voice trailed off, and I couldn't hear the rest of what he said.

The boat shifted, and I knew Art had sat down hard. The hollow footsteps sounded again on the quay and a car door softly closed.

I heard that peculiar, characteristic sound of the starter on an old Ford flathead V8 being cranked. I touched my fingers to Darcy's lips and leaned forward to the little cabin port to see an ancient, wood-paneled Estate Wagon back into the gravel and start up the winding drive.

Darcy and I had been still as church mice throughout the entire exchange. We remained seated on the bunk, holding each other's hands, not moving.

Then I whispered. "Stay here." I stood up as far as I could in the little cabin and reached for the companionway hatch.

"Jack, wait. Don't."

"Shhhh. It'll be okay. Just stay here a moment till I talk with him."

I opened the hatch and heaved myself through, looking hard in the semi-darkness for the discarded pistol. Art was seated on one of the cockpit benches, staring over the rail into the black waters.

I walked toward him and my foot kicked into the pistol where it lay on the cockpit sole. I quickly knelt to pick it up, and my hand encountered one of Art's crutches. I laid the crutch beside him and took a step backward, concealing the pistol as best I could.

"I'll start the motor, Art. We need to get back. It'll be dawn before we're at the marina."

He nodded, but said nothing. I had no place to put the pistol, so I went back to the cabin and told Darcy to hide it in a locker.

"We're leaving." I said, quietly. "Come up on deck when you're finished and help me with the lines."

I went back to the stern and Art moved slightly forward so I could get at the Seagull. The engine was still warm, and I topped off the fuel and wound the rope and pulled, and it started immediately. Darcy came on deck and loosed the bow line and the sloop backed quickly away from the dock.

We slid past the other boat, and I could see its shark-like form partly concealed with a deep green boat cover. The word GarWood was emblazoned in gold lettering on the polished mahogany planking.

The wind was still fresh and the Bay rough and choppy from the evening's storm. I set the boat on a run with all canvas flying and we sailed beautifully, with little heel and no blinding, freezing spray as on the earlier trip across.

We had passed the mile buoy and changed course an hour back. Art had still not uttered a single word.

The ride was smooth, and the boat was practically steering herself. Darcy stood up and asked if we wanted clam chowder. I voted an enthusiastic yes and she went below to open cans and light burners. Art said nothing. After a few moments, Darcy called from the barely lighted cabin.

"Art? Do you have a sweat-suit or something that Jack could put on?" I could see her silhouette, outlined against the glow of the lamp, rummaging in the lockers beneath the little bunk.

"Under the bunk," Art said. He spoke absently. "There are some things in one of the lockers."

I stood up. "You okay to steer?"

He didn't speak, but moved over and took the tiller under his arm. I went forward and closed the companionway hatch behind me.

The atmosphere below was charged with tension. Since the Englishman had departed, Darcy and I had been about to explode, bursting with questions and almost sick with a strange, quiet fear. It was like waiting for a bomb to go off. I had taken care to hide the pistol. Now the thing that bore so heavily upon us all could do nothing but wind down slowly leaving the nasty film of its memory.

"Jack." Darcy whispered in the darkened cabin. "He's acting so creepy. I don't like this at all. What's going to happen to him now?"

"I don't know. You heard what that Victor guy said to him."

"He's been giving all this stuff to British Intelligence the whole time? That man back there. He completely suckered Art."

"Sidney Reilly? He completely suckered everybody."

Darcy gave an angry pull on my arm. "Jack, that was *not* Sidney Reilly. Don't you, of all people, start acting insane. Not tonight. I couldn't stand it." She put down the can of chowder and hugged me in the cold wet rubber suit.

I'm not going insane, Love. I've just got to get warm," I said, and stripped off the yellow oilskins.

Darcy found a pair of sweatpants and shirt in the locker and I got a towel from the head. I scrubbed myself with it for about five minutes, then slipped into the dry clothing.

"Now, if he only has another pair of dry socks," I said, rummaging through the drawer where I'd found the first pair during the storm.

"I'll ask him," said Darcy and she climbed the little ladder and opened the companionway hatch.

Three seconds later, she shouted "Jack!" and leapt up the stairway, looking wildly around the boat. Barefoot, I followed her up the stairs. The sloop was holding course with the tiller lashed amidships. Art Baldwin was gone.

I frantically dived for the tiller. "Get ready to come about!"

We reversed course, running on the reciprocal. I stood ready with coiled rope and life ring, while Darcy went forward to the bow pulpit with a six cell flashlight and probed the waning darkness.

I had not been below more than ten minutes, probably closer to six or seven. Art couldn't be much more than a mile behind us, probably less. We went almost two miles and came about again. Then began a crisscross search pattern in accord with what I perceived the current to be. We were still searching at dawn. Darcy had traded the light for a set of powerful marine binoculars, and she tirelessly swept the horizon as we rounded and tacked through an area of several square miles. As the sun rose, the horizon was still packed solid with receding storm clouds and the sea was gunmetal gray.

Darcy focused on a spot in the water about one hundred yards distant and shouted, "Jack! I see something! I think it's him!"

She came aft with the glasses and we both took turns looking. Some object was riding the crest of the two to three foot chop, visible one moment and gone the next.

"Could be a duck. Pelican or something."

"Oh Jack, I'm afraid. I know it's him."

We came up fast, Darcy at the helm and me standing ready to drop sail when we rounded into the wind and heaved to. At about fifty feet we could see the bright dayglo orange of a life vest. I grabbed the boathook and shouted to Darcy. The vest was floating, spread wide over the dark waves. The orange strings and white webbed belt hung loosely in the water, trailing their bright metal fasteners. I leaned out far over the side, hooked it and slung it easily on board with a cascade of water. It landed in the center of the cockpit sole. Darcy threw her hands over her face and broke down in wracking sobs.

We notified the Coast Guard as soon as we reached Annapolis and search boats were sent out immediately. We told them mostly the truth. We had gone for a midnight sail after the storm had waned, laid over for a few hours in an inlet on the north shore and were returning early this morning when he simply disappeared over the side. Art might have been upset about something, probably at work, but didn't confide in us. I gave them our names and addresses and told them that Art was a federal employee. This last revelation seemed to be of particular interest to the Coast Guard to which it was first revealed. Later that morning, the police department sent two detectives down to Coast Guard headquarters to interview us.

Darcy and I were exhausted and deeply saddened, and this fact was immediately appreciated by everyone who talked to us and asked us questions. The boat was in good shape and had clearly encountered no difficulty at sea. I took the detectives aboard and showed them Art's gun. It was loaded and unfired and I said simply that he had kept it on board for protection. Everyone was genuinely sympathetic and treated us kindly.

There were a few "routine"(Were we drinking?) and embarrassing questions about the nature of our relationship with Art; but since there were no signs of foul play, and it was explained that Darcy and I were engaged to be married and that Art was a mutual friend, the death was almost immediately regarded as one of accidental drowning.

Of course, we were asked if we believed he had committed suicide, but we had no answer to that any more than they did. During the period when he must have gone overboard, the boat was pitching and heaving a little. He had badly sprained his ankle the week before playing touch football. In fact, Darcy and I were both along so the boat could be properly handled, as much as anything. We knew his lifeline had been left unattached after we started back. None of us had worn them when the storm abated. Was his life vest left untied? We simply didn't know. We'd only been wearing them because of the storm the night before. Darcy and I were no longer wearing ours. Art left the tiller tied off amidships. Perhaps he had done this in order to come forward to the cabin and had taken a fall because of his crippled leg. We simply didn't know.

His family, of course, was notified immediately, and the search by the Coast Guard was ratcheted up about five notches. The Baldwins also saw to it that the newspapers kept a respectful distance and did not engage in lurid speculation. The occurrence made the front page of the *Washington Post* but only a few lines near the bottom. ***Heir to Paper Fortune Feared Lost in Boating Accident.***

On the evening of the second day, Darcy and I were interviewed at the Harrises by two gentlemen from the FBI They were appropriately apologetic, carefully polite and extremely professional, showing the proper respect automatically accorded members of the ruling class; particularly those living in *that* neighborhood, undoubtedly mindful as they were that the entrance to their boss's estate lay just down the hill and a few hundred yards through Rock Creek Park.

One had the feeling that they knew quite a lot about the Harrises, Darcy, Art Baldwin and me; and that it was all good. Their queries centered on the question of Art's demeanor, his possible depression. Had he mentioned problems at work? Did we think it likely that he had, after all, slipped and fallen? It was certainly possible. We simply couldn't say.

We simply couldn't say, of course, because we had discussed the question non-stop for about 24 hours and had immediately come to the inescapable conclusion that we simply *mustn't* say. If Art's bosses at the CIA were onto him, as seemed to be true, they would draw their own conclusion about his sudden disappearance without any help from us. His family and friends would probably draw a different conclusion.

Our grief was completely genuine as grief always is when death comes to someone in the second decade of his life. It was made all the more poignant by the utter futility of his actions over the past six months, and the fact that he crowned the farce by this fatal act. Art Baldwin was many conflicting persons, and each of them was only twenty-three years old.

A fishing trawler, heading out of port the next morning, discovered the body. It was floating face down about three miles from where we figured he'd gone overboard. This checked out almost to the yard with the Coast Guard's earlier prediction after they had factored in drift and current and the time elapsed.

The funeral was held in Schenectady, New York. We met and were frequently on the phone with the senior Baldwins throughout the ordeal of waiting. They sent a company plane, and Linda, Darcy and I flew up for the service and burial the following Sunday afternoon.

CHAPTER TWENTY-SIX

The return from Art's funeral placed a period at the end of summer. The days began a headlong rush through a brilliant fall and on toward winter that was barely noticed by Darcy and me. The anticipation of Christmas and the wedding were uppermost in our minds and hearts as well as those of family and friends. But along with the joyous anticipation, and the sense of release from evil that grew out of the midnight sail and Art's drowning, there was also a profound sadness and confusion by this act of self destruction. We looked back on that most important summer of our lives with bittersweet longing tempered with a fearsome unease.

The newspapers finally freed themselves, somewhat, from the curtailing influence of the Baldwin family millions. There was the occasional article speculating on whether the death had been accident or suicide. A statement was eventually issued by a spokesman for the government to the effect that Art Baldwin had served his country valiantly and would be sorely missed. Since he had not been wearing his lifeline and was on crutches at the time, the verdict, not seriously contested by anyone, was of death by accidental drowning.

Neil, the son of the owner of the Arlington Yellow Cab Company, whom I barely knew by sight and with whom I had endured two unpleasant conversations, was profoundly moved by the mention of his cab company as my employer, in the same newspaper article with that of the scion of one of the richest families in America. So moved, in fact, that in a lost moment of ecstasy, he sent flowers to the funeral and extended his condolences to me and the other members of my family over the loss of our brother. I didn't bother to set him straight on the relationship, believing that, as with all other things regarding Neil, it was wiser to let sleeping dogs lie.

Art's body had been recovered on the birthday of Miss Withersby's grandniece, Priscilla. Miss Withersby, of course, postponed the festive occasion to a more appropriate time; and, on a Saturday afternoon about two weeks later, Darcy and I found ourselves again riding the elevator up to the second floor at 4000 Connecticut Avenue.

Alonzo let us in, and we were quickly greeted by Priscilla, whom we had met briefly when Miss Withersby had arranged a little gathering for her earlier in the summer. There were about 30 or 40 guests, all standing around the apartment rooms juggling drinks and little plates of hors d'oeuvres in the typical cocktail party stance. Miss Withersby had even laid on extra help in the form of a Negro maid who trundled back and forth between the kitchen and sideboard buffet carrying trays of goodies while Alonzo manned the bar.

About half the guests were college students and friends of Priscilla's. The rest were divided more or less evenly between those of my parents' generation and several handfuls of elders.

Miss Withersby was seated on a sofa in the living room with several old ladies and an elderly man who sat hunched over a cane. The old man's hands lay atop his walking stick and were terribly twisted and misshapen with arthritis. He had an enormous lionine head adorned with thick rimless spectacles and covered with snow white hair.

This nucleus of elders evidently constituted the center of the gathering and the nub of what amounted to a receiving line, as couples and individuals talked and stood around and worked their way toward the seated ones in order to pay their respects.

Uncharacteristically, I was not my usual cheerful and ebullient self and was in no mood to pay respects. The reasons for this departure from normalcy were clear and sharply defined. Darcy and I had failed to hit it off particularly well with Priscilla when we had first met. She was simply too young to have interests in common with us once we'd made attempts to cover the Beautiful/Sportsy theme; and though she performed all the social functions flawlessly and had beautiful manners, she exhibited a distant, aloof demeanor that was almost tragic in a 19-year-old. There was an element of snobbery in it, but more than that, there seemed to be an utter lack of desire to extend herself or take the slightest interest in others. I was absolutely positive that deep down inside Miss Prisilla's barely used brain, there resided the unshakable belief that 5 or 10 million dollars in old, gilt-edged securities meant that she would never have to.

Beyond having to endure Priscilla and her friends, the thought of Miss Withersby making inquiries about Art Baldwin and his death and having to tell and re-tell the horror story to every little clique of half-drunk party guests did not appeal to me in the least.

Finally, and worst of all, I did not have anything to wear, and I was extremely annoyed at myself for caring about the sort of thing that only women cared about. My Brooks Brothers travel suit was doing yeoman's duty. We were still in the dog days of Autumn and the weather had not yet really turned cold. Despite this, I felt totally awkward and stupid in this ice cream costume while all the other men in the room were properly attired in dark blue and gray worsteds. Darcy had actually gone with me to Lewis & Thomas Saltz on my lunch hour several days ago; but, alas, the alterations had not been ready when promised, and I now presented myself at a late fall afternoon birthday party dressed like a buffoon.

"It doesn't matter," Darcy said, trying to soothe me after the disappointing news from the haberdasher. "You're so handsome, it makes no difference what you wear. You could go in blue jeans and every woman there would be envious of me." She put her arms up on my shoulders and kissed my mouth, both cheeks and the whole line of buttons down my shirt front.

I thought about her last comment for awhile and decided that, if I appeared in blue jeans, every woman in the room would *not* be envious of Darcy. Every woman in the room would think I was a hick, a bumpkin and, probably, a day laborer or a filling station attendant. I was not to be appeased by flattery and kisses, no matter how welcome.

"I'll just feel extremely self-conscious. You're not going to be wearing some summer outfit."

Darcy laughed. "Jack Norton, I can't believe I'm hearing this from you. You normally don't give a damn about what you wear or what people think. You've been wearing khakis and your old moth-eaten Harris tweed every night for weeks now. Why not just wear that?"

"It would be rude to Miss Withersby, that's why. I'll have to wear the damn suit."

And so I did, but not before going over to Higger's Liquors, conveniently located right next door to Higger's Drugs, and buying a six pack of Heinekens and guzzling the first one in the car on the way back to the Harrises.

When I returned, Sam and Darcy were tossing a football around with some kids down the middle of Chesterfield Street, a cul-de-sac mostly devoid of traffic. Since I had reached the age of about 15, I had ranked throwing a football around somewhere below being strapped in a chair and forced to watch basketball games. Nevertheless, I joined the activity because Darcy was doing it and having so much fun. I kept the Heinekens on the seat of the VW with the window rolled down and helped myself liberally throughout the next hour or so.

About three o'clock we broke off to dress and get ready. After I had donned my Dacron and cotton wonder suit, I came down to the kitchen to wait for Darcy. After a couple of minutes of nervous waiting, I fixed myself a whisky sour because it was Saturday afternoon and Charles Harris invited me to have one with him. I finished it quickly as we were discussing the continuing problems in Cuba.

When Darcy finally made her appearance, looking ravishing with her hair up and wearing a dark blue sheath thing cut low and clinging, I was so impressed and excited by the sight of her that I had another whisky sour in celebration. Every man in the room would certainly be jealous of me, and it would have nothing to do with what I was wearing.

Having successfully insulated myself against what I felt would prove to be a tedious and unpleasant two hours, talking to rich adolescents and telling the story of the drowning to strangers for the thousandth time, I sallied forth with my beautiful Darcy into the elegant rooms at 4000 Connecticut Avenue.

We were introduced to those of Priscilla's friends whose paths we happened to cross, and then to a series of parent types and relatives, and were soon engaged in standard Washington cocktail party chatter centering on politics and the Berlin Wall. No one asked about the drowning or even looked askance at my ridiculous suit. As soon as we came into close proximity to any little knot of partyers, all eyes locked onto Darcy.

I stood there with a silly look on my face and just watched her. Oh God, Darcy was so achingly beautiful. Not only beautiful, but brilliant, sensible, wise, kind and absolutely everything. And she was mine. All mine, body and soul; and, I thought morosely as I lifted my glass, she was totally in love with me, Jack Norton, Drunken Oaf.

I began to regret having gotten tanked before coming to the party, but was too far along now to just stop. About every ten minutes, there was Alonzo standing with a tray of fresh, perfectly chilled martinis. When I tried to decline, coherent words simply failed me.

Darcy was busy enthusiastically enchanting a group of admirers when I espied a tray of delicious looking little somethings on the grand piano and wandered immediately in that direction. I was helping myself to a number of little toasted spinach puff things when I noticed the old picture of the young people in the speedboat.

All the girls were pretty. Pretty in the way you might imagine your mother was pretty when she was young, but certainly not in the way Darcy was pretty. Darcy wasn't just pretty. Darcy was the most beau . . . . And then I noticed the men. They all looked alike, of course, in the grainy black and white with undershirt bathing suits, the trunks or pants coming down to their knees, and their hair slicked down with Brylcream or some disgusting thing and parted in the middle.

I tried to picture Darcy and me dressed for the period and sitting among this crowd on the gunwale of the speedboat. The two of us just wouldn't look like that. I knew we wouldn't. Even with my hair slicked down and parted in the middle I wouldn't look like that smug bastard sitting at the wheel. I picked up the silver frame and stared hard at the image of the young man. Darcy had said that everybody in these old pictures looks pretty much the same, like they were all pod people. Visions from *The Bodysnatchers* swam before my somewhat glazed eyes.

"She was very beautiful, wasn't she? Would you believe she was forty-five years old in that picture."

The voice came from just behind me, and I turned and vigorously nodded agreement, although I had no idea what was being said or who was saying it about whom. It turned out to be Priscilla's mother or one of her aunts or somebody I had met soon after we had arrived.

"Aunt Bess was a real flapper. Did you notice the coquettish smile beneath the bobbed hair?"

"Yes!" I laughed. "Isn't that something!" I still hadn't the faintest idea what this woman was talking about. At first, I assumed that she must be paying a compliment to Darcy. Then the reference to 'Aunt Bess' and 'bobbed hair' threw me, and I thought she was referring somehow to Priscilla until she took the old picture from me and picked up a big round antique magnifying glass with a long handle from among the clutter on the piano.

"They certainly jump out at you when you use this," she said, and placed both objects in front of me. A blurry, hopping image of one of the girls jumped out at me. Her head was thrown back, in the manner of Franklin Delano Roosevelt working the crowd. All that was missing was the long cigarette holder. Maybe the jaunty, thrown-back head was a universal gesture among the well born of the flapper era. I made a resolution then and there to ask Darcy to do it to see how it looked. This girl had gone far beyond Roosevelt, however. Her lips were slightly parted with a come hither look, and she was seated especially close to the driver of the boat, one of her slim and not very appealing alabaster limbs thrown casually across his shoulder.

"Aahhh!" I said, not knowing what I was supposed to be seeing.

"Wasn't she too cute for words?"

'Cute' wasn't the word I would have selected, but I started to say something like 'Indeed!' or 'Oh yes!' still not exactly knowing who the girl in the picture was. Then I shifted the glass and focused on the driver of the boat. It was him! It was the Sidney Reilly character from the GarWood, from Middleburg, from the Arena Stage production; and, suddenly, I knew with complete certainty that this was the man who had stood on the dock that terrible night and pronounced a sentence of death over Art Baldwin.

I stared drunkenly at the man in the picture for several moments, trying to make sense of it. I turned to my admiring companion who was apparently growing tired of the old picture and wanted to move on to other topics.

"Who was that guy she has her arm around?" I suddenly asked.

"Oh, that was one of her many beaux. I think he was an Englishman." She said dismissively, starting to replace the picture on the polished surface of the Steinway.

"What was his name?" I asked abruptly.

"His name? Oh heavens, I haven't heard it in years. When we were small, we used to sit on her lap, and she would take down all the pictures and point out everybody in them by name. He wasn't anybody in the family, so I don't remember just who he was."

I turned and stared closely at the woman for what must have seemed a very long time as she smiled and looked confused and then looked away a number of times.

"I'll find out his name." I said, none too crisply.

"Yes. Well, I'm sure Aunt Bess remembers but perhaps now isn't the best time." She motioned around her to the guests and the long sofa where the queen and her court were receiving mostly sober, serious people.

"Oh, don't be silly. This is the perfect time." I took the picture, having to exert a tiny bit of effort before she released it.

"Yes but . . . ," she smiled awkwardly, "I really don't think . . . ."

"Oh, don't worry." I stood closely, looking into her eyes. "She'll love talking about it. Everyone will be charmed."

She started to protest again, but I simply leaned over and kissed her on her powdered cheek and patted her shoulder as I moved off toward the Withersby enclave, brandishing the picture.

Miss Withersby saw me coming and held out her hand. "Ah, Jack Deah, where is our Darcy? What have you done with our lovely young lady?" She turned and began to explain to everyone who we were, and that our forthcoming marriage was planned for Christmas time.

Since our betrothal, I had been promoted from Mr. Norton to Jack Deah. Alonzo had also upgraded me from Mr. Norton to Mr. Jack. Both of them, however, made no secret of the fact that Darcy was clearly the more favored of the two of us. They had long ago upgraded her to Darcy Deah, Our Darcy, and Miss Darcy; and, when we came to call, it was difficult to escape the feeling that I was somehow mostly regarded as a necessary escort; and, later, as something that Darcy loved and which made her happy and complete.

I came into her circle nodding, bowing, smiling, and shaking hands at the introductions, none of which I heard or remembered. Miss Withersby introduced me to the white-haired man, and I noticed that his twisted hands did not leave the perch on top of his cane. He remained seated and merely nodded slightly with only a trace of a smile. Miss Withersby was going on and on about the wedding and where it would take place. There was some inane bantering about people who were not Episcopalians. Finally she turned to the white haired man and said, "But they're both perfectly good Presbyterians, just like you, Allen."

The white-haired man simply nodded and smiled faintly. He looked up at me and then softly offered some sort of congratulation. I had the feeling he was finished with me. I turned to Miss Withersby, holding the picture so everyone in the gathering could see. "I'm sure you all know who this is," I said, pointing at the girl beside the driver of the boat.

No one did, or pretended not to know, until one middle-aged lady said, "Why Miss Bess. That's you!"

Everyone oohed and aahed in admiration, and Miss Withersby silenced them all by saying, "Almost fawty yeahs ago, and *even then* Ah was too old to have been runnin' with that crowd of kids.

A chorus of protestations, what-do-you-mean's, you-were-all-the-same-age-weren't-you's were followed by the punch line triumphantly delivered by Miss Withersby, herself.

"I was fawty-five yeahs old when that picture was made."

This was followed by a scramble for closer scrutiny of the picture and the inevitable chorus of you-don't-mean-it's, isn't-that-amazing's, crowned by a flurry of you-look-exactly-like-a-teenager's.

"The rest of that group practically were," cackled Miss Withersby.

I saw my chance and went for it. "That's no teenager driving the boat. Who was he?"

Miss Withersby laughed and explained primly to her companions. "He was one of my beaux when that picture was taken."

"What was his name?" I said, but nobody heard me.

Someone chirped in, "He was very handsome. What did you say when he asked you to marry him?" Everyone laughed politely.

"How do you know he asked me?" replied shrewd old Miss Withersby, playing her audience like Helen Hayes.

More polite laughter and someone said, "We know he must have asked you. The question is, Miss Bess, what did you tell him?"

Miss Withersby laughed along with her guests. "Ah told him, No."

There was a chorus of disappointed sighs. Miss Withersby took a sip from her glass of sherry and glanced about as if to make sure none of this would get to the wrong ears. She looked at each of us around her and said in a stage whisper. "You see, he was Jewish. In those days . . . ." Everyone nodded knowingly. The subject was quickly changed, and the man who currently had the picture in his hand quietly laid it back on the grand piano.

I stood staring at Miss Withersby, looking for an opening, but she was earnestly engaged with a middle-aged couple who had maneuvered their way in front of me. My hour seemed to have passed. It was all right, I thought. I would find out the man's name. I would just sit and drink and wait till all the other guests had left, and then ask Miss Withersby his name.

I sat down uncertainly in a small chair near the sofa and plucked another martini from the tray now being passed by Alonzo's female assistant. A man who looked like my idea of the President of General Motors came and sat near me and interrogated me about my background, where I had gone to school, what I was planning to do with my life and so forth. Since all this was about me, I was a most willing participant. I think I told the auto magnate rather more than he wanted to know about John Robert Norton, His Life and Times.

At some point, Darcy rescued me, or rather, rescued the magnate who shook hands, smiled and hurried away. Apparently, it was time for the unveiling of the cake and the opening of the presents. We all moved toward the dining room. I was unable to see or really hear what was going on. Someone eventually pushed a plate with a slice of cake on it into my hand.

The opening of gifts proceeded as these things always do. The guests oohed and aahed at the unveiling of each magnificent present, the small silver pin that Darcy had selected for our gift going practically unnoticed among the more opulent offerings. Chief among them, of course, was the present from Miss Withersby. We had returned the Jaguar several weeks earlier, and Alonzo, apparently, had spent most of the intervening days washing and polishing the thing until it shone like the winning entry at a *Concours D'elegance.*

All the guests had to troop down to the lobby of the building to see the actual presentation. Alonzo had drawn the car up under the port cochere at the grand entrance and had affixed a large red bow to a corner of the windshield. Everyone was suitably delighted and not at all shocked at so extravagant a present. Priscilla seemed pleased with the car but certainly didn't gush about it. After all, it was only a car. I had the feeling she was probably expecting a horse. An Irish hunter, or maybe an Arabian stallion.

The car presentation also provided an opportunity for about two-thirds of the guests to leave. The remainder were those of Priscilla's circle who were hanging out with her while she was visiting her great aunt for several days. I didn't want to leave until I had received an answer to my question, but it was clear that this was not to be. Darcy and I said our good-byes and thank yous and headed for the VW in the hidden parking lot at the side of the building.

Darcy automatically went to the driver's door. I tossed her the keys and flopped down in the passenger seat. Of course, I immediately told her about the picture.

"Jack, you've seen that old picture before. It doesn't mean anything except that a friend of Miss Withersby's owned a GarWood speedboat about 40 years ago. That's all." She leaned over and patted my frowning face. "You got a little bit drunk, Love. Things, people all look different when you're drunk."

"Do I look different to you when I'm drunk?"

Darcy laughed. "No."

"I bet I do. I bet I look like Charlton Heston or somebody."

She pealed her wonderful laugh. "You're much better looking than Charlton Heston."

"Gregory Peck!"

"Close, but your hair is the wrong color."

"Darcy, I know that man was Sidney Reilly."

"No, he was really Ian Fleming. Listen, you know as well as I do that the photograph is almost forty years old. Even if it had been Sidney Reilly, he'd be in his eighties now, as decrepit as Miss Withersby. He certainly isn't the 'Sidney Reilly' we've been bumping into all summer. You're just drunk, Sweetie. You're happily drunk, and you're very sweet, and you're like a little boy."

"Sidney Reilly," I said. "I know it was."

"Jack, it just all came back to you at once," she said.

"What came back to me?"

"Being drunk. Seeing that old picture with the boat again and then meeting the great spymaster. All at the same time."

"What do you mean?" I asked. "What spymaster? Sidney Reilly was the great spymaster?"

"Darcy sighed and shook her head. "No, not Sidney Reilly. Don't you know who that was sitting next to Miss Withersby? The old white-haired gentleman?"

I shut my eyes and slumped down in the seat. I was suddenly getting very, very sleepy. "Who?" I slurred. "Who was it?"

"That was the founder of the Central Intelligence Agency. That was Allen Dulles."

CHAPTER TWENTY-SEVEN

The next day, Sunday, was an extremely painful one. Once while in college, I consumed nearly a half case of malt liquor during some festive event. Then as now, the physical consequences experienced the following day were hideous beyond belief and carried an indelible memory as almost permanent proof against over imbibing.

Darcy delivered me to my room shortly after the party at Miss Withersby's. The notion of returning to her parent's house with her future husband dead drunk was not altogether appealing. She arrived at the sickroom on Sunday about midmorning bearing ice-cold orange juice, aspirin and a thermos of hot, strong coffee. Through her selfless nursing and ministrations, I was almost ambulatory by late afternoon.

I was so embarrassed about my behavior at Miss Withersby's, so terrified that I might have said or done something truly awful, that I didn't bring up the matter of the name of the man in the photograph with Darcy. It would also be a long time before I could broach the subject with Miss Withersby, and so I let it slide down behind other debris in the back of my mind.

This really wasn't difficult because, in the glaring light of sobriety, I immediately saw how silly the whole thing was. The Englishman who had manipulated Art was in his early or mid forties. Sidney Reilly, in the photograph or not, would be in his eighties now if he were alive; and, of course, the best evidence was that he had disappeared into Russia and was murdered by Stalin nearly forty years ago. Still, it was fascinating to speculate . . .

That Sunday morning, Darcy and I began to speculate on more immediate, concrete things. Darcy did not scold or wag her finger, nor did she apparently feel any criticism of my actions the night before; but I felt that I had been unfaithful to her by getting stinking drunk; and I was now particularly receptive to any and all ideas and plans she had for our future.

We had already given a deposit for the apartment which would be ours on January 1st. November would be the month of travels. We would visit my family in Kentucky. We would visit Darcy's family in Pennsylvania. We would visit Princeton University because I had been asked to come for an interview. There were also parties to plan and receptions to attend right through the next month, and, of course, all the festivities of Christmas.

On top of all of this, the Reverend Dr. Playfair needed to see us both for weekly sessions leading up to the wedding ceremony. During these little interviews, he would instruct us on our mutual responsibilities which must be assumed when we entered into a state of Holy Matrimony. I could hardly wait. Nevertheless, in my weakened and penitent condition, I said yes to everything that Darcy brought up.

The trip to Kentucky required five days if we drove both ways and spent any time there at all. This was reconciled somewhat with the Arlington Yellow Cab Company by taking the trip over the Thanksgiving holidays.

I had already informed the dispatcher of my forthcoming marriage and the need for time off around Christmas and had received a favorable dispensation from Neil. Neil was still enamored with my imagined close ties to the Baldwin family. He apparently had thought, all along, that Darcy had been Art's sister and managed to convince himself that my marriage into all this wealth and splendor was somehow good for the Arlington Yellow Cab Company. Maybe he would make me a partner someday. I made a mental note to have Darcy and Sylvia send him an invitation.

The drive to Kentucky took twelve hours, and we left on Friday night in order to minimize the time away from work and to take advantage of the short Thanksgiving holiday week.

For my family, it was love at first sight with Darcy. They forgave her immediately for being a Yankee and received her as one of their own. Amid the Thanksgiving celebration, there was a non-stop parade of parties, luncheons and breakfasts to attend, china and silver patterns to be discussed and left at the local shops, and lots and lots of people to meet. By the time we left the following Friday, Darcy was better known in town than I had ever been.

Snow had been in the forecast for several days, and we had cut short our trip by one day because of the fear of traveling in it. What we actually got was rain, in the same manner as on the night of the midnight sail; and, as we forged our way up the Shenandoah Valley toward the Nation's Capital, the thermometer began to fall.

We had been on the road fourteen hours by the time we reached Tyson's Corners and heavy snow had been coming down for the last two. We fell in behind salt trucks from the highway department, then an array of minor accidents and lumbering snow plows slowed us further. It was almost eleven p.m. when we made Georgetown and found a parking spot directly in front of the rooming house.

The back seat of the Beetle had been folded down to hold our bags and all the stuff that had been gleaned from my mother's house, and we carried the essentials into the room and left the rest for later deposit at the Harrises. While Darcy was unpacking, I went out on the little front stoop and checked the mailbox. I noticed that the VW had already acquired a solid dusting of snow.

The mailbox contained mostly junk mail and a few magazines. There was also last week's letter from my mother which contained a check that had been sorely missed before we left, as well as while we were on the trip, and again this evening when we had stopped for a bite to eat in Culpepper, Virginia.

I took the contents of the mailbox back in the room and tossed it on the bed. As I did so, a white legal-sized envelope fell out from among the junk circulars. I picked it up, feeling that familiar tingling in my lower belly.

It was just like the one that I had received during the summer. *Mr. John Norton* typed on the front with no return address and delivered unstamped. I glanced at Darcy who was enthusiastically unpacking and putting stuff into the bureau, and rapidly tore open the envelope. A plain white sheet of paper with boldface type.

Welcome Aboard. Information Received. Will Make Contact.

"Shit!" I stood there staring at the thing.

Darcy turned around quickly. "What is it, Love?"

I crumpled up the paper and flung it on the bed. "It's that fucking Russian again."

I wheeled toward the open bedroom door and slammed it with a bang, firing off a stream of good, short Anglo-Saxon expletives. When I turned back, Darcy was sitting on the bed staring at the message. She looked up at me, totally puzzled.

"*What* is going on? What does this mean? 'Information Received'? What is he talking about, Jack?"

I lunged for the bureau and tore open the top drawer. Nothing. Nothing was apparently missing or had been put there. I had left some socks and a couple of pairs of undershorts that I didn't like and didn't wear. They were there, undisturbed. Everything else in the drawer and been taken on our trip. The message that I had originally left for the Russian had sat there, undisturbed and forgotten, for more than a month, and I had finally thrown it out, sometime after Art's death. There was no note, no message, no can of Ronsonol. Nothing. I looked quickly around the room. We'd taken almost all the personal items with us. Nothing else seemed to have been disturbed.

"Jack?" Darcy was looking at me anxiously.

"I don't know, Love. I don't know what's going on. Nobody's been here, in the room. I haven't left any 'information' or anything else."

"What should we do? I can't stand having those people after us again."

I sat down on the bed beside Darcy and took her hands in mine. "They're not going to be after us again. They're not coming back into our lives at all. I promise. I'm going to end this right now before it gets started again."

"How? What can you do?"

"Listen to me, okay? This guy cannot hurt us. We have nothing he wants. We are totally unable to supply him with anything that he wants. I will not have him playing his spy games and breaking in on us and the rest of it. I'm simply going to leave him a message, arrange to speak face to face with him and tell him to get lost."

Darcy came off the bed in a rush. "Face to face with him? Jack, you can't *do* that! He could kill you, for God's sakes."

"Why on earth would he kill me?"

"How do I know? For spite. Because they're evil. Because they go around killing people and thinking nothing of it. I don't know, Jack." She was almost screaming now, and the tears were starting to flow.

"Darcy, Sweetheart. Listen to me. I have nothing that he wants. He couldn't have received any 'information' from me because I didn't send him any, and neither did anybody else. It's just a ploy. He must think I had something to do with Art or his work. I don't know. Maybe he's like Neil and thinks we're members of the same family or something. It doesn't matter."

Darcy sniffed hard and wiped her eyes. The tears had stopped and she looked straight at me, hard as nails. She said softly, evenly, with full control, "Jack, you are not going to meet with this man. Whatever happens, you are not going to meet with him. You can leave him another note. The same sort of note you left before. There is nothing a meeting could achieve that can't be done just as well with a note. Something in the bureau drawer or the mailbox; but whatever happens, my dearest love, you are not going to see that man again."

Argument with Darcy on this topic was futile, besides which I suspected that she was probably right. Once before, I had left the KGB agent a note in the bureau drawer. If he had bothered to pick it up, he might never have left the one that lay on the bed at this moment. My initial response had been foolish and ill considered. It had been born of the gut feeling that the spoken word delivered with all the attendant personal outrage and emotional baggage would carry more force than a well penned *no*; but this was just fear and anger overriding common sense. I decided to pen the note.

I wrote two identical pieces, one for the mailbox, in case he was able to open it, and the other for my top drawer. Darcy censored my impulse to address them to: The KGB Cocksucker, and we settled for, To Whom It May Concern, as we had the first time. The notes read: *I have sent you no information on any kind. I am not CIA. I have no information for you. Stay completely out of my life.*

We were dead on our feet from the endless drive and the shock and new anxiety engendered by the Russian's note. By the time we had discussed all the possibilities we could think of and had actually written our reply, it was long past time to retire.

The ancient steam radiator was making lots of noise and steadily dripping a puddle of warm water into a pan on the floor while putting out very little heat in the freezing room. Darcy sat in the big armchair with a blanket around her shoulders and watched as I made the necessary preparations. When billows of steam began to emerge from the bathroom, we flung off our clothes, sprang across the hall and jumped shivering into the hot shower. After the hot water started to wane, towels and robes came with us as we made the return dash and burrowed frantically into the tiny bed.

We awoke the next morning buttoned up to our chins and buried under about four inches of sheets, covers, spreads, blankets and two overcoats. I kissed Darcy on the tip of her red nose. It was as cold as a bloodhound's. An extremely unusual silence hung over the place. The normal subdued background noise of cars on the street and the muffled roar of traffic on Wisconsin were simply not there.

After we had indulged in our personal warming-up exercises, I threw on pajamas and robe and crept out to the front door. At least two feet of fresh snow covered everything. The black VW sitting practically in front of the door had been transformed into an unrecognizable lump, sunk clear past the headlights in the white blanket. The street was as still as a tomb. Even the streetcars were absent from Wisconsin. Far down O St. I heard laughter and voices and saw a man and two children floundering along with a snow shovel and sled. The snow seemed to be almost waist deep on the man.

I scooped up a big double handful of the stuff and carried it back in the room. Darcy was peeking out from under the mound of bed clothes as I came through the door with a large smile on my face.

"No!" She shrieked. "Don't you dare!" And immediately disappeared under the pile.

I carefully deposited the mound of snow in a bowl on the table, doffed my robe and pajamas and, despite squeals and protests, climbed under the mound of covers with my ice-cold hands and feet.

An hour later we discovered that the phones were still working, and we called the Harrises before setting out on foot in that direction. Washington, in those days, came almost completely to a halt with the arrival of a major storm. Although heavy snowfalls were almost an annual occurrence, the blizzard the year before had almost prevented the inauguration of President Kennedy, the snow removal equipment owned and operated by the District remained approximately equivalent to that owned and operated by Atlanta, Georgia.

Some sort of effort had been attempted on the main arteries throughout the night. We discovered that once we had made it out to Wisconsin, the snow there was less than half as deep as on the totally socked-in side streets; and passage, though exhausting, was at least possible. As we huffed and puffed up the avenue, red cheeks and noses blowing puffs of steam, the gray ceiling cleared, giving us blue sky and bright sunlight and creating blinding glare on the white drifts. By the time we had worked our way to Westmoreland Circle and were able to cross over toward Connecticut using Albemarle, it was almost mid-afternoon and the clouds were gathering once more.

In the residential districts, the atmosphere was like a holiday. A few hardy souls were manning snow shovels at front walks, but, in the main, no one was moving except for happy little groups of kids and young people building igloos and snowmen and pulling sleds.

We crossed a very subdued Connecticut Avenue with bundled-up people walking up and down the middle of the road just as darkness began to close in. I looked up at the street lamps and saw new flurries of snowflakes swirling in the bluish glare. None of the side streets was cleared past Connecticut.

It was another ten minutes before we floundered onto the broad white space lined by uniform rows of black tree trunks and the big, warmly lighted houses that made up Chesterfield Street. We had dressed warmly, in long johns and blue jeans and boots and mufflers and mackinaws. We had gloves and wool caps as well, but our feet were frozen, we were bone tired and wet almost to the waist. The trip had been as exhausting as running uphill through deep sand.

The house was toasty and the Harrises had a fire going in the living room. We pulled off our boots and outer garments and crouched in front of the hearth, mesmerized like primitives by the dancing flames. By that time, it was snowing heavily again.

The blizzard had also brought out the first signs of Christmas in the Harris household. The place fairly reeked of pine and spruce. Wreaths and fetching little coniferous arrangements festooned with red and green and silver had begun to sprout on tables, doors and windows all over the house. The family had also reached that marvelous latter stage of Thanksgiving when both turkey soup and turkey sandwiches garnished with cranberry sauce are available in abundance.

While Sylvia and Charles prepared food and drink, we peeled off our icy wet bluejeans and socks and hung them over the radiator in the solarium, then trooped back into the livingroom in longjohns and woolen shirts and collapsed on the rug in front of the blazing fire.

An hour later, surfeited with soup and sandwiches and hot buttered rum, the two of us were fast asleep, side by side, our heads sharing the same cushion gleaned from the sofa.

There was movement and soft noise. My eyes suddenly fluttered open as something covered my body. The lights had been extinguished and only the dancing flames lit the room beyond the brass firescreen.

Sylvia Harris was kneeling beside Darcy and me. She had pulled a down comforter over us and was gently stroking our hair. Darcy was sleeping like a child. I could see tears glisten in Sylvia's eyes as she leaned down and touched my forehead with her lips.

"Darling, Jack," She whispered softly. "She loves you so terribly much. Always take care of her, Dear."

I nodded and smiled faintly at her. Sylvia kissed my cheek and patted me, and then she was gone. I felt Darcy's soft warmth against me and drifted back to sleep listening to the sizzle and pop of hickory logs and watching the infinite pattern of shapes in the dancing flames.

When I awoke again, the room was bright. Darcy had crawled half on top of me and was still asleep with her head nestled on my shoulder. Coffee smells and sounds of breakfast activity emanated from the direction of the kitchen, and I experienced an acute twinge of embarrassment that someone had come downstairs and had seen us asleep together.

As if on cue, Sylvia's voice rang out. "Jack? Darcy? Are you two awake in there? Coffee's ready."

As rapidly and quietly as possible, I rearranged Darcy and slipped out from under the big comforter. My bluejeans and socks were toasty warm from the radiator, and I scrambled into them and went immediately to the kitchen.

Sylvia was pouring coffee into two mugs. We said our good mornings. We chatted a bit about yesterday's trek from Georgetown and the visit to Kentucky as well as the state of the weather which now seemed to have stabilized. Bright sunlight flooded every window, and snow had drifted, in some places, as high as the lower stone casements of the first story windows. I picked up the coffee cups and headed back toward the livingroom.

"Oh Jack, dear," Sylvia called after me. "There was a phone call for you last night, just as we were getting ready for bed."

I laughed. "Someone from Kentucky, wondering why we hadn't called?"

Sylvia looked puzzled and a trace of concern was in her voice. "No, dear. Not your family. I talked to your mother yesterday morning. No, it was a strange man. A foreigner. European accent. He just asked for Mr. Norton and when Charles told him you were already asleep, he hung up. Just like that."

That awful tingling in the belly zapped me like a cattle prod. "He didn't even leave his name or any message?" I managed, knowing, of course, that he had not.

"Nope," replied Sylvia, buttering slices of toast, "He just hung up without a fair thee well. Maybe it's the language problem." She laughed. "He didn't seem to have mastered the etiquette of the telephone in English."

He hasn't bothered to master the etiquette of the telephone in any language, I thought, not even his native Russian. "I can't imagine who it was," I lied. "I suppose he'll call back if it's important."

I brought coffee and kisses to my Darcy love who was enjoying the slow, languorous process of waking up on a sunny bright morning after a long winter night. She raised herself on one elbow, and I seated myself on the floor by the sofa cushion and set the coffee on the hearth. After a further exchange of little secret words and morning kisses, I gave her tiny sips of coffee from my mug.

After a few minutes, she sat upright and reached for her own cup. As she brought it to her lips, I whispered, "That Russian telephoned last night after we were asleep. He knows I'm here right now."

CHAPTER TWENTY EIGHT

Darcy's first question wasn't a question at all. "He must have already found the note."

I shook my head. "Hard to see how. He *might* have been to the room, yesterday; but I very much doubt it. The whole city was completely paralyzed. Nothing was moving except plows around the main arteries and government buildings. It's going to be the same way today."

Darcy and I had come to the kitchen for breakfast, and had then gone out into the solarium for another cup of coffee. Other members of the family were upstairs getting ready for the day.

"I bet the call was just to see if we'd gotten back to town," said Darcy. "He hasn't found the note yet."

I nodded in agreement. "It's really better this way; to talk to him directly by phone, I mean. When he calls back, I'll let him know exactly where we stand. I'll be a whole lot clearer than any note."

Darcy was staring solomnly into her empty cup. "What, Love?" I asked.

She looked up at me and sighed. "I just can't understand why he thinks you have anything for him, and it worries me. It worries me a lot."

We heard Charles coming down the stairs, shouting for Sam who had made a late appearance at the breakfast table. Clearing the walkways around the house and a path out to the street were the first order of business. I quickly got into my boots and gear and followed Charles down to the basement to break out the big snow shovels. After a while, Sam joined us and we worked steadily piling the snow waist high and opening up narrow little paths all around the place.

By mid-afternoon, despite a long lunch break, or maybe because of it, we were about worked out. Almost half the walks remained to be cleared; but, at least, we could walk unobstructed out to the street. The trouble was that, once there, about all you could do was turn around and walk back to the house.

Chesterfield was one of those anointed streets that were always among the first of the residential lanes to be cleared. Why this was true, no one seemed to quite know, but I had no doubt that the excessive number of governmental big wigs of various stripes who made Chesterfield their home were somehow a factor. Even so, no side street would be touched until the larger thoroughfares were plowed, and there was an awful lot of snow to move and very little equipment with which to move it.

Inside, Darcy and Sylvia were all atwitter with more decorations. Boxes, paper and ribbon were strewn all over the dining room table while wonderful, warm baking smells crawled out of the kitchen and permeated every corner of the house. The log fire was kept going all day and phonograph music resounded through every room.

Charles Harris seated himself before the fire and started removing his icy boots. "You girls are going to be finished with Christmas before it even gets here."

"Christmas is going to be a little different this year, dear," responded Sylvia. "We're going to need about twice as much time for it. Best to get an early start."

Charles winked at me, and I ambled into the kitchen to see what Darcy was up to.

She was up to making a pecan cake from a recipe that my mother had given her and was having trouble finding the necessary ingredients. Sylvia had quietly compiled a list of things needed from the grocery store, should one be open. We called around and found that the wonderful new Safeway just below Chevy Chase Circle had managed to get its lot cleared. A skeleton crew of employees had faithfully managed to straggle in and the place had finally opened for business about 3:00 p.m. It was quarter till four and Darcy and I quickly suited and booted up. Pulling the Flexible Flyer behind us on the frozen, bumpy trail, we made for Connecticut Avenue and the supermarket.

Although the neighborhood streets were still unplowed, a number of the main residential thoroughfares were now passable with a thick layer of hard-packed snow and buried lines of cars parked at the curbs. Connecticut was open and very light traffic was gingerly making its way to and fro along with the city buses to the clank and rattle of snow chains. We set a good pace once we reached the Avenue, keeping off the still clogged sidewalk and walking in the street like everybody else. It was almost 5:00 p.m. when we saw the lights of the Safeway store and the bundled figures shuttling in and out like refugees.

Thirty minutes later, we put three bags of groceries in a cardboard box and secured it to the sled with a bungee cord. It was dark by the time we left the store. However, the sky was clear and the moon full and, with the additional illumination from the street lamps, we had no trouble navigating our way toward home. A scattered number of stores had managed to open late in the afternoon, the plows having made slow but steady progress since early morning. Most of the people we had seen were on foot, blowing clouds of steam in the frigid air and pulling children on sleds and innertubes. We finally reached the side street cut-off from Connecticut which would take us along Rock Creek Park and then down to the vicinity of Chesterfield.

It was eerily silent after the relative bustle out on Connecticut. There, a few cars had been limping along with a depleted cadre of buses from the District transportation system. Now, as we made our way onto the lesser streets, almost all the cars we saw were still buried at the curb. Caught there by the driving snow two nights ago, they had since been further inundated, and the relentless blades of the plows now penned them solidly with dirty white walls of half-frozen slush.

With the sled behind us, we walked happily down the middle of the darkened street. Darcy was gabbing a mile a minute about Christmas. As a properly brought up young wife-to-be, she had already begun compiling a Christmas List of all those friends, relatives and important people in our lives who would, forevermore, receive Season's Greetings from Jack and Darcy Norton. This master list was designed to serve as a sort of social rhumb line during this joyous season of the year. It became the basis for the more exalted registers which would be limited to the various blood relatives, inlaws and intimate friends who would actually receive gifts from the Nortons in addition to cards.

Darcy absolutely loved this sort of thing as she absolutely loved doing everything that piqued her interest. Amazingly, these chores were not seen as oppressive social duties but as wonderful opportunities to bring a little happiness to others. I was genuinely delighted that Darcy had been so heartily endowed with this saintly quality: in a peculiar way, I felt it absolved me for my utter lack of interest while, of course, maintaining the necessary social standards. Her voice rose in surprise and laughter as she thought of this one and that one, of grandmothers and small cousins and friends who had been with her at school. I walked by her side, hand in hand on the sled rope, loving the sound of her voice and delighting in the beauty of her enchanted being. We enjoyed the sense of being completely alone in a silent, softly rounded, white world lit only by streetlamps. When she paused every so often to let me make a comment, we could actually feel the crisp, cold silence of the darkness and hear our breathing and the swish of the sled runners augmented by the squeaking tempo of our boots on the hard-packed snow.

Behind us, an engine roared to life. I turned while Darcy was still talking and could see nothing but an isolated cloud of exhaust smoke drifting upward toward a street lamp. About a hundred feet back, the gray plume rolled up from among the line of socked-in mounds at the side of the street. No lights were visible from the vehicle. It was impossible to tell exactly which of the cars had been started.

There were no houses on the street. The long brick sidewalls of upscale apartment buildings lined each side of the road, lighted faintly here and there from windows three and four stories above the ground. We had just passed the place, less than a minute ago, where the exhaust cloud now plumed. As we had come down the street, not even the tires or windows of any of the parked machines had been visible. Rather, a continuous, unbroken snow bank stretched all the way back to the intersection along the side of the plowed roadway.

Now, suddenly, the engine note swelled and I heard the hoarse, rattling scratch of tire chains on the packed surface. A twenty-foot section of the snowbank broke softly away and moved out onto the street. With it came the rasping whisk-whisk of wipers against an icy windshield. A long dark object, carrying a foot-thick blanket of snow, began to move slowly in our direction.

I reached over and took Darcy by the arm, and we quickened our pace to the far side of the street. As we did so, the car picked up a little speed until it had moved up to about fifty feet behind us. Darcy stopped talking about Christmas Lists and anxiously glanced over her shoulder as the two of us sped up.

The street ahead was a long smooth corridor, its sides blocked by four-foot-high walls of snow filled with parked cars. The first exit came at the next intersection, almost fifty yards distant. Both of us instinctively recognized that this represented the only immediate door to safety. We broke into a fast jog, the sled lurching along behind us. The car behind us increased its speed and began to close the distance.

Darcy glanced back. "Jack!" she screamed.

I let go of her arm and dived for the box of groceries on the sled, grabbing the necks of two bottles of red Spanish wine.

"RUN!" I bellowed. "Don't stop for anything! RUN!"

Darcy let go of the sled rope and took a few steps ahead, then turned again. "Jack!"

She was still screaming when the first bottle of wine exploded against the windshield.

The big car slewed sideways to a halt and both front doors were flung wide. Two large men wearing heavy overcoats and fur hats stepped out behind the doors. I reared back and threw the second bottle as hard as I could at the head of the driver. It smashed into a thousand fragments on the doorframe and the big man was down on the ground, crying out in pain and shouting to his companion.

I glanced over my shoulder. Darcy hadn't moved an inch. A flashlight snapped on, the beam sweeping across my face. Then the light fell against the snow-covered car and I could see that the entire front end was drenched in dark liquid. The downed driver was still on his knees, furiously wiping at his face. The man with the flashlight backed up, shouted something and came fast around the vehicle. Skirting the rear corner, he slipped on the ice and landed flat on his back, spread-eagled in the road. I reached out for Darcy's hand and we ran for the intersection as hard as we'd ever run in our lives.

The intersection marked the first of the side-boundary entrances into Rock Creek Park. To continue down the same street on the snow-blocked residential corridor would bring certain disaster. They wouldn't need a clear windshield in the car to run us down in about thirty seconds once they had gotten under way. We turned off toward the Park and ran like hell through broken snow down the steep hill that I knew led to the National Zoo.

The big iron-barred traffic gate was pulled across the roadway at the entrance and locked. The place was obviously closed. We began to circle the fence working our way around the broad perimeter, looking for any place to hide or lose our pursuers.

Snow removal in the area had proceeded indifferently. Sections of roadways had been scraped. Here and there, certain parts of sidewalks had been half-cleared so that a sort of one lane passage was possible. A lighted gateway appeared in the high fence only a few hundred feet ahead of us. As we approached it on the perimeter walkway, I could see that it was slightly ajar, a no admittance sign displayed at chest height. We were through in a flash and slammed it behind us with a loud, metallic clang. There was no padlock but I doubted that the two Russian goons would try every little gate if they thought the whole Park was closed.

I squeezed Darcy's arm reassuringly and murmured "okay" as we struggled along inside the barrier. We had covered perhaps thirty feet inside the solid, comforting fence line when we heard the rasp of tire chains on the hill behind us. We lunged ahead through the broken snow and ran for our lives.

The National Zoological Park was located entirely within the boundaries of Rock Creek Park, less than a ten minute drive from the Harrises. Darcy had been going there all her life. The two of us had ambled through the place a half dozen times over the summer, and I was, at least, familiar with the central layout. Now, of course, everything was different. The heavy blanket of snow had erased and camouflaged most of the familiar points of reference. The Zoo was quite large, perhaps one hundred sixty acres, and was laid out, in so far as was possible, within the context of the natural setting. Like most of the rest of Rock Creek Park, construction had been held to a minimum or cleverly concealed so as to preserve a feeling of unobstructed wilderness. Buildings, animal enclosures, moats and waterways were cunningly set among the low rolling hills and gullies. Two main paths, The Olmstead Walk and The Valley Trail ran down through the zoo from the main entrance near Connecticut Avenue and were interconnected by a series of little winding foot paths. I knew that somewhere near the Harvard Street entrance at the opposite end of the zoo lay a small building which housed a detachment of the Park police. Surely someone must be there, even on a night like this. Animal keepers and night watchman had to be on permanent duty.

We stumbled and slid and ran on, trying desperately to find some familiar spot or landmark. There were lights by the rear entrances of some of the buildings in the distance, but, in the white silence, everything actually looked pretty much like everything else.

The splash of water and the sound of honk-like barking sounded just ahead of us. Both of us recognized it instantly.

"The seals and sea lions," I whispered to Darcy.

"They're feeding them? Can you hear anyone?"

We stopped, trying to hold our breathing and to listen. Apart from the intermittant sounds of heavy bodies hitting water and the honk of the aquatic mammals, the zoo was absolutely silent. The huge outdoor pool was ringed with snow and the building adjacent to it could hardly be seen at all. The place looked dark and deserted.

"I don't think anybody is there," I said. The sea lions are just enjoying the weather, that's all."

"What about a fire alarm box? I've seen them all over the zoo.".

"They're either in lockboxes or inside the buildings. I thought of that as soon as we came through the gate. We need to find the police station. Even if it's closed, there are pay phones along the walk just in front of it.

Darcy whispered as we ran along, gasping for breath. "Jack, the bears." She inhaled hard and continued. "The bears are just beyond the seals. Down the path next to the creek on the other side of the building. If we follow it past the bears, it comes out up on The Olmstead Walk. We can follow it to the police building."

I nodded and tried desperately to remember and recognize the layout. The moonlight cast each feature in pale blue and draped black shapes and shadows on every sculptured form. I had the general map of it in my head now but the unfamiliar shapes did not conform to memory. It was worse than driving a Yellow Cab in Arlington.

We slid and stumbled down the little path that ran behind the cluster of buildings in which the bears were housed. Along the footpath, caged enclosures abutted out from each section of the compound, now still and deserted with a heavy covering of snow. A series of steep, concrete steps just beyond the row of enclosures brought us out onto the main thoroughfare of The Olmstead Walk.

We stood at the top of the stairs for a moment to catch our breaths, feeling relatively safe in the shelter of the snow banks atop the surrounding heavy foliage.

Just ahead of us, across a broad expanse of snow-covered lawn, I could make out two buildings that I knew housed the gibbons and great apes. Beyond the walkway which led between them lay Olmstead walk. If we followed it down the hill, we should come upon the little police building not much more than a quarter of a mile away. The administration building lay in the opposite direction just inside the Connecticut Avenue entrance. I took Darcy's arm and we left the sheltering foliage and started across the open space.

We had just reached the walkway between the two buildings when the Russian stepped out of the shadows.

"Remain silent. If you utter a sound, I will shoot you now."

Darcy made a sharp intake of breath and grabbed me hard. I half turned, putting myself between her and the Russian.

"You've made a mistake," I gasped trying to find my breath. "I'm not who you think I am. I have no information for you."

The Russian spoke as dispassionately as he had that night in the cabin. "You will be silent. You will come with me now. The car is waiting."

We stood stock still at the first sound of his voice. The Russian was moving toward us when we saw him and continued his advance until he was standing only a few feet away. There was some sort of pistol in his hand.

He raised the gun toward my face. "You will come now."

He stood to one side and gestured quickly with the pistol for us to move.

Darcy and I held each other tightly and started forward.

"Listen please," I said, not looking back at him. "I will explain everything to you."

"Oh yes. You will certainly explain everything. Only now you will keep moving, and you will not speak."

We traveled the fifty or sixty feet on the shoveled-out path between the two buildings. When we reached the far corner, the Russian gestured toward the left, away from the cluster of administration buildings and toward the perimeter road bordering the empty parking areas.

We took two steps in the new direction. From behind us came a sickening smack and the frantic, helpless scraping of shoes against the ice.

I spun around and the Russian was on the ground, his body twitching and his feet jerking in little spasms. His fur cap had fallen off and his eyes were wide and bulging above his open mouth and protruding tongue. A man was standing quietly over him. It was not his companion from the car. The man stooped quickly and retrieved the pistol where it had fallen from the Russian's quivering hand.

Darcy let out a little shriek and I grabbed her even more tightly. We stood there, in total shock, holding on to each other. Half crouched and paralyzed with fear, we watched the man and were unable to utter a single word.

He calmly watched us as he unscrewed the long silencer from the barrel of the Russian's pistol, then slipped both pieces into his overcoat pocket.

When he spoke, it was the same Oxbridge accent that I'd heard that night on the dock. "I very much regret your involvement in this business, Norton. These people won't be annoying you again. Take your young lady now and go home. Exactly as you came, mind you, and you must go quickly." He gestured to the man lying in the snow. "His comrade is waiting, not far from here."

He stood watching us, dressed in a tailored overcoat with a heavy fir collar. He wore a fir hat like the one that lay beside the dead Russian. We moved back the way we had come, treading gingerly on the ice and silently clinging to each other for support. A few yards along the narrow pathway, I turned abruptly and called out, "Sidney!" But he had vanished.

We retraced our steps as fast as we had come. Still numb with shock, we had not spoken a word since leaving the Englishman. We came rapidly through the little gate on the far side of the Zoo. Three times before reaching the white corridor where we had first encountered the Russians in their car, we had to stop and lie down in the snow, panting as though our hearts and lungs would burst.

When we reached the spot, the contents of the two wine bottles along with a lot of glass were still in the roadway. The Flexible Flyer was sitting just at the side of the street where we had left it, the box of groceries still intact.

CHAPTER TWENTY NINE

The Wednesday morning edition of *The Washington Post* carried a minor article about a Soviet deputy assistant trade representative who had apparently slipped on the ice and broken his neck at the National Zoo. Hidden by snowbanks, the body had lain unnoticed for almost a full day before being discovered by a maintenance crew. Foul play was not suspected, and the body had been released to the Soviet embassy for return to Moscow.

A hundred times, I saw him sprawled out on his back. The bulging eyes and mouth stretched wide in agony, the protruding tongue and the legs that twitched and jerked, helplessly convulsing on the icy walk. What the hell had the Englishman done to him?

I scanned the papers in vain for news of the other one, the driver. There would be no tidy notice of an accidental fall in the snow for him. I knew that somewhere in the City, at this very moment, perhaps even out on 16th Street in front of the Soviet embassy, sat a long black Cadillac car, snow-covered and wine-spattered with a smashed windshield and at least one dent in the door. I knew that the driver sat like stone, slumped over the wheel, a line of clotted blood running from his right ear. Pinned to his heavy overcoat would be a note: *For Gregovnia* . . . The accounts had been squared.

Darcy and I had almost had a collective nervous breakdown when we returned to the house that night. The place had taken on an even more festive air with the addition of a tree and ornaments and the non-stop sounds of Christmas carols. Darcy went into a sort of controlled manic state, bouncing around the kitchen and turning out cookies and holiday goodies like a short-order cook. I went into the living room and sat with a drink in a big easy chair by the fire. I watched Sam and Sylvia decorate the tree and gave little snippets of advice when called upon. Otherwise, I simply stared for long periods into the dancing flames and saw the image of that helpless twitching man, already dead in the snow.

Sylvia Harris asked each of us, at least twice, if anything were wrong; and, of course, we cheered up and came alive and behaved normally and said no, we were just tired from our trek. Darcy didn't act tired. She behaved as if she had just eaten a bowl of amphetamines. I didn't really act tired, either. I behaved as if I were totally preoccupied with some very unpleasant memory. The family didn't press it; although, at dinner, Charles Harris asked me, at Sylvia's secret prompting because it was a Sylvia kind of question, if I had heard any news from Princeton, which, of course, I hadn't.

I was nominally assigned to one of the guest bedrooms while staying at the Harrises. That this arrangement entailed hypocrisy and a mutual conspiracy of denial by all parties bothered no one. We all knew it was hypocritical, but the hypocrisy was more than offset by the correct observation of the moral and social conventions. As proper Calvinists, we revered the proper forms.

Darcy and I lay awake in the guest room bed not speaking for a long time that night. Finally, She turned to me and said in a whisper, "Jack, I'll never forget what happened tonight. Never."

I kissed her wonderful dark honey-gold hair and nodded. "I know."

"That Englishman. He just used us to get at them."

"That's right." I said. "'If you want to catch a lion, first tether a goat'".

She was crying softly. "That's horrible."

"Yes."

"That man in the snow."

"He was a killer, Darcy. He murdered Gregovnia, and he would have murdered both of us."

"Oh God, Jack." She turned her head into my chest, and I could feel the wetness of the tears and the sobs that shook her whole body in little tremors. I said nothing and stared unseeing into the darkness at the grotesque visage of the deputy assistant trade representative until it faded with the night.

The wedding took place on Saturday morning, the 30th of December at the First Presbyterian Church of Chevy Chase. The weeks leading up to the big event were so frenetic that they will always remain a blurry, half-remembered dream.

For my Darcy love, they seemed to involve a continuous display of energy. Running here and there, trying on this, being fitted for that and picking out enormous quantities of both. Linda Townsend and a delightful covey of mutual girlfriends were recruited *en masse*. The dining room table at the Harrises was fitted out with all its extra leaves and served as the center of operations.

On this mahogany field of honor, gifts were wrapped and opened, lists were scrutinized and invitations sent out. Endless details were discussed, patterns were cut and menus were created. By the time my mother arrived and became part of the dining room clique, the place bore a certain resemblance to Churchill's map room in the bowels of No.10 Downing Street during World War II.

My former roommate and other friends from school had arrived late in the week after Christmas. Along with my family and childhood buddies from home, they ensconced themselves in a suite of rooms at The Shoreham and conducted a marathon bacchanalia in which I was expected to be both honored guest and chief participant.

I took leave from the Arlington Yellow Cab Company on the day before Christmas eve. The dispatcher enlivened his radio communication throughout the day with all sorts of vulgar and earthy advice pertaining to my forthcoming nuptials. Apparently, the question of maintaining adequate sexual energy bore acutely on his mind, and he had a great deal of practical wisdom to impart regarding the measured and ongoing disbursement of my precious bodily fluids. These unsolicited gems were proffered in what he, no doubt, considered highly humorous style and had the effect, at least, of putting him in the best humor I'd seen since taking the miserable job.

At one point during the seemingly endless day, I almost suffered cardiac arrest when the voice of Neil cracked over the loudspeaker. He again offered his most profound sympathies on the terrible loss of my brother, Art, wished me a merry Christmas and Season's Greetings and, of course, congratulated me on my impending marriage.

He went on to say that he had received a very nice card from my family for the flowers he sent to the funeral, and that he would always treasure the message which had been personally written by Gwendolyn

Baldwin, herself. Apparently, it was the next best thing to a hand-written note from Jackie!

I thanked him and signed off. Later, I learned that he had spoken by radio to each of his drivers that day. Just his way, in lieu of more tangible benefits, of saying Merry Christmas and thanks for a job well done at year's end. I mused over the likelihood of some fifty bizarre automobile accidents occurring in Arlington Yellow Cabs on the same day in response to a surprise Christmas message from Neil.

On the eve of our marriage, Darcy was whisked away to those ethereal and mysterious climes which are the sole province of mothers and assorted women, dress makers and wedding mongers. In the late afternoon, amid gathering darkness and the beginning of the long holiday weekend traffic rush, I got into the VW and drove, for the last time, over to Georgetown and the rooming house at **1435** O St. N.W..

Most of my belongings had already been transferred to the Harrises' garage and basement, but a few articles of clothing and the odd possession still remained. I carried a large, empty suitcase up the front steps and stopped to remove my nameplate from the little mailbox, empty for the past week save for a few junk circulars.

In the room, I laid the bag on the bed and filled it with sheets and towel, the few remaining personal items from the bathroom and cleaned out the bureau drawers. On an impulse, I walked out into the hallway and stood for a moment at the door of Art Baldwin's old room. I tried the knob, but it was securely locked as prescribed by Miss Withersby. I glanced back down the darkened corridor, at the hall floor where once, dainty naked footprints had adorned the worn boards. I walked the few steps and leaned hard against the doorway of the wretched little bathroom trying to inhale the now vanished fragrance of roses but smelling only the mildew and age of paint covered plaster and ancient wood.

The place was cast almost in darkness now, and the only sounds were from the muffled din of traffic in the far background. I looked back and forth at the two bedroom doors, mine still ajar and Art's closed and locked forever. Oh God. Art.

Near the casing at the base of my door, I could almost see a bottle of Chateau Latour, wrapped with red ribbon. I recalled the flood of surprise and delight when we had first discovered it. I glanced toward the street door, its little panel of glass near the top bringing in the only light to the building. The shadowy figure of Sidney Reilly was standing just inside the hallway.

"Checking out are we, old boy?" The English accent brushed smoothly along the dingy walls, and I could see the faint trace of a smile on his lips.

I nodded, not speaking.

The figure held a tightly furled umbrella. He shifted it and raised his right hand to slowly remove the dark homberg. The light from the door reflected on his slickly parted hair. He slipped a button, and I could see the high starched collar and the flash of a diamond stickpin and the gold watch chain draped across his waistcoat.

"Pity about poor Baldwin," he continued evenly.

I nodded again, and tears welled in my eyes. Reilly stood there silently, waiting. I saw him cast his glance at my feet, and I followed his gaze to the small, wet footprints which led from the bathroom. The scent of roses was strong in the hall.

"We both loved her, you know."

I struggled against the tears and my choking throat. "You damn well sent her out to die."

"She knew the risks. She was a professional. Those people forgot that. *They* forgot to follow the rules."

"What rules?" I shouted in the darkness. "You're all a pack of killers."

"Really now, old boy. We never kill each other. Weren't you aware of that? *They* certainly were."

"You almost got my Darcy killed," I cried, breaking into wracking sobs.

"Oh, there was little real danger. I was watching all along" A light flared, and I could see the cigarette in his lips. He quietly exhaled and continued. "They wouldn't have come otherwise, you know."

I was crying uncontrollably. "Her whole life has been fucked up because of this. She'll never be the same. Her sweet innocence . . . . God damn you," I screamed. "She'll never be able to forget . . . ."

"Steady, old man." The voice was calm and soothing. "Your Darcy will forget. It will be as something which occurred long, long ago. As time passes, she'll only have memories of you and the life you build together. Those are the memories upon which she will construct her life." He returned the homberg to his head carefully and buttoned his tailored greatcoat. "Off for good now, are we?"

I wiped my eyes. "I'm never coming back here again. I hate this fucking place, that room."

"Oh come now, Jack. I can understand that the place has left a bad taste in your mouth, but never is a terribly long time. I might have even said that once, myself, long ago. Now, as you see, here I am."

I looked hard at the dim figure. "What? What do you mean? Were you here before?" I took a step toward the door. As I approached, the little vestibule became empty, containing only shadows.

I stood quietly in the darkness for a moment, then became aware of a pounding headache and an overwhelming need for air. I threw open the street door and stepped out onto the little brick stoop. The fresh coolness flooded my lungs. From across the street, the sounds of voices and laughter as a group of teenage boys shouted and roughhoused along toward the lights of Wisconsin Avenue. I closed the door and went back in the room. The place was as dead and silent as before. I zipped up the bag, locked the door to my former room. On the brick stoop, I carefully locked the street door, as one who listens does when instructed by Miss Withersby, and skipped briskly down the steps to the waiting Volkswagen.

I spent the night of my wedding's eve at The Shoreham Hotel rubbing elbows in the dining room with the rich and famous as well as with the sodden drunks of my own party. A double scotch and soda almost instantly cured my headache. From the bar, we repaired to a private room in the restaurant for a final evening of male camaraderie, of food and drink, of giving of gifts, of talk with good friends and of the remembrance of things long past. There were definitely no naked girls jumping out of cakes.

Everyone said that it was the most beautiful and touching wedding ceremony ever witnessed. I would have said that everything went off without a hitch, except that was, of course, exactly what happened. The church was bedecked with flowers. Almost everyone over the age of fifty cried. Especially the parents. Even Miss Withersby's rheumy old eyes were glistening. Darcy and I remembered each other's full Christian names as did the Reverend Dr. Playfair. My best friend and college room mate, William Carter Longworth Ogilsvey, was a tower of strength and Virginia manhood. He charmed the pants off every woman in the house and, somehow, managed not to lose the ring.

And my Darcy? My Darcy came down that aisle on the arm of her father. She wore her grandmother's old-fashioned wedding gown with a train and acres and acres of white lace. She came down that aisle with orange blossoms in her hair looking as radiant as an angel. Standing before God and the congregation, we promised ourselves to each other for richer for poorer, in sickness and in health, till death do us part.

At the reception, parking on Chesterfield Street was impossible. The cars were backed up in double rows all the way back to the intersection. Miss Withersby's great long Packard V12 sat by the curb exactly in front of the house, Alonzo having preempted the place of honor by sheer presence. Both a Lincoln and a Buick belonging to cousins of Darcy had to be moved down the street to make way for the ancient behemoth.

We had reservations for an afternoon flight to the Island of Eleuthera and Miss Withersby had graciously put Alonzo and the Packard at our disposal. We stood and met people and accepted congratulations and good wishes for what seemed an awfully long time. Later, we drank glass after glass of champagne and went from this little clump to that little clump all over the house and met people and more people. I had no idea who most of them were. At some point, Carter Ogilsvey mercifully tapped me on the shoulder and pointed to his wristwatch. We collected Darcy for the cutting of the six-tiered cake and the taking of more pictures. In another hour, we were allowed to go upstairs and change and finish packing.

Alonzo came quietly and unobtrusively into the room and collected our bags. I went downstairs to wait for Darcy and to start saying the good-byes and kissing all the relatives. Part way through this process, I spied Miss Withersby who, for a moment, had been left sitting by herself on a small chair in the hallway. I came quickly to her side and seated myself on the chair next to her.

"Well, Jack deah, you have certainly got yourself a lovely bride." She beamed at me, taking both my hands in hers and telling me how much she loved us both and how happy we had made her and on and on.

I thanked her for her generous wedding present, and said all sorts of pleasant things. I particularly mentioned the loan of the Jaguar during the summer, and how I hoped we'd all see a lot of each other during the coming year.

She pooh-poohed any talk about the Jaguar or the gift and insisted that I let her know if there was just anything that we needed or that she could do to make our lives more complete.

Sensing an opening, I leaned forward and said, softly, "This may seem like a funny question at a time like this, but what was the name of the man in the boat picture who asked you to marry him?"

She looked at me rather strangely for a moment, then said, "His name? Oh, Sidney! Sidney was his name. He was the most charming man you evah met. Attached to the British embassy, you know."

I looked quickly into the kindly old eyes, at the wrinkled face, liver spotted and soft with age. Suddenly, behind it formed the clear, youthful image of the girl in the speedboat, head tossed back, laughter pealing from her lips. Bare arms draped carelessly across the driver's shoulders. Attached to the British Embassy, I thought. And attached to you as well on secret afternoons in a certain old rooming house way out in Georgetown.

There was a round of cheers and a burst of applause as Darcy descended the stairs, dressed for winter vacation travel in a tan skirt and tweed jacket. I stood up as the crowd gathered around. I helped Miss Withersby to her feet, and went forward, holding out my hand to my Darcy love.

The End

AUTHOR BIO

Although a native Kentuckian, James Haley was educated in Virginia at Hampden-Sydney College and lived in Washington, D.C. during the Cuban Missile Crisis and at the height of the Cold War. He went on to receive graduate training at the University of Cincinnati College of Medicine and at the University of California at San Francisco where he conducted medical research for many years. Mr. Haley writes, sleeps, eats and has his being with his wife, Ann, and beloved Airedale Terriers at their home in the central coast mountains of California, a land flowing with milk and honey.